The Crimson Claymore

Claymore of Calthoria
Book 1

Craig A. Price Jr.

CLAYMORE
PUBLISHING

Dedicated to Mary Quimbey,

Thank you, Mom, for always believing in me.

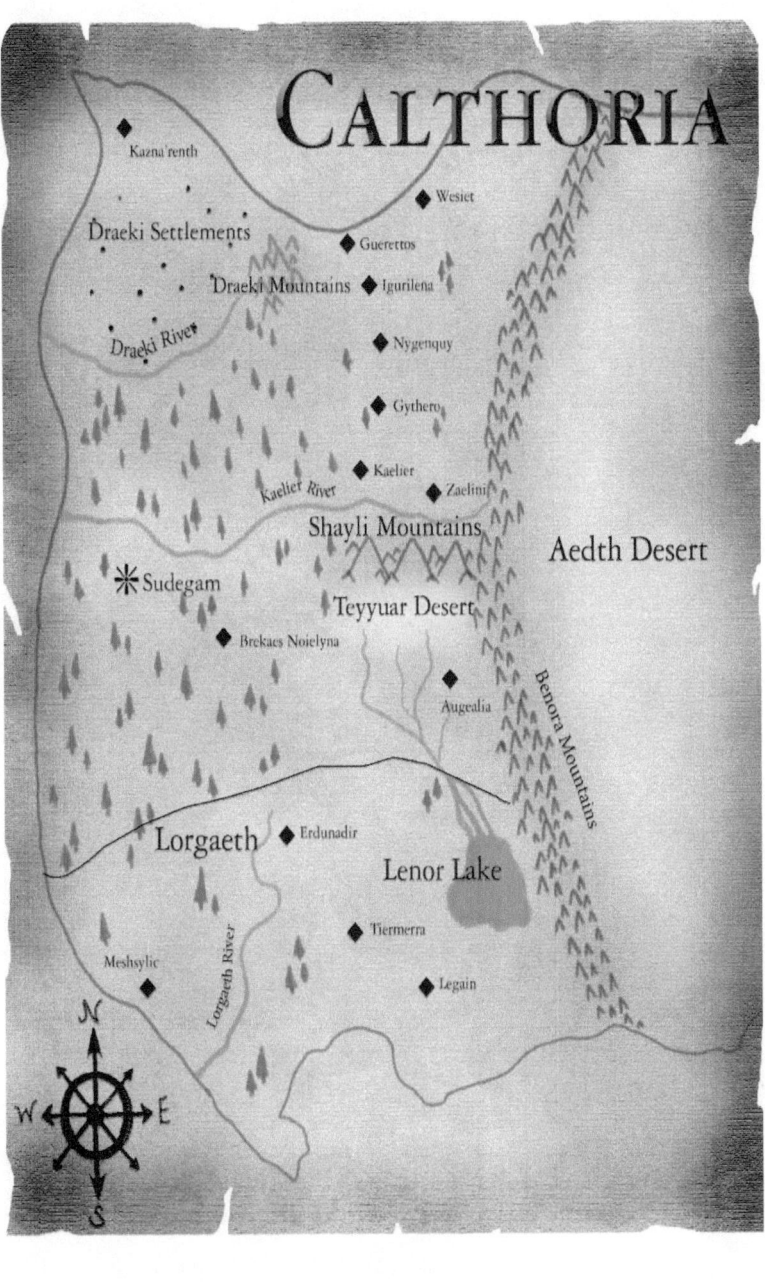

Prologue

Searon ambled through the alleyways of crowded Augealia, completely ignoring the merchants who hounded him with their entreaties. He knew that they had seen him giving a small bag of coins to a poor beggar woman and her children and no doubt figured he had plenty to spare. He dared not meet their gaze, but kept his steady pace as he walked past them. Suddenly, something walloped into him from behind that made him stagger and nearly tumble to the ground.

It was a young girl, grown barely higher than his waist, with a loaf of fresh bread in her arms. The smell taunted his stomach as she looked up at him with her watery blue eyes. He understood her fear—he was probably the most intimidating man in the crowd in his plate mail and scabbard, except, of course, for the two guards with short scimitars in pursuit of the girl. He glanced back down at her. She cowered in fear. He reached down to grab her arm, but she was too quick, and she dashed away through the crowd, stopping only long enough to stick her tongue out at him.

Searon gaped at the girl as she receded into the distance. She had some nerve, although it was hard for him to judge: Was she was merely a thief, or a true survivor? She didn't look as if she had any money, with her torn cotton and leather dress, and her dirt-stained hair, about which he could only wonder—had it once been blonde? Her smudged face looked as if it hadn't been washed in months. He tried to catch up to her, sprinting now, but she was far too quick for him.

The guards had reached him and bumped into him, but ignored him and sprinted on, intent only on catching the girl. In their loose chain mail, they made entirely too much racket and seemed mere footmen compared to Searon, with his finely honed tracking skills, and it was amusing to watch them fall behind the clever girl. Searon knew by the way they chased the girl from behind, with little regard for tranquility, that their intellect wasn't very high; he knew well that was never the best way to catch someone.

Searon cut through a few shops and into an alley. He figured if the young girl had been stealing food to feed herself, she'd have made a roundabout back through the shops to lose the guards. Instead of foolishly joining the chase, he decided to intercept her when she headed back.

Every stone wall in the nearly deserted alleys was spiderwebbed with cracks. The village did not appear to have spent money to fix them for a long time. It had just stopped raining, and water draining down was even now eroding the cracks ever deeper. A few crows looked down at him from the rooftops. Searon followed a small gravelly path through the still puddles. When ripples began to form on the surface of the puddles, Searon looked up to see what could be making them. Fast footsteps echoed in the water in a chill whisper.

The young girl splashed into plain sight from a side alley. Searon swiftly turned and dashed into the next alley. His ears were keen, and he was able to discern her position with more certainty than most other humans. He rushed out from his hiding spot and grabbed her. She kicked and bit but did not scream. Her mouth was glued shut so she would not divulge her location to the guards, who were most likely lost in another alley. But Searon couldn't hold her for long. Her tiny foot connected with his groin, hard, and she wriggled away.

The excruciating pain sent shivers down his spine, and he dropped to his knees, his vision blurring. This tiny girl had grounded him worse than anyone ever had. The games were over, and he unsheathed his claymore. The silver blade glowed crimson in the shadows. Tears like sparkling sapphires welled up in the girl's soft blue eyes.

"What is your name?" Searon said in a tone as gentle as he could muster, hoping to not startle her.

She stared up at him, quivering, holding herself in a firm hug. "Charlotte."

Searon sighed and sheathed his claymore. He wished no harm to come to the little girl, but she seemed too frightened to give him any helpful information, especially with the guards still on her trail.

"Where are your mother and father?" His voice was soft as a warm autumn rain. But somehow he knew that no parents in their right minds would be letting their daughter run aimlessly through the markets to steal food.

"They are no more," she whispered. There was no sorrow in her voice, only irritation—a true sign of her having been on her own for far too long.

Searon nodded. He knew if they were still alive they'd be risking their own lives for food rather than their daughter's. At least that was how it would have been if he were her father. He felt sorry for the little girl. She didn't need to be living like that from day to day, each day draining a little more of the innocence from her youth.

"Come, you must pay for this food. It is not right to steal," he declared, holding out his hand to her. She dared not budge. He didn't really expect her to; he only wanted to guide her along her way.

"But I have no money," she spat out, almost crying. He looked at her rags. If she'd even had a pocket to keep money, once upon a time, anything that might have resembled one had been torn away.

"Do you know where the captain of this village's army is?" Searon asked politely. He held his chest high, as if to impress her.

"Yes," she muttered, and backed up a few steps. She appeared confused. She was frowning, and he could tell that she wanted to show him that she wasn't afraid, no matter what he did or said.

"I must meet with him. If you lead me to him, I will pay you," Searon said. He lay down his claymore to show her he meant no harm.

"Why?"

"There are some very bad creatures out there. The captain may know where I can find them. Can you take me to him?"

He unclipped a bag from his sash and handed it to her. Heavier than the one he had just given away, it was all gold coins, his emergency fund. It should be plenty for her to buy food for some while. Besides, he didn't need it half as badly as she.

He observed her closely. The bag was so heavy that she staggered and had to grasp it with both hands. She gazed up at him in blissful wonder, her eyes still full of tears, but also gratitude. Her face glowed. She had the biggest, brightest smile now, and her teeth were perfectly white. Despite everything else she had been through, she knew how to take care of her teeth.

"Follow me," she said with a giggle. She dashed away through the alleyways as gleefully as though she were skipping through a meadow of beautiful flowers. Searon followed her only a few paces behind. Even though he was clad in silver and crimson plate armor, he barely made a sound. Finally, Charlotte turned from the dirt pathways into a main road, completely empty of traffic. Searon stopped and stared. Ravens glared down from the rooftops at a pearly, octagonal building at the road's end. Charlotte nodded at the building and made a tiny gesture with her hand.

A few men talked among themselves. They barely paid heed to either Charlotte or Searon standing there. Blacksmiths' hammers pounding steel echoed up and down the road, which was made of colorful stone rather than dirt, in tans, blacks, grays, and reds, all laid out in a very precise pattern.

She stood behind him. Her voice shivered. "Sir Knight...please do not make me go any farther."

Searon turned around and smiled at the young child kneeling in front of him. "Thank you for your help, child. You may go now, but promise me you will get yourself a fine meal and a good night's sleep."

"I promise!" The little girl beamed up at him.

"May the stars shine over you and light up your path for the future," he whispered.

"Thank you, sir!" She bowed, dashed back into the alleys, and disappeared.

Chapter One

Searon's claymore was in his hands, glowing red, sparkling as he twirled it about to deflect blows from axes all around him. And yet, even as he defended himself against the black-scaled reptilian draeyks, the blazing orange eyes he saw in his dreams the night before were still the only thing on his mind. He felt as if those eyes were watching him still, and he could almost swear to have seen them through the thick forest enveloping him. Three draeyks lay dead on the ground. The stench of distilled vinegar and rotten eggs brought an awful taste in his mouth, taking away the scent of pine that he treasured so much.

Only two of the creatures remained, both cunning warriors but frightened at his skill with a blade. He didn't understand why he was having such a hard time killing the savage creatures. For the past three years, Searon had been slaughtering a few each and every day, yet it never seemed like it would be enough. There was only one of him, and there seemed to be thousands of the wretched creatures. Sometimes, it felt as if they would never be destroyed but would keep coming back to haunt him in his nightmares.

He charged the two draeyks in front of him, focusing all of his rage for the creatures. Anger bled from Searon's veins to his clenched fists, passing through them and into his claymore as it grew brighter and brighter, with such ferocity that it cast a crimson gleam to his weapon that was nearly blinding, even to himself. Searon's blade only glowed

5

while being used, almost appearing as if it was on fire. The crimson claymore was cool to the touch, but its steel was harder than any other sword, and if Searon pushed it a certain way it could fracture any other metal it came to contact with. Each of the creatures blocked his incoming strikes with so much precision that it baffled him. He tried changing the degree at which he slashed the blade, but the attempt seemed even more useless than what he was doing before. A flash of orange stole his attention as he looked into the oak trees beyond. Before he even heard the click of the crossbow, he felt the searing heat of a bolt puncturing his left shoulder. Gritting his teeth over a shout of pain, Searon tried to shake off the tingling burn that was running through his veins. He stepped forward, ready to finish off the bloodthirsty beasts.

Now three stood in front of him, two with axes held high, and another, farther back, with a crossbow in its grasp. He stood calm, teeth bared, soaked by raindrops under a blanket of storm clouds while thunder rattled the ground around him. His boots felt slick against the wet leaves and mud, yet he held his ground. He took a step back and sheathed his claymore in its scabbard. The two creatures in front rushed at him now that he was weaponless. He quickly ducked and leaped away from them as the third, with a crossbow, locked a bolt into place.

One draeyk brought its axe down toward Searon's head. He reached up and grabbed the weapon as another bolt pierced his forearm. His teeth clenched as a great moan of anguish escaped his mouth, but he did not let go. Despite the agony, he continued forward, allowing his rage to turn his pain into numbness. He kicked the draeyk in the gut, causing it to drop its weapon, which he was able to snatch before it hit the ground. Searon twirled the axe in his hands and chopped the overgrown lizard's scaly skull in two. Closing his eyes, Searon heard the crunch of scales and bone. Grimacing, the warrior wiped from his face the black ooze that filled his nostrils with the scent of spoiled milk and vinegar.

The other draeyk charged at Searon, delivering swift blows, which struck in such an odd pattern that made it difficult for Searon to deflect. He let the handle of the axe slide down his hands as he blocked another attack. Searon spun the axe around, feeling the imbalance of the weapon, and used the blunt side to slam into the creature's knee. A loud ding in his left ear echoed from where an arrow struck his crimson-and-gold helm. The draeyk in front of him collapsed to his injured knee in the mud, clearly defeated at the hand of Searon. Before Searon finished the creature, the warrior stared deep into its soulless red eyes with such hatred that the wretched reptile nearly flinched. Searon nodded approval at the defeated creature's distress before slashing its throat, causing thick ebony blood to pour down the creature's body before it collapsed onto the ground.

Searon turned to the remaining draeyk still holding a crossbow, and heaved the axe at its throat with inhuman speed. The reptile stepped aside with only millimeters to spare, and the axe pierced into the side of an oak tree, its handle wobbling from sheer velocity. Without a moment to spare, Searon ran forward, tackling the creature before it had a chance to reload its crossbow. They wrestled for a moment, the lizard's sharp yellow teeth unable to puncture Searon's armor. Drawing upon his superhuman strength and speed, Searon grappled with the draeyk a minute longer before growing bored with the struggle and rolling away while unsheathing his claymore. The creature, timid, attempted launching one last bolt toward Searon's face. Swiftly and without much effort, Searon curved his blade to intercept the bolt's tip, causing it to ricochet away, but the shaft still found its way to Searon's face, smacking against his jaw. His chin throbbed, and a deep red welt began to form. He sliced the creature's crossbow in half with annoyance and took another step forward where, with a sneer, he sliced its reptilian head from its shoulders.

He groaned heavily, sheathed his claymore, fell to his knees in the mud, and thanked the creator. When he opened his eyes, he noticed those same orange eyes that were so unsettling in his dreams the night before. No longer was he dreaming of them, but they floated in front of him, growing closer.

The thundering ceased with the rain; chirping birds and squeaking crickets were the only sounds that breached the silence surrounding him. An elderly man appeared from the shadows between trees, startling Searon. Despite his keen hearing and sight, he never saw nor heard the old man approaching. Long, wispy salt-and-pepper hair graced the stranger's shoulders, falling down in thick curly strands. A raggedy brown robe draped down past his shoulders to his feet where he wore thick brown leather boots. He walked with the aid of a tall, thick wooden staff that masked the color of bark and seemed to be made of hardened wood that nearly resembled glass. The tip of the weapon (as

Searon saw it) was five curled limbs that reminded him of fingers claw-ing for an unknown object. Searon clenched the hilt of his claymore and watched wearily as the old man approached him, radiant orange eyes glowing brighter with each step.

"Put that blade away, you fool," the old man said with a serene voice.

"Who are you?" Searon asked, staring deep into the man's demonic orange eyes.

"Someone who is much more attractive, and much smarter, than you are," the old man said with a gravelly voice.

"You're asking for it, old man." Searon's eyes narrowed in frustra-tion.

"No, if I were asking for it, I would simply ask. However, you may call me Karceoles," he said, folding his arms over his staff and grinning with lowered eyebrows.

"You must be wandering in the wrong forest. There are draeyks all through here," Searon said in an attempt to frighten him off.

Karceoles kept his smile. "You underestimate me, boy. Besides be-ing more attractive and smarter than you, I'm also exceedingly strong-er."

Searon grew tired of the old man now, and the way he talked with-out the slightest hint of respect in his voice. He studied the man's face: full of hard lines, a strong, rounded jaw, swirling flames of orange for eyes, and, although he seemed aged, his wrinkles made him appear more wise than old.

"What do you want?" Searon asked, growing weary of the old man and ready to be on his way.

"Some help. I'm looking for someone to start a war, and I've found you. That is a lovely horse," he said.

Searon turned to see his black-and-white striped stallion approach-ing, saddle and bags secured tightly; the mighty steed apparently obvi-ous to the old man. It nuzzled its cheek against Searon's palm, which the warrior stroked before climbing atop the magnificent beast.

"I want no part of any war," Searon said.

"I'm afraid it's too late…" Karceoles's eyes wandered off, as if searching for something.

Searon began to wonder what the old man was talking about, but before he came to an answer, four draeyks jumped out from the trees with axes raised. He raised his claymore and blocked an incoming blow at the same time. Karceoles raised his staff and blocked the strike of the axe. Searon found it strange when the axe didn't slice through the wood, but the old man blocked it, creating sparks with his staff as if it were metal. Karceoles swiftly moved his staff with ease, blocking every strike by the draeyks and adding offensive parries of his own at an ungodly speed. Searon, already in a weakened state, had a tough time battling the draeyks. They outmaneuvered him, and then one struck him in the knee and caused him to fall off his horse.

Searon continued to fight from a kneeling position and was able to overcome a draeyk and strike it down. As he did, there was an incoming blow from behind that he wasn't fast enough to catch. An axe sank into his shoulder, forcing him to fall flat on the ground, his face in the dirt. Searon tasted crunchy leaves, with a bit of blood in his mouth. At that moment, Karceoles slew his draeyk, and he raised his staff to point at the last two creatures by the warrior. Searon rolled over to stare at the two lizards above him as a swirl of orange flame escaped the tip of Karceoles's cane and tossed the two draeyks at lightning speed into a thick tree. Their piercing screams were the last sounds of their existence.

Karceoles walked up to Searon and offered his hand. The fallen warrior hesitated. Sighing deeply, Searon accepted the help and got to his feet with the old man's aid. He looked around to see four dead draeyks, and his eye twitched when he looked at Karceoles.

"What are you?" Searon asked tilting his head.

He studied the old man and noticed his deep-brown cloak covered his tan robes with a hood. The old man's eyes were no longer orange but a dark brown that seemed to flicker with slight hues of orange every few seconds. With his tangled-salt-and-pepper hair, he looked strange without a beard to warm his face. It was custom for most of the older men of the land to grow beards, but this man seemed to make a point of keeping it shaved.

"I am a wizard. As I have said, I am stronger than you," Karceoles said, lowering his cane to rest upon it.

Astonishment came to Searon, as he'd only heard rumors and stories of wizards. If they'd ever existed, they were supposed to have gone extinct at the same time as the dragons. He couldn't be sure if the old man was telling the truth or not because he had never seen a true wizard or knew what they looked like. The only thing he remembered was they wore robes and cloaks and held a staff. It was also known that their power resembled their eyes and robes. However, Searon considered how ridiculous orange robes would look upon the strange old man.

"What is that?" Searon asked, pointing to the large wooden scepter. It was the plainest weapon he'd ever seen that held so much power.

"This is called a zylek, which means *channel of energy*. It is customary for wizards to carry one so we can focus our power instead of using it blindly," Karceoles smiled. "It also shows how much smarter I am than you. Now, you can make a comment about how great-looking I am, and all three things I've said about myself being more superior than you can fall right into place."

"I don't know how your mind works, old man, but no woman would find you attractive ahead of me," Searon beamed at the old man's confidence.

"We'll just have to see about that," Karceoles said, taking a step toward Searon and twirling his zylek with his strong, wrinkled hands.

"Aren't you supposed to have orange robes? Or are the stories false that match powers with robes?"

"My robes *are* orange."

Searon looked again.

"They're old…and dirty."

"Why do they have to be the same color?" Searon asked.

"If not, the magic that burns through me will burn through whatever clothes I wear. Therefore, wizards have learned to wear the same color, lest we wander naked."

"Are there a lot of wizards?" Searon asked, watching the old man closely, unsure if he could trust him.

"I am the last one left of Calthoria who is worth a grain of salt," Karceoles explained. The wizard raised his zylek, inspected it closely, and watched with concentration as it transformed from brown to orange.

"Are there more lands across the seas?" Searon asked, never having heard such tales about other continents. He was sure it was plausible, and there were some tales of people traveling to other continents, but he hardly believed those stories.

"There ought to be. How else might the kheshlars have migrated here?" Karceoles said, pulling his hair out of his glowing eyes and raising his eyes at Searon.

"There are kheshlars here? Where are they?" Searon asked. His heart raced. "I've only heard stories of kheshlars showing up here and there but never knew there were any here."

Tales of kheshlars traveled across the land, but none had ever been seen, and Searon wasn't sure it was any more than a story. His past few years had been filled with relentless traveling through human villages and cities, searching for draeyks to slay; he had never come across any kheshlars. He stroked his horse's mane as he pondered these thoughts.

"There's an entire section of their territory deep in the forest here in Calthoria. They have a capitol there called Sudegam," Karceoles said.

"That is unreal," Searon said, trying to remember the old stories of kheshlars that he heard.

"What is unreal is a foolish man trying to seek out all the draeyks of this land by himself. The draeyks of this land more than triple the numbers of humans," Karceoles said with confidence.

"Don't preach to me, *wizard*; I can handle myself," Searon said, gritting his teeth. Talking to the old wizard had grown exhausting, and he was tired of wasting time.

"Everybody has problems with the draeyks, boy; you're not the only one who has lost something because of them," Karceoles said as he sighed and drooped his head to one side.

"I don't know how you know so much about me, wizard. I live my own life. I don't need you telling me what is stupid or not," Searon murmured, reminiscing on his haunted past. He wondered if he was that transparent to the wizard and would have to do better guarding his emotions.

"You don't need anyone to tell you that facing them alone is stupid, boy. You already know that. This is another reason why I am much smarter than you," Karceoles smirked, expanding his chest to show his masculinity.

Searon clenched his eyes and held back his anger, remembering his family and how much he missed them. "Despite what you think, I will not quit hunting the draeyks."

"I'm not asking that you do. I'm merely suggesting that you be smarter about it," Karceoles said, holding his zylek from his body and letting it glow the brightest orange. Flashing swirls of orange magic enveloped the top of it; those swirls seemed to dance.

"And how is that?" Searon asked. He was interested in any information that would lead to the death of draeyks.

"Go to the kheshlars, and ask for their help. There is a great war coming soon, and if you humans can get the kheshlars to ally with you, you can defeat the draeyks once and for all," Karceoles said. The swirls cascaded out from the zylek and disintegrated into the crisp air.

"From what I heard about the kheshlars, they do not ally themselves with anyone who is not kheshlarn," Searon said, remembering the stories of old. It was often said that to ask a kheshlar for help was asking for a woman to be quiet during the birth of her son.

"You must try," Karceoles pleaded, eyes less focused and more concerned, watery in the sunlight.

"You are mad, wizard. I must do nothing. You cannot burst into my life and make demands of me; now leave me be," Searon said before putting his claymore back into its scabbard and turning away.

"Actually, I can, and I have. You will go to Sudegam, and you will ask for the aid of the kheshlars in the upcoming war against these reptilian creatures," the wizard said with hardened eyes and pursed lips.

"I will not. What war?"

"A leader has risen. It is time we have one as well."

Karceoles raised his zylek, and orange magic trickled from it that caught Searon's plate mail on fire, burning through to his flesh. He dropped to the ground and rolled until the fire put itself out in the brush, but the hot metal still burned against his flesh.

"Fool, do you think torture is going to work on me?" Searon growled. He could always handle pain; he had already lost everything he cared about, and physical pain meant nothing to him anymore.

"Yes…Yes I do," Karceoles smirked deceivingly.

Another swirl of orange magic flowed from his zylek and froze Searon in a block of solid orange ice. He was still conscious and stared at the wizard in disbelief, his eyes shifting but his body unmovable.

Karceoles shook his head, allowing his tangled white-and-gray hair to seemingly float in a breeze of magic. "Some fools never learn."

Chapter Two

Shivers traveled down Searon's partially frozen body as he stared through the orange ice that gave the world a lightened appearance. The color made the trees look a dark brown, almost black, eerie. He shivered as the cold ice encased his body. The surrounding orange clouds and deep-brown sky infused him with a lifeless feel. His face was finally free of the ice, and what he heard was far from lifeless. The sounds of animals hit him like a loose pebble tumbling from a cliff, and at first he felt overwhelmed. Life seemed to flow more there than he had ever imagined before. Each plant made a different sound and moved in a different way, as if they whispered to each other as they stared at Searon. Birds of all kinds sang in chorus with each other instead of the sonic competition that he'd grown so accustomed to. He could hear the contrast of blue jays, robins, doves, eagles, and so many others that he couldn't name.

Searon looked to the trees surrounding him and realized that he wasn't in the same place. His shoulder no longer pained him, and he wondered if something in the ice had healed it. No longer were there bare autumn trees with scattered colorful leaves; now he was looking at a forest of pine trees. The smell was so overwhelming and minty from the pine needles that he could taste in his mouth. He allowed the pleasant smell and taste to settle through his nostrils and mouth, soothing his mind. He recognized the white-and-red cedar trees, thick and bushy with leaves that were soft to the touch. There were also white fir trees, tall and thinned through the trunk. The needles were small, filling each branch. Red fir scattered the area, as well, and had different traits than the white fir; they were thicker and held longer needles. Most impressive, though, were the sequoias that draped the land surrounding Searon. The sequoias scraped the sky, nearly touching the clouds. Searon felt like a gnat in comparison. The trees looked older than time.

Searon struggled as he broke an arm free of the ice and fought to rip chunks off of his body. When he was free, he took a few steps forward and stumbled on the rough ground covered in pinecones. He noticed that he was alone and that the arrogant wizard was nowhere to be found. His horse was also nowhere to be seen, and besides the animals and chilled breeze, sound remained absent. He rubbed his neck, looking at the various bushes on the ground with small green leaves and red berries. His hand brushed against one plant that he'd always heard tales of but had never been so deep into the forest to see. It was a fern, one of the most beautiful plants that Searon had ever seen. The branches came out with a scattered variety of leaves that tapered off the long branches and grew shorter until reaching the end, each branch looking like a long triangle. A smile reached his face as he studied the forest surrounding him until his stomach rumbled from hunger. Behind him, hooves patted against pine needles, crushing them. He felt the hilt of his claymore and swiftly turned around.

Behind him he saw the wizard riding a large, shining brown horse, and his own white-and-black striped horse traveled alongside. The wizard held three rabbits in one hand and two ducks in the other, with a grin upon his face. He tossed the animals toward Searon, who was about to say something about being dragged to such a place, but fell silent as his stomach grumbled even louder.

"Well, don't just stand there. Prepare a fire!" the wizard barked.

Searon hurriedly organized small branches and logs in a cube, wedging dried pine needles and bark between the legs. Carefully, he pulled out his flint and steel, making sparks to light the dried needles. His stomach barked with hunger, and he carefully tied the rabbits and ducks to branches that he spun around the fire.

"What is wrong with you, old man? You can't just force people to go where you choose," Searon spat.

"Of course I can. I'm a wizard. You're just being stubborn," Karceoles smirked.

"Who's more stubborn, the one who doesn't agree, or the one who drags him along anyway?" Searon grumbled staring at the orange pool of water at his feet.

"You'll learn that I always get my way. If you weren't going to come of your free will, then I knew I would have to pursue other avenues of convincing you," Karceoles snickered.

"What is it going to take to get rid of you?" Searon snapped.

"Come with me to the kheshlars, and ask for their assistance," Karceoles said, motioning forward.

"What makes you think they will join our cause?" Searon asked. The course of action the wizard wanted to take seemed useless, knowing the stories of kheshlars. Searon remembered the stories told of a selfish race that only cared for themselves and the trees.

"*They* won't…but *one* will."

"One? One. You froze me in a block of ice to drag me halfway across Calthoria for *one* bloody kheshlar!" Searon spat.

"Yes," Karceoles paused. "Let me explain," he sighed and pulled out a long-stem pipe that he carefully filled with tobacco. "A long time ago, a kheshlar touched the untouchable. She did what every other kheshlar was too scared to do, in an attempt to save her own mother. For the kheshlars, dark magic is forbidden, but that was precisely what she studied. Foolishly, she thought dark magic was the only way to save her mother. The problem with dark magic is it is too powerful for a single person to control, and she was consumed by it. Her sister was forced to murder her to prevent her use of the dark magic further. When they looked for her remains, they were nowhere found.

Dark magic is a powerful thing, and it very powerful. It can reverse death, but it comes with a cost. The dead walk in a shell of their former selves. That particular kheshlar, filled with dark magic, strayed away from the other kheshlars until she found the draeyk settlements. With her intelligence, she united the draeyk tribes with her as their leader. Then she launched an attack against her own kind. The only thing she had left was revenge, revenge for the kheshlars killing her. This was nearly a hundred years ago when the kheshlars defeated her. She fled, injured, never to be seen again. Her sister still lives. I have a feeling that for the kheshlars, there is still a need to know what happened to their kin that strayed away from the path of the light."

"And this sister is the one you seek?" Searon asked.

"Ah, yes. You are smart indeed, boy. Blood is thicker than water, they say. Well, I say they are fools. Blood is thicker than molasses, and twice as sweet.

"What is her name?" Searon asked.

"Starlyn is her name. What do you think this remaining Starlyn desires more than anything?" Karceoles asked.

Searon thought for a moment before stating the obvious. "She wants to find her sister. Depending on her condition, help her come back to how she was."

Karceoles grinned, "Yes, you do learn quickly."

"And her sister is with the draeyks?"

"She was, years ago. I do not know where she is now, but Starlyn thinks she is, and she spends a lot of time hunting draeyks. The sister does not matter, what matters is an alliance with the kheshlars, and if they believe she is with the draeyks that can be an advantage."

"And if she's not?"

Karceoles grinned from ear to ear, "We'll improvise. Kheshlars are very protective of their lands…and all those who tread on it."

"I can see your logic, wizard, and so I will assist you, but if this doesn't work, I'm off on my own way," Searon said reluctantly.

"Fair enough," Karceoles agreed.

"So where is this kheshlar?"

Chapter Three

A slight breeze tickled Searon's unshaven face as he quietly crawled up the hill. The reek of vinegar and spoiled eggs rotted in his nostrils and mouth, and he had to use all his energy to block out the nauseating sensation. The clattering together in the distance sounded too much like swordplay. He knew the sound too well, and this echo wasn't practice; it was a struggle. His claymore gleamed crimson in the morning sun as he peered down the hill. At the bottom, Searon noticed a woman wearing clattering plate mail that formed a skirt above her knees, with thick plated turquoise boots and a large diamond of gold in front.

On the woman's sides were five draeyks, all with high-held one-sided axes with large spikes on the opposite side. She defended herself well, parrying from one to the next, with a complex technique that resembled a graceful shadow-sword technique, except that she carried a hammer. With the way she fought, it seemed she was twirling a feather. It was a sight to watch her singlehandedly battle five draeyks at once. She swirled her hammer and twisted her body, sometimes spinning through the air between two axes with only millimeters to spare. Searon watched in awe as she spun in the air, twirling as her left leg collided with the jaw of a draeyk. The draeyk fell to the ground just before she used her hammer to bash its head in. As she fell, she struck another in the chest. Both fell, lifeless, before her feet touched the ground.

Only three draeyks were left, and they battled fiercely against their skilled opponent. Searon debated rushing to her aid, but she seemed to be doing a decent job by herself. Besides, he didn't want to seem like a threat to her, as he didn't know the woman's personality or her allegiance. The two on her left struck at the same time, and she impressively blocked both with the same defensive stroke. She held her hammer steady with her left hand, grabbed a shuriken from her pouch, and bolted it into the neck of the third, causing loud gagging from the wound before the creature crumbled to the ground. Then two battled her, rage showing in snake eyes, and she backed up for a better position, tripping on a fallen axe. Without a second to lose, the two draeyks jumped at the opportunity. She grabbed one of the crossed armor straps on its chest, and her fingers scraped against hard scales as she tumbled to the ground with the draeyk on top of her. A dagger pierced through the rough scales of the creature's back as its carcass lay upon her.

Searon slid down the hill and mounted his stallion, shaking his reins, causing his pearl-and-onyx steed to gallop down the hill. The final draeyk glared at Searon as his horse rushed down the hill toward the creature. He held his claymore in his right hand, its weight making him lean slightly on the right from its heftiness. When in range, he jumped from Stripes and collided with the creature, knocking it to the ground along with its axe. He rose to his feet and placed both hands on his claymore, steadying the two-handed weapon, and swung it to each side of him before holding it secure in front of his face. The draeyk rolled and got to its feet with an axe in each hand, obviously taken from a fallen comrade. Both axes spun in the creature's hands, moving so fast that it was hard to tell whether the draeyk was about to slash at Searon with the two weapons or throw them at him.

Want to dance? Let's dance, Searon thought as he gripped his claymore tighter and swung the long blade at an toward the creature's left temple. The axes stopped twirling, and the one in its left hand abruptly shot up and blocked Searon's strike while the right swung toward Searon's armor. He was caught unexpected, and the axe crushed in his plate mail on his left shoulder. He quickly backed away and felt pain and blood dripping down his arm. The pain didn't slow him and he kept his composure more than he, even, expected of himself. He changed into defense and blocked one strike then the next. The axe struck short of reaching him and was harmlessly deflected.

Searon dashed forward now, growing impatient; and turning himself onto offense, he knocked an axe to the ground—along with the draeyk's hand who'd held it. The creature snarled, showing its sharpened yellow teeth. Nothing but rage came from the creature, and Searon held his own against the quickened attacks but had to come up with a new plan to end the battle—and quickly. Many options circled his mind, and he picked one quickly, tossing his claymore toward the creature that leaped out of the way to avoid being struck. Searon dove to the ground, gripping an axe from a fallen draeyk and launched it toward the last draeyk, impaling it in the head. The creature's jaw opened slightly before falling backward the ground.

Without a second thought, he rushed to the dead creature and sheathed his claymore. Surrounding him, he noticed, were nine dead draeyk. Vinegar and vomit attacked his nose again, and he looked around. With nine dead that meant the woman had defeated four before he even noticed her. That was quite impressive, and Searon didn't know of anyone besides himself that shared such a feat.

Searon rushed to the body that had fallen on top of the woman and jerked it off, tossing it to the side. He was surprised to find nothing underneath the creature but flattened grass.

"Looking for me?" a deep female voice asked.

Searon turned around abruptly and saw her standing before him with her teal-and-gold helm wedged between her elbow and breast. Blonde hair hung behind her head in a tight blue silk ponytail with two thick strands falling in front of her ears and down past her breastplate. Her skin was pale blue but radiated light that made her armor glow brighter in the sun. A loose shorter strand of hair that was considerably thinner than the other two fell upon her cheek. She had dark-scarlet lips that added to her beauty. Her eyes were a deep silver sapphire that sparkled as strongly as the gem itself, but the strangest of all were her silver eyebrows.

She wore tight midnight-blue chain mail with gold patches of plate mail throughout her arms, and golden swirls upon her chestplate. A blue-and-gold plate mail skirt hung at her waist that stopped just above her knees. Her boots didn't start until her knees, leaving a few inches of exposed silk skin that glittered in the morning sun. The chain mail was skintight, showing the definition of her body, including her tight stomach and belly button. On her sash at her waist was a dagger with a mix of topaz and sapphires in its hilt. There was also a large hammer shaped like a triangle with a thick spike at its tail. His eyes traveled back to her chestplate where they lingered for several minutes. Her chain mail was tight, and Searon had a hard time keeping his eyes away.

"My face is up here," she snapped, annoyed.

"Ah...yes...I am sorry. I was merely inspecting your armor. It is impressive."

He knew that she knew better than that, but he felt compelled to have an excuse. Even after being caught, he felt himself having a hard time keeping his eyes away from her body but held his gaze on her face. It became harder to look away from her face than it was from her bosom, as her eyes sparkled so beautifully that he couldn't gaze away from them.

She arched an eyebrow and smiled, "Of course."

Karceoles trotted down the hill and held the reins close to Searon's side now. "Oh my, are you hiding melons under that chain mail?"

She glared at the wizard with intensity in her eyes.

"My name is Searon. I'm a warrior hunting the draeyks. This idiot next to me is Karceoles, a wizard," Searon said.

Searon's head shook in despair at the remark the wizard had made. He should have expected as much coming from the sarcastic wizard, but even he didn't think such a rude comment could come from the old man. He should have known better. *Fool of a wizard.*

"My name is Starlyn of the high kheshlars of Sudegam," she bowed slightly, showing a sign of respect.

"What are you doing out here?" Searon asked, still not finding an opportunity to gaze away from her blazing eyes.

"I may ask you the same question. A simple human and an old wizard, hardly threatening to these wild creatures," she said.

"I think you would be surprised," Searon said, eyes darting to the wizard.

"I see...and why are you after the draeyks?"

"They are foul creatures that have been striking humans for too long, and it is time for their demise," he snapped.

Memories flooded his mind like overflowing rivers collapsing over cliffs in waterfalls. It pained him to have such thoughts circle in his mind, and he gritted his teeth using all his will to push the horrors of his past away.

Starlyn nodded. "I have been keeping the draeyks contained so they won't strike Sudegam."

Searon noticed that she seemed to withhold as much information about her reasoning to fight the draeyks as he did. He quickly brushed it off, as he wasn't ready to tell her the reason behind his bitterness either toward the creatures. Every time he did speak of it, he felt on the edge of fresh tears that he wouldn't allow to fall.

"You're not doing a very good job protecting the humans from them," Karceoles snapped with bitterness.

"Excuse me?"

"By keeping the creatures away from the kheshlars, you have provoked them into killing humans," Karceoles spat.

"That is not my concern; I am a kheshlar," Starlyn snapped.

"Congratulations, you know what it is that you are," the wizard said softly.

"I don't have to stand here and listen to this," Starlyn barked, turning away and clenching a fist.

"Wait," Searon beckoned.

He knew that the wizard didn't have a way with words, and he wasn't even sure if he could convince her of anything. He did know that he had to try. The wizard seemed clouded in judgment with his newfound bitterness toward the kheshlars. He hadn't realized the wizard cared so much for humankind before, and he didn't understand why. The woman in front of him seemed to be the only kheshlar that was actively fighting the draeyks. With her help and skills, they would be able to confront many more draeyks.

She turned around to look at him and bit her lip before licking it with her tongue. An eyebrow rose on her face, and she waited. There seemed to be a lack of patience on her face as she glanced a few times toward the wizard.

"If you don't like these creatures, why don't you help us? We're on our way to attack their camps and settlements," Searon said, appearing sincere.

"Only the two of you?"

"Yes, I've been told the kheshlars wouldn't bother helping us," Searon said.

He tried to keep his voice as neutral as he could to avoid discrimination against the kheshlars but still wanted it to remain clear that they would be denied for help. She looked from Searon to Karceoles a few times with doubt on her face.

"How do you expect to kill them all with one human and an overly annoying mage?" she asked glaring at Karceoles now.

"Wizard," Karceoles corrected with annoyance in his voice.

She glared daggers at him with eyebrows crunched together and eyes swollen.

"With the element of surprise on our side. We will move too quickly for word to get out. Victory has never been my objective. I have fully expected to not come back from this, but with your help we may be victorious. With or without your aid I will do this. The wizard seems to think there will be a war and with your help we can destroy them once at for all. I had my doubts, but that was before I saw you fight. I believe he is right. If you will not aid us, I will continue my plan, and I don't expect to return. Until now, that has always been my goal," Searon said.

Searon gulped as he finally admitted what he had always known since he set out on the quest. He probably wasn't coming back, and he hated to realize it. There was only the need to take as many of them down with him as he could before he would be struck down. Then he could rest in peace and meet his family once again in the afterlife.

"Can you keep the wizard in check?" Starlyn snorted with a half smile.

"No...probably not. You'll just learn to tune him out like I have."

He looked back to the wizard, who was smirking at him now. He was sure that the wizard knew that much of what he said went in one ear and straight out the other.

"All right, I'll help you, but there's something I must tell you first." Starlyn shuffled uneasily.

"What?" Searon asked.

He looked genuinely concerned as if hoped he could accept what she had to say. She shifted her eyes, looking at him hard in the face and quickly blushing. It seemed as if the kheshlar had been checking him out, and he shifted uneasily. He could tell what she had to say to him was hard for her, and he knew that if they were to travel together that one day he would have to tell her about his life.

"My sister...changed years ago...she left with the draeyks. She led them in a war against the kheshlars, and I injured her to protect Sudegam. I believe she is still with them. I want to destroy the draeyks as much as you but…but I will not kill my sister. She is not to be harmed. If we encounter her, we capture her and bring her back to the kheshlars," Starlyn demanded.

She sighed as she seemed to reminisce of her times with her sister. Her eyes closed and opened with fresh tears drizzling down her cheeks.

"As you wish," Searon said.

He couldn't imagine what it would be like to lose a sibling to the draeyks like that. At least his family had only been destroyed instead of turning them as dark as Starlyn's sister now apparently had become. He didn't know if he could bear something like that to happen to him.

"Good, now I have something more attractive to look at," Karceoles smirked.

Starlyn stood and glared at the wizard with ice in her silver sapphire eyes.

"Shut up, Karceoles," Searon said.

Chapter Four

The human, kheshlar, and wizard traveled relentlessly through the meadow without conversation. Searon was thankful that the wizard had kept his mouth shut during the journey. There were fewer trees to travel through ever since leaving the kheshlarn territory, and it made their path an easier one to follow. It also meant that they held less cover from wandering eyes, and so they made pace carefully. Searon only hoped the tales of the kheshlars were true—that they had sensitive hearing—and only that rumor kept him at ease through the open path.

Often he looked back at the kheshlar with scattered glances, where he studied her. He noticed her looking back at him and smiling without the attention of the wizard. Her smile was sincere, and she seemed to be studying him as much as he studied her. She had long blonde hair that sparkled in the sunlight, with waves that bounced with each stride. His eyes remained on her as often as it did the beast she traveled with. She rode on top of a jaguar, and he admired the beast's bronze fur with black spots. At first, he had been afraid of the creature when it had approached shortly after the start of their journey. Soon, he realized that the kheshlar had called the beast and she climbed atop it like he would a horse, but without a saddle! It kept high pace along with their horses, and so she hadn't slowed them in the slightest.

When the light from the stars touched them, she only seemed to glitter more in their glow. Her namesake was true, and she shone with their same intensity. It was almost as if she glowed at night, but it came and went with each smile that graced her lips. Searon wished he could get her to smile indefinitely because it brought such a profound beauty to her that he could never even dream of.

They agreed to stop to rest for the night, or at least for a time. There was nothing past their plan besides to stop and rest to find food. The kheshlar took off west through a small forest without a sound despite the scattered broken branches that lay among the bare trees. Searon decided to head east to search for wild game. His stomach was grumbling for something besides dried meat and water that filled his saddle.

He stalked the bare forest for what seemed like an hour before he heard the faint footsteps and the sound of a trickling stream. Peering through a prickly bush, he noticed a large wild boar drinking water. It shone black with stiff bristles and fine fur. Searon hadn't seen such a large boar before, and his mouth watered at the savory flavor it could create over a hot fire.

His hand dropped to the back of his sash where he grabbed an arrow from his quiver and detached his bow from his back. Its fine oak exterior molded in his hands as he remembered handcrafting it as a young man. The smooth texture rested in his left hand as he notched the steel arrow with his right. He hardly used the bow for more than hunting, and most of the time it stayed with his saddle and horse. Keeping his aim steady, he licked his left index finger and checked for wind. It was blowing to his left slightly in the same direction the small stream was heading. He held his bow tight, aiming to the right of the boar, and let go of his arrow. It whistled through the air with barely a sound, and before it could reach the boar he already had another out and notched. He didn't need the second arrow, as the first one struck the boar in the heart.

He walked to the large beast that lay by the stream, taking its last drink. *At least it became hydrated at its death.* With struggle, he hefted the beast onto his shoulders and struggled forward one step at a time. He didn't expect it to weigh so much, and his mouth watered even more at the amount of meat he would have.

Back at the camp, Karceoles sat on a stump with his long-stem pipe in hand in front of a fire. Both the pipe and the fire were smokeless, and Searon set the boar down beside it. The wizard laid his pipe on the stump and rose to his feet, tying the boar to a few large branches he seemed to acquire with twine.

"Magic trick?" Searon asked, glancing back at the fire.

The fire burned the wood, and it turned black, but there wasn't any smoke or the smell the smoke would produce. There weren't even any ashes or sparks traveling from the wood, and the tasteful crackling that Searon enjoyed so much was absent as well. It was rather impressive, and he was fascinated by the useful tactic for traveling.

"Well, you don't expect me to let them know our whereabouts, now do you?" Karceoles bit his tongue.

Starlyn approached and sat on the opposite side of the fire, where he now sat roasting the boar, with some vegetables and fruit that she picked while he hunted. She quietly ate from a shaped wooden bowl and made no notice of the others. It seemed she was deep in thought as she slowly picked at her food.

Searon filled his emptied water skin from the stream into a tin kettle. He added a few thick black leaves from his pouch before placing it next to the fire. It would be nice having some hot black tea with the fresh boar for once.

"Want some boar?" Searon asked with a disapproving look at her bowl.

"I do not eat animals," Starlyn said, still avoiding his gaze, and her nose seemed to cringe in disgust.

"Why not?" Searon asked, bewildered.

"No kheshlar does; it is cruel to end the life of a living creature just to settle our stomachs. We can better ourselves and don't need meat to survive," Starlyn said, looking deep into the wizard's eyes now.

"Yeah, but what about those poor plants? You tear them to shreds, and they are living as well. It would be better off if we all just starve and die," Karceoles said.

"Plants still live when you take from them; animals *do* not," Starlyn said.

"Not all plants continue to live after picked. The animal's offspring are like the plants seeds; when the plant dies the seeds are left to carry on the family. The same goes for animals. All creatures die one day, and animals are meant to be eaten; it's the circle of life. Meat makes us stronger, as we are not naturally strong like your kheshlarn kind. We must have more energy to feed our bodies for the strength that we need," Karceoles defended.

Silence filled the air, and Searon often checked on the boar, eagerly awaiting it to be cooked. Once it was fully cooked throughout, he and Karceoles set the beast down and began carving it with knives. There was much that the two set aside to be dried out and packed back in their packs as travel food, but they immediately carved their favorite parts for their meal of the night. Searon cringed as he noticed the wizard had taken the hog's brain, heart, and other organs to feast upon.

When their stomachs were full, Searon pulled out his pipe, followed by Karceoles. The wizard held his zylek next to his pipe and began puffing, allowing it to ignite the tobacco and herbs. Searon held out a taper he ignited from the fire and placed its tip on his tobacco, inhaling the soothing mixture of raspberry leaves and harsh tobacco with whiskey spice. Smoke encircled them before disappearing with the wizard's magic. Searon was glad to have the aroma linger in the air for a few moments making a pleasant smell to go with the boar and the fire.

"Why are you really after the draeyks? I know there is more to it than you will let on. There is a personal hate toward these creatures. I know there is because I share that same quality with you," Starlyn said. She looked at him with interest and seemed to scoot forward slightly.

Searon nearly choked on his pipe and coughed a few times, allowing too much smoke to escape his lungs. He looked at her and opened his mouth in an attempt to speak, but no words came out. Closing his eyes in frustration, he rested his head on his clenched fist that turned white from the blood draining from it. When he looked back up to meet her gaze (that hadn't faltered), he attempted to speak again, but still no words would flow. Exhaling deeply, he cursed and rose to his feet and walked away from the camp without looking back.

Shivering from the cold night, he walked just far enough out of earshot from the camp and stabbed his claymore into the ground. Leaning on its handle, he looked at the stars that shone extra bright that night. They blurred in his vision, and he fought back tears from falling. His heart pounded inside his chest, and he shivered at the haunting memories that sank back into his mind. He knew the time was coming to divulge the information to the helpful kheshlar, but he didn't think he was ready yet. It was hard enough having the burden to bear, but sharing it was even harder.

With only a few minutes of silence, he heard footsteps treading the ground behind him. There were three distinct presses against the ground, and he knew it wasn't her. Turning around, he saw Karceoles staggering up to him, using his zylek as a walking stick. He stopped in front of Searon and leaned on his zylek. The wizard shook his head and spat on the ground before taking his pipe out and giving it another puff.

"Do not take your suffering out on that innocent kheshlar who only wishes to help you. She wishes to connect with you because the both of you have a personal interest against these draeyks," Karceoles said, brushing his long grimy hair out of his face with his right hand.

What the wizard said caught Searon by surprise, and he swallowed hard. He had never heard the wizard speak with such serenity and compassion. Surely, there had to be an ulterior motive for it, otherwise the wizard would be provoking conflict instead of trying to resolve it.

"Since when do you care?" Searon challenged.

Frustration baked Searon's bones, making them feel like they were aflame. He wasn't cold anymore, but he still shivered at the haunting thoughts seeping through his mind. Every time his past came up, it only got worse for him. All he wanted to do was bury it and move on without glancing back through his personal history.

"She can be a great ally for fighting the draeyks and eventually connecting the kheshlars to our cause!" Karceoles spat.

Realization struck Searon now, and he contemplated on the wizard's wisdom. Wisdom? He had never known the wizard actually had any. Most of the time, it seemed the wizard spat out of his mouth before he could think, but Searon realized every foolish move the wizard did was a part of his greater plan. *Where do I stand in this fool's plan? I don't want a part of this. I only want to kill the draeyks and go home...home...No, I want solitude, not a home.*

"Is that all you care about?" Searon asked.

He cursed himself inside. If the wizard didn't know everything he seemed to about the draeyks, he could ditch him. But *could* he ditch the wizard? It seemed the wizard knew every button to push and where to find anyone that held problems with the draeyks. Perhaps the old man had only been lucky so far, but why take that risk? Searon knew he had to follow the old man—and into the war he was creating. *I want no part of any war. Curse wars.*

"There are other reasons, but yes, to be blunt. Now go apologize, you fool of a human."

Searon cursed himself in his head again. It was a strange feeling to be wrong about something and especially a strange feeling for the wizard to be right. He knew there was little chance of receiving any help from the kheshlars in the future, but with Starlyn...there was a chance. No matter how little of a chance, it was still a chance. The wizard tilted his head toward the campfire and cleared his throat.

The memories he kept suppressed for so long drowned him in such a rush that he could barely breathe. He remembered the first time that he had seen Victoria, his love.

* * *

They called him the captain of Legain, and they attacked the city of Tiermera. Tiermera had sent mercenaries into Legain that had sabotaged and stolen their food supply. There was little forgiveness in the city of Legain, and they placed Searon in charge of storming the city of Tiermera with an army of warriors at his side.

He remembered the battle well as it was his last; at least he'd promised himself that it would be. Storming the city, they left no male survivors. Every warrior and every man that bore arms Searon and his men struck down without even a thought of pity.

With the city in ruins, they had cheered their victory, taunting at the faces of the women and children before riding off. Searon waited back to be the last to exit the city as was accustom for the captain of the force. Without a sight of any of his men left, he'd trotted his horse forward, nearly pitying the women and children of thieves. Something had caught his eye, though, before he reached the outskirts. It was a glistening ruby necklace attached around the neck of a young lady. Searon pulled his brown mare to a stop and glanced at the young woman. Tears filled her eyes and dropped into her hands that held prayer in front of her.

Curious, Searon had edged his horse forward toward the young woman. She didn't flinch or even pay him heed even when his horse stopped right at her side. She continued to pray with her eyes closed and tears gently falling down her cheeks. He looked to the ground at which she prayed and saw a graying man with a clean stab wound through his chest. Searon recognized the man as one of his killings. The old man actually had impressed him in battle and was quite a formidable foe.

"Father, may the light shine on your soul," the woman's voice said shakily.

A lump seemed to get caught deep in Searon's throat as he dismounted and stood next to her. Her eyes opened, but she did not look at him. The expression of knowing that it was he that killed her father was clearly shown on her face. She did not make an attempt to strike at him or curse, or even glance at him in any way.

"I am sorry," Searon whispered.

"It is not your fault. You did as you are told, and you were told to storm our village," she whispered.

Her voice was soft like a wind chime soothing in the night. Searon seemed captivated by it as well as the young woman's beauty. Her straight, glossy brunette hair hung just below her shoulders, and her lips seemed small but firm with the bottom one twice as large as her top. She glanced at him, and he was taken aback by her swirling brown eyes like shimmering pools of delicious chocolate. Her eyes did not carry hate or displeasure of any kind toward Searon, and for that he was relieved. Her nose was small and full of freckles and seemed to twitch when she looked at him.

"What is your name, my lady?" Searon had asked calmly.

Her thin eyebrows drifted at his question, but she'd looked at him in calm wonder nonetheless. "I am Victoria, daughter of Joseph."

Searon was both taken aback by the mention of her father's name and relieved at the same time. With her using that title, it had meant that she had not been married and so he had not killed her husband. It also gave the fact that had killed her only family and the one that meant dearest to her.

Something about her had an effect on Searon unlike any other, and he didn't quite understand it. He felt like he could travel to the end of the earth for her. For a taste of her lips he would circle the earth time and time again if he was able. His heart pounded hard in his chest at such thoughts. Never before had a woman affected him so. He had never taken a woman, and most of his time was spent in the glory of the battlefield, but now he wasn't too sure of himself anymore.

He knelt before her, and she looked down at him in surprise. "My lady, I am truly sorry for your loss. My name is Searon, and if you take my hand I solemnly promise to never cause harm to any again unless it is in defending you."

Searon looked at her eagerly for an answer. It did not come, though, and she stared down at him in seemingly disbelief. She seemed to be taking her time in considering his request. Searon did not budge in the slightest and kept his stare at her eyes true.

"Why should I trust in the word of a brutal warrior?" she asked.

"I had almost left this town until something caught my eye. I saw you standing alone over here and felt something inside of me that told me to come see you. I have never seen anyone or anything as beautiful or as kind as you, and if you let me I will spend the rest of my life proving my worth to you..." Searon said softly as he looked at her.

She blushed thickly, making the freckles on her cheeks seem to sparkle. "What makes me more special than another?"

"No others have caught my eye like you have. I feel that once I have you, my life will be complete."

"And no more killing the innocent?" she whispered.

"You have my word, my lady. My sword will only strike those who wish to harm you." Searon bowed his head.

She smiled slightly and nodded, "I accept, Sir Knight Searon."

With that, the first smile that wasn't from bloodshed came across Searon's face. He leaped up from being on his knee and took Lady Victoria into his arms. Gently, he placed her on the back of his horse before getting atop the saddle himself. He rode off into the blood-red sunset with her arms cautiously around him.

* * *

Chapter Five

Searon exhaled deeply, knowing the wizard was right. He knew he needed to talk with Starlyn and open up to her. There would be a use for her skills, and he knew it. It was hard remembering the past that haunted his dreams every night, and he tried to remember the last time he woke up without a cold sweat.

He paused for a moment before leaving the wizard behind to walk back to camp. Starlyn still sat in the same spot she had before he left, with her back to him. Her legs were crisscrossed on the dirt a few paces from the fire, her hammer in her hand. She sharpened the edges with a stone, creating scraping sounds that echoed through the camp and sent chills down Searon's spine.

"I'm sorry. I was out of line to walk away from you."

She looked deep into his eyes, her own silvery eyes swirling with understanding. He knew that she had her own feelings toward the draeyks and imagined it was just as hard for her to talk about.

He sat down next to her, holding his legs tight in his arms and inhaled deeply. A trail of ants paced the ground in front of him, and he stared at them with interest. Grabbing a small stick on his right, he poked at them, causing a disruption in their pattern. Looking back to Starlyn, he saw she was still staring at him, and yet a word had not escaped her lips. It would make things easier if he didn't have to look into her mesmerizing eyes.

"It's just hard talking about it…about my past," he sighed.

He looked up to her for only a moment before casting his eyes back to the ground and scattering ants. Words were harder to get out than he thought. He knew he had to get it out or it would eat at him from the inside. Still, there was nobody that he had told what had happened to his family. Even the wizard didn't know, yet somehow there was knowledge in his eyes that Searon dared not think about.

"Sometimes, it is better to let things out. It can become unsettling inside our minds, clouding our judgment," Starlyn said softly, still staring at Searon.

"I haven't told anybody about what happened," Searon shook his head as haunting memories dawned on him once again.

"Not even the wizard?" she asked.

"No…but I think he knows. I don't yet know how…curse wizards," Searon said.

He began to ponder if the old man could read minds with magic or see the happenings around the land with it. There was still question as to how the old man knew so much, but he didn't feel up to asking.

"If you don't wish to talk about it, I understand." Starlyn twirled a flower in her hand between her fingers. It was a beautiful blonde lily that glittered from the starlight with the same hue as her glistening hair. She held it back to where she picked it from, and it seemed to mold itself back to life. When she removed her hand from the flower, it was attached back into the ground and life flowed through it once more.

"No…you are right. I need to talk about it. The nightmares haunt me every night, and it is hard to willingly think about that night." Searon took a deep breath and looked back into her eyes. They were inviting, willing him to continue.

"What happened that night?"

"Forty months, three days, and twenty-one hours ago was when I woke up." Searon shook with shivers.

"You keep track?" Starlyn asked, bewildered.

"No…I just know…somehow…I know exactly how long it has been, and yet I never think about it."

"What happened?"

"I came home and ate dinner with my wife as I always would. After dinner, I went into my son's room and kissed him goodnight. It was like every other night. I didn't suspect…I…there was no warning," Searon brushed his hands through his thick brown hair. "That night...draeyks broke into our home and slaughtered my family. I watched them as they mercilessly murdered my family while I tried to fight back. Never had I faced a draeyk before and thought they were only a campfire story. By the time I had killed all the draeyks, my family was already dead. Since that moment, I have vowed to hunt down all the draeyks I could find and slaughter them one by one," Searon said, quickly feeling the weight lift from off of his chest. Tears filled his eyes, but he quickly dabbed them away, not wanting to shed any more tears over that night. The past would not change, but he could look forward to the future.

"I am sorry you had to endure that; it must have been terrible," Starlyn whispered.

"If I dwell on it too much, it only gets worse. I try to stay focused and keep going forward. Nothing can be done about the past, but I can do something about the future. I will keep fighting draeyks until I die," he said with anger replacing his grief.

"Something doesn't make sense," Starlyn said.

"What?"

"You had never seen draeyks before that night. They had not been a problem in nearby villages? There were no rumors of them in the area?"

"No...humans were oblivious to their existence before. We knew only of daerions...and they are long extinct now. History books told us of the Battle of Lenor Lake where we defeated the daerions. Humans only battle each other, and that was why I left the cities in place of a small village."

"For what reason were you attacked first?"

Searon looked at her, puzzled, and dropped his eyes down deep in thought. He hadn't ever thought of it before now. Still now, his family's slaughter rattled in his brain with every detail he could fathom, but his mind still wouldn't delve into the reasons it might have happened.

"I do not know...it wasn't just me...our entire village was destroyed. I think I may be the only survivor. After burying my family, I traveled back to the village to find it in ruins. There were a few draeyks still lingering there, and I slaughtered them before leaving, never to turn back."

"It seems our friends were searching for something in that village. I wonder if they ever found it," she whispered.

She had given him something new to ponder, and he lost himself in thought. There was a lot of wisdom in her words, and he realized that men were more people of action while women thought about the bigger picture. Perhaps it would be good to have her travel with them.

"We are alike, you and I; both of our families have been lost to the draeyks." Starlyn wiped a tear that threatened to fall down her face.

"It is good to have a friend," Searon nodded.

He rose to his feet at the same time as she did. She stepped closer to him, and he flinched as she gave him a hug before she disappeared into the night. The wizard stepped into the area and gave a thumbs-up before lying down in the grass to watch the stars. Searon propped himself up against a large smooth stone that rested near the fire before he closed his eyes for darkness to consume him.

Searon awoke in the middle of the night startled as Starlyn slid behind him to lie down. She put her arms around his waist, sliding under his armor to feel his fit abs. At first, it made Searon uncomfortable, and he shivered at the sudden affection. But after a moment, he grew fond of the closeness and smiled, closing his eyes once again. It had been a long time since he had known the comfort of lying down next to a woman. He wasn't ready for a relationship, or even anything close anytime soon, but it was still nice to have someone that close to him. When he closed his eyes yet again, the cruel nightmares didn't haunt him anymore that night.

Chapter Six

Sun rising through the trees created a blazing yellow light that blinded Searon. He woke with a yawn and realized for the first time that he had woken up after the sunrise. It truly had been a relaxing night after Starlyn joined him. There was no recollection of nightmares for him from the previous night, and he smiled, tossing his arm behind him. He found that the space was empty, and he shivered turning around to see Starlyn was nowhere in sight. She could have just wanted some comfort in the middle of the night, as their previous conversation most likely stirred bad memories for the both of them.

Reluctantly he rose to his feet and stretched out his muscles. It was something he tried to accomplish every morning to prevent strains. He stopped in his tracks to watch an exotic blue-and-red butterfly flutter by. It landed on a low branch in a nearby tree and flapped its wings a few times. The creature appeared to not have a care, and Searon often wished he had such a carefree life. He marveled at its simple beauty as it flapped its wings to hover for a moment before traveling north. His eyes continued to follow the creature until it flew past Karceoles.

Searon stalked over to the wizard, who was staring north after the butterfly. His zylek was in his right hand and his pipe in his left. The pipe wasn't hot, as he wasn't smoking it but simply holding it. Searon stood next to him and looked into the sky where Karceoles was looking. There was a thin trail of smoke rising through the trees into the sky in the far distance. It was barely noticeable through the morning mist, but it was still clearly smoke.

"Draeyks?" Searon asked.

He didn't imagine they were that close to the settlements, as he thought they were still several leagues away and the smoke came from a league or two, max. The smoke that rose in the distance wasn't fresh but a smoldering remnant of a previous fire. It meant there was something traveling out there.

"I don't think so; that isn't the location I remember from the map of their settlements," Karceoles said.

"We ought to check it out then. Where is Starlyn?"

He looked around in hopes to spot her somewhere, but there wasn't any sign. The last he had seen of her was in the middle of the night. She hadn't given him a reason to distrust her, but he still was unsure about her.

"I am unsure; she was not here when I awoke this morning." Karceoles wrinkled his nose.

"Well, I don't think we should wait on her; if that smoke comes from either humans or kheshlars, there may be more allies out there for us." Searon fidgeted his hand around the hilt of his sword, touching the sharp rubies.

He was ready for another battle and could taste the blood on his lips. It had been far too long, at least for him, and he looked forward to the next time he could slash his claymore through the air. His mind would wander too much when he would keep still.

"You are right. Let's go, keep an eye out for the babe," Karceoles attached his zylek to his pouch and nodded his head.

The two saddled up, jerking the reins of their horses to trot forward. It was still early morning, and fog clouded the horizon. Condensation covered the light grass on the ground, and their horses were very gentle and quiet as they galloped. The morning air felt cool through their nostrils, almost too cold, as Searon began to shiver.

Suddenly, the fog cleared a small area, and someone appeared before them. Searon raised his claymore while Karceoles lifted his zylek and took aim. As the fog thinned, they recognized Starlyn standing before them, hammer raised and stained with blood. She had heat rushing through her body, and her face held rosy cheeks and luscious red lips that Searon found tempting.

"Humans, fighting draeyks, they need help," she gasped.

Three draeyks lay on the ground, dead before her feet, and she swiftly attached her hammer to her sash. She faced north and glanced back to the two of them before dashing forward back through the fog.

"Let's go!" Karceoles called.

Starlyn kept well ahead of them despite her being without an animal to ride. They were blindly galloping into the fog and had to trust their horses' instincts that followed Starlyn's scent. His horse, Stripes, suddenly stopped unexpectedly, and he was tossed from the saddle where he collided with Starlyn. The two tumbled onto the ground with Starlyn falling on top. Searon's eyes never made it all the way up to her face, and Starlyn rolled her eyes before getting off of him. He froze in place for a moment after she was gone before shaking his head from the memory and rising to his feet. She pulled her hammer from her sash, and Searon followed suit, grabbing his claymore from its scabbard.

In the distance, Searon noticed a clearing through the fog and watched as a human was struck down by a draeyk. There were two dead humans sprawled on the ground now among four dead draeyks. There were still two humans left standing that were putting on a fierce battle against the last three creatures. The last two warriors both battled without helms. Searon figured they had been caught by surprise or their helms had been knocked to the ground during the battle. One, with straight black hair that nearly touched his shoulders and a clean-cut face, held a higher skill with a weapon than the other. His fighting companion wasn't as skilled and held an axe instead of a broadsword. He blocked attacks fiercely with the wind tossing his thick brown dreadlocks across his face.

The two fought well with each other and had obvious practice in teamwork. However, the man in dreadlocks that held an axe began to slip on his strikes. He injured two of the draeyks in the shoulder, but they snarled and jumped at him using their own axes to slice him down. His voice cried out in pain just before his body went limp.

Searon jerked his horse's reins, causing the animal to dash forward. He looked to his side and noticed Starlyn next to him with her hammer drawn and a fierce look upon her face.

The lone warrior struck hard with his sword, holding it only with his right hand. It was shaped like a broadsword but seemed to have a smaller blade allowing him to maneuver the sword with only one hand. He stabbed at one of the draeyks while punching another one. The third he was able to strike down after a series of blows, leaving him only two left. One jumped forward and struck his head with the backside of the axe, and the warrior fell to the ground.

Searon's stallion slid in front of the two draeyks before they could give a deathblow. He blocked their attacks and was joined by Starlyn at his side. The two battled perfectly together against the draeyks. Their strikes were almost in unison with each other, and they switched opponents. When they switched, it confused the creatures, and their guard was let down. It was long enough that both were able to deliver deathblows at nearly the same time. Searon's blow came from overhead, slicing the scaly creature's skull in half while Starlyn's was an uppercut that shattered the creature's jaw with her hammer. Starlyn turned to Searon and grinned, causing him to smirk back before nodding.

Karceoles finally arrived next to Searon as he got off his horse to hold the young warrior up. He checked his pulse and found the man was still alive. There were cuts across his arms and a stab wound into his stomach. Searon looked up to the wizard.

"Can you heal him?"

"No, I'm not that type of wizard. Most of my energy I focused on learning flame, not healing. I can heal to an extent, but most of it will be external," Karceoles said.

"Perhaps now would be a good time to learn," Searon rumbled.

Starlyn moved closer to the human warrior and began tracing her hands across his wounds. She ran her fingers across his stomach, arms, and face. They had stripped him of his armor to his cotton clothing underneath that was stained red. His abdomen was fit and scrawnier than Searon, but he still held strength enough for battling. The wounds weren't too deep, but his injuries were still threatening if he didn't have medical help.

"I can heal these, but we need to find some herbs. Some can be found in this meadow, but others we need to head back to the trees for," Starlyn said.

"There is a forest to the west, not far," Karceoles said.

"Come, Searon," Starlyn grabbed Searon's hand and nearly dragged him to his feet.

He felt the cool of her soft skin touching his now that his gauntlets were attached to his sash. A warming smile graced Starlyn's lips as her eyes met his. It was strange having another hand in his, and he looked at it reluctantly before glancing to the wizard.

"Will you watch him?" he asked.

Glancing back down to her hand, he noticed how much paler it was than his own. It was cool in his hand but it wasn't cold, and he found he liked the presence of it.

"I'll be the babysitter this time, but hurry, there's not time for **fun**," Karceoles glared at the kheshlar, who only smiled back at him.

Searon slid back onto his horse, and surprisingly, Starlyn jumped on behind him and clasped her arms around his waist before resting her head on his shoulder. A half smile found his lips before he tugged the reins, making Stripes gallop off.

Chapter Seven

Searon's horse pranced forward through the small meadow with Starlyn at his back, clutching hard onto his plate mail. She seemed uneasy at traveling on a saddle and behind Searon. It could probably be assumed that it was both her first time on a saddle and riding behind someone. When they reached the end of the meadow through the thickening sun, she whispered in his ear to stop. He clutched the reins, causing Stripes to halt, and he looked around. The meadow was clear besides a few fluffy white clouds above them that only blocked enough sun to withstand being completely blinded by its bright yellow rays.

She gently dropped to the ground and stalked over to a small bush with large leaves and violet flowers. Searon kept on his horse, stroking his mane for comfort while watching Starlyn out of the corner of his eye. She brushed her hands through the five large flowers as if searching for the perfect one. Finally satisfied, she pulled two and held them tight to her chest as she made her way back to him. She handed him the two flowers, and he studied them curiously. Both were deep blue in color and turned bright green near the petals. The two flowers must have been hard to find when the majority of them on the bush were violet. He cautiously wrapped them in a red linen handkerchief and stuffed them in an empty saddlebag.

She lifted herself back onto the saddle and sat behind him, tugging at her hair.

41

"What are those called?" he asked.

"Adueur… they are rare in these colors and hold more healing potency than the purples…and they're less bitter."

Searon watched as her glittering sunflower-blonde hair fluttered in the wind. Her electric silvery eyes resembled jolts of electricity that bolted outward from her pupils and sparkled to match the stars at night. Her beauty outmatched any human that he had ever met, and yet he felt nothing for her. Nobody could tear away the love he had felt for his wife, and even though her physical beauty hadn't compared to this kheshlar before him, in his eyes Victoria was absolute perfection.

He became lost in thought, and her body faded out of existence, replaced with memories.

* * *

Victoria clutched at his waist as he rode off into the sunset to begin his life anew with her in it. There was something about the way she clutched at him as they rode into the sunset atop his brown mare. She seemed to want the closeness with him but was still afraid of what kind of person he was. He knew he would have to prove himself to her before she fully trusted him. She had accepted his proposal, but she was still reticent about accepting him as a husband.

When they arrived at his small gray slate home, he noticed her anticipation. Worry stained her face at what his intentions were, and he had to prove himself to her that he was kind. After dismounting, he gracefully lifted her into his arms and pushed open his front door. Inside, candlelight lit the room, and it was larger than it appeared from the outside. He strode into the bedroom with her still in his arms before he rested her on his bed. She looked up at him with concern on her face, and he leaned down to kiss her on the forehead.

"Rest well, my darling fiancée."

Without pausing to see her reaction, he left the bedroom to rest in his chair in the front room. He pulled out his pipe and lit it carefully, pondering the events of the day. In his room rested the most beautiful woman he had ever come across. It wasn't only that, but she glowed unlike any other as if the heavens were making her known to him. He rested his pipe on the small table and shut his eyes to patiently wait for the next morning.

The next morning, he awoke to the smell of fresh porridge lingering under his nose. He opened his eyes to see Victoria dressed in loose cotton clothes of his, setting two bowls of porridge on his cedar table with two cups of fresh squeezed orange juice. His eyebrows rose as he got to his feet and approached her.

A smile brightened her face when he secured his arms around her and relaxed his jaw on her shoulder. She motioned for him to sit, but instead he pulled out her chair for her and set her down properly before relaxing in his own. The soothing smell of cinnamon, brown sugar, and oats relaxed Searon.

"This is a surprise," Searon grinned.

"It is gratitude, for not pressing consummation last night."

"We have not made our vows for each other yet; my fiancée and I have no interest in consummation until after our marriage. It will not be until you are ready."

An exhale of relief spread across her face, and a slight smile appeared. Searon nodded and silently ate his scrumptious porridge before directing his attention back to Victoria. He chuckled as he glanced back over his loose clothing she was wearing.

"It seems I must take you shopping today; besides, you must pick out a dress to marry in."

A smile lit her face, and she swiftly washed the few dishes before sliding back into her freshly washed black silk dress. She strode forward into Searon's arms, who took her wholeheartedly. Looking into his eyes, her face lit up, and she bit her lip. Her freckles glimmered in the candlelight, and he fought the urge to kiss her. There was nothing more that he wanted at the moment than to feel her soft lips upon his, but he held his desires back. Searon did not want to act hastily with her. He knew waiting for marriage would be the hardest thing he would have to do, but somehow in his heart he knew that it would be worth it. For the moment, he was at his happiest with only her in his arms. He felt complete, which was something he had never known before.

* * *

"Searon?" a familiar voice whispered unseen.

His memories swirled back into nonexistence, and reality consumed him. Looking down, he saw Starlyn at his back on his horse, staring at him with concern. Sighing heavily, he pulled at his hair and coughed. He wondered how long he had been lost in a haze of memories.

"Are you all right?" she asked.

"Yes, I am fine," Searon shrugged and cracked his neck. "Starlyn...about last night."

His mind flashed again back to the memory of her arms around him throughout the night. Even though he felt warm and peaceful through the night for the first time in ages, it still wasn't something he was ready to get used to. He had been alone for too long, and his memories still faded to Victoria every chance they could.

She dropped her grip from her ear and bit her lip, eyeing him. Her eyes either filled with hopefulness or surprise.

"What about last night?" she asked with innocence.

"When you came in the middle of the night and slept by my side. Either to comfort you or me, or perhaps both of us from the past memories that still haunt us. First, I would like to thank you for the comfort. I haven't slept so well in such a long time. Now, you are beautiful, of that there is no doubt, bu—"

Starlyn didn't allow him to finish his sentence as her lips met his. At first, he resisted, but soon he molded into the kiss. Her lips were so soft and tasted so sweet that he couldn't find it within himself to pull away. The kiss seemed more comfort than passion, and it lured him in.

* * *

By midday, they had arrived at the thick pine forest to the west. Searon slowed his horse now that they couldn't see too far ahead. Birds conversed with each other from branches, and Searon noticed several nests where mothers fed their hatchlings. They sought only two more plants in the forest: a purple-leafed plant and a scarlet flower.

"Starlyn...about what happened back there," Searon said.

He hadn't soberly lost control around a woman in so long that he wasn't sure how to act around her now. Complications rolled in his mind at his stupidity that he had seemingly become involved with a woman that traveled with him. Not just any woman, but a kheshlar for that matter.

She smirked with a blush but said nothing as she continued looking for the plants.

"What about it?"

"What happens now?" He turned away from her.

"The two of us were lost in a moment of comfort and passion. It stays at that."

He looked at her now, and her face was stern without emotion. Her blush was gone and so was her smile. She stroked her blonde hair from her eyes and tugged it behind her slender ears.

"What do we say?" he asked.

Her grip on him tightened, and he imagined if he didn't have thick steel armor on that he would be able to feel her claws digging into his flesh. She shifted abruptly behind him in the saddle and cleared her throat.

"Tell no one."

Her eyes stared deep into his, colder than he had ever seen them. She left it at that, but it seemed to carry weight that it was important, that it was to be kept secret. Turning her head to the north, she smiled slightly before hopping off the saddle. She knelt to the ground and picked up a few large purple-bordered leaves from a plant.

Searon slid off the saddle and soothed his horse before approaching Starlyn from behind. Before he reached her, he noticed a scarlet flower from the corner of his eye lost in a patch of vines. Gently, he plucked it and walked over to Starlyn, tapping her on the shoulder. Abruptly, she turned to face him and stared into his eyes. Her heart caved and lips parted as she studied him. Finally, she saw the flower he held in his hand. She blushed quickly before snatching the flower from his grasp and rising to her feet. Smelling the flower, she smiled before placing it in her hair.

"That's the last one; now we can get back to heal him."

She disappeared through the trees ahead of him. Searon raised his eyebrows slightly before following her. He noticed his horse wasn't where he had left him, and Starlyn was nowhere to be seen as well.

Something didn't feel right to him, and he edged forward, keeping a hand on his claymore. He knelt to the ground and brushed his gauntlets on the scattered branches. They seemed slightly out of place and crushed in the middle. He hadn't heard anybody approach, but someone had stepped on the branches.

"Starlyn?" he called out, unsheathing his claymore. Silence filled the air without even the gentle chirping of crickets or birds. Something or someone had been in a hurry to step on those branches hard enough to crack them. Cautiously, he looked around to search for more signs.

The Crimson Claymore

A foul scent lingered in the air that reminded him of both death and cloves. It was odd that a pleasant smell could be surrounded with the smell of death. He clutched his claymore tighter as he stepped through thick shrubbery into a clearing.

He nearly collided with something and was taken aback when he noticed it was Starlyn that was before him. She wasn't alone; behind her was a kheshlar that held a curved dagger close to her throat. Her eyebrows were silver and matched Starlyn's, but her skin wasn't pale blue as other kheshlars. Instead, it was a light charcoal shade that he had never seen before. Her hair was pearl white and tangled atop her head, coming apart at two thick strands stopping just below her chest. He looked into her gunmetal eyes and had a hard time looking away.

Chapter Eight

There seemed to be an aura of power surrounding the woman that Searon couldn't explain. She resembled a kheshlar ranger with a bow attached to her back next to a quiver. Her black steel armor caught his attention with thick pointed shoulder pads and stripes of white to match her hair. Strangely, she only wore a steel gauntlet on her right hand while her left was bare, showing long fingernails. The armor on her bosom was half the depth of Starlyn's. Silver scale mail covered her legs before they were met by parted boots just above her knees. Three sharp points like daggers rose to her knees from each boot, looking deadlier than the dagger she kept at Starlyn's throat.

Despite her exotic appearance, nothing kept Searon's attention more than the woman's face. It was very similar to Starlyn's with high cheek bones, a small nose, and lips that nearly mirrored each other. The ears were also very similar with each other, but Starlyn's weren't quite as sharp on the tip.

"Let her go."

He didn't let his voice falter in the slightest, but inside he could feel chills run down his spine. For the woman to be able to capture Starlyn so easily he wondered how little of a chance he stood against her. Still, he clutched the handle of his claymore until he was sure his knuckles had turned completely white. He kept his eyes focused into the woman's with as much courage as he could while trying not to be mesmerized by them.

"Ah…you are attractive. I can see now how my sister lost control in your presence." Her voice was cold and harsh like grinding nails.

"Sister?" Searon breathed, shifting his eyes from the woman to Starlyn's fearful expression.

He knew Starlyn had told him about losing her sister to the draeyks. She had never told him of her change of appearance, though, and he had imagined the woman to be similar to Starlyn. Indeed she was similar to Starlyn, but the change of skin color took Searon aback. He was intrigued at how the woman could have changed so much. Now he knew that he hadn't been given the full story of what had happened to her sister.

The woman grinned, showing perfect white teeth. Searon half expected her teeth to be rotting like the charcoal skin on her body. Her skin didn't appear rotten; in fact, it appeared smoother than Starlyn's, and he had a craving to touch it. The same craving dwelled in him to feel her cold violet lips upon his.

"Yes. I assume she's told you about me."

She loosened the curved dagger, which held a blade similar to a flamberge sword, from Starlyn's neck only slightly. Starlyn appeared to be partially relieved but still didn't attempt to make a move. Her blazing silvery eyes watered and pleaded with Searon.

"Some, still I have yet to learn your name." His hand vibrated slightly from the pressure his grip sustained on his claymore's hilt.

"Arria." She masked a smirk that was far from innocent. "And yours?"

"Searon," he avoided her eyes that now seemed to be boring deeper into his, almost luring him to her. However, looking at her body now didn't help matters much.

"If you don't mind, I would like some alone time with my lovely sister." Her eyes seemed to glow slightly at the end of her sentence.

Searon looked away from her eyes again and fought the urge to do exactly as she asked. There seemed to be a power lingering from her to him, and he wished for nothing but to please her. He felt the urge to bow to her there and ask her for guidance on her bidding. Shaking such thoughts from his head, he held firm.

"I'm afraid I can't do that; forfeit her now, or prepare to fight."

"Mmmm…you would make a good pet. I now understand why my sister likes you so."

She tossed Starlyn into a tree, knocking the kheshlar out before unsheathing a large flamberge from her scabbard. The blade glistened purplish black in the light, and she held it steady, flaunting the black diamonds encrusted in its hilt. Searon held his claymore high, now noticing the crimson glow that surrounded his blade.

Arria rushed at him, delivering strong offensive blows that took Searon aback as he hurriedly maneuvered to defend. Each strike of her wavy flamberge against his thick claymore was deadly, as she was able to slide her weapon farther down his blade toward his hilt. He jumped back and spun, thrusting his claymore at an upward angle toward her face, only to be deflected. The curves on her flamberge were able to catch his claymore between grooves, slowing his assault. Vibrations ran through his claymore that disconcerted him and began to make his hands feel numb.

It was clear to him that her skill outweighed his, and adding her unusual weapon choice, he fell back. Ideas tried to push through his head, but he came up blank. There was nothing in his mind that he could do to outsmart the corrupted kheshlar.

In a blind haze, she rushed at him with a tackle that caught him off guard, and they both tumbled to the ground. He fought to push his blade up, but her body kept it lowered. She let go of her flamberge for a moment to thrust her right fist into his face—a blow that held enough bite to make his head spin. Biting his lip, his eyes blazed in fury as he continued to fight to free his weapon. When the two finally stopped sliding across the cold dirt, Searon rolled out of her grasp quickly to grab his claymore. In an instant, she was up in front of him with a dagger in her left hand that sliced through the top of his right gauntlet, causing him to drop his weapon.

He took a step back, rattling his mind for a way to get his weapon back safely when she lurched forward with a slice across his left cheek with her curved dagger. Blood dripped down his face, and he held his hand to it for an instant, feeling the flows running down his cheeks. His teeth bared, and he clenched his fists, preparing to not go down without a fight.

Her eyes met his, and all his thoughts suddenly vanished. He stared into her gunmetal eyes that lit with such intensity and power that he nearly forgot his own name. His claymore that lay not a pace in front of him vanished from his mind, as did Starlyn, and it was only her. Arria.

She is so beautiful, I am not worthy. Thoughts of ecstasy traveled in flows through his mind with hundreds of different outcomes if the two of them touched. None involved death; well, at least not at first. He imagined a black widow circling a web and waiting patiently for her prey. A male widow came into view, and the two locked in a moment of passion. The two arachnids were lost through the spinning of silk and dance until at last the deed was complete. In a sudden burst, the male leaped to escape, but the female was faster to snatch him in her long legs before biting her mate. Great hunger consumed her now, and she couldn't let him escape. His dying thoughts were shunned through his dying breath. *It was worth it.*

That was how she seemed to Searon as he stared at her with lust in his eyes. She was a black widow to him, an exotic beauty with a poisonous bite. It would be worth the fatal bite at the end, though, and he knew it. There would be no better way to die to than spend a moment in her naked charcoal silk arms.

"I thought someone as courageous as you would put up a greater fight. Perhaps the next time we meet you'll be more prepared," her fiery voice whispered.

He didn't say a word but kept still with anticipation as she moved mere inches from him. The exotic smell of death, cloves, and a pinch of ginger lingered at his nose. No longer was it a strange smell that was both foul and intriguing, but now it was lustful. She leaned in closer, and her luscious violet lips sprang onto his.

The breath caught in his throat when their lips touched, and he nearly gagged with the lack of oxygen. He could taste blueberry clove on his lips that replaced his need for oxygen, and he molded his lips into hers. His right hand unconsciously rose to graze her cheek gently before tangling in her hair. Her lips were softer than any he had ever set his lips upon, and her skin was softer than the finest silk. He had thought Starlyn's skin was soft, but it had only been as soft as silk, not softer. The pearl-white hair that his hand tugged at felt as soft as snow. A slight moan escaped her lips before she dove farther into the kiss to play with his tongue and bite his lip. He was lost in complete ecstasy.

Suddenly, energy seemed to drain from him, and he began to feel weak. It was slow and seemed to have been happening the entire time. He had not noticed before, lost inside her eyes and lips. Even though he noticed now, he didn't care. She seemed to gain strength as he grew weak, and it pleased him that she became stronger. He was weak compared to her, only an insect to a spider.

The sound of hooves echoed in the wind along with a roar that shunned all silence. Arria broke away from him and took a step back, glancing to the west. Her hand still interlocked with his, and his heart kept racing. Reluctantly, he turned away from her beauty to observe a jaguar prancing through some thick bushes with a black-and-white striped horse balking close behind. The cold touch of her hand in his vanished, and eagerly he looked back for her. There was nothing; she was gone.

He dropped to his knees, at a loss for words as his heart quivered in pain. His hand shook in his memory of her hand in his. He needed to find her and snatch her back in his arms. Across from him, Starlyn rose to her feet, clutching a hand to her head. She tried to walk forward but waivered from side to side. The jaguar, her friend, leaped to her and knelt to the ground so she could climb atop.

"Arria," Searon whispered.

Starlyn looked at him now, her electric silvery eyes blazing with concern. He paid her no heed and searched through the empty forest. There was no sign of her, and he felt heartbroken, longing for the taste of her lips again.

"Come back," he whimpered.

The jaguar crept forward at the instruction of Starlyn until she was directly in front of him. She stared cold into his eyes for a moment, and he quickly turned his gaze. A hand smacked across his face so fast it was almost unseen. The pain welled up on his cheek and inside his mind. His face didn't flinch, but his eyes blinked before he placed his hand on his now-red cheek. It stung beyond any sting he had ever felt in his life. Reality crashed back to him, and he seemed to be falling out of a haze.

Blinking one more time, he tried to stand, but his body crumbled back to the ground, lacking the strength he needed to rise. He searched for his claymore and saw it not a pace in front of him. Crawling, he grasped it in his hand only to find Starlyn's hammer directly in front of his face.

"I'm back. Her control over me has vanished."

The hammer withdrew, but he noticed she still clutched it tight in her hand as she watched him. He clutched his hilt and used the blade to steady him to his feet. Stripes ran by his side, and he was able to lean on the horse so he could sheath his sword. Clutching the reins tightly, he climbed on the horse's back. There was little strength left as he followed Starlyn and her jaguar east. He could only wonder what it was that her sister, Arria, had done to him.

Chapter Nine

Pacing from north to south in long strides, Karceoles held his hands behind his back and stared solemnly at the ground. Beetles scurried about, and he was careful to avoid them. Some were small, clicking beetles and others tri-horn beetles. Sighing, he lifted up a small clicking beetle by its backside and held it close to his ear. He heard the continuous clicking it created by snapping its head in an attempt to jump. Letting go, he watched as it snapped once more, diving into the air.

Something felt wrong to him, very wrong, but he wasn't sure what it was. It had been a great while since both Searon and Starlyn had left to search for herbs. They shouldn't have been gone so long, since they'd traveled by horseback, and already the sun was setting. Cursing under his breath, he tore his long-stem pipe from the pouch on his robe. After lighting it with magic channeled through his zylek, he puffed heavily, feeling the calming tobacco and herbs settle his mind. His head spun only slightly, but at least he wasn't as worried anymore.

A whisper in the distance startled the wizard, and he turned, only seeing a dark shadow scurry by. He focused his mind on fire, and from within he felt his power bind at his zylek, ready to be released. The energy streamed through him, bringing him more alive. Whatever had passed through him was now gone, and he let his power dissipate regretfully. He loved the burn of fire he felt within him whenever he channeled it. It was probably the reason he only chose to bind with the element of fire. Many wizards preferred water or earth, but not Karceoles. He was the first wizard in thousands of years that preferred fire above all and wasn't corrupted by it.

He stalked back to where the unconscious man lay and looked at him. *Is this single man worth all the risk? I do feel something in him, something great. He is still not as important as Searon...but he is important. Yes...the risk is worth it. Where are you, Searon?* His mind rattled, and he knelt down to check the man's pulse. It still beat strong, although it was slow at pace. He heard a crow in the distance, and fire pulsed through him again into his zylek, and a small but effective fireball emerged from its tip that chased the crow away. Crows were scavengers that often brought death even when it didn't seem near. He did not know if they were evil creatures or not, but he wasn't willing to take the risk.

Hearing hoof beats in the distance, he turned abruptly, holding his zylek high and awaiting anything that scurried through the bushy trees. He saw a jaguar emerge carrying Starlyn, who clutched tightly at the animal's fur. Directly behind her was the white-and-black striped horse of Searon. The human seemed to clutch tightly to the reins of the horse, as if for dear life, and slumped ever so slightly in his saddle. He was injured, or at least weak, and Karceoles clutched his zylek in a frenzy, feeling the pinprick of a thousand needles travel through his hand.

The horse and jaguar stopped abruptly, and Starlyn slid off the animal and got to her feet. She proceeded by helping Searon off of his saddle carefully. Karceoles watched in horror as Searon limped forward to meet the wizard. There was something else too, something that both seemed to be hiding. Karceoles was no fool though and could see the radiance in Starlyn's eyes and hair that showed affection toward Searon. It was affection past that of a travel companion, and the wizard knew they had shared a moment. However brief it might have been, the two were connected now, and it tied their plan in knots. He only hoped the two of them had enough sense to keep their minds clear.

"What took you so long?" Karceoles's eyes squinted to look from one to the other.

"It took longer than expected to find all the herbs and flowers," Starlyn spat.

Karceoles watched as Starlyn blushed ever so slightly before regaining her composure. It was long enough for him to see her rosy cheeks and all the confirmation he needed. She glared at Searon with a warning glance, and he shifted uneasily. Looking at Karceoles now, Searon nodded.

"We ran into Starlyn's sister." Searon shivered.

Starlyn immediately took out the herbs and flowers to mash into a wooden bowl that she had carved during the journey. She mixed them with a wooden spoon that she had also carved. Snatching a canteen from her sash, she poured water in the bowl. Karceoles dismissively created a smokeless fire in front of the two of them through his zylek. He felt more alive than he had all day as he directed the power.

"You saw Arria?"

Starlyn jumped at the mention of her sister's name. She stared blankly at the wizard with an open mouth. No words left it before she closed it but then opened it again.

"How do you know about Arria?" Starlyn asked in a stern voice.

"I know who and what she is. An undead kheshlar. The only one of her kind. She died that night, but now she lives." Karceoles looked back at Starlyn, who held a terrified look on her face.

Shaking her head, she removed the bowl from the fire. "Open his mouth."

Searon stumbled over to the warrior's head and held his mouth open for Starlyn to shove a spoonful of slimly burgundy paste into. She tickled the man's throat, causing him to swallow. Pulling the water skin back out, she mashed the rest of the substance and mixed more water into it, creating a liquid. Removing the wool blankets from the man's body, she felt at his scars, adding the water to each one.

"Okay wizard, you are welcome to heal his wounds now."

Karceoles held his zylek steady, feeling pulses of energy flow into it from his body. It took more energy than fire, a lot more, but that was because he spent the majority of his knowledge studying the use of fire. He had spent little time learning anything to do with healing. If he had studied more of it, he could have healed the human completely without breaking a sweat. The wounds closed slowly but surely, and he could feel them healing slightly. Even the inside of the wounds healed a fraction from his power, and that surprised him. It would still be Starlyn's herbs that would make the difference.

"How long until this works?" Searon asked, staring down at the pale human.

The Crimson Claymore

Starlyn crouched by the human to feel his pulse and check his forehead. There was a cold sweat across his exposed body, and she frowned. Without a pause, she put his armor back on and wrapped him up with as much cloth as could be found. His body was limp all the while she positioned him for warmth.

"He has entered a coma state. The rest is up to him," Starlyn whispered uneasily, looking back at Karceoles.

The wizard shrugged knowing there was nothing more that he could do. There wasn't time to sit and wait on the young man anymore, and all three knew they needed to continue on. The longer they stayed in one place, the more likely it would be that the draeyks could find them.

"We can't wait on his recovery. If we are discovered, our element of surprise against the draeyks will be ruined," Searon trailed off looking into the distance through the trees.

Searon began gathering his things and packing them tight on his stallion. A few times he checked his scabbard to make sure his claymore was secured tightly. Turning around, he arched an eyebrow at the wizard before securing his crimson-and-gold helm and climbing atop his horse.

"He's right, we need to leave. What are we to do about this human?" Karceoles looked from Searon to Starlyn, growing impatient.

"I will carry him," Searon said, reaching out for the man.

Karceoles eyed him curiously, but Starlyn quickly nodded and pulled the unconscious man to his feet and onto the saddle in front of Searon. He held onto his limp body securely while still able to handle the reins with ease. Nodding to the others, he led the way.

Starlyn and Karceoles were able to swiftly get on their animals and follow Searon close behind. Searon only seemed to struggle slightly with controlling his stallion, but it was clear that his horse put his faith into the rider. He seemed to whisper to his horse, Stripes, soothing the animal that neighed in response.

"Are you sure you can handle him with you?" Starlyn asked with worry on her face.

"I will be just fine," Searon smiled.

Searon led the way north with Starlyn traveling on his right side on her jaguar companion and Karceoles on his left with a brown mare. The added weight only slowed Searon's steed slightly below a full trot.

There wasn't enough room for a full gallop through the forest, but they kept a steady pace.

Several hills scattered the horizon that had to be climbed slowly with caution. Stripes seemed to be noticing the tension from Searon and was extra careful during the climb. At the top, the view was indescribable. The sun shone brightly with only a few scattered powdery white clouds, and everything could be seen a league in almost every direction. Sweat drizzled down Searon's face as his teeth gritted from holding the human so tight to climb through the hills. At the bottom, a river could be seen with a ruined bridge.

When they arrived, Karceoles crept to the gray stone bridge and stared at it for a few moments. The current was exceptionally strong with several silver-and-blue flying fish jumping from the water to snap flies that scattered the air. Carefully, he grasped his pipe from his brown robes and gently put some chocolate aroma tobacco inside. After a few puffs, he looked to both Searon and Starlyn, who seemed to be waiting on his call. Starlyn's eyes were wide, blazing like hot fire. She stared from the river to Searon and bit her lip intensely. Searon's eyes merely squinted as he let his horse trot to the bridge to stare at it. There were at least ten paces between broken parts of the bridge. It may have been jumped had his horse not been forced to carry extra weight, but it was risky now. He still appeared as if ready to attempt it.

"Halt," Karceoles rumbled, looking from east to west at the river.

The width of the river didn't seem to change no matter which direction the wizard looked. Instead, he concentrated deep to think of something he could do to help them across. Twirls and binds of magic rattled in his mind as he tried to think of spells.

"We have to cross," Starlyn said defiantly.

Searon's dazzling green eyes glared deep into the wizard's orange ones. There was no doubt in the wizard's mind that Searon wasn't going to leave his fellow human behind. It seemed that Searon felt that, had their places had been switched, he wouldn't have wanted to be left behind himself.

"Yes…I know. Give me a moment, and let me try something."

Karceoles closed his eyes and let flows of magic encircle him, bringing new life through his veins. He felt so alive with growing power as his magic flowed through him and into his zylek. Bright-orange sparks formed at the tip of his zylek that intertwined with each other, forming a web toward the river. The magic flashed and fizzed out of focus before disintegrating into dust particles. He attempted thrusting the magic harder through his zylek, causing his body to sweat profoundly. It did not fail this time and created a web of laced fire that tied both sides of the bridge together.

"Go!" Sweat poured down the wizard's strained face, and he began to weaken. His entire body began to shake, but he kept his eyes open and his mind focused.

Searon glanced at the bridge one last time in doubt before seizing the reins of his horse to gallop across it. Starlyn followed him close behind holding her jaguar tight. As the both of them reached the end of the chain of magic, the opposite side of the bridge began collapsing. Searon's horse, Stripes, nearly fell down by its hind hooves, but he urged the horse forward, and it was able to climb through the collapsing stone before crashing into the soft mud of the shore. Starlyn's jaguar fell into the river just short of reaching Searon. She grabbed her supplies and braced herself for a jump from the animal. With a flip through the air, she spun and landed behind Searon with her two legs and one hand on the ground before looking up to him and smiling. The jaguar was long gone without enough strength to swim through the current, and it was swept downriver, roaring profoundly.

As soon as both Searon and Starlyn made it across along with Karceoles's horse, the flows of magic vanished, making the web disintegrate in a flash. With a gasp, the wizard inhaled deeply before directing more magic at his feet, creating a swirling orange ring. The hollow space in the center filled with various shades of orange before he stepped onto it and floated into the air. He kept his zylek aimed at the strange disk as it glided across the large river until he landed perfectly on the other side and the magic faded away.

"How come you wouldn't do that for us?" Searon arched an eyebrow.

"It's much harder channeling power for others than ourselves." Karceoles ran his fingers through his curly hair. His blazing orange eyes relaxed a bit, and some of the fire seemed lost in them. "Also, when there is no magic flowing through your bodies, it makes it harder getting magic to work for you."

Searon turned to Starlyn, "I'm sorry about your jaguar."

Starlyn smiled weakly, "I will miss him, but I do not fear for him. He will make it, the mother will watch over him, and one day we may cross paths again."

The three continued traveling north through the small meadow at the end of the day. They watched as owls flew through the night sky with a kind of carefree quality that they wished they held. The air was hot, and the heat was getting to them so that they slowed their pace to a slow trot. Starlyn kept up just fine without her jaguar but denied Searon's request to hop on his horse with him. She claimed the poor horse had already carried enough weight with the unconscious human.

A large stone blocked the path as the meadow thickened into a forest. The stone was over fourteen paces high and seven paces thick with crows circling around the top of it. It was something strange to see such a large slab of stone in the middle of scattered trees without any more rocks in sight. However, it blocked their path, and they had to travel around it.

When they reached halfway around the stone, they bumped into five armed draeyks that stood waiting for them with smug looks upon their black scaly faces. Starlyn sharply turned around to find another five cornering them in. It seemed the three of them had stumbled straight into a trap.

Karceoles rose up his zylek and held aim sharply at a draeyk. Starlyn drew her hammer and spun in circles, studying all of the creatures. Searon looked at all of them, cautiously holding the man in front of him steady on his horse. There was nowhere to set down the human where he would be safe. Instead, he secured the man on the saddle and drew out his glowing crimson claymore, holding it with one hand while daring the creatures to step forward.

Chapter Ten

"**D**rop him, you fool!" Karceoles yelled into the wind as he turned in his saddle to face Searon.

Searon ignored the wizard as he wielded his claymore with one hand. He kept the other secure around the human in the saddle in front of him. The weight from the large sword was nearly throwing him off balance. His attacks were slower than normal with a higher focus on defensive parries rather than offensive strikes.

His body felt weary as he moved around in a flow of defensive maneuvers against the draeyks. He wasn't at his full strength after what Arria had done to him, but he didn't let it show. The muscles in his arms ached greater than they ever had, and he clenched his teeth hard to distract himself from the pain. He knew he was still stronger than the creatures he faced—mentally if not physically.

Searon's eyes flickered as his blade crossed an axe of a draeyk. There was tension and anger that swelled through his body more than ever. His blade shook slightly at its weight, and he tried to shift his balance while keeping hold of the human in front of him. Each time he faced draeyks, it enraged him with new passion to destroy everything that they were. The shiny black scales of the creature in front of him shimmered, only making him angrier. His blood boiled as he fought with newfound passion. He saw a flicker of Victoria's face in the distance, and he blinked, hoping to see her wonderful smile again, but she was gone. *Murderers.*

His arm was becoming weak as his body was tiring, but he would not let go of the human; he wouldn't give up on him. He'd seen too many people around him die, and this time there was something he could do to prevent another death. The creature in front of him snarled in impatience at being deflected. He stared into the creature's eyes with boiling hate. *There is no forgiveness for murder.*

At his side, Starlyn performed exotic moves, twirling her hammer in patterns of stars. It almost appeared that her attacks would strike herself as her hammer moved around her body. She stepped on another's head, hearing the crunch of its black scales, before landing perfectly behind them all. In one quick motion, she heaved her hammer into the skull of a draeyk before it had the chance to turn around. Before the creature fell to the ground, Starlyn leaped into the air and dashed along the side of the large stone until landing alongside Searon once again. The way she slashed the air with defensive maneuvers seemed as soft as a feather. She didn't feel or think during the battle but became one with the hammer and let it guide her. She was one of the few that could show speed and grace with a hammer.

She observed Searon, wondering why he cared so much for a fellow human he had never met. The emotions of his kind were hard for her to understand. Searon's strength impressed her as he fought. She knew that he was strong, but to be able to hold onto the human while battling with a large claymore with only one hand stunned her. Even though she was a kheshlar with more strength than a human, she still knew she would have dropped the man so she could better balance her hammer. A smile tugged at Starlyn's lips as she realized that once Searon's mind was made up that there was no changing it. Instead of debating with herself at his reason, she instead decided to help him protect the human and stood by his side.

There was only one thing lingering in Starlyn's mind as she fought. Her sister, Arria, flashed through her thoughts, and it kept her concentration high. It seemed as if every draeyk she battled was her sister. Their faces only changed back to those of the scaly creatures as she delivered their deathblows. She could not kill her sister, and she would not. There was little chance she could ever have her sister back the way she was before the black magic grabbed ahold of her. Yet inside her heart Starlyn knew that she had to try. Arria did not deserve death, no matter what her crimes were. If it came to the worst, she would imprison her sister until she could find a cure. She owed it to her. Her sister had saved her so many times in the past, and she knew that somewhere in the soulless demon her sister still lingered. Every now and then when she saw the undead kheshlar that was her sister, she saw a flicker in her eyes that belonged to Arria. It was the only thing that kept Starlyn going. She had to have faith.

With her mother gone now, all that she had to cling to was the knowledge that her sister was still out there. She did have one good friend back near Sudegam, but besides her…Starlyn seemed to be an outcast to the kheshlars. With great struggle, she had led the kheshlars in an attack against the draeyks in the second kheshlarn war. The first was rumored to be against strange flying creatures with scales—a race that became extinct. It took great effort to unite the kheshlars against the draeyks, and after the war was over everybody seemed to look at her differently. She was considered the impatient one for dragging the war forward. It had all started because of her mother's illness and her rash decisions did not save her. Perhaps there was still a chance to save her sister. All the kheshlars told her that she held her emotions too high, but she could not abandon her mother. Now it was her sister that she could not abandon. She no longer cared for acceptance from the other kheshlars. That was why she was alone in the wilderness fighting the draeyks.

She turned to Searon, noticing him dancing with his claymore in hand. The skill of his blade excelled hers, yet that was why she chose a hammer. At least she had found someone who hated the draeyks with the same passion as she. Her family was all she had left in her life. There was little choice for her. She never knew her father, but her mother and sister were everything to her. One was already lost, but she was not about to lose the other. Her sister had known their father, but he died from a blade when Starlyn was just a babe. She did not understand why her mother took ill when kheshlars were supposed to be immune to such things. Unless it was poison—yet who would poison her mother? She fought so hard against the draeyks because she couldn't handle losing another family member. Arria had to be captured; Starlyn had to have her back. It was what kept her strong.

The wizard fought off to the side, forming orange spheres of light. He formed them one at a time and bolted them at the enemies. It was very effective at blasting the creatures off their feet. Karceoles relished in the power that flowed through him. He felt incredibly alive as the burning energy shivered through his skin down to his bones. Without the power circling inside him, he felt so dull, so lifeless. Yet when the power flowed through him he felt like he was invincible. It almost felt as if he could jump and fly at a moment's notice. Which he probably could if he channeled energy from his zylek to his feet to levitate. In fact, he liked the idea of flying into a battle as an entrance. He decided to add that tactic into his battle tactics.

The speed of the wizard's magic was as swift as that of a sword strike. He may have seemed an old man, but his wits were just as fast as a young warrior. A draeyk rushed toward him and raised its axe in an attempt to block his magic. Karceoles shot a powerful glittering sphere that pushed the axe back, followed by another quick blast of sizzling orange flame that blasted the creature. Its lifeless body incinerated in mere moments before dropping to ash on the ground. Next, he shot a wave of energy that blew two draeyks off their feet and tossed them several paces back. One rose quickly to lunge at him, and he barely had enough time to hammer his zylek forward into the skull of the creature. He lit it with fire as it shattered the creature's scaly skull into two before the body cremated. Swiftly, he shot out an orange lightning bolt at the creature that still lay on the ground, electrocuting it until nothing remained but a steaming pile of bones.

Karceoles kept a watchful eye on Searon as the human fought. He found the human foolish to continue fighting while holding onto the unconscious man. His attacks were slowed to half their normal pace, and holding onto the wounded man had kept him from being more effective in battle. It was true that he could hold his own just fine, but he hadn't been able to slash down as many enemies had he fought without carrying an injured man. Karceoles had chosen a human to lead the effort against the draeyks because humans were weak minded, but above all because they were selfish. It seemed of all the humans he could have chosen, he happened to find the one who cared about others more than himself. Though it was to be expected when the poor man had little in his life to be proud of. There was little left for the man to live for besides revenge. It was what also made him a perfect candidate to be the leader of his army. And there *would* be an army soon, of that Karceoles was sure. He understood now that kheshlars were the true selfish race. They were the ones raised in the shadows of the world, oblivious to the dangers that encircled them. Even though the wizard despised Searon's rash decision to protect the human, he knew that it was power. It was evidence that Searon could make it, that he could be saved. It started now, with him putting the human's life above his own. With an army by his side…he would be unstoppable.

The wizard had lived for far too long to watch as the land turned into chaos. The draeyks seemed to come from nowhere, a dark spell long ago. There seemed to be a greater evil upon the land that created it all, but he could not place its origin. He had tried bringing it up to the council, but they had paid it no heed. They dismissed it as quickly as he had mentioned it, claiming that they would discuss it at a later time. However, the council had soon disbanded, and chaos had soon come to the land. It was up to him now to control the threat and smother it into nonexistence. He couldn't stand by and watch as the draeyks took over. Besides, something tugged at his soul that something darker was at work, yet he had not discovered what. It was his last mission for himself. He would make the world right once again before his time expired.

Next to the wizard, Searon battled fiercely and effectively despite his only using one hand. A claymore was a tough weapon to handle with only one hand, but he wielded it with such skill. He wasn't effective on the offensive, yet he still held his own quite well against three draeyks that enclosed on him. Two of the creatures slashed with axes while the third preferred a spiked mace. The piercing weapon held a weight advantage that set Searon off balance with each block.

Soon, the creatures realized that Searon would not fall despite their numbers and decided on a different approach. The creature with the mace bashed the weapon into the horse's shoulder, causing the animal to dash forward in rage to knock the draeyk down. When his horse leaped forward, both Searon and the unconscious human tumbled to the ground. His claymore was gone, and he was left defenseless. Without much thought, Searon heaved the human on his back and used his steel boots to knock one draeyk out of the way. The other dashed at him, but he dove back, still protective of the man on his shoulders. He held to the human tight as he made a spinning heel kick that caught one creature in the jaw. Another was on him in moments, swinging an axe above its head. Searon only had enough time to grab the axe at the haft with his left hand to stop the blow. Without thinking, he was left with little choice but to punch the creature with his right hand, causing the human to slide imbalanced on his back. He dropped to the ground in an attempt to catch the man. The draeyks closed in on him quickly as he tried prying the human's sword from its scabbard. There wasn't enough time, and he could feel the pinch of an axe blade slamming into his lower back.

The pain shot through his nerves, and he shrieked loudly, causing a disturbing look to come from both Starlyn and Karceoles. However, both were too far and too busy to come to his aid. It was the first time he let the creatures catch him off guard, and he cursed himself silently. He knew he should toss the human off his shoulders and end the lives of these creatures, yet he could not bring himself to do it.

Searon dashed to the side to avoid being entrapped by the creatures. The pain shot in his back again, causing him to stumble and lose his grasp of the wounded man. In a matter of seconds, the human fell to the ground and rolled. Searon grasped the small of his back and gritted his teeth in agony. When he brought his fingers to his face, he looked in horror at his blood-stained hand. He also felt a large bruise forming on his lower back that hurt more with each step.

A draeyk dashed toward the human's body, and Searon quickly slid in front to protect the unconscious man. He wished he could reach his claymore, but it was ten paces away. Furiously, he kicked up some dirt, blinding the draeyk for a moment. In those mere seconds he was able to elbow the creature's jaw with his left and jab with his right. It knocked the creature down and in turn granted Searon able to snag the axe from its grasp. A smile brushed his lips at having a weapon in his sweaty gauntlets again. There was little concern that it wasn't his claymore. He had studied a wide range of weapons throughout his time as a warrior, and some thereafter when training students.

With the creature weaponless, Searon was able to cleave its skull in two with the axe blade. He studied the axe for a moment, admiring its bronze glow. Laughing started now that he couldn't believe was his own. Two draeyks jumped at him, and he dodged both swipes, followed by shearing the tip of his axe blade into an uppercut that shed a draeyk's scaled jaw in half. The last one took a step back and looked at him.

He stared hard at the creature, daring for it to come forward to its death. Deep inside its black eyes, it almost seemed soulless. There were often times he wondered what went on through the creatures' minds, what provoked the creatures to do such things. It almost seemed that they were afraid to fail because they feared something worse than death. The draeyks were simple creatures that enjoyed violence but were not intelligent enough to craft their own war.

Searon had known the draeyks had been led into a war before against the kheshlars. Starlyn hadn't told him much, and Karceoles was worse to pry information from. Back then, it was Starlyn's sister, Arria, that had united the reptilian creatures. It seemed that someone had learned from her efforts and took it upon themselves to unite the creatures again. There were differences now as the humans had been involved in their skirmishes. Arria was still out there, and he only hoped that she didn't get back involved with them. If she did, then the kheshlars truly were in danger once more.

"Diiiee," hissed the creature.

"After you!" Searon barked.

He heaved the war axe with one hand, watching as it spun in the air like a boomerang. The action almost seemed in slow motion as the creature gasped in effort to bring its axe up to block. Its effort was in vain as the axe blade penetrated into the skull of the creature. Searon dived at the chance to retrieve his claymore and felt complete once the crimson glowing blade was back in his hands.

Fifteen paces away, Starlyn busied herself against three draeyks. Surprisingly to Searon, she held her own very well. With a slide of hand and a flick of her wrist, she was able to deflect two strikes at once. When the third draeyk struck, she had to quickly move aside the blow and strike. On occasion, she blocked an attack with her foot, creating an echo through her plate mail. Her helm was tightly secured and so only fragments of her straight blonde hair shone through.

Suddenly, Starlyn rushed west and climbed up the towering rock. The creatures behind followed her to the rock and stared up in disbelief. She pushed her feet from the rough surface of the stone and somersaulted backward. When she landed behind the three creatures, she bashed in one's head with her hammer and crushed the hand of another. The third charged at her, managing to knock her to the ground. Without a chance for a breath, she pulled out shurikens from her pouch and launched three into the skull of the reptilian creature. It skidded headfirst toward her, and she rolled out of the way before rising to her feet. Her grip loosened on her hammer as she readjusted it to face her last opponent.

Another twenty paces away, Karceoles stood no longer wielding magic. Instead, he used his zylek like a weapon. He was able to block blows from both sides of him and twirl in complex patterns that showed off his skills. It was strange seeing such an old man attack with such incredible speed. His zylek blocked the axe blows as easily as a sword would without taking a single mark. His blunt weapon didn't cause as much damage as a sword, yet it was still efficient.

A few times, he knocked them down with a whack of his zylek. Other times, he channeled a pulse of energy through it that jolted the creatures back several paces. He could sense a draeyk trying to sneak up on him from behind. Spinning his zylek swiftly in his hands, he knocked it in the side of the face, breaking its jaw. With a loud thud, the creature hit the ground, clenching its broken bone. As his back was turned, another draeyk swung its axe toward his face that he was not able to sidestep in time. The blade grazed his cheek, creating a three-inch line of blood. A sharp pain tingled through his body, and he cursed his own foolishness.

Karceoles hadn't been so foolish to add a scar to his collection in years. He felt the blood trickling down his face with his fingertips. It had been a long time since he had been overwhelmed in battle. Without trying, he could feel energy channeling from his body into the zylek. The weapon was charging in response to his anger. His nose winced, and his lips parted to show snarling teeth. He dashed at the two draeyks in front of him with stronger blows that took the form of a dance. An illuminating orange light radiated from the zylek that had previously been absent. He pivoted the weapon so it collided with a draeyk's skull. The blow tossed the creature a span back, surrounded in orange flames. He fought the next as he pivoted his zylek and proceeded to break every bone in the creature's body.

The wizard stared coldly at the last one as fire came out of his eyes. He held his zylek forward, creating a glowing orange whip from its tip. Without a second's delay, he slashed it at the creature. The creature shrieked so loudly that it made everyone want to cover their ears. It made a dent in the side of the draeyk's black scaly skull that smoldered.

He slashed at the creature again. The draeyk brought its axe up, attempting a block, but the whip melted through the axe. Another strike caught the handle to incinerate it in mere seconds. Horror stuck the draeyk's face, and it backed up awestruck. Karceoles stepped forward, the whip growing even longer, until with one last slash of his zylek it wrapped around the draeyk.

There was utter shock on the creature's face with eyes wider than ever seen before. Its mouth hung open as the pressure of the whip tightened, causing flames to sprinkle out. Within seconds, the entire draeyk was engulfed in flame, burning it alive. Karceoles whispered unintelligible words that seemed to echo in power while grasping his zylek tighter. The whip sawed at the creature's body, cutting into its flesh until it shattered the body into dozens of pieces that flew in every direction. Each piece that exploded out was aflame and burned quickly to ash. Karceoles was weak now, drained of energy. It had taken a lot from him to perform such complex magic, but his temper got the best of him.

Only five draeyks remained on the field, scarred with battle. Karceoles faced one, his zylek being used as a weapon once more. Starlyn fought against three, and Searon faced a single opponent. Starlyn battled smoothly against the three creatures without taking a break between blocks and attacks. Her skill with a hammer was uncanny. She kicked one in the jaw, knocking it back several paces as she crossed blades with the next. The third dashed at her as she snatched a shuriken from her pouch and launched it into its neck. She stood facing her last draeyk as the one she had kicked had fled. Without having several enemies to worry about, she was able to control her slashes better and quickly got the kill by severing the creature's neck.

Searon fought with brilliant skill against his lone opponent. There seemed little concern to finish the battle and more for practiced sword play. It felt great for him to wield his claymore once again. The glow of it reflected in his green eyes behind his battered gold-and-red helm. He switched the position of his hands so his left hand rested on the top of his hilt. His attacks were able to shift in different ways, with his left hand guiding instead of his right. It also increased his muscle strength for his lesser arm. The draeyk suddenly attacked him in a frenzy of slashes and uppercuts that he was able to extinguish instantly. Even though Searon wasn't left handed, he was still able to defend nearly as well. He dropped to his knees, spinning his claymore to shove the creature's axe down before he impaled the draeyk through the heart.

His eyes closed as all he heard around him was silence. It seemed that both Starlyn and Karceoles were done battling as well. He enjoyed the quiet, as it reminded him of simpler times. A twig crunched not a pace behind him. Searon turned around abruptly, still on his knees and jerking his claymore to a defensive position. It wouldn't have been enough time, as he saw one last draeyk with an axe already raised ready to drop it on his skull. Instead of feeling the abrupt pain of death, he saw a sword pierce the creature's heart from behind. A low gurgling was the only thing he heard as the creature tumbled to the ground. Behind the creature stood the human he'd spent most of his efforts protecting. The man held a sword in his right hand that shook uneasily. A cold sweat drenched the man's face, and he shivered before dropping his weapon. He looked hard into Searon's eyes until his knees gave way and he sank to the ground, losing the last ounce of strength he just had.

Chapter Eleven

Searon rushed to help the weak man and strained his back in the process. He was still injured from the blow to his lower back, but he knew that the human in front of him was weaker. With an easy touch, Searon was able to shift the human onto a log. His claymore still resided in his hand, and he put the no-longer-glowing weapon into its scabbard.

The man tugged at his long black hair now tangled with waves. It hung just past his shoulders and appeared that it should be tied in a ponytail. His eyebrows were thin and his face shaved clean. Even with the days he'd been unconscious, there was still little facial hair to be noticed. He had a baby face as if he was young, but his slanted eyes told his age of long experience. They were hazel and harder than any warrior Searon had known. His body seemed fragile with barely enough meat to cover his bones, but there was still muscle in his arms. Still, he held his pointed chin high with pride. Muscles were only seen if he shifted the right way or likely if he flexed.

"Thank you," Searon shifted his gaze to look deep into the cold hazel eyes of the man.

Searon was amazed that the man held enough strength and courage to strike down a draeyk when just waking up from a coma. He may have seemed thin and weak, but his strength went beyond his muscles. It seemed the warrior had heart, and that was one thing that Searon himself was lacking.

The man only nodded silently with obvious strain. Sweat drizzled down his face, and his long black hair frizzed with moisture. His hand pulsed in effort to make a fist, and he stared at it blankly. Strength would not come back to him, though, as it seemed he used the last of it to save Searon.

Searon held his bottom lip down and whistled deep into the wind. In a moment, the gallop of his horse could be heard. Stripes appeared within minutes and nudged at Searon's hand. He smiled, briefly petting the animal behind the ear. Reaching in the saddlebags, he pulled out dried meat and an apple, which he handed to the man. At first, the man looked at the food with a blank stare before reaching for it. With barely a chance to swallow, the food disappeared into his mouth.

Karceoles stalked up slowly with his zylek. He put out his hand to assist the man to his feet. The man looked at him reluctantly before accepting his help. Strangely, the wizard gave up his zylek to the human, who gratefully accepted it. Karceoles appeared strange in brown robes without his zylek in hand. He appeared weaker as he hunched over, but he still stared down his nose to look at the human.

"What is your name?" Karceoles asked, raising an eyebrow.

"My name is Andron of Guerettos," he said in short breaths. Karceoles noticed the man had dark bags under his cold eyes. His accent sounded nasal, as if he spoke more through his nose than his mouth. Each word seemed to connect together with barely a definition of sound from one word to the next, and that gave his voice a flowery tone.

"What are you doing this far west?" Starlyn broke in with wonder.

It was strange to see humans that crossed the Aedth Desert. Most who attempted such a feat were later found as bones sprawled out on the desert floor. The Aedth stretched on for so many leagues that it was deemed an infinite amount by the standards of humans. Starlyn stared at him strangely as if he was the first human she had met. Likely, Andron was her second. There were also rumors spread throughout Calthoria about the other side of the Aedth being more dangerous than the desert itself.

"The village I come from is strong, but it was attacked by savage draeyks. The finest warriors were gathered and sent out to cleanse the land surrounding us. We were led astray until we became so lost that we had no choice but to continue traveling." He paused briefly to wipe sweat from his brow and catch a breath. "Our numbers dwindled, but we could not stop. Everywhere we went we found draeyks, and our bloodthirst was great. We were destroying the creatures that brought chaos and fear to our homes. It seems I am the only survivor of the hundred sent."

"And you were their leader?" Karceoles brushed his knotted white hair from his face to better inspect the warrior.

Andron croaked a laugh and shook his head. "Hardly. I come from a mere peasant family. It is merely luck that I am still alive."

Andron's face turned grim now with memories of his fallen comrades tormenting him. He seemed to be holding onto himself with barely a thread. His face buried into his knees, and he began to rock back and forth. Chills tensed his body and traveled down his spine as he sighed. There was little left for him but his home, yet it seemed enough.

Karceoles looked at him with respect glowing in his orange eyes. The wizard did not believe Andron could be a mere peasant. Surely, he was a captain, a lord. His fighting skills were more than enough proof of his importance.

"Luck has nothing to do with it. I saw you battle out there. There is much skill in you, and I would gather that you are superior in swordplay to the rest of your party." Searon flinched his nose as he spoke.

He had trained thousands of warriors over the years, and none held as much skill as he saw in the young man before him. Even the captains that Searon trained for various legions did not seem as skilled as Andron. Searon knew he only saw little of Andron battling and would have to test his skills when he regained strength to be sure. Warm thoughts crossed his mind as he realized he would have someone to sword practice with. It was good exercise to dance with a blade at least once a day.

"Let's just say that I'm faster to learn from my mistakes," Andron said, disregarding their compliments.

"Do you have a family?" Starlyn asked as she sat down next to Searon.

"Wow, a kheshlar! I've heard stories, but I've never known they were true. I mean…you are a kheshlar, are you not?"

A smirk broadened at Starlyn's rosy lips. There was a slight blush that streaked across her face that quickly faded. Instead of seeming offended, she appeared proud. In fact, she brushed her golden hair behind both of her ears and grinned profoundly. She looked a fool. Andron's eyes widened as he was able to get a closer gaze of her thin tall ears shaped like long leaves.

"Yes, I am." Starlyn continued to grin sheepishly.

"The stories are true then that kheshlars hold appearances beyond beauty."

Her cheeks reddened deeply. "Do you have a family?"

"Yes...yes, I do."

His eyes watered as his mouth tightened. No tears fell, but he sighed and stared at the ground. Strength enough to snatch a switch from the ground found him, and he began twirling it, drawing figures in the dirt. He shivered as he looked at a picture of a woman and three children.

"I have a wife and three kids. I am eager to get back to them, yet I do not want to head home until I know those savage beasts will do them no harm. I wish to see these abominations destroyed."

"It seems...today may be your lucky day," Karceoles nodded with a twinkle in his eye.

"Do you hunt draeyks as well?" Andron asked with a hint of excitement touching his breath.

"We more than hunt the draeyks. We have maps and locations of all their settlements. We plan on annihilating all of them." Karceoles pried a scroll from under his horse's saddle and handed it to Andron.

The man's eyes lit up with excitement. His hand seemed to touch the hilt of his sword for a moment before shakily drifting back to the scroll. He paused a moment to study each one of them with bewilderment in his eyes. There was doubt in his expression but hope as well.

"What are your names?"

"I am Karceoles the Wise, fire wizard of Calthoria."

"Wise?" Searon barked a laugh.

"Fool, I *am* wise!"

"As you say, old man," Searon grinned before turning back to Andron. "I am Searon De'Athaniel of Calthoria." His voice faded before lowering to a whisper. "No longer do I have a city to claim myself to."

"I am Starlyn Nightsky of Sudegam."

Andron nodded patiently as he continued studying the three. "A human, kheshlar, and wizard...and you seem to have quite the adventure ahead of you. Still, it does not seem possible with only three."

"Perhaps with four we could manage," Karceoles grinned.

"Are there warriors in your city of Guerettos that may aid in our battle?" Searon asked.

"Better than that. There are two neighboring cities that would leap at a chance to destroy the draeyks." Andron slid a dagger from his sash and began to sharpen it on a stone.

"Perfect. Perhaps with an army of humans by our side, the kheshlars will follow suit," Karceoles reasoned.

"Not true," Starlyn admitted with saddened eyes.

She had experience with the kheshlars before, leading them to their last war. Adding to the fact that she was a kheshlar and even though she no longer thought the way they did, she still knew. The king put her in charge of keeping the borders of Sudegam safe from draeyks because he knew nobody would take the role more seriously. Yet despite her efforts, the king wouldn't allow any forces outside the borders.

"Karceoles raised his left eyebrow. "How so?"

"The kheshlars will only ally if personally threatened by the draeyks. For it to be a full-scale war, there would have to be a large force directly threatening the capital."

"Kheshlars are one of the most foolish and stubborn races on this world," Karceoles muttered under his breath.

"There are more stubborn?" Searon asked warily with an odd glance toward the wizard.

Karceoles's eyes twinkled for an instant as he grinned. "Only one."

"There might be a way to arrange an attack against the kheshlars," Searon nearly whispered.

From what he'd learned of draeyks he knew that they would not back away from a battle when provoked. On the other hand, the kheshlars would not attack but only defend. It was clear what had to be done, but the only question was how.

"What are you proposing?" Starlyn asked with a raised gold eyebrow.

"Once attacked, the draeyks will follow; I wonder how far they will chase."

"Are you suggesting we lead them into kheshlarn territory?" Karceoles asked.

"If we do not have an army to battle against such odds, then we have no choice but to lead them to an army that can defeat them."

"Your theory is stupid enough to work…I like the way you think," Karceoles grinned.

"We need a large settlement of draeyks to infiltrate. How far is the closest?" Searon asked, patiently looking at the wizard.

"Ten leagues north." Karceoles stood brushing hair from his face to check his saddlebags. He turned to Andron with a grin still staining his face. "You may ride with me, boy."

"It's settled then," Searon said, rising to his feet.

"It seems I have arrived just in time for the action," Andron smiled.

Andron didn't have enough energy to rise to his feet. Starlyn helped him and walked alongside of him to Karceoles's horse. The wizard held out his hand and heaved Andron onto the horse behind him so he could steady himself by holding onto his back.

The two horses trotted the majority of the way but were allowed to walk for rests a few times. Searon's mind was blazing with revenge against the draeyks, and it was nearly all that he could think about. Nothing or nobody was going to get in his way. He knew that he needed more allies in order to overcome the draeyks, and no longer was it a needless quest of revenge until his death. Now he would be able to destroy them completely and put them back into the ground where they belonged.

The horses were paced at a medium walk now with Karceoles and Andron next to Searon and Starlyn. Andron stared at Searon with curiosity on his young face. There was respect in the young warrior's eyes.

"Were you a leader of an army?" Andron asked.

Searon glanced at the man with an eyebrow raised. "No, my people never went after the draeyks. We were oblivious to their existence. In my town, I was the weapons trainer."

"What was it that brought you here?" he asked with a twist of his lips.

"Revenge," Searon growled through gritted teeth.

"I'm sorry; I didn't mean to bring it up."

"Tell me about your town."

Andron smiled. "It stands at the brink of the sea, with birds that soar high above, squawking into the distance. The sound of the ocean is the most mesmerizing sound that echoes with running water and waves that crash into the sand. There is a large lighthouse that overshadows the tallest buildings of the town with a giant flame during the night so vessels can find their way to shore. It is truly a sight you must behold yourself, Sir Searon."

"It truly does sound amazing."

Searon remembered the first time he saw the ocean. It was with Victoria when Kellen was five, and it was the grandest sight to behold. He remembered the look on Victoria's face when she stared at it, holding his hand as they both had sat on the beige sand. Kellen had pranced through the water, splashing about without a care in the world.

His mind was lost to thought of the current situation as he flashed back in time into the arms of his love.

* * *

"It is wonderful, Searon. There is so much water."

"Yes, my love, it goes on farther than the eye can see, for leagues. Right now, all of it belongs to only you and me."

She had smiled. "The world belongs to us, my love. Anything we want, it is within our reach."

He had returned her smile and placed his hand just below her jaw to raise it up. Her swirling milk chocolate eyes froze him for a moment as they always had. Leaning in, he brought her face to his and gently kissed her soft lips. The sound of the ocean echoed in his ears as their lips melted together to become one.

* * *

"Searon?" A familiar voice seemed to come from nowhere.

He snapped out of his daze and turned to look at Andron. The man looked at him with concern in his eyes. "Are you okay, Searon?"

"Yes...I'm fine. It was just another fond memory. One day, I will have to come to reality that those no longer exist," Searon said with a small smile.

Searon tightened his reins and sped Stripes forward. He had little patience anymore for idling. Revenge was the only thing on his mind after the memories of Victoria came flooding through. His teeth clenched, and his body tightened. He felt Starlyn grip tighter on his waist to reassure him, but he disregarded it.

Chapter Twelve

It was near dusk by the time they arrived at the hilltops to glance down at the draeyk camp. Searon brought his stallion to a stop and climbed from it to glance down upon the settlement. He was cautious to remain hidden, which was a difficult feat without any surrounding trees to hide behind. Still, he could clearly see the camp that still stood a league and a half away.

The camp was unsettled, as draeyks scurried about, tormenting each other and getting into fights. There seemed to be little control between the creatures, proving they were more like animals than men. Fires blazed in several areas throughout the camp where they carelessly cooked animals from bison to rabbits. They ate like they were complete savages, tearing the flesh with their sharpened yellow teeth and even devouring the bones.

"Less than a hundred armed," Starlyn whispered.

He turned to spot her crouched down on the hill next to him. Andron was on his other side, squinting his eyes hard in an attempt to see anything. Searon shook his head, realizing the kheshlar came there to help be his eyes. He wondered how she would react if she knew he didn't need her.

"Yes, but you are forgetting the fifty crossbowmen in the back of the camp. They spread out swiftly with an attack, and a retreat will be near impossible."

Starlyn stared at him now with eyes wide. "You can see them?"

"I can hear them as well; they are uneasy shifting their loaded crossbows with loose bolts. I'm afraid this will not be an easy task to accomplish without much cover. There appears to be four hundred total including those in the tents."

"We will need something creative," Andron whispered.

"My turn for an idea," Karceoles grinned as he walked up behind them.

He stood behind them, looking down at the camp. There seemed little concern for shielding himself. Searon eyed him warily before getting to his feet and gesturing the wizard back away from sight.

"We need something that will work. Not just something that you consider fun," Searon snapped.

"Ah, but this idea *is* fun, and it will work. Draeyks are more animal than human. It is bloodlust that they crave. If we merely spook them, they will chase us as far as we want them to."

"No, Karceoles. A plan must be discussed."

Karceoles paid him no heed and walked past him to the edge of the hill. Searon tried to stop him but burned his hand when he touched the wizard's zylek. An orange glow surrounded the zylek, causing the wood to steam. A sphere of light appeared at its tip that was at first blinding white but soon changed to orange before catching aflame. Karceoles jerked his zylek forward, releasing the magic, causing the fireball to swirl into motion at incredible speed toward the draeyks' camp.

Searon knew he should have run like the wind in that instant. It would have only made sense to jump onto Stripes and pull the reins with all his might to take the horse on a full gallop. Instead, he took two steps forward and watched with interest at the speeding fireball. Andron stepped next to him with a gulp in his voice and a shudder flowing through his body.

The fireball struck at the main campfire, disintegrating everything in its immediate area. There was no longer a roasting bison there nor the dozens of draeyks that were crowding the fire. The gray tent that was behind the fire vanished in milliseconds as the flame devoured it. Ashes seemed to scatter the ground everywhere in the center of the camp. Weapons were lifted promptly as snarls echoed from the creatures. The creatures looked around furiously before staring directly at Searon. He felt hate flash into his eyes, and he cringed and took a step back.

"Time to run," Andron whimpered in a hoarse voice. He clutched onto his sword's hilt tucked tightly in its scabbard before turning the other direction and fleeing.

Searon was the first to jump on his horse, with Starlyn directly behind him, clutching her arms around him tightly. Stripes dashed off at a pace that nearly knocked them from their saddle. It seemed the horse knew danger as surely as they did and took no time to delay. He glanced back to see Andron and Karceoles saddling up before looking back ahead to steer his stallion. As long as the two were secured, Searon didn't have to pay them any more heed. The fool of a wizard had really got them into a pickle now. There was at least a league of open terrain before trees could cover their tracks. At least without the cover of trees Stripes was able to run at full gallop, and without obstacles.

After traveling all day to reach the draeyk camp, now there was no time for rest. The fool wizard couldn't even wait a day for them to rest before moving forward with his foolish *plan*. Searon had his full faith in his horse, Stripes, that had got him out of tight spots in the past. With a glance behind, Searon was glad that none of the draeyks had horses or four-legged beasts of any kind to ride and perhaps catch up with them. The creatures were fast enough on their feet that he could only imagine how quick they would be with mounts.

Searon shifted in his saddle, making Starlyn get in front to ride. She was reluctant at first, pleading that she couldn't ride like a human. With much effort and dire need, he finally convinced her. She would not touch the reins, though, and tied them to the saddle. Instead, she gently caressed the horse behind the ear and whispered to it. Strangely enough, the horse seemed soothed by her words and continued at its hard pace.

Searon loosened the longbow that hung from his saddle and grasped a quiver that he hung on his back. He noticed that a few of the creatures were drawing close on Andron and Karceoles. Licking his lips, he notched an arrow and released. The arrow sped forward, missing Andron's face by millimeters and struck into the skull of a leaping draeyk. It was two hundred paces away but not too far for Searon's range. He didn't like to use the bow that often, but he would in dire need. The creature tumbled harmlessly to the ground instead of reaching the wizard's mare.

"Quite a shot for a human," Starlyn whispered.

The Crimson Claymore

"Don't watch me, drive Stripes forward!" Searon croaked.

He notched another arrow and looked hard before releasing it. There was a break between the wizard and the human that the arrow traveled between, missing both of them by millimeters and striking down another draeyk. Notching a third arrow, he studied the following party hard. He counted the creatures coming to a total of 338. That meant the wizard's magic killed sixty and he killed two—but Karceoles didn't have the luxury of using any more magic while he fought his horse hard to speed up. He settled on another target and released, watching with pleasure as the arrow struck two draeyks and both dropped to the ground. The arrow pierced the first through the throat and the one behind it through the eye.

Searon had spent a lot of time developing an arrow that could penetrate the creatures' scales. He did have several years of hunting them to try new things, but it wasn't something new that worked. Instead, he used their own scales to create arrows. They had to be sharpened for hours until they were sharp enough, but they were harder than steel and notoriously difficult to shape. The bow he used was specially crafted as well so it could shoot farther than most.

He released another fifteen arrows, dropping twenty of the creatures before he attached the quiver back onto the saddle. There were only thirty arrows remaining, and he didn't want to waste them all in case there was a future need for them. They were still a long way away from being free and clear, and most of the night had passed, coming onto morning with them still running. The draeyks would not give up easily, if ever.

When they reached the wide river in the meadow, there was no time for magic. Besides, Karceoles was still several paces behind, and Searon wasn't going to waste time reaching a decision. He nudged Starlyn and motioned her to get back in passenger position. She nodded reluctantly, still eyeing the approaching river. To Searon's amazement, he watched as she stood on the horse and leaped into the air. He slid forward to grasp the reins and soon felt her arms back around his. An eyebrow arched in surprise, but he disregarded her acrobatics quickly. *Bloody kheshlars,* he thought.

The river in front of them was calmer than usual, and he could see a span of dirt amid the current, just past the grass on its nearest bank. Searon thanked the new moon from the night before. Goats scattered about as they neared, which explained the well-trimmed grass and shrubs in the area. However, rapids still furiously clashed against sharpened stones making the river treacherous. Searon stared uneasily at the roiling blue water and rubbed Stripes behind the ears.

"Come on, boy, I know you can do this. Leap hard, and tread fast."

Stripes seemed to nod approval before Searon flicked the reins. The horse leaped far through the air by five paces, enough to bring jealously to any horse rider, before splashing into the river. They were only halfway across, and Searon urged the horse forward. He felt Starlyn release him, and he glanced in surprise to her swimming across with incredible speed. Within seconds, she was already across and standing to look back at them. Stripes pulled through, and after a few minutes they were across and soaked from head to toe.

After another few minutes, Karceoles's mare approached the river, and to no surprise his zylek rose into the air to glow orange. His lips moved in a chain of words that caused the water to separate in front of him. His horse dashed through in quick strides before he released the magic to turn the river back into its natural state. There were draeyks trailing him too close, though, and several of them got through. Searon counted seven that snuck through the river's opening. The rest watched the water in fury and began to spit hissing curses.

Karceoles kept on for a few paces until he reached Searon and turned his steed around to meet the draeyks. His zylek was attached to the saddlebags, and he pulled his sword out to strike down a draeyk through its skull. Searon grinned as he pulled out his claymore to strike at a creature, quickly decapitating it. Starlyn leaped from the saddle as Andron did, and the two of them together fought in unison side by side. Andron was using the fighting style Searon knew as fanning peacock, which consisted of a series of overhand blows that mirrored the range of a peacock's spread feathers. Starlyn's style, however, was strange to Searon. She used her hammer, but it consisted of only side blows to the left and right of the creatures with no overhead or underhand. It was peculiar to Searon but quite effective as he watched her drop three creatures with ease as Andron struck down two.

Searon slid off his mount and watched as the draeyks across the river scurried around its back farther away from them. They did not seem to want to risk a crossing but instead traveled alongside the river, hoping to find a path across. The bloodlust had not settled in them, and they were determined to reach them.

"They will not stop until they cross and find us," Searon whispered.

"Or until they find someone to fight," Karceoles grinned.

The sun was rising now in the horizon, and Searon yawned loudly. Tiredness could not be afforded, though, and he had to press Stripes forward. Soon, they would be in the cover of the forest where they could hide until the draeyks passed by. After they were clear of the creatures, they would be able to take a much needed rest, but not before. Searon's eyes burned red with bloodshot, but he urged Stripes forward. Starlyn seemed to be the only one unaffected by fatigue, but even she didn't hold onto Searon's waist as tightly as before.

Rain began to crackle in the sky, and it first came in small drops that felt soothing in the morning sun. Soon, the rain picked up, and it began to pour frantically and with such ferocity that it was hard for them to see clearly. Searon, however, was still able to see quite far through the rain and spotted a cavern. He kicked the side of Stripes with his left foot, causing the horse to steer east. Stripes soon caught on when he saw the cave and fixed to a trot until they were safely inside.

It was dark but did not look very deep. There was a scarred area on the ground where another had used for a campfire. Searon and Starlyn slid off Stripes and unsaddled the horse. After several minutes, they had everything organized against the wall when Searon frowned to look around.

"Where did that bloody wizard go?"

"Try looking a little harder," came a voice that echoed through the cavern.

Searon stared deeper into the cavern where the wizard appeared in complete serenity. His body was dry without a drop of rain covering him. He held his zylek tight and limped forward unsteadily. Andron appeared at his side as well as their horse.

"What took you?" Andron smirked.

Searon shook his head and stared Karceoles with anger swelling in his eyes. "If you ever do that again, old man...I will kill you myself."

The wizard's grin only broadened.

Chapter Thirteen

A chilling breeze swept the cavern followed by thunder that shook the ground. Small pebbles broke and collapsed from the top of the cavern that brought chills to even Searon. Starlyn kicked rocks as she huddled over to a corner to shiver. She seemed to be trying to find warmth where there was none. Andron quickly followed her removing his thick, plain brown leather embroidered jacket to cover her. She looked up to him and smiled with gratitude. Each had taken their heavy armor off now to be rid of the metal that might attract the storm. Instead, they wore leather armor of lighter weight and greater warmth that Searon kept in his saddlebags.

Searon stood his ground, still staring at the wizard without a flinch. "I mean it, Karceoles."

"What ever do you mean?"

"Don't you *ever* do anything like that again."

"What was it that I did?"

A vein appeared on Searon's temple that trembled fiercely, to match his green eyes, colder than ice. He rubbed his partially overgrown goatee with frustration as he nearly snarled openly. Brushing his tangled shoulder-length brown hair from his face, he tugged at it tightly, biting his teeth.

"Don't you ever do something stupid like that again. There is no use endangering all of our lives. Next time, I will take that zylek from you and whack you in the head with it. We will make a plan that is agreed upon; then, and only then, will we proceed."

"Now where is the fun in that?" the wizard asked with a crooked grin.

Andron croaked a laugh, brushing his long black hair from his eyes, "This man is something else."

Searon eyed Andron harshly, causing the other man to quickly close his mouth and continue brushing his hair. Of all the things he kept in his sash, a brush seemed to be his most important. His hair was looking rather better than it had since waking from the coma, and his brush was to thank for that. It was a span long with a thick wooden handle that had three distinct chips in it on the bottom, and it was crafted from stained cherry wood. He hadn't stopped brushing his hair for the past few hours, and instead of a mess of tangles it was very nearly straight once again.

"Just you wait, I am full of surprises," Karceoles winked with a smirk.

"That is exactly what I'm afraid of. One of your thick-skulled surprises is going to get us all killed."

"Before you met me, you seemed to embrace death."

"Death will come whether we want it to or not, and I chose to face it head on."

"Why do you choose differently now?"

Searon turned around and stared at the ground, "Now…there is a chance. Finally, a chance has arisen to strike the heart of the draeyks." He turned back to face Karceoles dead in the eyes. "I fully intend to ensure the draeyks are no more."

"As do I," Starlyn said, standing up.

The black leather armor that she wore was tight on her skin, showing her cleavage. It clung skintight to her. Her blonde hair was tangled, and she often glanced toward Andron's brush as if she wished she had one to tame her own hair. She shifted slightly before glaring at the wizard with clear distaste.

"I stand with you as well. I swear to fight alongside you until we have vanquished these creatures from the land and bring peace once again throughout the kingdoms."

It was Searon's turn to shift uneasily now. "I do not know about bringing peace between the kingdoms. They have always seemed at each other's throats, with clashes and raids. My only wish is to destroy the draeyks."

"And how do you propose to do this without uniting the nations?" asked the wizard.

Searon shifted uneasily, again staring at the ground to kick a pebble. He watched as it rolled unevenly until a thin foot stomped on it. Looking up, he saw Starlyn with a serious expression on her face. She glowed of beauty that was undefined, past any human he'd seen. Yet he knew that she was not for him.

"I may regret to say, but the wizard is correct. The only way to wash the land of draeyks and…" she paused, and her eyes shifted. "The only way to destroy all the draeyks will be to unite everyone together, or most, and march upon them. Humans will have to be a part of this as well as the kheshlars. How it will be possible, I do not yet know. But I stand with you."

Searon nodded and pulled out his long-stem pipe along with his tobacco, which he proceeded to pack into it. The aroma that let off when he lit it with a branch was intoxicating, of maple and cinnamon. He sat down against the wall of the cavern to ponder how he would do just that. The storm outside was still at its peak with lightning filling the entire cavern from time to time. He pulled out his claymore and began to polish it with silver shine from his saddlebags.

Andron lingered over to sit down next to Searon. He watched Searon with interest as he sharpened his blade. His hand seemed to play at his now-straight hair that draped past his shoulders. He twirled it around his right index finger and pulled from time to time.

"That is a nice sword. I quite like the rubies in the hilt." Andron's eyes sparkled with delight as red rubies shone back in them.

Searon looked at his hilt in admiration. The crossguards were a crimson silver metal and slanted toward the blade slightly. Both ends extended to a diamond where a large encrusted ruby rested an inch in diameter. The grip was made of crimson-stained shagreen with darker spots scattered throughout. There were dozens of small rubies encrusted in the pommel that glittered whenever light touched them.

"I have held my claymore for a long time now. The blacksmith was a friend of the family and made it special for me."

"Is that why it glows when wielded?"

"No…that another did for me, as a gift. So I would never forget, as though I ever would."

Andron nodded with obvious question lingering in his eyes. He pulled his own sword from its scabbard to study it. His sword was plain with a much smaller hilt than Searon's and very little color to it. The grip was black leather, and the blade was black steel rather than silver. It was a great sword and a well-balanced weapon that would be easier to wield with one hand than Searon's claymore. His crossguards had a few encrusted diamonds that sparkled, and they appeared as if they had been added after the initial forging of the sword.

"My sword is so plain. I never achieved any high rank, so I still hold my first sword." Andron rubbed his fingers on the diamonds. "The diamonds I put in myself from those I found from my journey, to distinguish it a bit."

"Diamonds are strong, yet they aren't worth much because there are so many. It almost seems wasteful to have a colorless gem, but you're right. You probably have the only sword with diamonds encrusted in it."

"Do not give gems disrespect. You never know where they might be of use. These diamonds may be worth something somewhere," Karceoles said, laughing slightly.

The two men cackled loudly before shoving their swords back in their scabbards. Searon proceeded to fondle a bottle from his saddlebags and poured himself half a cup in a steel container.

"What do you have there?" Andron asked.

"Bourbon, to warm the mind. Would you care for a cup?"

"Please," Andron smiled.

* * *

Searon rode his steed ahead to gain himself some fresh air and some time to think. They had rested well in the cavern, but it was time to go. It was uneasy to rest during the day after having traveled all night. Searon found rest hard to come by once the light was out. That was part of the reason he opened his treasured bottle of bourbon. Either bourbon or another type of whiskey would settle his thoughts enough to gain some rest. He knew they couldn't rest too hard with the draeyks still scurrying about. They still had to be cautious in case the wizard's foolish plan was to fail. Searon suggested they take turns resting while one watched the entrance. Karceoles agreed to take upon the first watch, and he cast a globe of shadow within the cavern with magic. The darkness made it easier to sleep, and Searon was the first to pass out, with bottle still in hand.

It was morning now of the next day, and Searon considered plans to continue. He wasn't sure how far he would be able to take his quest or where to go next. It was obvious that they should find these home-lands of Andron, but after that where should they travel? They might not yet find a direction until they saw how many Andron could rally. He didn't seem to be a general, or noble, of any kind, and so his ties might not stretch far. Men of Calthoria were divided, with several different lords or kings. He knew in order to defeat the draeyks, to truly defeat them all, the nations would have to unite under one banner. Searon did not wish to hold that banner, but if he could find another that would unite them....All he wanted to do was lead the attack as general. There were no designs on leadership from him.

"What burdens you?" a sweet, calming voice asked as smooth as wind chimes.

The voice came from behind him, and it was familiar. Starlyn sat on the saddle behind him, and he almost forgot she was there. He turned to look at her calmly. She was beautiful, with straight glistening blonde hair that hung well past her shoulders to match the stars. Her eyes were shimmering pools of silvery blue that looked electric, like sparks of fierce lightning. Light leather armor, black in color, now covered her instead of the heavy plate mail as she had worn before. Riding would be much easier with such items packed away. Searon himself kept most of his underarmor on but kept his heavier plate mail packed away in saddlebags. Chain mail, boots, and gloves that all glittered with a faint crimson to match his glowing sword. The claymore only shone with color when he wielded it in combat.

Starlyn's cheekbones were higher than any human. Her lips were small but puffed red without any hint of lip gloss. Kheshlars didn't use fruit and plants to enhance their features like some human women, but they didn't have to, for their faces seemed perfect in definition of color. She had rosy cheeks, golden eyelids, and a pointed jaw. In every human's eyes, she was absolute perfection, except for Searon. She was too perfect in appearance for him. Besides that, he felt more drawn to brunettes rather than blondes. It was an oddity when compared to most men, who seemed to flock to blondes like pigeons to bread.

The Crimson Claymore

"I do not hold the burden on my shoulders, but I often wonder how we can unite the nations. Humans aren't as tightly held as your king keeps your kheshlars. We're divided across the country, and I feel we will have to bring unity to destroy these evil creatures."

Starlyn didn't speak, but she nodded with understanding. Finally after a moment of thought, she said lightly, "The kheshlars aren't as tightly woven as you would believe. I nearly stood alone in my journey against the draeyks. It was with great struggle that I was able to convince aid against them."

Searon fished around at a pouch at his sash until he came across his worn pipe and lifted it to his face. He inspected it carefully before packing it with Goldwater tobacco. It was well-flavored tobacco with a hint of clove, cinnamon, and mint. The flavor was relaxing when smoked, and he hastily pulled his flint and steel to light a small twig. He pressed the lit twig to the tobacco in his pipe and inhaled deeply, letting the soothing mixture calm his nerves.

"It seems we have quite the journey ahead," he whispered.

Karceoles caught up now with his horse and looked questionably at Searon. Andron sat behind the wizard, his young face looking hopeful at the surroundings. The sequoia trees were growing less and less the farther they traveled from Sudegam. They were replaced with smaller pine and even a few oaks.

The chilling wind came to an end, giving the air a warmer embrace around them. Searon sighed heavily, still considering everything that there was yet to do. It would not come easy, but given the help of his allies he was sure they could formulate a plan. So long as they disregarded any of the wizard's advice.

They traveled hard and steady throughout the day, with little talk, although Karceoles could be heard bickering now and again. He seemed to be much like a child, complaining about the length of a journey, with little patience. Searon hoped there was only one wizard in Calthoria because if there was another like him wandering around, he was sure he would go insane.

When the sun settled below the trees at the brink of the horizon, leaving only a glaze of orange light for travel, Searon frowned. He looked ahead with questioning eyes, but they were naught for the fading sunlight. His eyes were good enough to see at dark nearly as well as traveling at day. There was something odd in the air, a smell that wasn't full of evergreen leaves, pine, and sap. The air smelled and tasted like stone, not just of boulders and rocks, but of granite and marble. He knew there shouldn't be such a large amount of such stones in the middle of the forest with no civilization around. Bewildered, he shifted his steed south rather than east and kicked at the horse's back. Stripes paced forward abruptly, and Searon began to notice slight changes in the forest.

Trees and bushes grew slightly closer together as if they were planted by man rather than Mother Nature. Searon studied the forest with suspecting eyes, noticing animals were scarce around that particular part of the forest. There was an unsettling calmness to the air that surprised him. It seemed as if all the animals were missing from the area; their sounds and calls could not be heard. Searon pulled the reins, causing Stripes to come to an abrupt stop.

"What is it?" Starlyn whispered.

"Something is not right about this place...It seems too calm. Even a pond has a ripple within it."

"Yes, I was thinking the same."

Searon edged Stripes on but at a much slower pace. Even Karceoles had stopped bickering to Andron and had grown silent. If the wizard was quiet, then something was definitely wrong. That man never seemed to shut up. Through the tightly compacted bushes and trees, Searon saw a stone shape that had the appearance of a building. It intrigued him enough to continue forward, but with caution. It was still too quiet; this time at dusk even crickets should be heard, but the area was completely deprived of animal sounds. The only sound that could be heard was the horse hooves from the wizard's mare pressing against the ground. Stripes couldn't be heard over that loud horse, as Searon had trained the animal in the art of stealth.

Suddenly, Searon burst through a clearing to a city of stone. Buildings were everywhere, packed close together and covered in the wilderness. There were hundreds of them organized with careful skill. Each one seemed covered in its entirety with moss. They weren't maintained in the slightest, and it seemed that nature had taken them over. A total of seven rows of roads stacked south in perfect alignment with each other, which left eight perfect rows of buildings on each side of the roads. The buildings seemed to be organized from smallest to largest in every row, starting with homes and ending with businesses. Each road forked into one main one that led to an immaculate stone palace that seemed to touch the clouds. At the top were three golden globes with spikes traveling into the darkness of night. Besides the three sphere cylinders that led up to the globes, the rest seemed to be rectangular with dozens of windows covered in cobwebs.

Starlyn gasped, "What is this place?"

Chapter Fourteen

Karceoles pushed his horse to gallop alongside Searon and studied the city with intensity. He removed his pipe from his top pocket of his dusty brown robes and tapped his zylek to it, causing it to go alight. A pleasant honey-cinnamon aroma filled the air in puffs of smoke around them. Searon pulled out his pipe next and tipped it toward the wizard. Karceoles rolled his eyes lazily before tapping Searon's pipe, which he hastily began puffing on.

"The lost city of Brekaes Noielyna. Finally, I have found it. All these years, and I could never add the location of the rumors to my books."

"What is this place? It feels…corrupted," Starlyn nearly whispered.

"It was, though it should be safe now. It is a place of nightmares."

"Nightmares?" Andron asked, shivering.

"Yes." Karceoles puffed on his pipe, still staring at the palace.

"Karceoles…for this once, would you please expose the secrets you're keeping locked in your brain? We need to camp, and I think we'd better know of this place before we settle down," Searon said.

Karceoles sighed. "Very well. It began over six thousand years ago, or so I'm told."

Each turned to him with interest and wide eyes. They shivered in turn as a chilling, almost haunting breeze blew across the group. Karceoles puffed on his pipe a few more times before settling it back into his robe pouch and pulling his greasy white hair from his eyes to behind his head.

"The legend tells of another race that existed here well before the humans, kheshlars, draeyks, and even the wizards. They were a race of stone itself. I do not know much about them other than that they were a force to be reckoned with. It is said they were the ones to fight the dragons and bring them into extinction, before they themselves became extinct. They were the first of this land. Rumors say finally, after much fighting, either the humans or the kheshlars finally slew them all, but others tell of them abandoning this land to seek another. Still others claim that one day they disappeared. Not much is known about these people, as not much has been discovered to study, certainly not their city of origin. There are scripts found that seem to be written by them that are dated generations back. Some scripts speak of the city Brekaes Noielyna. It is strange that the kheshlars have never discovered it with how close it seems to be to Sudegam."

"I have heard small legends of the same, but they are not much spoken of. Most who speak of it are punished by our king," Starlyn said.

"Most?" Karceoles asked, rubbing his brow before taking his pipe in his mouth once more. "And the rest? Strangely disappeared?"

"Yes," Starlyn said.

"Most interesting," Karceoles said with another puff of his pipe.

"Is this place safe?" Searon asked.

"I would assume so, though we should keep one eye open through the night to be sure," Karceoles answered.

"Good enough for me; let's explore the city some and settle at that palace where we can keep an eye on it all."

"Searon…" Karceoles whispered.

"Yes?"

"How did you happen to stumble upon this place?"

"I caught something in the air. It smelled like…granite…and…marble mixed in the air. I found it a strange scent to be in the middle of the forest, and so I followed the scent."

Starlyn stared at him wide eyed and glanced from him to the wizard awkwardly. Karceoles's eyebrows simply raised, and he nodded. Andron's mouth hung open wide, and he had to push it closed before shaking his head.

"The only marble and granite that I can tell is that palace. That is quite the nose you have, Sir Searon; it may continue to prove useful," Karceoles said.

Searon nodded and tugged the reins of his horse to urge the animal forward. He kept a hardened eye at the buildings as he traveled down the third road from the left. The air was calm besides that of a low twirling breeze low on the ground. There was an unsettling silence as they walked, for none decided to speak. Instead, all gazed their heads about to gather in the sights of the long-abandoned city.

When they reached the end of the main road, both horses stopped, and the warriors stared up at a dark palace that the fading sunlight cast in shadow. It was haunting and disconcerting to them all to be but as a mere grain of sand compared to such a large building. The size seemed to outmatch any palace or castle of men, and the only one that surpassed it was the palace of Sudegam, but only by a fraction. Marble walls rose for leagues of height, and tall pillars of black and tan freckled granite made an entrance at the front with dozens of stone steps.

"Do we dare go inside, or shall we rest outside this night?" Andron asked.

"There is a pit here for a fire. I say we stay outside of this daunting-looking place at night. Perhaps we can get a better look in the morning, but even abandoned there is little comfort to spend inside a place as great as that, without knowing what lurks in the shadows," Karceoles said.

Starlyn hopped from the saddle behind Searon and stared up at the glorious palace. "This almost looks kheshlarn made."

"Perhaps it was, though these kinds of kheshlars have not dwelled in this land for many centuries," Karceoles said.

"Shall I go find food then?" asked Searon.

"Yes, please do, my stomach grumbles at me in such a way, I think it will hinder me if I don't settle it soon," Karceoles said.

"May I come with you, Sir Searon?" Andron asked.

"You may."

Before Searon turned his stallion around, he felt a soft hand graze his forearm. He turned to see Starlyn looking up at him fondly. "If you are to come across fresh fruit or berry."

He smiled. "If I do, I will not hesitate to fetch them for you."

With that, they were off into the night, leaving Karceoles and Starlyn to study the exotic palace. Soon, they were faded shadows in the night, next to an already blazing fire that the wizard created. Chills began to run down Searon's back as they wandered back through the darkness toward the forest.

They traveled a few hundred paces back into the trees with barely a word, for both were observing and listening for any sign of life. The night air was quiet of most sounds, including those of birds and owls. Searon could not smell much because the wind was blowing away from him, and so he could not smell far. At the least he knew there was not scent of any animals from behind. Andron gently tapped on his shoulder, and he bid Stripes to a stop.

Searon turned around to see Andron snatching a leaf from a thick bush to inspect. He held it up to observe and quickly passed it to Searon. With a glance, he noticed a bite mark at the end of the leaf and nodded.

"The bite appears that of a deer, and it is not long old either. Feel with your bare hands, there is still wet saliva near the edges," Andron said.

Searon shot an eyebrow up but quickly took a leather glove off and felt at it. Indeed the other man was correct, and he wiped his moist finger dry on his reddened leather. Andron leaped from the saddle behind him and began glancing at the ground. Searon followed in short order, but not before Andron seemed to find something.

"Look, Searon, for I have found it."

Searon stared down to a notice two large teardrop shapes embedded in the ground, side by side, next to a few others. Andron pressed his own foot next to the print and inspected the two of them. He felt the moistness of the dirt of his new print, and that of the deer. Both tracks had edges with a similar sharpness to it, and Andron nodded approvingly.

"Less than an hour ago this track was pressed. Let's continue forward."

Searon nodded and leaped onto his horse, followed quickly by Andron. The two set off again at a quickened pace, yet not a full gallop. Stripes could trot for haste and yet still barely make a sound. Searon fingered at his saddle as his horse trotted, and found his longbow.

He was impressed with Andron's tracking skills, and he realized that he put too much confidence in his smell and sight abilities instead of his knowledge. Andron might not be able to smell or see as far as him, yet he did know what kinds of things to keep an eye out for. Searon had been too accustomed to searching for draeyks, but they made such a rampage through the land that it was impossible to mistake their whereabouts.

Still, he saw the deer well ahead through the trees, even when Andron could not. He pulled an arrow from its quiver and patted Stripes to calm the horse back to a brisk walk. There were dozens of trees between him and his quarry, yet his skill outweighed such an obstacle. The deer stood two hundred paces ahead when he released, and the arrow soared through the air at an incredible speed until it struck the animal's heart. Such a shot it was that the deer didn't stagger or cry out in pain. Instead, after a second of shock, it tumbled to the ground.

They galloped up to the animal, and on their way Searon found a tree of peaches and one of plums, some of which he gathered for Starlyn. Searon leaped from his horse and cleaned the bloodied arrow before tying a strong rope to the deer and attaching it to his saddle. Many horses would not be able to travel swiftly with two men in the saddle and a deer tied on top, but he knew Stripes could still gallop in haste, even under the extra weight. After everything was secure, he jumped back onto his horse, and they rode back toward the abandoned city that Searon could still smell in the air.

When they arrived down the empty streets and to the front of the palace, they noticed both Karceoles and Starlyn deep in conversation. As Karceoles noticed them, his eyes widened in surprise, and he fed a few more faggots to the fire that he had brought with him in his saddle. Searon leaped from his horse and detached a long metal pole he kept secure for such a roasting. Searon, Karceoles, and Andron struggled to secure the large deer over the fire.

"Quite the buck you two found; very impressive. This food shall last us a while, and tonight we shall have a feast before the rest of our journey," Karceoles said.

"Andron is one bloody good tracker," Searon smiled.

Andron laughed, rubbing his stomach. "Only for food."

Searon handed a basket of fruit to Starlyn and noticed her eyes were cast down in gloom. No longer were they bright electric blue of serenity and joy, but instead seemed haunted. She looked from Searon to Andron with near disgust forming on her lips before taking a glance at the fire and swiftly casting her eyes aside. Searon was about to ask her what was wrong when she suddenly turned around and walked into the darkness without so much as a thank you for the fruit. He could definitely tell that something was wrong now, for she was too polite a person not to thank him for her meal.

"What is wrong with Starlyn; is she ill?" Andron asked from behind.

"Do not be foolish, boy; kheshlars do not suffer illness as you do," Karceoles barked.

"I do not know what is wrong with her, but she seems greatly upset," Searon whispered.

"Go to her then, but beware of the secrets of kheshlars. Do not ask her what it is that troubles her at first. Only show that you have come to listen, and soon her mind will be spoken," Karceoles said.

Searon nodded, listening to the advice carefully. He then wondered about how right the advice seemed, despite the source from which it came. Perhaps the old man did know a thing or two. He noticed that the stars up above, which only moments ago had shone brighter than even the moon, were dull in comparison. Many of them had vanished into the darkness while even the brightest seemed dull. If not for his keen eyesight, he would have been blind in the darkness.

He walked down the alley, leaving his horse behind, and wondered where it was that Starlyn had fled off to. She didn't seem to be anywhere it the streets, yet she did not seem to run away the last he saw her. Soon, he found himself staring at the various buildings of different shapes and sizes, now shrinking in order as he walked away from the palace. The shapes were not all too different, as all still seemed to have a rectangular appearance. It was on top of a medium building that he noticed a glint of sparkling steel.

Turning, he walked into a building, what appeared to be a home. The door was pushed open slightly, and he pressed it another span until he was able to fit in himself. Inside, it did appear like a home, but it was not empty as he expected. Cobwebs formed in every area except a direct path to the stairs, but that was not what he found strange. Surrounding the area were wooden chairs and tables, unmoved through time. Nothing appeared to be changed in the slightest, as if it were exactly as the people had left it. Yet nothing seemed taken from place, and even paintings and bowls of food on a kitchen dinner table seemed unmoved. He walked forth, casting spiderwebs from his eyes as he made his way to the kitchen, where he peered into the bowls that sat on the table with silverware. The food inside seemed crusted and hard, but it was still within the bowls. He shivered and backed away to start stepping up the stairs. It seemed as if whoever left had not only walked out, but seemed to do so without provisions or even finishing a meal. That was the best of the thoughts spinning through his head. Surely, these people couldn't have just plainly vanished. Another shiver came over him, but he cast his thoughts aside and continued up the stairs to the roof.

There, sitting on the ledge with legs dangling into the air below, sat Starlyn. Tears seemed to be glazing her face, causing the few dim stars to make her face sparkle with terror. Searon walked slowly now until he noticed Starlyn turning her head back at him. His movements stopped, and he stared at her.

"Are you all right? What are you doing by that ledge?"

"Do not consider me weak, Searon. I am not some mere depressed human with a fancy of ending my life for the pointlessness of it."

Searon nodded firmly and took cautioned steps forward. He sat on the ledge next to Starlyn and stared down. The height was well over a hundred paces and a nasty fall had he ever seen one. He looked away from the drop and put his hands behind him to stare up at the night sky.

"I'm sorry... I should not have snapped at you."

Still, her words tore at his heart, for it was not long ago that his mind was mixed up in thoughts of peril. He often bore thoughts of ending his own life to cease the pain. He would not do so on his own accord of course, for he knew if he did that Victoria would never forgive him. Instead, he sought battle; he sought it more than anything else. He could survive without water or food, but without battle he was lost. Without battle to occupy his mind, it became lost in thought and memory of Victoria, and so he kept himself busy. He continued searching for the draeyks in hope that one day he could forget the number that continued rattling around in his head. Forty-one months, six days, and eighteen hours since he'd buried Victoria and Kellen. He did not count, he refused to, yet still he knew the number, and it sickened him.

"It is the deer. The cruel habit of men slaughtering animals is something I cannot get past," she finally said.

Searon turned to her and noticed her eyes sinking deep into his. "What of the boar? You did not seem as ill when we fed upon it."

She turned her face from his gaze and muttered lowly, "This is different."

"How so?"

"You would not understand."

"Starlyn, I have come here to listen. I have come to understand. Hunger weakens my body right now, and yet even though the food that I know to be awaiting me is grand, it is not worth the tears of my companion."

She turned back to meet his gaze, and respect filled her eyes. They seemed to gleam bright electric blue for almost a second before returning to their dull state, and yet they did not seem as dull as they once had. Taking a deep breath, she sighed heavily and brushed her blonde hair from her face.

"For me, it is like you slaying a brother of your dear horse, Stripes."

Searon looked at her puzzled now with an eyebrow raised. She kept his gaze, and his eyes did not stray.

"Kheshlars are friends of the animals of the forest. No matter what animal it be, we are to treasure it. Whether it be a small pestering mouse that steals our bread or a large cat that we praise. Yet, like you, there are some for which we hold in higher respect. You as a human would not let harm fall upon that of a cat or dog, but above all else, a horse. A horse is a companion that you ride and travel with. One that you trust with your life. There are many animals that will come to us when we call, and of those many there are few that will let us ride them to rest our legs. Of those there are, of course, the wild horses, but also deer, antelope, elk, wolfs, tigers, panthers, and other large cats.

Deer has always been my second animal of choice to ride beyond that of a large cat. There was one I grew to love beyond any other. Her name was Moonlight, and for years she was my companion of travels. She was with me during the years I fought against Arria and the shadow of the draeyks. I do not know where she has gone in the years since. Either she has disappeared, or perhaps age has taken her. This deer you felled was not Moonlight, but who knows? It could have been her father, her brother, or even her son."

The stars above became darker until only a few inches could be seen in the cold night. It almost appeared as if every cloud imaginable covered the sky, and yet above was clear and the stars were dim. They flashed a couple of times above until resting on total darkness. Tears streamed down Starlyn's face as swiftly as a river rapid, and despite her many attempts to swat her tears away, more still fell.

"We cannot survive as you do. You must know that. If only fruit and vegetables we had, we could not gain the meat we need for muscle. Without muscle, we cannot be strong enough to wield a sword."

"I know; that is why I said nothing, but I had to come get fresh air."

"What would you have me do?"

"Nothing. Do not be burdened on my part."

"That is not a compromise. I am here to compromise. Surely, there is something we could work out together that could make all of us happy. How about if I promise to you that as long as we are in your company, from now on, no harm will befall the animals you named by our hands? Instead, we will hunt the smaller game, or those unworthy of the saddle."

A faint smile pressed her lips now. "You would do that for me?"

"Aye, I do believe all of us would. We do care for your feelings, Starlyn, despite our lack of showing it."

"I think a compromise is met; thank you," she leaned in and kissed his cheek.

He blushed slightly. "What of cattle and bison, surely they are not saddle worthy if we are to come by them by chance."

"I do think that shall be all right, so long as I am not part of the killing or witness of the eating. We are not shallow to the need of meat eaters. For one of our favorite allies is the large cats, and we know they must eat meat to survive."

"My body grows weary, and I must go eat now. Do not fear, your friend will not come to waste. Anything we cannot eat will be dried and packed, and the bones we will bury in his honor."

She nodded, and as he walked away he noticed that the stars were shining brighter. He also noticed what appeared to be a small yet faint smile upon her lips. The stars weren't as bright as they were before, but the sky was shining once more. As he walked back through the building, he thought he heard her voice, soft yet soothing, sing a song into the night.

"This dark night is haunted no more.
No more tears are needed to fall.
Fire ablaze to light the night.
And feed the stomachs of hungry men.
A kheshlar here sits intrigued in thought.
With berry and fruit to keep me strong.
We need no meat, no friend or foe.
Yet strong forever we shall be.
Others are weak and need the strength.
And we accept the fate they cause.
This night dawns and casts anew.
For no longer will they fall a friend.
This night it is agreed upon,
That those that hold so dear to us,
Are now given leave to roam.
They will be free in both shadow and light,
And I shall rest without a frown,
For I know these words to be honest and true,
And forever on the stars remain bright."

Chapter Fifteen

Searon held the final watch into the morning and was relieved when he saw the sun glistening through the few openings of the trees. The eerie, near-silent darkness of the abandoned city was chilling to say the least. He nudged Andron first, who awoke with a stir and a yawn. He rose to his feet and then croaked loudly, covering his mouth. His finger sprang forward to point as his eyes bulged. Searon turned to see what he was pointing at and found the wizard lying on his back. His arms were bent at the elbow with hands by his shoulders folding forward like a dog. He twitched in his sleep slightly, and his mouth was open with hanging tongue, drool pouring from his mouth. However, the oddest thing about it was that his eyes seemed to flutter between half-closed and half-open.

Barely containing laughing for a few seconds, Searon finally gave in and chuckled loudly, which stirred both Karceoles and Starlyn. Andron soon joined in, and both croaked so loud with laughter that tears came to their eyes. Both Starlyn and Karceoles leaped up, fishing for weapons to hold in their hands. The wizard appeared upset at being awoken in such a way, but Starlyn seemed amused.

"What! What is it?" Karceoles asked.

Both laughed harder now, and Searon fought the tears from his eyes with his hand. "Nothing, nothing, my friend."

"Should we be off then?" Andron asked with laughter still in his voice.

"Yes…yes, I think so," Searon replied with a more solemn tone. "Do we dare take a peek inside the palace?"

"I say nay, I have been inside one home already and have not liked what I saw."

"The spiderwebs?" asked Starlyn.

"No…that was to be expected. It was not the decades of spiderwebs that brought cold bumps to my arms, but what lay within the room itself."

"What did you see?" she asked.

"I thought kheshlars were to have the fairest eyesight of them all; did you not glance upon the room yourself?"

"My thoughts were clouded, but I should have. I should not have let my emotions get the best of me." She lowered her head as if in failure.

Searon set his fingers beneath her chin and lifted it up. "You had reason for thoughts to be astray. Do not deem yourself at fault, for I will not have it."

She nodded, and her appearance seemed to brighten slightly.

"What I saw was that of an abandoned home. Everything in the home seemed to still be in order, paintings and furnishings alike. Also, the kitchen held bowls of a meal that appeared to have only a few bites missing. All the remaining food was crusty and old from centuries. It almost seemed as if they left suddenly, without taking a scrap or moving anything. Either that or…"

"Or what?" asked Andron.

"The only other thing I can think of…is that they simply vanished. I do not like this place; let us be gone swiftly."

Karceoles stepped forward now with a raised gray eyebrow. His grip on his zylek seemed to tighten, and yet he peered at the buildings and palace.

"I know of that look, Karceoles. No, I will not stay here, and neither will you if you wish to continue on my journey. I know of your curiosity, and we shall not be burdened with it now. If this war comes to an end with us victorious, feel free to travel back here and try to put to rest the questions rolling in your head. For I, I do not care, and I value my life right now too much to chance it here when I can do good elsewhere in a fight."

The wizard nodded and held his head high with pride. Soon, they were packed and saddled up, and by midmorning they had left the abandoned city. Searon was glad to be away from the cursed place, as were the rest—besides the wizard, who continued to peer back behind his steed to glance upon the city.

They traveled for a few hours in near silence before Searon heard something in the air. At first, the sound of birds calling for each other and singing soothing songs grew louder, but as they approached it became dim. The chirping of crickets seemed to come less only slightly, but it was enough that Searon grew aware. After a few dozen paces, his horse came to a stop, even when he didn't bid for him to. He turned and noticed the wizard's horse had as well. Starlyn's eyes scurried about, and her hands swiftly found their way behind her neck, where they rested. Searon followed suit, felt the hilt of his claymore tightly before setting his hands behind his head to wait.

From behind the thin pine trees appeared six kheshlars, three with bow, two with sword, and one with hammer. Starlyn seemed to look at her own hammer from the corner of her eye. The kheshlars did not seem to embrace their weapons, but instead only stared at the company. One with shining silver hair stepped forward.

"An odd company if I've ever seen one. Two humans, a wizard, and a kheshlar kind." His gray eyes seemed to stare only at Starlyn.

She looked back at him, but she did not speak a word. Her body kept still, and her breathing stayed calm.

"Starlyn I believe it is…Yes, Starlyn. Long ago did I fight alongside you in your claimed war against the draeyks."

"Vaelmirr."

"Ah, so you do remember me. Tell me, Nightsky, why do you travel with a company as ill as these?"

"They are not ill, for they seek a common enemy."

"Are not ill? They are friend killers. Only last night they have slain a friend of ours, a native to our land, and a dear friend of mine."

"They were unaware of our customs, and yet now they walk in the light of knowledge. No longer will they torment the animals we call our friends."

"It is too late, as blood has already been spilled on our land."

"Think them not as humans, but as tigers roaming the land without knowledge of the rules. Were they tigers, no punishment would become of it."

"Ignorance is not an excuse. They must be set in trial."

"That is not fair."

"Be silent."

Karceoles slid his zylek from his robes and held it high. He chanted words, and soon the silvery haired kheshlar was lifted off the ground. Three arrows loosed in a fraction of a second, but each was blocked with three small orange spheres of light.

"Do not stand in our way!" Karceoles bellowed.

Searon leaped from his saddle now and cast aside Starlyn's arm as she tried to grab him. He turned to the wizard and shook his head. "Stand down."

Karceoles looked at him, but the glow of orange around the kheshlar disintegrated into sparks, and he lowered his zylek. He continued to stare with stern expression at the kheshlar as if ready to do it again if any harm were to become of Searon. Searon turned to the kheshlar who was still serene in appearance and knelt to the ground before him.

"I, Searon De'Athaniel, the leader of this party, do beg forgiveness. We did not know what crime we did commit, and once it was explained to us after the fact, we were greatly sorry. We made sure none of the sacred creature went to waste, and we buried the bones in sorrow."

The kheshlar looked down at the human in bewilderment for a long moment before speaking. "Rise, Searon De'Athaniel."

Searon rose to his feet and cupped his hand on the hilt of his claymore. Starlyn walked to stand next to him, followed by Andron and Karceoles. The four stood before the six kheshlars, who seemed intrigued by the party.

"True it is that your leadership is strong. You have tied yourself to a kheshlar and a wizard who both show obedience to your will. Perhaps there is more to you than meets the eye." Vaelmirr paused to glance at the rest of the company before looking back at Searon. "Very well, this once we shall grant you what you humans call a warning. Do not take it lightly, for if we meet again in these circumstances it will not be so. Starlyn tells of a common foe you seek."

"Yes…we are setting forth to destroy the draeyks."

"Ah, a worthy task indeed. Starlyn herself once tried, but they are more cunning than they seem."

He turned to Starlyn. "Nightsky, I know of your desire and need to fight these creatures in an attempt to soothe the memories of your sister. I fought alongside you before, and I know what it is that you seek. Be cautious, as in groups these beasts are dangerous, but perhaps a friendly eye will serve you when in need."

Turning to his kheshlarn companions, he motioned for one to come forward. The kheshlar had long red hair and held a sturdy long-bow. He bowed to Vaelmirr before turning to look at Starlyn. He seemed to glow a slight red as he looked at her and quickly turned away.

"I lend you Erenuyh, archer of sharp eye, to join you on your journey. May he serve you well."

Erenuyh bowed before Starlyn and nodded to his leader before joining the party. Starlyn bowed and thanked him, as did the rest before they continued through the kheshlarn land. There were still hundreds of leagues to go yet before they could gain much rest in their party. Men were near to the other side of the land of Calthoria, and they dared not rest much until they could have a full force behind them.

Once out of the kheshlarn territory, Karceoles bid them to stop. He got off of his steed and beckoned Andron and Searon to as well. Erenuyh had sprinted alongside them instead of saddling up because no horse could fit another. The wizard waited for all of them to come close to him when he spoke.

"It is now time that we separate. For the land of men is spread aplenty, and for us to rally enough it would prove more effective if each could find a territory. We already know of Andron's homeland, Gueret-tos, but there are other nations that if we could only convince to ally with us, we could truly become a formidable foe against the draeyks."

"What do you suggest?" asked Searon.

"I have already told Starlyn of a short way that leads close to Andron's homeland in the north," he said, addressing the group. "The journey is perilous but necessary for haste. Searon and I will head south to the cities of men and make east for a large city where we will pay a visit to Searon's brother and see if he can lend us aid."

Starlyn and Andron both turned with questioning glances to Searon. Searon didn't notice either one of them, however, but instead stared at Karceoles in disbelief. He quivered as his memories haunted him.

"How is it you know of my brother?"

Chapter Sixteen

The middle of summer had finally arrived where the days grew hotter and the nights shorter. Seldom did they decide to travel during the day but instead chose the coolness of night to carry them more swiftly. During the hottest hours, they discovered what little shade could be found to rest and nap. Andron rather enjoyed Starlyn's cheerful company, but he was unsure about the other kheshlar. Erenuyh did not seem to speak much or acknowledge him at all. He did peer at Starlyn from time to time, but he hardly even spoke to her. It seemed a spell took him each time he looked upon the fair kheshlar. Andron did admit that Starlyn's beauty outmatched any other he had ever seen, but he thought it was common among the kheshlars. Perhaps she was even a treasure in their eyes, and Andron didn't doubt it.

He always fancied the old Wiseman tales of kheshlars while sitting at a campfire smoking pipe weed, but he thought they were more a myth than reality. Starlyn was the first of her kind that he'd seen, and he had been entrapped by her beauty. In the stories, they were the fair folk, fair of both appearance and tongue. It was also said they had strange ears and thin but strong bodies. He had also heard that they did not eat meat, were friends of the forest, and immortal of life. As far as he could tell, the stories did not go astray. She was the first he had seen, but he was hopeful she wouldn't be the last. Erenuyh would be the second kheshlar that Andron laid eyes on, and the first male. He noticed that there was little difference in the appearance between the men and women, for he had studied when the six had surrounded them. The men had stronger jaws, larger ears, and thicker cheek bones. Still, these comparisons were small and had to be closely observed. The clearest detail would be the body shape and slightly less pale face of Starlyn. He wondered if all the kheshlars had as fine a bosom as Starlyn.

They traveled near relentlessly once they exited the large forest of the west. The plains were bare now but a few scattered trees within giant meadows. Most of the ground was bright-green grass with goats and sheep aplenty grazing upon it to keep it trimmed. Large mountains could be seen far in the distance to the east, and they seemed to travel straight for them at a northern slope. Andron had remembered seeing mountains as tiny specks to the south of where he lived, and so he gathered Starlyn was using them as a marker. They did not travel all the way to the mountains but instead kept a league away atop small hills heading north.

Andron dearly wished he was back upon the saddle of a horse again, for his feet grew weary sprinting across the hills. He soon realized how much more energy kheshlars had than men and how out of shape he was. True it was that he was thin, much thinner than Searon perhaps, but his endurance was low. It had not always been, but after such a journey that he had, he did grow tired. After that, he grew perhaps lazy as he sat upon Searon's fair white-and-black striped horse.

On the morning of the seventh day, they began to slow and were at a quick-paced walk. It seemed like a standard walk for the kheshlars, but it was quick in pace for Andron. Each morning, they seemed to slow in pace to relax with the morning breeze. Then they would search the hilltops for close area of shade or water to rest during the hot summer day. That day, they found both a large oak tree with shade and a pond only fifty paces in front of it. Andron smiled broadly when he sat down in front of it.

Soon, when his back was relaxed against the stern trunk of the tree, he pulled out a long-stem cedar pipe and packed it with pipe weed. The plant was called Klitheaur, and a common weed that grew in the outskirts of his village. It was used by most for its healing and potency of relaxation. The smell was good and the taste even better. He found a few twigs that he lit with his flint striker and dipped into the opening of his pipe. After taking a few long-desired inhales of the fresh pipe weed he leaned his head back in relaxation. Erenuyh's nose seemed to twitch at the stench of the weed, but he said nothing. Starlyn, however, looked intrigued.

"That is different from the leaf that Searon smokes," she said.

"Ah yes, this is called Klitheaur; it's a weed, it is better for relaxation, especially after a long journey. However, it is not good for a fight, and I assume that is why Searon does not smoke it."

"It calms you then?"

"Yes, it is often used for healing wounds, as well as a soothing aroma to help numb your body and relax your mind. After this journey of relentless sprinting, it is a much-needed calmness. Would you care for a smoke?"

She smiled. "No, but thank you."

He looked at her then and marveled at her entire beauty. She seemed flawless, like that of a glass sculpture too fine to touch. Her fingers ran through her shining blonde hair as she sang to herself in a voice so low that he couldn't understand the words. Andron had to clear his head from the thoughts that tormented it. He had a beautiful wife at home and many children. Yet the kheshlar's beauty was unmatched, and he found that he could not help himself from staring.

Suddenly, a singing blue jay leaped from the branch where it sang and landed on Starlyn's outstretched index finger. It whistled a beautiful humming tune that Starlyn matched in whistles. Together, the two seemed to perform a duet as Andron had never seen before, and his gaze didn't falter for a second. It seemed a dream of absolute perfection, and he could not believe that what he saw was real. His eyes did not deceive him, however, for even after he rubbed them he continued to stare at the marvelous sight.

There were still many questions swirling in his head, and he knew he must ask if he were ever to find answers. He waited patiently until the bird and kheshlar finished their song. Starlyn giggled softly as the bird bowed to her and fluttered off. She looked at Andron after and smiled. It moments, he felt his cheeks grow warm, and he had to glance his eyes away for a moment.

"Have kheshlars always dwelled here in Calthoria?" Andron finally asked, looking back up at her.

Her eyes were astray glancing upon the calm pond that lay outstretched before them. She turned and met his eyes with her own and smiled.

"My knowledge is not great. Yet from what I've come to learn, our king Elsargast sailed across the sea many thousand years ago. He arrived with a small party of kheshlars, and they were wary from their journey, and they did not know a land here. They searched the land and were surprised to find no dragons and a race of mortal men. Their hearts stayed true to the forests of their origins, and so they settled in the west of the land. I do not know if the wood kheshlars traveled with us or came from elsewhere, but for many generations they have been lost to us."

"Younger race? How old is the race of kheshlars?"

"That even my knowledge does not know. Our assumption is that we are the elder race, and yet since we were not kin to here, we do not know for certain. I do believe that we have been here since nearly the dawn of time, but again, I cannot be sure."

"You did not speak of the draeyks; were they not here when your kin arrived?"

"I cannot say. I think another was noticed, but their numbers weren't great enough to spark our interest. There was another race back then, though, that our stories do tell. They were called daerions, or those of horns. Those were nasty and strong creatures with rough blue skin and large ram-like horns that fell from their forehead to their jaw."

"I wonder where the draeyks came from."

"Do you want opinion or fact?"

"You have given me fact; what is your opinion?"

"From the appearance of these draeyks—with their elongated snouts, sharp teeth, long claws, scales, and tales—it seems a close similarity to the legends of dragons. Yet these creatures are much smaller. The legends of my race tell of fearsome large, scaled beasts with wings that flew through the skies and caused death and destruction to anything in their path. These draeyks do not seem so different, do they? The description is right, yet they are not as large as a palace, nor do they have wings. I come to wonder if through the dragons' destruction of these lands, perhaps they've adapted in some way to a new kind, a new race."

"Do many of your race hold your same beliefs?"

"Only a few. There are not many theorists among the kheshlars these days. Instead, they like hard facts that are written in history."

A small humph came from Erenuyh, who sat on the far side of the tree with legs crossed. He seemed to turn to look at Starlyn for only a moment until her eyes met his, and he soon cast his aside.

"A very few," Starlyn whispered.

"Is it true that kheshlars live forever?" Andron asked.

"We cannot die from natural causes and will live on until either sword, bow, or poison claims us. We do age, even if you human folk cannot see it. When we feel we have lived as long as we will, we become one with the trees. We may go to them and ask them for a chance to become a part of the nature that we so love."

"How old are you, Starlyn?"

She hesitated for a moment. "Three centuries and twenty years."

Andron stumbled as he looked at her. Her face did not nearly look so old. Indeed, she did not look young either. It was a strange appearance as he studied, but it was neither young nor old. Instead, it seemed to have an ageless appearance.

"Do all of you appear ageless?"

She smiled. "No, that look does not form until after our first hundred years, when we have reached full maturity."

"Are there many kheshlar children?"

Starlyn laughed. "You are very intrigued in our ways."

"I'm sorry, am I asking too many questions? Not but a month ago did I think you as an old Wiseman's tale. It seemed you appeared out of a storybook, and I am eager to learn as much as I can."

"Do not fret, you dare not speak too much, I will answer your questions as I can. Then perhaps I shall have questions of my own."

"You may ask any you wish."

"To answer your question, no, right now there are naught kheshlarn children. Though there are a few young kheshlars."

"No children? In our villages, there are dozens outside playing with each other, either making kites or wagons to play. I have three myself, three beautiful children. I am very eager to see them once again."

Starlyn laughed. "I have no doubt you are. You must remember that kheshlars live much longer than you. We do not need to be hasty to bear children. Our king has set forth strict rules about when we are to conceive children."

"Rules? There shouldn't be rules of such things."

"For us there are. We are to only bear children once a century, on its dawn. Therefore, at each new century dawn, each of us has grown exactly a hundred years apart. It gives easy knowledge to each other's age and how long they have been around."

"You say you are 320, and it is true to my calendar that it is twenty years in the century. So the youngest of your kin are but twenty?"

Starlyn smiled once more. "Other kheshlars may say what they will of humans, but I will know the truth. You are a race quick to thought and mind. Yes, twenty is our youngest."

Andron opened his mouth but soon closed it. Starlyn stared at him with wonder, but he tried again to no success. Finally, he wiped sweat from his brow and spoke at last, "Has a kheshlar ever been committed to a human?"

Starlyn's expression darkened, and even Erenuyh looked over with wonder. It was hard to say whether it was at the question or for the answer. Starlyn shook her head as if fighting a battle with herself from within her mind.

"It is forbidden by our king. None have tried to my knowledge, though even if they had, I would not assume I would hear of it. The act is considered treason, and the penalty is death. We are to remain within our borders, with our own race."

"That is sad, for you seem so free, and yet so trapped at the same time."

"Yes…I have often felt as such. Please, may we change the subject?"

"Of course, I cannot think of any more questions. What questions do you have of me?"

"Not many, though I wish to know of your family. Tell me of your wife and kids, if you may."

Andron smiled. "Ah, how I do miss them."

He took a drink of cold water from his water skin and pulled his pipe out once more. Igniting another twig, he dipped it to the pipe weed and inhaled smoothly. After another few puffs, he sighed and closed his eyes, leaning his back upon the tree.

"My wife, Ketharine, is fair with fiery hair well past her shoulders. Freckles cover her cheeks that turn red when she smiles. She is both kind and gentle, and I am truly rewarded to have her love. Though, being redheaded, it seems she does sprout a temper from time to time that is fiercer than the thick fires her hair takes color from."

"Does the color hair alter the personality of the humans?"

"No…I do not think it does. Yet the tale passed from generations of men has always been: blonde the fair, brunette the wise, and redhead the fierce. It does seem to hold true in many a circumstance, but nay, it does not hold true to everyone. Yet Ketharine does seem to heat with temper from time to time if she does not have her way. Although I find that true for all women. She was quite angry when I told her I was going to leave to fight, yet she seemed to settle when I told her that I would not be able to rest until the creatures were dead and unable to harm our children and her."

"What of your children?"

"I have three, two little girls and a young boy. Kierra is my eldest at the age of nine, and has fiery red hair and freckles to match her mother. Adreamera is but five with long black hair and few freckles upon her beautiful face. My last, my son Aneldon is but a year old with very few hairs on his head, yet they are already fiery red. I do miss them dearly and am eager to spend time with them again. I hope we do not have to leave so soon after we arrive."

"We may have time to stay a little while," Starlyn smiled.

"Good."

"What is it like?"

"What?"

"Children, being a father, a parent."

His eyes widened with wonder as he looked back at her. He didn't think to ask about her personal life, but now he wondered of it. "Do you not have children?"

"No…I do not. I think I have always wanted, yet each time the century comes close I find that I have nobody to share it with, at least nobody that I wish to. There are many kheshlars that have tried to win my affection, but my heart has never set." She closed her eyes. "And I fear it never will."

"Do not fret, fair Starlyn, if your heart has not been claimed, it is only because you have not met the right one yet. As my father told me as a lad, 'Son, there is a special someone for everyone. The trick is not to search, but let yourself be found.'"

"Strange advice, yet it seems soothing in a way. Perhaps I have spent too much time searching for someone that wasn't there. Between that and searching to destroy these draeyks, I have kept myself quite busy."

"Perhaps it is time that you take a rest, and instead of searching for others, you should search within yourself. Find out who you truly are, and then the rest of the decisions you will find much clearer."

"For one so young, you seem to be wiser than those of old."

Andron laughed. "Not I; I am not wise. Yet I listen to the words of wise men, and I keep them true to my heart."

Both were quiet for a while, and Andron took to smoking his pipe weed. The sun rose high in the sky, and the head of midday was upon them. Soon, the scorching heat would make them drowsy, and they would take a great sleep.

"It is a wonderful feeling, far past what mere words can describe."

"What's that?" Starlyn asked, seeming to break from thought.

"Being a father. You crave to be around them all the time. To play with them and teach them things. Every time you teach them something, your heart warms with pride. For to you they are unlike any other. They are yours, and when they grow they will look up to you. In their eyes, you are everything that they should be. And so each deed you do, each step you make, you must make certain that it is the correct path. For they will always be watching you, and they will learn from your successes and your failures."

"It almost seems a burden."

"Burden? Yes, it may seem so. Yet it is not a burden to drag you down, but a burden to boost you up, and make you a better person for it."

"I can see that in you, for I see you as a great person. Your quality of good surpasses that of many kheshlars I know. There is no selfishness in you but instead selflessness. This is a trait I have seldom seen within kheshlars."

"I thank you for your kind words, yet I am far from perfect."

"As are we all. I'd like to ask, if I may, what is it like having several younglings only years apart? It is a question I cannot even ask a kheshlar, for they do not know, as we cannot have children so often."

"The only word I can fancy to find is joy. Watching them play with each other and treat each other with kindness, and sometimes spite. It is a warming feeling. Together, they learn, and together they play. It is easier to have a few children than only one. For one child demands your full attention at every waking moment. Yet when there are a few, there are times they would rather play with each other. They learn from each other and teach each other, which is also a help in times of stress."

"It sounds enlightening, and sometime in the far future I would not mind at all to be a bearer of children."

"I think you would make a fond mother."

She smiled. "Thank you."

He yawned loudly and tucked his pipe back in his pouch. "I'm afraid we've stayed up too long, and my body grows weary. I will rest now, for I know this evening you will want to be off again at the same swift pace."

"Rest well, Andron," Starlyn said as his eyes closed. She smiled at him before closing her own eyes to rest against the tree.

Chapter Seventeen

Searon rode long and far five days southeast alongside Karceoles with barely a word of conversation. Flashbacks of his brother and the time they'd shared together occupied his mind. He still remembered the confused expression on his brother's face when he returned from Tiermera. Searon's hard battle-worn expression had changed since he came back from the city, and Noraes was the first to notice it. Noraes was many years younger and still craved the thrill of the fight, while Searon grew in mind and wanted more peaceful things. There was a time when he thought he would never want such things, but when he had stared upon the face of the tear-struck Victoria through the smoke of Tiermera, everything changed. He no longer cared for the wars, the battle, and the foolishness of men attacking men. It seemed that during all the long years of fighting he was searching for something, and it was found when he first glanced upon Victoria.

At first, Noraes had bid Searon to see the foolishness of his ways, and told him that the phase would pass. Searon tried telling him otherwise, but the young hardheaded brother would not listen. Until the day he beheld Victoria for himself. Searon had kept Victoria from him at first because he was still unsure if she did trust him. He would not force himself upon her because he treasured her beyond all else. First, he would allow her to fall in love with him, and then they would marry. For many months, did he hope and wish for that day to come, but he kept true to his word and didn't leave for battle when all else around him did. Instead, he stayed, but he did train men in the art of swords, to all those who would wield one. He told Victoria that he trained them so they would not be defenseless in an attack, but he did hold back death-blows that he had once taught.

It was the third month when Searon noticed Victoria's kisses returned with passion, and the glint in her eyes and smile upon her face. That's when it was time for her to meet his brother for more than a glance—a true meeting. He wanted his brother to understand before marrying so he could accept his wife without resentment. He wanted his brother to be by his side at the wedding. The memory was carved in his mind like that of a perfect glass sculpture, and it came to him every night in his dreams since the wizard had mentioned his brother.

* * *

Victoria stood in the kitchen, stirring the large steel pot of soup she'd made. A smile was on her lips when she turned around to find Searon setting the table with bowls and spoons. Searon only smiled back as he continued to make sure everything was proper with his seat across from hers and his brother's on the side of the oak table. The smell of fresh vegetables, chicken, and spices loomed inside and made Searon's mouth water. She made some of the best soup he had ever tasted, with cabbage, potatoes, chicken, garlic, and other ingredients that he could not guess.

He walked up to her from behind and rested his head on her shoulder. She turned into him and clasped her arms around his neck. Her face lit up in a smile, and she bit her lip. Searon smiled down at her and was surprised when she stepped up on her tiptoes and kissed him passionately. A knock at the door startled them, and Searon left her to open it.

Noraes stood, dressed in a blue silk shirt and slick black breeches with a bundle of flowers in his hand. He seemed to shake nervously, and his eyes kept wavering side to side. His dirty-blond hair was partially brushed as well as any single man might hope to achieve without a mirror. He smiled slightly looking at Searon, but he remained still.

"Please, come in," Searon beckoned.

He nodded and stepped inside, glancing at Victoria who was in a crimson silk dress and red slippers. She began filling the bowls that

Searon handed her as Noraes took a seat. Searon sat down and watched his brother.

"Thank you for inviting me."

"You need not thank me, but Victoria: She is the one who beckoned me to meet you. It is also she who slaves in the kitchen without allowing help."

"Uhmm...Thank you, Victoria."

"It is my pleasure," she smiled. "I have been very eager to meet you, as your brother speaks well of you. There is much pride in him to have you as a brother."

"He is too kind, but perhaps, he always has been."

"I am surprised he has not invited you to meet me sooner."

"I did not want to push my family on you, dear, but I decided to wait until you were ready to ask," Searon said.

"You take my feelings into too much thought, darling, for I was yours as soon as you swept me upon your horse."

"Yes, that is true, yet there was still doubt within you, and I have allowed that to pass."

"It has passed," she smiled.

Noraes looked at their exchange with unease and fondled his soup spoon.

"Would the guest like to say grace?" Searon asked.

Noraes looked up suddenly, and his eyes widened. "Uhmm, yes, I could do that." He shifted in his chair slightly. "Dear whoever may be higher than us, the mighty one who gives us all that we have. We ask that you continue to enlighten our lives, and we bid thanks to thee for the meals on our table, and the ale for our thirst."

Searon laughed. "That was blandly put, my brother."

"What...you know better than to ask me. I could never say it right when growing up; what makes you think I can now?"

"It was good enough for us; we may eat."

The three ate, and Noraes seemed quite pleased with his soup and impressed by Victoria as well. He had never had such a fine soup before, and besides, he was used to eating bread and simple food, for it was always only him. Once the three had filled up on soup and bread, both Searon and Noraes went outside to smoke their pipes. Victoria stayed inside to clean the table and dishes.

"So, my brother, what do you think of her?" Searon asked.

"She is a fine cook."

Searon laughed. "Yes she is."

"She is nice, Searon, beautiful and kind, and I find her to complement you well. I am sorry I spoke ill of your changes, but some part of me still wishes to grasp for my brother that would join me on the battlefield."

"I understand, but I've come to realize that these battles and wars are futile. We are destroying our own kind, and for what? All those innocents caught between the few who do the harm to start it all. Can't you see the waste?"

"I can…but it cannot be avoided."

"Perhaps not, but I will take part in it no more," Searon paused. "Brother…I am in love. When I first saw her, I knew that she was the one…I do not know how I did, but somehow I was drawn. I did not love her then, but I knew that she would be the one that I could love, for any others my heart wouldn't allow myself those feelings. With her, it has come swift but sure, and now I know that I love her. I believe she loves me as well, and I told myself that when that moment comes, I would marry her. I have given her time, and I think she's nearly there."

"Brother, you are blind, as you've always been. She isn't nearly there," Noraes laughed. "She is there already, I can already see with the way she looks at you. She is in love, and you should ask her, but ask her proper."

Noraes looked about the evening city where most stayed in their homes but a few traveled the streets in search of pubs. He stood and walked a few feet forward to pluck a violet from stem and bring it back. Handing it to Searon, he smiled, "Go, and ask her."

"Now?"

"Yes, now, you fool."

"I want you to be there, by my side."

"I will be."

Searon smiled and opened the door, leaving it open, so Noraes could bear witness. Victoria had just finished up with the cleaning and turned to him to stare, puzzled. He hid the violet behind his back and went to kiss her. She was taken aback at first, but she soon melted into the kiss, not caring that Noraes could be seen from inside. When Searon withdrew, a smile brighter than the biggest full moon was upon her face. He knelt down to one knee and looked up at her. She seemed puzzled until he pulled out the violet and held it in front of her. It was then that her eyes widened and lit up with her mouth dropping slightly.

"Victoria, when I found you, I knew that you were the one. I knew that I had to have you as mine, if you dared take me. I asked for your hand and promised I would never again stain my blade with the blood of innocents. Yet still, I gave you time, so we could get to know each other. I deem that time over, and I come to you in confession. I love you. My desire burns for you with every ounce of my soul, and if you would have me as your husband, I would like you to marry me, and then no longer will beds separate us. I want to be with you, mind, body, and soul."

Crimson stained her cheeks in a blush, and she covered her smile. She spoke no words but instead fell into his arms. With all of her might she hugged him, sucking all the breath from within him until his face turned blue. She released and kissed him with such passion that Noraes averted his eyes.

"I accept."

Noraes stepped inside and smiled. "I, Noraes, have born witness to the proposal between Searon and Victoria and deem the two shall marry one week from today."

Searon clasped his brother's shoulder and murmured a thank you before returning his attention back to his fiancée. He held her in his arms and never wanted to let her go.

* * *

Searon shivered as he remembered the day he proposed to her. It was both a fond and a sad memory for him. The day was grand, and he had been so happy that his brother had given his blessing. It was the start of a perfect life for Searon. Yet it was sad now because his perfect life was over. Victoria was gone, and nothing he could do would ever bring her back. He shivered and cast such thoughts from his mind.

He stirred from his sleep on the night of the fifth day and tried to shut his eyes again to meet Victoria in his dreams once more. Karceoles nudged him, and he growled before reluctantly rising to his feet. It was now time for him to go on watch, which meant it was nearing morning of the sixth day. He stood and yawned before going next to the smoke-less fire and warming his hands. The weather wasn't freezing, but there was a chill in the air at night. It was the middle of day that carried all of the heat, but it began to drop in temperature the farther south they went.

After warming himself for a moment, he got to his feet and unpacked some deer meat that he'd brought to the fire to warm. He kept his rations of deer calculated as not to eat too much. Neither he nor Karceoles wanted to stop during the travel to find food, when they were trying to make haste. From what the wizard said, it was a longer journey south than north, and so their horses made great speed during the day.

Searon was eager to see his brother again, and he often wondered what he was up to. He wondered if his wild nature had finally been tamed by a woman and kids. It was a pleasant thought, but Searon wouldn't believe it unless he saw it for himself. Noraes was too outspoken and loved the thrill of the chase, whether it be in battle or of women.

Through the rest of the darkness and into the sunrise it was mostly calm besides a few howls of wolves that seemed to be too far north to worry about, and the hooting of owls. The sun came over the mountains to the east, and Searon watched it for a long moment. It was a beautiful sunrise with an orange sky, and glittered light appeared through the clouds that covered the sun. The winding river glittered with the light as it snaked through the thick trees toward the flat plains and mountain. Searon stood on the hill amid the trees for a long moment watching the sunrise and smoking his pipe before turning to wake up the wizard.

Karceoles woke with a yawn and stumbled to grab his zylek to help him rise. His white hair was tangled, and he brushed it, annoyed, with his hands to settle it away from his orange eyes. He grabbed some provisions of food and water from his saddlebags that he finished rapidly before putting the saddle back on horse and securing himself on top. Searon followed his lead and put the saddlebags back on Stripes.

The horses began at a walk, as they were weary as well. Searon had been silent for the past few days while he rode with Karceoles because his mind had been occupied with memories of Noraes. Yet the wizard had still not answered his question.

"How do you know my brother?"

Karceoles's eyes darkened as he looked back at him. "I am a wizard; I know everything."

Searon grunted, but he expected such an answer from the wizard. "I haven't seen him in years; I didn't know he was still alive. I would have figured he would have ridden himself to battle and death long ago. Either that or pissed off a woman enough for her to kill him."

Karceoles laughed. "Yes, I could see that from the little I know of him. He is alive and well the last I left."

The wizard took his pipe from his robes and took a long puff. Honey-cinnamon aroma filled the air surrounding them that mixed with Searon's delightfully aromatic Cavendish blend. Both sat silent for a minute as their horses walked side by side through the cover of trees.

"You have met him?" Searon asked with blood growing hot.

"No, but I've wandered long and far during the years of my travels."

"Where does he live, what city has he run off to?"

"Run off? You two may be brothers, but he isn't like you. He likes what is comfortable. There were a few times he tried relocating, but each time he came back to Legain, and there he stays."

"Legain? I do not know if I'm ready to see all of my old friends. The questions…they will ask of her."

"Sometimes, the best way to grieve is to face it head on and get it over with. Only then can you continue on in peace."

"Perhaps you're right…but don't expect to hear that much from me. I should be able to hold myself together…but as soon as I meet my brother, I will be in need of a pub with whiskey."

"As will I, my friend."

"Hold up…I don't know if you have earned calling me that yet."

Karceoles looked back at him with question, but Searon was only smiling with a playful face. Instead of growing heated, the wizard only laughed and clapped Searon's back. They continued on in mostly silence.

By midafternoon, the horses grew weary of galloping, but neither Searon nor Karceoles let them rest yet. Searon had a feeling, and so he pressed Stripes on. His horse wasn't nearly as tired as the wizard's was, and there were many days that Searon had pushed Stripes even harder. It seemed as if ahead of them was a pure bright light, and Searon strived to reach it.

Finally, Stripes burst through it with Karceoles's horse close behind. Searon's eyes widened with wonder, and he tugged his stallion's reins to bring Stripes to a stop. Karceoles stopped quickly after and guided his horse next to Searon. In front of them the forest was gone, to be replaced with a meadow as far as the eye could see. Perfect bright-green grass covered the distance for leagues. A large river could be seen winding south between dozens of villages. Smoke from chimneys could be seen above every village.

"One step closer, yet still many days away from Legain. Still, it is nice to see civilization once more," Karceoles whispered.

"You're only excited to have more people to torment," Searon laughed.

"That may be so, yet I would not mind that whiskey you spoke of either."

"Then let us be off, slowly this time, for our horses need the rest. The river I see is three leagues south, and we should stop there for drink before we continue the final league into the first village."

"A sound plan, though I could have come up with a better one myself."

"Is that so?"

"Yes, though you will never hear it now. Your plan it shall be that we follow."

Searon chuckled and nudged Stripes forward.

Chapter Eighteen

Starlyn awoke as the sun edged toward the trees to the west. Twilight covered the ground now, and many of the afternoon hours had passed in rest. No longer was the blazing sun making her weary, but instead the night chill gave her comfort. She did not sweat but a few droplets even during the highest point of the sun, but she noticed Andron drenched in it even when covered in shade. Kheshlars were different from humans and didn't strain from the temperatures of either hot or cold. When kheshlars would sweat it was because of thought and not heat. Still, she was parched, and she drained the contents of her water skin into her mouth. She walked forward to the pond where she filled it to the top, unaware of how much farther it would be until another fresh water source could be found. The lands before her were strange, and even during her adventures in battle against the draeyks, she had not traveled this far.

Andron still lay peacefully against the tree, snoring lightly with mouth open. She smiled as she nudged him, and his eyes opened slowly with strain to glance at her.

"Has it reached our hour to go already?" he yawned.

"I'm afraid so. Do not fret, for we shall start slow."

He yawned again and took his water skin to his mouth. It emptied quickly, and he frowned. Walking to the pond, he filled it quickly and stretched lazily.

"Aw, but I wish we did not have to leave so hastily. I would very much like to smoke my pipe once more. I deem we take a fitting rest once we arrive at my city."

"It shall be. Yet if you wish, you may smoke once more before we travel forth."

"There shouldn't be too many enemies about hopefully. Perhaps only a little, though when we reach a city I will be in dire need of an ale."

Starlyn smiled. "When we reach a city, I will buy you the first ale."

"My foot will press faster with that news; will you drink with me?"

"Kheshlars do not drink ale or beer."

Andron frowned with the saddest face he could fathom, and Starlyn laughed.

"Perhaps I will have a glass of wine."

"That will suit. But we've talked too long; let us be off."

Andron walked alongside Starlyn, and she could smell the rich aroma of pipe weed beside her. Erenuyh hung back ten paces watching them, but he did not speak or make a sound. His eyes seemed ever moving, as if searching the darkness for any friend or foe. Starlyn did not know much about the strange kheshlar other than his skill with a bow. His leader, Vaelmirr, had been a good friend of hers in the war of shadow against the draeyks, and she trusted his counsel of taking this kheshlar with them. As of yet, his usefulness wasn't known.

The stars above shone brightly as happy thoughts fluttered her mind. Soon, she would travel into a human town and make her presence known. She would be the first kheshlar revealed to the outside world. Fear and pride both overtook her as she thought. The king, Elsargast, would probably greatly disapprove of her quest. She did not seem to mind or care, though, because her focus was blind to those of the kheshlars. All that she wanted was to cause death and destruction to the draeyks. They were despicable creatures that warped the mind of her sister. Beyond all else, all that she wanted was her sister back. Not this new "undead kheshlar" that Karceoles had called her, but the true Arria, with the heart of gold.

The moon was a crescent that night, yet beautiful amid the stars. When all else failed of bringing a smile to her face, the night sky was always there to cheer her up. Every time she would glance upon it, there would be a smile to meet her face. She felt stronger during the night than at day. In that way, she was different from her sister. Her sister had always seemed stronger during the day with the bright sun about her face. Still, many nights they enjoyed watching the stars together.

A sudden howl in the wind caught her attention and shattered her thoughts. She stared to the east toward the mountains, but she could see nothing. Wolves didn't often howl when there was but a sliver of a moon, unless they were to attack. More howls echoed it, and each came from the east. Erenuyh behind her paced up and withdrew an arrow but did not notch it. He peered around both north and east for a long while. Andron shivered next to her and grasped his sword.

"If battle approaches, I'll wish I never smoked," he whispered.

The sun was only minutes from the light being completely extinguished, and Starlyn felt the long handle of her axe. Suddenly, snarls could be heard from the north, and from the hilltops came a force of draeyks sprinting forth with haste. There were a lot of them, much more than the three would be able to handle.

"Erenuyh, how fare your eyes? How many do you see?"

"Fifty dragon creatures. I do not yet know if the wolves will join them."

Andron's sword unsheathed, and the blade became transparent with the darkness. He held steady and breathed slowly, casting his eyes from side to front. Starlyn pulled her hammer from her belt and felt at the long spike along the back of it before holding it steady with its face in front. She unclasped the pack at her back and quickly attached her armor in place of her lesser leather. When she let the leather fall to reveal her nearly naked body, she caught a glimpse from Andron for only a second but let it pass.

"A few more paces. Reach the top of the hill, and hold. We must have the high ground against this many," Starlyn said.

Andron leaped forward and stood atop the hill, ready for the worst to come at him. He seemed focused with more intensity than Starlyn had ever seen him. Time seemed to slow for her as well, and she stood alongside him. Erenuyh stood to their left, still glancing at the mountains to the east as he loosed arrows.

Seven draeyks fell before the party reached the top of the hill thanks to Erenuyh's arrows. Starlyn hit with the first strike, knocking a creature down the hill to tumble into many foes. Andron brought his sword forward to block incoming axe strikes from the draeyks. He held well, and each of his blocks was met well. Starlyn was thankful for his protection as she hammered foes back with force. She held the offensive while he held her defense. He saved her from many blows, and his speed with a sword impressed her greatly. He was faster with sword than any she had ever seen, even Searon. Yet Searon didn't rely on speed but strength, and Andron lacked much of that strength.

Soon, they were overwhelmed by foes, and Erenuyh had to toss his bow back over his shoulder to bring forth a kheshlarn short sword. He fought valiantly next to Starlyn, and hope seemed in their favor for a moment.

Then the sound of howling wolves grew closer. Starlyn tried calling to them, but they would not listen to her pleas. Instead, she whistled out as loud as she was able, and the sound echoed through the valley of the west. Soon, a pack of eleven wolves was upon them and swiping at them along with the draeyks.

It wasn't the draeyks that proved the deadlier foe, but the wolves that were menacing. They were not normal wolves, but seemed tainted by the dark. Each had thick black fur and deep red eyes instead of yellow. Their fangs were twice the size of a standard wolf and seemed coated in green venom. Starlyn suffered many swipes of black claws as well as several bites. Her armor was thick and strong, but still some scratched flesh. The wounds burned beyond that of any other, almost feverish, and a cold sweat fell upon her forehead. It felt like fever, and it slowed her down, but she did not stop.

Next to her, Andron suffered many scrapes and cuts from both wolves and draeyk alike, but his pace didn't slow in the slightest. His eyes seemed haunted with pain, but through each breath he took he fought through it. He seemed intent on keeping Starlyn safe no matter what the peril. His sword moved swift and true, and as Starlyn saw a wolf leaping for her face it suddenly vanished as its head fell away from its body by the mark of a black blade. Andron stood with bloody face and heavy breaths, but he continued on.

Erenuyh fell and fought from the ground with three fingers from his left hand bitten clean off, and blood staining the once green grass below him. Starlyn pushed herself through the crowd to his aid and fought off the two foes that tried to overcome the kheshlar ranger. Andron was at her heel, knocking off any that wished to attack her from behind.

From the darkness, roars came instead of howls, and even the remaining six wolves seemed to cower at hearing such a noise. Andron looked afraid as he listened, but by the grin on Starlyn's face, hope restored his fear.

"Do not fear, Andron, for that is the sound of ally, not foe."

A new hope sprouted in the human warrior, and he fought with more intensity than he had before. It appeared they would not last long, and the hope might be in vain if it reached them too late. A wolf leaped at him, and he sliced a paw off, but the wolf leaped at him again with rage and bit off the tip of his right pinky. He howled in pain but stabbed the wolf at the neck, and it whimpered to retreat.

Starlyn turned her hammer around and used the spike instead to embed foe after foe of draeyks. Suddenly, all the attention of the dark force changed, and all leaped toward Starlyn, as if noticing that she was the leader of the company. Andron tried to fend them off but was quickly knocked to the ground with sword falling out of reach. Erenuyh as well had fallen, but neither the wolves nor draeyks paid him any heed. All set forth on Starlyn, and her defense was fading.

Andron crawled for his sword, but a stern foot pressed against his back kept him in place. He fought against it as well as he could, but his body was too weak. Erenuyh had been struck several times in the back and legs until he dared not try and get up. Both watched with despair as Starlyn's hammer was finally knocked from her hand.

The wolves and draeyks stopped for only a second to celebrate their victory in triumph. It proved an ill second for them because as they did so a shadow passed over Starlyn in a great leap followed by three more. Draeyks fell to the shadows in quick order, but the wolves fought on. The creature that kept Andron down ran forward and quickly met his doom in a scream. Andron was weary now, but he had strength enough to crawl the rest of the way and grasp his sword.

All around, it appeared wolves fought against a shadow with deep-yellow eyes and thick white claws. It was a masterful fight with strikes back and forth, but finally the wolves fell, and the shadows conquered all. One last shadow appeared that was taller than wide behind Starlyn as she picked up her hammer. She didn't seem to see it, and neither did the friendly shadows that came to her aid. Andron sprinted forth, and in the last moment before an axe could cleave her head from her shoulders his sword pieced the heart of a draeyk that screamed into the night louder than any other. Instead of having a complete black lizard appearance, there seemed to be orange spots under its jaw and all the way down its abdomen, as well as horns above its snout and below its jaw. Most likely, the captain of these evil creatures, and it seemed to hide in the shadows when battle seemed lost, to commit one more ill deed. Andron's blade left its chest, and the creature fell to the ground, unable to harm anyone anymore.

Starlyn's eyes grew wide, and she leaped forward to catch Andron's weary body that nearly fell to the ground. She held him up and carried him with arm under his shoulder to set him down at the top of the hill. Erenuyh moaned, and she hastily helped him over next to Andron. She was tired, but there was energy still left within her.

The shadows that came to her aid finally finished killing the remaining creatures. They seemed to nudge at bodies to ensure their demise before coming forth to Starlyn. Before her sat four black panthers that only now could they be seen through the darkness for what they were. She kissed her hand and pressed it to each of their noses, repeating, "Emknaht unildir."

Andron stumbled forth to stand behind Starlyn, and she turned to him with sorrow in her eyes. "You should rest, Andron."

"Yes I should, as should you. Yet I could not rest, not until I came to thank those who have come to save us."

He looked at the four panthers that stared at him with curiosity. Each yawned in turn and stretched out on the ground before purring. He took another step forward with hand held out.

"May I?"

Starlyn smiled. "Yes, you may."

He took another step forward and put his hand on the first panther's ear, scratching it slightly. The animal at first stared at him in wonder for many long seconds, before tilting its head to embrace the affection. It purred fondly. He petted each in turn and finally spoke.

"Thank you."

Each came to their feet and encircled him purring loudly and rubbing against him. He laughed and turned to Starlyn.

"Do we dare rest? Are there more out there?"

"We may rest for tonight, and tomorrow as well before we journey forth again. My friends here tell me there are no more for many leagues. Most of the path is clear to the cities unless something changes. Go, rest, I will find herbs to aid in healing. My friends here will stay with us through the night to watch while I find what we need to heal."

"Rest…good. I need a smoke."

Chapter Nineteen

The sun was setting beyond the western trees as they arrived at the tall gray stone gate of the first village. It appeared as if it was the only one to have such a gate, but it was to be expected since it was the closest one to the trees, and closest to possible attack. Nobody wandered outside except the two guards who held position as still as a statue. Both were clad in thick silver plate mail armor, square steel helms with wide visors for eyes, and an opening that traveled thinly down to the jaw so only an inch of the mouths could be seen.

"Halt, who comes to Erdunadir, and what is your business here?"

Searon faltered and looked at the wizard.

"We come from the far city of Guerettos near the sea of the north. We travel this way, as it is the swiftest way without boarding ship, and we are passing through to the city of Legain for urgent family business."

The two guards looked at each other for a moment before nodding. "Very well, you may pass through, but if you cause any mischief, your weapons will be forfeited."

Searon nodded and urged his horse forward through the now-open gate. He stopped short and turned to the guards. "My throat is quite parched after such a long journey; tell me, if you may, where is a good tavern to wet my throat?"

"The Dancing Donkey is a fine inn and pub three hundred paces in and on the east."

"Thank you kindly sir," Searon nodded and flipped a gold coin in the air that the guard caught and nodded.

Inside, the village was simple, and only a few traveled the streets. It was probably only those trying to make it back home for meals, or those who attempted to find pubs to eat and drink. The buildings were rustic stone of mostly gray and tan in various sizes throughout the streets. There were a lot of stands on the side of the streets, but not many were manned for selling goods and probably wouldn't be until the morning arrived. Searon did have to shake his head at a few merchants that tried to sell him weapons or jewelry. Black smoke seemed to appear from every chimney that was a home rather than business, although a lot of businesses were breathing smoke as well because of the owners that probably lived somewhere inside.

The night air grew cold around them, and Searon shivered slightly, hoping to find a warm tavern and inn soon. Now that they were so far south, the nights were brisk with chill indeed. After another few minutes of enjoying the homely scenery of the village; they arrived at a red sign with a white donkey standing on two legs and smoking a pipe. *The Dancing Donkey Inn & Pub*. Searon smiled and got off of Stripes, grabbing a small coin bag, to look inside. He petted his horse behind the ears before pushing the two wooden swinging doors in.

Inside of the pub was loud and obnoxious as men hollered about, clapping their hands and stomping their feet to the beat of music. The floors were dark stained wood with only scarce stains from beer and ale, showing that it was well maintained. Nearly a dozen serving maids wearing red cloth dresses with white lace and lining patrolled the areas to bring new drinks and clean messes. Every now and then, one would jump after passing by a table of men due to a hard-pinched bottom. Some of them would glare back, but most continued on to their jobs.

There was a large stage in the back where on the side of it was a band of four playing upbeat music. They had a fiddle, flute, saxophone, and clarinet. Each played in perfect harmony with each other, making such a song that made you want to tap your foot. On the center stage were two women scarcely clothed dancing exotically to the music. The brunette was wearing blue silk, and the blonde was wearing red. Everybody cheered for them while others made ill-mannered comments about what women that fine could do besides dance.

A serving maid approached him and bowed slightly. "Welcome to the Dancing Donkey, would you care for an ale, or a bed?"

She spoke loudly because of the constant cheering and music, yet she was still barely heard, and Searon stepped up closer to her. Her hair was auburn, and freckles stained her face with small lips and creased jaw. She wore a white baggy hat that complimented her dress's white lining.

"Yes. Actually, I have another with me; we have traveled far and have two horses outside. We would like a stable for them and a room to stay in tonight. But before we head to our room, we would like a table and whiskey."

She smiled. "I will take care of that for you."

Searon stepped outside, and she followed, still eyeing him and smiling. A blush appeared on her face as she saw him look back at her. He only scratched his head and felt at his beard that was well overgrown and now had begun to cover his cheeks and neck some with an incredible itch.

She grabbed both reins and headed down an ally south of the pub. Searon nodded approvingly before stepping back inside with Karceoles trailing him. He walked to a table in the back corner where he sat down to watch the dancers. The tables surrounding them were empty or with only a few that did not outwardly yell or dance too much. Some far ahead were up and dancing, circling with each other arm in arm as they hollered.

"You sure know how to pick the tavern," Karceoles smiled.

"It is a bit ill mannered, I'll admit."

"Ill mannered? This place is marvelous. Those are two fine women, and can't you just see the way they are eyeing me?"

Searon rolled his eyes and leaned back stretching. He grabbed his pipe from his sash and began puffing on it slowly after Karceoles lit it for him. His foot began to tap to the music quietly though, and he smiled. The music was good.

After scarcely ten more minutes of dancing, the music faded to a slower tune. The two dancers stopped to rest before walking to the tables to talk to the patrons, in effort to ensure a nice tip. The maid with auburn hair and loose hat approached the table and smiled.

"You said you two would like a room?"

"Two rooms, make them adjoining if you wish, yet I do not wish to sleep too close to this man, to ensure my good looks and charm don't dwindle," Karceoles said.

She smiled and bowed as Searon dropped his head back to roll his eyes again.

"You may stay in rooms sixteen and seventeen. What shall I get you two to drink?"

"Whiskey…a tall whiskey and some food, if there is any left," Searon said.

She smiled and left the two to talk, yet talk they did not. Searon instead closed his eyes and leaned his head back. He was weary from the journey, but he wasn't ready to sleep yet, not until whiskey could settle in his stomach. It was only a few minutes when a plate of steaming pork and potatoes reached him with his whiskey.

"Thank you so much."

"If there is anything else you need…"

"I won't hesitate to ask," he smiled.

With that, she winked at him and was off again to greet guests.

"Did you see that maid wink at me?" Karceoles asked.

"Old fool, she was winking at me, not you."

"Whatever you wish to believe in to boost your confidence."

Searon laughed and ate every bite on his plate. It was hard to manage because of his scarce meals in the past weeks, but he accomplished it. His stomach began to growl at him in anger with how full it was, but he smiled and smoked his pipe to ease digestion. The soothing music was helping as well, and after a few more minutes he began drinking.

The music was still light when the two dancers walked up to their table. Both smiled and looked from Searon to Karceoles.

"You two seem like you have seen a long journey," the brunette said.

"Yes, we have. Too long," Searon smiled.

"It is but fate that we traveled so long and far to stumble into this place. Both of you are so skilled with graceful dance, and beautiful faces, that it puts our minds at ease after such long traveling. We may now rest easy this night knowing that we sleep in an inn where there are kheshlars or angels, for surely you must be one of the two because your beauty and grace surpasses all," Karceoles said.

Searon turned to glare hard at the wizard, but he seemed not to notice as his attention was turned toward the dancers with a courteous smile. There seemed to be an aura of charm about the wizard, and he seemed to glow. His face was stern and his smile genuine, but no wrinkles stained his face as Searon had thought did on the road. It was a clean face, still without beard or mustache, and it seemed to be mature, as if he knew more about the world than anyone.

"You are too kind," the blonde said, curtseying at her knees. "What is your name?"

"I am Karceoles, and what are such fine women as you two called?"

"I am Berethana, and this is Annettera. We are both pleased to meet you," the blonde said.

"My name is Searon," he said, but neither seemed to notice him in the slightest.

Both were blushing as they looked at Karceoles with large smiles on their faces. Searon shook his head and took another long drink of his whiskey.

"Perhaps we'll see each other again," Annettera said shyly.

"I count on it."

The two women giggled and walked off, with glances over their shoulders at him, and holding hands to whisper in each other's ear.

"That's it, I'm ready for bed," croaked Searon as he finished his whiskey.

"So soon? I believe Berethana and Annettera are going to sing next."

"I'll pass this time, be sure to tell me how they do, as I'm sure you will anyway."

With that, Searon rose from his seat and stumbled past the bar to the stairs on the south side of the tavern. He held the rail carefully as he made his way up, and he walked down the hall, searching for his room with heavy eyes. Finally, when he found room sixteen he opened it up and crashed headfirst on the bed without bothering to remove his chain mail.

Chapter Twenty

Starlyn awoke in the morning to smoke coming from Andron's pipe. She yawned and noticed the sun not yet rising to the east. Andron kept the bandage made from Starlyn's torn cotton shirt secured on his pinky. She had brought the clothing to change into while in towns and cities so she wouldn't have to always wear armor. It seemed that fancy had gone and passed after the attack the night before. Andron seemed to barely notice his half-bitten off pinky as he smoked his pipe. Though Starlyn assumed the pipe weed took some of the edge off.

The four panthers were gone to hide during the day, and she got up to sit next to Andron. They were between two small hills at the bottom, so rest would come easy leaning back against the slope. He smiled at her as she sat down, and she returned the smile. Erenuyh was still asleep with a fever that was beginning to break. He clutched at his left hand with his right, feeling his index finger and thumb, which were the only two fingers left on his left hand. Starlyn had wrapped the hand tightly to prevent any more blood loss, but she knew that the kheshlar would not be comforted without his fingers. She also knew that despite how weak the fever and loss of blood made him, he was a kheshlar, and would not let any weakness show.

She was uneasy about being in the open without the cover of trees. All kheshlars stayed in cities in the forest and seldom traveled outside of the wilderness. Yet among her race she was considered the most adventurous. She never imagined herself to one day journey so far but since her sister has been gone many things had happened. Andron seemed to be studying her, and she turned to him with suspicion in her eyes. He wasn't like most men, or at least men of the kheshlars, that stared at her body with eyes barely straying from her bosom. Andron seemed captivated by that as well, but he was inspecting her entire body from head to toe as if trying to study her as a person. When she thought about it, she realized he always seemed to do it when looking at her.

She pulled her hammer from her belt and studied it carefully, grazing her hands across the handle up to the golden steel neck to the large face. The face of the hammer was as large as her palm and deadly to the strike. It had been her weapon for many years and was dear to her. The handle was long and crafted of beautiful oak with carved designs. At the neck, it transformed from a large hammer to a sharp thick spike a long span with a sharp point. She sighed heavily and turned back to Andron to see him still staring at her.

"Must you always stare?"

"I'm sorry…I don't think I can help it sometimes."

He turned away shyly and began to play with the rocks by his feet.

"What is it about me that intrigues you?"

She wasn't accustomed to someone so content to study her. Most of the time in the kheshlarn capital of Sudegam, the male kheshlars studied her, but their eyes didn't stray too far away from her bosom. This human in front of her, while his eyes did stray there from time to time, were content with studying her movements, face, hair, and anything else about her. She never felt she had much to offer besides a pleasant body for male kheshlars to look at. After all, her body was a bit more complementary in areas than most of the female kheshlars. Still, most of them found her as flawed, with too high of an ambition for adventure, or too high of a temper. Also, her mind wandered too much about other parts of the land that didn't concern the kheshlars.

"Everything really. The kheshlars are so mysterious to me. Your beauty, I've never seen anything like it. Most humans' beauty is like a flawed gem, where so much is so beautiful, but there are a few imperfections that make them who they are. Yet with you, you are a perfect gem, flawless in every way."

Starlyn blushed and turned her head away. She had never heard such words from anyone. "I have many flaws."

"Not that I can tell."

She smiled. "If you have any questions, ask."

"Is the armor you wear custom made for you?"

She wasn't wearing her helmet, so her beautiful blonde hair was exposed but tied behind her back, with the exception of a few long strands that fell forward onto her bosom. Above electric silvery eyes on her forehead was a gold circlet that hung low in the middle, falling down toward the center of her thin eyebrows. Her upper body was covered in midnight-blue-silver chain mail with gold lining. Plates of gold covered her upper and lower arms over the chain mail but left her hands bare. Her shoulders had thin gold pads atop them outlined in blue steel. Two beige plates covered her bosom with swirls of gold on each to hide what the nearly see-through chain mail would not. Her chain mail below the plates extended outward nearly a span with cleavage. Two small thin plates covered the sides of her stomach appeared as if two mouths were to eat her exposed bellybutton through the see-through chain mail. Her belt was in a tilted v shape where her hammer was clasped securely. Past her waist, she wore a brown metal skirt clad with blue and gold armor draped down in patterns that enabled her to move freely. Only part of her thighs were visible before her blue and gold steel boots began at the knee.

"Yes, each kheshlar must go to a blacksmith to be fitted. This chain mail would be loose on any other kheshlar who may try it. We choose our own colors and style that we wish. It is something we do on our hundredth name day."

"What about your weapon? Your hammer, did you get that from the blacksmith as well?"

"No…this was made by my sister," she felt at the thick gold hued steel. "It is enchanted, though I'm not sure how. She gave it to me before she fell to the shadow. I keep it with me as a memory of her. A memory of how she once was."

"Are we to continue traveling at night, or shall we head out now?"

"Let's get a few hours of traveling before midday since we are now behind. It is only a few more days to the villages of the north, and a day beyond that to your village, if Karceoles wasn't mistaken."

She nudged Erenuyh, who awoke with a start before slowly getting to his feet. He looked at the two of them and sighed, still weakened by his fever, before securing a few things into his pack.

* * *

The next few days, they pushed themselves harder since they were getting close. They knew they could take rest in the human villages once they reached them, and so they took little rest during the day. According to Andron's memory, they would have to pass through only three villages before coming to Guerettos at the edge of the sea. It was a bay that the village rested on, with more villages nearby. Larger cities headed northwest along the bay until reaching the ocean.

When nightfall approached on the eleventh day, all three were growing weary from traveling and decided to take a short break before continuing. The hills were a day gone, and they were to travel on flat terrain for the remainder of their trip. For some unknown reason, the flat ground seemed to take more energy from them than the hilly slopes they had come from. Andron supposed it was because without any changes the mind became drowsy faster. He led the group now, for his knowledge of the area was beyond Starlyn's, as she only knew which direction to travel, and he knew the land.

The sunset to the west was beautiful to say the least with pink and purple hues glowing across the horizon. Andron stared at it for a long moment as he smoked his pipe next to Starlyn. Erenuyh sat a few paces away, lost in his own thought. The ranger didn't seem to socialize and appeared as an outsider. Andron had tried to start a conversation with him several times, but each time the responses were but one word, and so he eventually gave up.

"How is your hand?" he asked, trying to spark a conversation with the ranger once more.

"Fine."

"Does it still hurt?"

"Yes."

"Mine does as well. I'm beginning to grow accustomed to being without my pinky."

Erenuyh sat silent, staring at the sunset without as much as a glance toward Andron.

"Can you still use your bow well?"

"Yes."

The Crimson Claymore

Andron sighed and began puffing at his pipe once more. The night was silent besides the few chirpings of crickets and hoots of owls. When the stars came out, he noticed Starlyn immediately staring upon them. She truly loved the stars, and he could tell when each night she spent most of her free time gazing upon them.

"I suppose we'd better get—"

Andron closed his mouth and listened with his ears. There was a sound like cracking fingers from the darkness. It didn't come from either Starlyn or Erenuyh. He stood and fingered his sword, grasping the hilt and looking around.

"What is it?" Starlyn asked.

"I don't know, but I heard something."

Erenuyh stood to look about and grabbed his bow with his two fingers of his left hand. His eyes snapped from one patch of darkness to another as if hearing something. Andron knew his hearing wasn't as toned as a kheshlar, but he could hear something out there.

Suddenly, he was tackled and fell to the ground, rolling several feet. He kicked at whatever it was, seeming to knock it off. Getting to his feet, he looked around but saw nothing. Unsheathing his sword, he ran back to where Starlyn and Erenuyh were fighting unseen foes. Andron blinked in surprise and tried to focus hard, but he still could see nothing. Suddenly, a warp in the air came toward him that appeared as if he was looking through bent glass or crystal. He shoved his sword upward and felt a force slash against it. His eyes widened with horror as he could hear the foe but could not see it.

No matter how hard he tried to study the warped crystal shape, he could still barely see it. He flinched with every blow that came upon him. There were only a few strikes that he was able to land true. Erenuyh dove backward and glanced at Andron, firing three quick arrows his way. Each arrow embedded into an invisible foe: one at a span from the ground, another midway, and the last a span higher than Andron's head. The creature appeared tall, and besides the warped darkness that could not be seen of its body, Andron now had three markers that moved with each strike it made. He was able to defend himself with better effort, though the creature still landed several attacks upon Andron's chest and stomach.

As Andron fought, he noticed there were only two of the creatures. There was one attacking Starlyn and the other in front of him. Erenuyh shot arrows at the two, making the two targets easier to spot, but still no complete shape was distinguished. Starlyn was fending hers off well with her large blunt hammer causing good damage, making the creature fall pack several paces with each true aim. Andron's sword didn't have the same power as a blunt weapon, and without knowing where fatal spots were to slash he was fighting blind.

An arrow pierced the front of the creature before Andron, and it shrieked out in pain. A loud humming growl came from in front of him, and Andron found himself flung back a dozen paces with what felt like a steel bar against his face. Blood trickled from his mouth as he crawled back toward Starlyn and Erenuyh without his weapon. He had no idea where his sword flew off to, but he couldn't leave the two of them there without his help.

When he finally got to his feet, he saw Erenuyh without bow in his hands, and instead his long dagger defending as many strikes as he could. Andron fished for his throwing knives in his sash, but was too late as he saw Erenuyh's head ripped from his neck and thrown into the darkness. The creature went for Starlyn next as he found his pack of throwing knives. He threw one after another with only two striking the creature. The strikes were true wherever they hit because the crystal creature came to a stop only a span from Starlyn and tumbled to the ground at her feet. She gasped as she saw it and leaped back as she delivered another strong slam to the invisible foe in front of her.

Andron ran to the invisible body and studied it careful to see where his knives hit. Even as it was still without movement it was as clear as crystal, but defined traits could now be seen. It was a large creature but humanoid in appearance except three times the size. The head was enormous with large clear eyes shaped like horizontal diamonds that didn't blink. One was pierced with an arrow that Andron assumed was what made the creature angry with Erenuyh. It seemed to have a large pointed beard that was a slightly darker crystal than the rest, but besides that it was still mostly unseen. One of the throwing knives appeared to be in the arm of the creature as far as he could tell, but the other was below the beard in what he assumed was the neck.

He pulled one of the knives from the creature and spun to watch as Starlyn backed up in defense. Her hammer was large enough to protect her from most attacks, but the creature still seemed to be overwhelming her.

"Starlyn, duck!" Andron cried.

She didn't question him but listened right away. He studied the pattern of the arrows on the invisible foe and with all his might he threw the knife. It hit true, and the creature shrieked one last breath before tumbling to the ground in a thud. Starlyn gasped and rolled backward before coming to her feet and looking at Andron.

He noticed that her left arm hung limp, and she clutched at it with her right hand. Her hammer was secure back in her belt, but she seemed hurt with gritted teeth as she came toward him. He reached out to her, and she whimpered slightly when he touched her arm.

"Are you all right?"

"I think it's dislocated."

"I can help it, if you trust me."

"I do."

"This might hurt."

She clenched her jaw. "Go for it."

He grabbed her arm and snapped it back into socket with a loud pop. She screamed out in pain, and tears came to her eyes. He removed the plate armor at her shoulder and began to massage it gently. She wiped tears from her face with her right hand.

"Thank you."

"What were those?" Andron asked.

"There is a legend in the kheshlarn records. I think they're called Caestlycs."

"Caestlycs?"

"Yes, it means the unseen."

"Poor Erenuyh…he saved our life with those arrows. Without them, we wouldn't have seen them well enough to kill."

"Yes…I am saddened that we didn't get a chance to get to know him more."

"He wouldn't let us."

"I think he may have foreseen his doom when he came with us," Starlyn said.

"Perhaps so; I fear that whatever is happening goes deeper than Searon knows. If there are wolves joining with draeyks, as well as these Caestlycs."

"Yes…I believe the wizard more and more now. Something is going on, and unless we unite the nations of human, and the kheshlars alike…it may be the end of us all."

"What are we still doing here then? Let's be off," Andron said.

"First, let's give proper respect to Erenuyh."

Andron nodded, and the two of them gently set Erenuyh's body and head to lay in peace with bow in hand. Starlyn then fished through her sash and pulled out a few seeds, which she planted in the ground next to his body.

"Let new life come from this saddening death," she said.

Starlyn and Andron sat for a long moment in silence. After a few minutes, Andron pulled his pipe and filled it full of pipe weed. With a few puffs, he noticed Starlyn reaching her hand out.

"Would you like some? It may help with the pain."

"I do not have any herbs to heal my cuts and scrapes, so if this helps, yes I will have a little."

Andron passed the pipe over and watched her with amusement as she coughed from the smoke. It was likely that she had never even smoked pipe tobacco. He chuckled lightly and began walking.

"Hold onto that, Starlyn, and follow me. Let's make haste to the villages."

Chapter Twenty-one

Aloud crash in the middle of the night woke Searon, whose eyes jolted open. He moved his head on the pillow and shrank it back when his face sank into a large puddle of drool. Licking his lips, he sat up on his bed and heard another crash followed by a scream. His eyes grew wider, and he yawned loudly before getting to his feet. He looked around for his claymore before discovering that it was still attached at his side. His head shook tiredly, and he banged on the door in his room that connected to room seventeen.

When there was no response, he opened it to see Karceoles stumbling to get his brown robe back on. He seemed to struggle, but he didn't look like he had been asleep yet.

"Did you hear that, Karceoles?"

"Yes, yes. I will meet you outside, and we'll investigate."

Searon nodded and was about to turn back in his room when he noticed the bed to his left with two women hiding under a white sheet. One was blonde and the other brunette, and both looked scared as they looked around each time a loud noise came from downstairs. He blinked his eyes a few times as he looked at them until he finally recognized the two. They were the dancers, Berethana and Annettera, naked under near-see-through white cotton sheets, cuddled together. Searon shook his head and slammed the door behind him.

Searon waited in the hall for a few minutes before Karceoles appeared with staff in hand and a grim look on his face as another crash of metal was heard. Searon sprinted toward the stairs, holding his head intact from the throbbing of drinking.

At the bottom of the stairs toward the exit of the pub there were three warriors behind an overturned table, looking outside. All had swords drawn and fear on their shaking faces. Searon and Karceoles ran up next to them, and they nearly jumped from their socks.

"What seems to be the problem?" Searon asked.

"Another raid!"

Searon sighed, "Conflict between the villages."

"No…there hasn't been any of that in years, not since the creatures came. It is they who raid our villages now."

"Draeyks," Karceoles spat.

"I've never heard of those, no, these are called daerions, and they are evil and strong. Too strong."

"Daerions?" Karceoles gasped. He stood and looked to Searon. "Come, we must stop them, but be cautious, these aren't mere draeyks you fight anymore."

Searon's eyebrows rose as he followed, but first he called back, "Do not cower in fear, help us, and fight!"

Searon stepped outside and unsheathed his crimson-glowing claymore. In the streets, half the warriors ran in fear as the others fought on. Most that fought fell down either injured or dead from such a formidable foe. Searon caught a glimpse of them in the faint starlight. The creatures were shorter than the draeyks, at only five feet, but were much broader and muscular. Their skin was rough, leathery, and dark blue in color. Each held a short sword or mace and slashed at anything that came close to them with more weaponry skill than any of the draeyks. They wore tight, ripped black breeches but no shirts or shoes. Their feet had four toes with long midnight-blue claws.

Rushing forward, Searon slashed his claymore forward to be blocked by a short sword. He looked into the large cold, unblinking oval eyes of the creature in front of him. They were pitch black in color and stared back at him in wonder. Its face was hard and cruel with two large horns extruding from the top of its head down to its jaw. They were black in color and similar to those of a ram except harder and thinner. It had a pointed jaw and large snarling black teeth at least two centimeters in length.

The Crimson Claymore

He fought the creature fiercely but barely gained any ground as each swift strike he tried was easily blocked by the quickness of the beast. Changing his fighting style didn't seem to help much as the creature was well skilled in each form. Instead of attacking with strength, he decided to take a step back and move into a defensive position. The creature seemed to snarl, showing a tall mouth of sharp teeth before it leaped toward him.

Searon nearly fell back as the creature hacked at him from the left to right with a mix of overhead slashes and uppercuts of its short sword. He felt like the creature was trained by him with its skill. It was unsettling to say the least. As he backed up, he tripped over a dead warrior's body and fell to the ground. The creature leaped at the chance and began furiously slashing down at him with attacks he was barely able to defend against. Many scrapes and bruises began forming on his arms through his chain mail when he wasn't quick enough to bring his long claymore to defend against a swift short sword.

When it seemed all hope was lost, a warrior leaped toward the daerion, seemingly from nowhere. The warrior was clad in purple glinting scale mail and twice as wide as Searon. He fought the creature back with powerful blows that seemed to flash with each strike of his mace. Searon slowly got to his feet and went to meet the new warrior. He wore no helm but had a great big, bushy black beard upon his ebony face. His attacks were quick and reckless, which was surprising for such a large man. Searon was surprised to see the creature holding a strong defense against the power of the mace with only a short sword.

Searon ran to his side, and the two of them fought side by side against the creature that seemed to be cowering away. Their weapons flashed in the torchlight in a brilliant array of twists and turns. After only a few more strikes each, the warrior next to him bashed the creature's hand, nearly tearing it from its limb. A sudden horror crept upon the creature's face as Searon stepped up to slice its head from its shoulders. He watched as it bounced harmlessly down the street, before turning to the man next to him.

"Hallo there! Glad to accept your assistance, outsider, yet you may need more training with weapon before fighting these formidable foes. Do be careful." He stopped and took a harder look at Searon.

"Searon?"

Searon's eyes lit up. "Yes…"

He took a step closer to inspect the younger man that seemed to be only a few years short of himself. His hair was thick but short and deep black in color; he had gray eyes, a rounded nose, and wide jaw. He was much larger than Searon with a rounded belly, though he didn't seem overweight but big boned and obviously strong. A faint scar traveled from his left eye to his jaw a medium-brown color on his ebony face. There weren't many ebony-skinned people in the smaller villages, though Searon's old hometown of Legain had a well segregated mix.

"Xython?" Searon gasped.

"Aye," he nodded and smiled, showing his profoundly white teeth. "When you left me, you were the master and I the trainer. It seems these days your teaching has granted me more skill than you!"

"Don't count on it! I am weary as I have traveled hundreds of leagues the past week and drank too much last night."

"Ah, Searon, always excuses! It was the same when you led us to victory against the cities. Every excuse as to why we didn't ride to victory with one less death on our side. It's good to see you again!"

"Yes, yes, it is. We shall catch up later, but for now, let's help the poor citizens of this village."

"Aye, but do not fall to the ground this time, my friend. Attack them swift but unexpected. They know all the moves, so you have to change the order of natural attack."

Searon nodded, and the two of them dashed farther into the village. In the midst of battle, Searon noticed there were fewer than a dozen daerions, but their power was overwhelming most of the village guard. Karceoles stood ahead twirling his zylek to strike from one creature to the next. He would back away every now and then to shoot orange glows of light from his zylek that tossed the creatures backward. His blasts of energy and fire killed at least five of them before all of them turned focus to him.

Searon dashed up and fought alongside the wizard, paying heed to his old friend's advice. He was much more effective with surprising blows of intermixed fighting styles. Sometimes, he would knock them back with the hilt of his claymore instead of a deathblow because it was easier to surprise them with. One daerion stood behind the rest with a crossbow and began firing arrows. A few men around him fell from the bolts, and he fought harder to try and reach the creature.

The creature noticed him and shot two bolts that hit his breastplate and bounced away. One of the arrows slipped down, and the backside slid up and smacked Searon in the jaw, so he nearly tasted the feathers attached to it. His teeth gritted, and he growled, growing angry before striking down another in front of him. He leaped to the daerion with the crossbow, but the creature tossed it to the ground and withdrew two long daggers. Searon slashed his claymore from the side, but it was blocked by both the daggers. The creature leaped forward and stabbed one of the curved daggers into Searon's stomach, breaking several links of chain mail. Searon gasped and stumbled backward in pain.

Searon fell to his knees, coughing, but he kept a hard grip on his claymore still. The daerion in front of him croaked a snarling laugh and leaped forward in an attempt to kill him. He rolled to the side and swung his claymore along the ground to an uppercut that split the creature's jaw in two. Thick blue goo dripped from the creature as it hit the ground with horns separated by split face. Xython was at his side in moments, defending him against any other creatures that came. Karceoles shot several balls of fire at the remaining three creatures before they fled from the village.

Searon stood there for a long moment before turning around to look at Xython and Karceoles. "Why does this not surprise me?"

"What's that?" Xython asked.

"That we finally get to a village after traveling for so long, and the wizard has all the fun while I get stabbed in the stomach. It doesn't surprise me one bit."

Karceoles cackled as he walked up. "Come, my friend, if the daerions are truly back, then there is much to discuss. I fear these raids on the north and south from two separate creatures are more than mere coincidence. I fear war is coming."

"You call yourself Karceoles the Wise, and yet I have assumed as much before this. When do I get to see this wisdom you so speak of?"

"Watch that mouth, boy."

Searon smiled. "Karceoles, this is Xython, an old friend from my battle days."

"The pleasure is mine," Karceoles said, shaking his hand. He turned back to Searon. "Is he to join us?"

"That depends," Searon said and turned to Xython. "Would you like to help us unite an army to rid the land of these daerions of the south and the draeyks of the north? It may turn into a full-scale war, but if these creatures are no more, there can finally be peace in the cities."

Xython thought for a long moment before nodding his head. "Yes, if you seek to destroy these creatures, then I think I ought to at least hear you out."

"Come then," Karceoles said. "The three of us have much to discuss."

He turned and walked back through the city toward the Dancing Donkey. People scattered through the village, disposing of the bodies of both men and creatures alike. Many of the guards that were helping in battle were heading for treatment of their wounds. The silence that had once filled the city was no more, and through the rest of the night murmurs could be heard from every corner.

Chapter Twenty-two

The next two days of travel toward the villages went by swiftly and quietly. Both Starlyn and Andron were silent during their journey as they reminisced about and mourned Erenuyh. The long plains they traveled across were dull and weary without so much as a wanderer to come by. Birds were scarce through the tall tan hay and grass. There weren't many goats or sheep throughout the terrain, and Andron found that odd. Usually, the last few stretches before the villages was covered in sheep, goats, donkey, and several more animals. He hoped the draeyk attacks hadn't scared them off, or that all weren't claimed as food by the creatures.

As they neared the first village from the field, Andron's anticipation grew with excitement at first. He was excited to see the few friends he had in the village, and for a fresh pint of ale. It'd been many long months since he'd set foot in home, and restlessness overcame him. The excitement didn't last long for as they neared closer to the village by a few hundred paces, he noticed all was silent. It was midday as they neared, and the village should have been humming with life. Yet an uneasy dread seemed to douse the village in gloom, as if the entire place was cast in shadow. He began to feel uneasy and slowed down, feeling at the hilt of his sword as they neared.

Starlyn noticed his uneasiness and touched the shaft of her hammer. "Something is wrong."

"Yes, very wrong. This is too quiet."

"These past few days have been too quiet."

The wooden gate was made of tall thin trees held together with metal plate at the top, middle, and bottom. It wasn't closed but pushed a quarter open without any guard to stand before it. A lone sign hung by the opening of carved wood in black letters that read, *Gythero*. Andron walked up quietly and unsheathed his sword before he entered. The sound of crows was distant but still disturbing. Starlyn trailed him closely and held her hammer in her right hand.

Inside, the streets were bare, without destruction, and without man. The silence was beyond eerie, and it unsettled Andron. He shivered as he inspected each street, yet nothing moved. There was no pattern to the buildings in the village, and most were made of wood with only a few stone. The ones made of stone were the large white-and-black octagon barracks and the rectangular city hall of red and black. Everything else was made from thin trees pressed tightly together in the same fashion as the gate. Some of the doors were open, but nobody was inside.

"No bodies; it seems they fled," Starlyn whispered.

"I hope with whatever came that they made it in time. There is no time to waste; let's leave this place and check on my village."

Dread filled Andron's mind as he lead the way northwest through the next village of Nygenquy. It was a close neighboring village—only a league's march—but they found it quick. Andron was no longer walking since he saw the first village. He nearly tripped over himself as he kept to a full sprint. With each new bit of scenery, he observed his pace only quickened. Nygenquy was as abandoned as Gythero with gate pushed open as well. Still, to his relief, there were no bodies to count along the streets or inside any homes as he could find. There was a defensive plan for the villages in case of great need to hasten to the great city of Wesiet north of his village of Guerettos. He hoped with all this might that his family had made it if there without peril.

The third village of Igurilena was empty of person and animal. It should have brought comfort to him that the three villages before his own were abandoned in the same fashion. However, Andron felt no comfort as he traveled warily. He wanted to travel throughout the night to reach his village, but Starlyn stopped him. She was still hurt and needed rest before going on. It was well past midnight as they camped in Igurilena. He found a familiar pub that he used to come to when he visited, and found it empty of patrons but not ale. Pouring himself a large mug, he made a fire on the outskirts where he and Starlyn rested. He lit his pipe and sat smoking it for a half an hour before he was able to find rest.

* * *

When the dawn rose on the fourteenth day, Andron was already up and packed. He was ready to set out and already had the fire out with the extra wood already cleaned up. Starlyn arose a half an hour after dawn and saw Andron ready and staring toward the north. She quickly packed her provisions and clasped her hand on his shoulder.

"Are you all right?" she asked.

"I just hope *they're* all right."

"I know."

"Part of me wishes to see them there, yet the other part hopes they're safe in Wesiet. It is still a day's march past Guerettos. I still dread showing up to our home. What will I find?"

"Then let's head forth and find out, shall we?" She smiled.

He nodded but didn't turn back to her. With a long, deep breath, he finally began walking at a swift pace north. She trailed next to him and appeared to have a struggle keeping up with him, when only days before it was he that had grown weary while she seemed fresh.

The day was the hottest day they had come across during the whole journey in the dead middle of summer with the longest day of the year. There was still little to no life in the fields, but the grass grew greener the closer they came to the sea. After a few hours of , the sea could finally be seen in the distance. The crisp water made both of them thirsty, and yet both had already finished three-quarters of their water skins from the hot day.

Even through the hotness of the day Andron did not stop but continued on. His mind was clearer than ever, and his ambition was unstoppable. Vultures cried out in the skies above as they circled them, but he wasn't going to let the heat or the birds get to him. He had a mission, and he would see it done no matter what.

It wasn't until dusk that they finally reached the stone gate of Guerettos. Unlike the rest, it was not pushed open but held solid. Yet there were no guards in front or behind as far as Andron could tell because his yells went unheard.

"The gate cannot be opened from the outside," he whispered.

"Lace your hands tight, and hold them out."

"Starlyn…I can't boost you that high."

"Just do it."

He reluctantly agreed but instead of coming toward him to step on his hands, she began walking backward. She didn't stop until she was at least twenty paces from him. Her lips moved as if counting to herself when she stopped, and then she began running. Andron almost flinched but kept his hands held steady. He could barely feel as her feet touched his hands and she leaped into the air.

She leaped high in the air and grasped at the seams of the stones in the wall and climbed with incredible speed. With a few swift reaches, she was up and over the stone. Andron stared at the sky where she had been in amazement. It wasn't but a few more minutes when the stone gate finally opened.

Starlyn stood blocking the entrance with a solemn expression. "Andron…I'm sorry."

"What for?" he asked but fell silent as he walked inside.

The village was of unorganized stone buildings sorted with no order throughout curvy rows of dirt paths. There were no buildings or homes of wood, yet if there had been they probably would have been burned to a crisp. It seemed each building had been of a white hue, but each was stained black from where they'd burned. Not one building had been left unscathed. Andron's eyes lit up in horror.

He couldn't feel his legs, his chest, or his head. Everything was lost, even thought, as he stared at his village in disbelief. His right hand twitched, and for the first time he thought he could almost feel his pinky once again. When he looked down at it, all that he saw was a stub. It was a scarred piece of flesh that had once been whole, much like the village that stood before him.

Skeletons with burned clothing were scattered all about the ground. None were piled, but all seemed to have died where they now lay. The bodies were less than a hundred and mixed with skeletons of draeyks as well. It wasn't the entire village, but it was a great number of them. Each body held a weapon as if in defense before their ultimate demise. All of them seemed dressed for battle like they knew it was coming.

Fear shook him, and his sword left his scabbard and held tight in his hands as he ran through the town. He didn't use caution as he ran and stepped upon many skeletons, hearing them crunch under his steel boots. His body trembled as he ran, but he did not stop. Starlyn followed close behind, but she was cautious to avoid any bodies as she sprinted.

He finally stopped before a charred gray wood door and knelt to his knees under the three stone steps. Tears clouded his eyes, and he began to weep openly. His home was destroyed. Everything that he knew and loved was gone.

"I'm sorry, Andron."

"Everything I know," he whimpered.

Starlyn's hand rested on his shoulder, and he clasped it in his. He wept openly for many minutes before rising to his feet and walking up the three steps. His hand paused on the doorknob for a long while before he finally turned it.

Inside, nearly everything was burned to a crisp. A large and wild fire had been set from within and destroyed all the furniture and everything else in its path. There was no light inside the home, only blackness. He walked a few steps and paused, looking at an overturned frame below a half-burned black-and-gray rug. Slowly, he walked toward it and picked it up.

It was a faded painting of a happy man with long black hair holding a woman with a fiery red mane. Next to the two of them were two young girls and a baby boy. A smile came across his face as he stared at it for a long moment. He tore the frame apart and held the thin paper painting in front of him to treasure.

Starlyn watched him from a distance as she inspected the carnage within. She didn't move or attempt to go to him. "I don't see any bodies."

Andron awoke from his trance and rolled up the painting. He glanced around before stuffing it in his armor. The place was completely destroyed, but it was true that there were no bodies anywhere, not even draeyks. He searched the home in each room and upstairs but still found nothing but charred walls and burned furniture.

"Perhaps there is still hope," he whispered.

He stepped outside and looked toward the sea, with Starlyn following him. She gaped as she looked at the vast body of water. A single dock stretched out into the water, and Andron went to it. It was still solid, and he walked out to its edge before sitting down.

The sun was setting across the western horizon, and its red rays glistened across the sea. Andron smiled as he watched the sun set. A mild sea breeze tickled his face. Starlyn stood behind him with her left arm wrapped around a tall wooden pole that stuck out from the side of the dock. Her eyes were transfixed on the sea as wide as they could be. Dolphins and small fish jumped from the water, making large splashes. Some of the dolphins began making hoarse, scratchy calls to one another as they jumped and played. Eagles soared through the skies and dodged the hundreds of seagulls that fluttered about.

"It is beautiful," Starlyn gasped.

"Yes it is," Andron whispered.

"There's something in the water!"

Andron looked carefully, seeing only a darkened shape in the far distance. He let his eyes focus on it for a few minutes before he could distinguish sails above a large ship. It was so far toward the north that he could barely make it out.

"A ship heading for Wesiet," Andron exclaimed.

"There is yet hope," Starlyn encouraged.

Andron stood up abruptly and swept past Starlyn back toward the village. She stayed for a few more moments to stare at the sea before she followed behind. He stalked toward the center of the village, unsure what he was looking for. They would have to camp there that night, yet his adrenaline was pumping so hard, he wasn't sure if he would be able to. In one more day, they would reach Wesiet and find out what was going on. The excitement and dread was nearly unbearable.

Chills ran down his arms, and he clutched at his hilt back in its scabbard. He turned east and saw nothing down the curved road. The chills seemed to come even sharper, and he abruptly turned to the west where the sunset was still blinding. He saw the shadow of a man in cloak and hood in the distance.

Unsheathing his sword, he sprinted toward the unseen foe and began running faster once he saw that whoever he was didn't look human. He had human traits in appearance with rounded ears, long straight blond hair with a deeper-yellow hue blond than Starlyn's, thick bushy eyebrows, and square jaw. Yet he also seemed inhuman with blazing green eyes to match his robe and cloak of deep green. He seemed to stare past Andron at something unseen. Andron didn't hesitate but continued running forward, preparing to fight and ask questions later.

As he neared within fifteen paces of the man, the stranger's focus found Andron, and he raised both of his hands in the air. His hands began to glow a soft green that quickly darkened as Andron could not feel his body anymore. He was lifted from the ground into the air and seemed to fly like a bird over the man clad in green. His sword grew hot, and it fell to the ground near the strange man as he passed over his head. He skidded in the dry dirt on his back as he watched the man in horror with the wind knocked from him.

When he was finally able to move, he got to his feet and began staggering down the dusty road toward the man. He was defenseless, but what weapon could cause any harm to such a foe anyway? As he neared, he noticed a thin dark-green cloth wrapped around the man's forehead that was tied at the back of his head.

Ahead of the man was Starlyn, awestruck as she looked at him. She didn't attempt to grab her weapon or speak but gently strode up toward the man to stop ten paces from him. There seemed to be disbelief in her face as she looked, and it was that that caught Andron off guard.

"Hello, Sh'on," Starlyn finally said.

"Hello, Starlyn, it has been a while, has it not?" His voice was thick with a rustic accent.

Andron took a few steps closer and watched as the man's eyes grew a deeper and darker green. He didn't move in the slightest or care to look back at Andron. Suddenly, a large, genuine smile appeared on his face. Starlyn didn't return the smile but continued to look at him with unease.

Chapter Twenty-three

Searon, Karceoles, and Xython sat alone around a table in the back corner in the common room of the Dancing Donkey. All was silent around them, as even the inn owner and most of the serving maids had gone off to bed. Only two remained; one continued wiping down the tables and cleaning the floor. She smiled at the three men from time to time but left them alone after they said they wouldn't care for a drink. The other was the same redheaded maid with the white hat they had spoken to before. She knelt next to Searon, cleaning his wound and bandaging it. Searon and Karceoles both puffed at their pipes as they leaned back in their chairs. Karceoles's pipe was thrice the length as Searon's with a long stem that he held nearly two spans from his face. Xython watched the two carefully with arms crossed.

"Where do we start?" Searon asked.

"The beginning is usually suitable," Karceoles said.

"How about where you have been the past ten years," Xython added.

Searon sighed. "Do you remember Victoria?"

Xython's expression changed from stern to worry. He looked around as if expecting her to come from the shadows. When he saw nothing, he turned back to Searon and studied him with caution.

"Yes," he said reluctantly.

"Well, fourteen years ago, we married. She grew with child after half a year, and we decided to move. We had a son, Kellen, who grew

157

to the age of ten when she was with child again. Before our family could grow, we were attacked by draeyks. I am all that is left, and a little over three years have passed. My life quest from then on has been to seek out these creatures one by one and destroy them. Nothing else has mattered."

Xython nodded but kept silent.

"Well?" Searon asked.

"What?"

"Would you like to join us in gathering an army to destroy them once and for all?"

"After nearly thirteen years, little has changed about you, Searon. You are still the selfish leader that took off to battle with little regard to anyone but yourself," Xython paused. "No, I will not join your quest. While I'm sorry for what grief you must be going through, your act is still selfish. Can you not see what these villages are going through? This daerion threat has only begun in the last few years, and it has been increasing rapidly. To ask us to abandon our armies that are needed to protect us here to instead run off and leave this village unprotected for thousands of innocents to die? You ask too much."

Xython got to his feet and slid his chair in. He took one last hardened glance at Searon before shaking his head and walking toward the exit.

"Wait!" Searon called.

Xython stopped and reluctantly turned back to look at Searon. His expression was unreadable, but it seemed borderline rage and sorrow.

"You're right; I am selfish. These people need protection as well. Please sit. I am not here to dictate. I have come with ideas and have come to listen. Your politics have always been appreciated in the past, even if I haven't always thanked you for them. Please, sit, friend."

Xython raised an eyebrow. "Perhaps you have changed a little. Fine, I will sit. Do not think to change my mind without a debate."

Searon smiled. "I would never. Have I ever?"

"Nope, and unlike you, I haven't changed."

"And that is the reason, my friend, that I wish to have you as my ally."

"Go on, tell me what you have to say."

"We need an alliance. Even if we aren't to take many on a journey to fight, the fact that an alliance is true against these creatures is security enough. If a bond can be created, with messengers to let each other know where there is trouble so that the other may come to aid. If we have a few thousand strong, and the city is being attacked, we would make haste to come defend. Yet if we find a camp where they dwell, we could send for aid and head in strong."

Xython's wide white smile appeared. "It seems you do still think as a general. Do you still play Crossguards?"

Searon frowned. He hadn't even thought about the strategy board game in years. It was an intricate battle of wits, where you had to break through a force of units that had special maneuvers of defense to breach the castle. As children, both Xython and Searon played it all the time together, as did most boys who wished to learn battle tactics. The carved wooden pieces took forms of cavalry, pikesmen, swordsmen, crossbowmen, archers, and a captain. There were fifteen pikesmen, five each of cavalry and swordsmen, two each of crossbowmen and archers, and one captain, making a total thirty movable pieces in the game. The board was fifteen circles wide and fifteen tall, making a total of 225 blue and white mismatched circles. There was only a true winner if one defeated all the pieces while keeping their captain alive. "You bring back fond memories, friend. But no, I have not played Crossguards in many years. In fact, I believe the last game I played was against my brother right before I left Legain with Victoria."

"A fitting last game then. I will not ask you to play until after we reach Legain and you play a rematch against your brother."

"So you will come?"

"Only to make sure you don't make an arse of yourself. Someone needs to knock sense in you from time to time to make sure you do the right thing."

Karceoles grinned. "I have been trying my best to do so myself, yet his head is as stubborn as stone."

"Tell me something I don't know." Xython smiled back.

* * *

When the morning arrived, Searon quickly packed his things securely. He wore simple brown breeches and a tan V-neck button-up shirt. His dark-brown hair fell down on each side of his face, and he looked in the mirror on the wall. The room was lightened through the cracked blinds at the window. It was a simple inn with brown sheets and blanket, dark stained wood floors, a desk, and an end table. His armor was secured in his pack, as he knew he wouldn't have much use for it. He felt like being comfortable rather than guarded through the rest of his journey. Besides, it had been too long that he had been without it. He now knew what type of attacks to fight the daerions with, and besides, he had his friend Xython with him now.

When he looked in the mirror, he frowned, feeling at the rough beard at his jaw. It wasn't clean as it had been so long ago. During the time he was with Victoria, he'd kept his hair neatly trimmed at exact shoulder length and his beard and sideburns trimmed perfect with thin lines up to his mustache and a single line traveling down from the middle of his lip. Now there were stray hairs on his cheeks and between his three goatee lines as well as scouring his neck. The neck was the worst, as those hairs itched, and he constantly felt himself scratching just above his Adam's apple. He fingered at the knife on his sash next to his claymore's scabbard. Dipping his hands in the bucket of water next to him, he wet his face and began shaving.

A knock at the door startled him, and the knife pressed into his left cheek, making it bleed. He cursed lightly under his breath before speaking.

"Come in."

Xython stepped in and nodded to Searon. He wasn't wearing his purple scale mail armor anymore but was clad in thick leather riding armor. Behind him stood a younger woman, ebony skinned the same as Xython, with a fearful glance in her eyes. She appeared to be dressed for riding as well with black leather armor and a cape with bow and quiver at her belt.

"What's this?" Searon demanded.

"My sister."

Searon inspected the young woman. She appeared to be in her twenties and frail in contrast to her large teddy bear of a brother. Yet her facial features did resemble that of Xython, with her small rounded nose, puffed lips, and fierce eyes. Her chin was different and pointed rather than rounded, probably a trait from their mother. She had long black hair that had two braids in the front, one with purple and white beads, and the other with green and white beads.

"The road is dangerous."

"I know," she said.

"I only wish to take her to Legain where there is more of our family. I do not wish for her to be in a small village with the attacks if I cannot be here to protect her."

"As you wish." He turned to her. "What is your name?"

"Taasheka."

Searon set his knife down on the table and stuck his hand out. She studied it for a moment before gently putting her hand forward. Her fingernails were painted a deep purple and held a few gold rings. Searon gently grabbed her hand in his and brought it up to his lips where he kissed it above the knuckles. She smiled and blushed, turning her head away.

"It is nice to finally meet you."

Xython nodded to Searon, "We will meet you downstairs. Oh, and Searon, I notice you still haven't learned how to shave without cutting yourself."

Searon laughed as his friend closed the door. He looked back in the mirror and wiped the blood with a towel. He continued shaving until it looked like he was ready to meet the king.

When he finally made his way downstairs, he noticed Karceoles, Xython, and Taasheka sitting at a rounded wooden table, talking. Taasheka seemed to be giggling at the wizard's words, and Searon sighed and shook his head. Xython had a large grin on his face, and Karceoles seemed to be in a good mood as well. Searon figured that would be the case anyway after what he had seen the night before. He did look twice at the pint of ale in the wizard's hands. He lay down three gold coins at the bar where the innkeeper stood for the rooms and walked to the table.

"A bit early to be drinking, is it not?"

"Not at all. I see it as a bit late to be drinking after what happened last night."

Searon's eyebrows rose and he chuckled lightly. "Let us be off then; the sun has already risen, and traditionally this is later than we leave."

Karceoles nodded and downed the rest of his ale before placing the mug on the tabletop along with a silver coin. When they walked outside, they noticed a serving maid holding the reins of four horses. Searon's black-and-white striped stallion, Karceoles's beautiful brown mare, a large strong black beauty, and a smaller gray horse.

Searon removed two gold coins from his bag and handed them to the maid. "Thank you."

The maid beamed at such coin and her deep-brown eyes widened below her golden hair. "Thank you." She smiled the whole way into the inn, clutching the two coins for dear life.

"That was a bit much. Perhaps two silver coins would have sufficed," Xython said.

"Yes, it would have. But two gold coins will give us better service the next time we come through here. Besides, I don't carry silver coins."

"You never have cared much for money. It was always the battle."

"For a time, yes. Then it was always Victoria."

Xython nodded and got on his large black steed after helping his sister onto her small gray horse. Her horse was at least a span shorter than all the others but an easier horse for her to ride. Searon avoided his old friend's gaze and climbed on Stripes. The four of them rode through the village to the south side.

The trails outside the village split in three directions: west, south, and east. They turned east, and the horses began walking at a fast pace. Searon looked south for a long time, longing to see the ocean once more. It was down that path, in the city of Meshsylic that he showed Victoria the ocean for the first time. The memory was troubling, but he wished to see it nonetheless.

He didn't wish to think of Victoria anymore, but he couldn't shut her out. The worst were the memories of that night. Every time he had a good memory of her, the worst would come crashing into him soon after. He hoped that the traveling and the quest would make him forget, at least the amount of time it had been. Yet it still circled in his mind without even thinking about it, without even counting. It was now forty-one months, fifteen days, and six hours since he buried both his wife and child. The torment of knowing, as each second passed by, was torture beyond any he had ever known. Perhaps seeing his brother would help.

"I think I've heard of these daerions as a child. They were always stories told by elders, scary bedtime stories, evil creatures that fought and killed humans. I thought they were supposed to be extinct," Searon said.

"They were supposed to be. The kheshlars killed most of them when they came to this land. When they were weakened, the council sent a few of us out to destroy the rest. I chased down a lot myself. These...seem stronger than the ones I fought before. It seems...somebody has been hiding them...and training them," Karceoles said.

"There is only one reason to train such creatures. War. It is strange to me that the daerions keep to the south while the draeyks keep to the north. So far, they have been separated, yet their goal is the same. I'm afraid of an alliance."

"Yes...that would complicate things. I have a feeling that the wizard who left the council has something to do with this...yet these daerions were trained like kheshlars."

"Starlyn's sister?" Searon shivered as the memory of her came back.

"Besides the time when you met her, I have not heard about her whereabouts since the war against the kheshlars. She led the draeyks during that time, and it seems clear she is no longer. Perhaps she found new allies to bully. Let's hope it is her, and not some new threat."

"Yes...still, the memory of her makes me shiver. I do not see her being a minor threat. If she's failed once, perhaps she has learned her mistake. If it is her I believe it will be even more difficult to defeat her."

"I agree...she is not to be taken lightly. Come, let us ride fast."

The four of them put their horses to a gallop through the flat terrain. The sky was blue with hardly a cloud in the sky. Farms went on for leagues with grain, wheat, fruits, and vegetables. Searon made sure to stop from time to time to buy fresh fruit from the farmers for their travel.

Chapter Twenty-four

Andron stood with his arms crossed half a dozen paces away from the smokeless green campfire. Starlyn sat on a log next to the strange man a safe distance away from him as she stared in disbelief. Andron's eyes were wide as they looked from Starlyn to the man in green robes.

"You two know each other?" Andron asked.

The man nodded his head toward Andron. Andron flinched and took a step back, unsure about the man before him. He seemed as if he wasn't human, and that scared Andron. Only weeks ago, the only creature besides humans that Andron was aware of were the draeyks that attacked his village. Then he met kheshlars and a wizard, and his entire world turned upside down. This man sitting in front of them appeared to be neither. His ears weren't rounded like a human's but seemed to have a slight point on the top similar to some kheshlars. He didn't appear to have a staff, or zylek, as the wizard had called it, so he couldn't be a wizard. Yet it was magic that Andron felt in the air surrounding him as he was tossed to the ground. He shivered as he took a step closer.

"He helped me in the war the kheshlars had against the draeyks years ago," Starlyn whispered.

Andron nodded slowly and turned to her. "What is he?"

The man stood, brushing his long straight blond hair from his eyes, and bowed before Andron, "My name is Shronan Onderon, but you may simply call me Sh'on. I am a mage."

"A mage?" Andron's forehead wrinkled in thought.

"Yes, a mage."

"How many different types of magic users are there?"

"Well…there are wizards, mages, witches, sorceresses, and warlocks. Those are the five stronger fields of magic—while there still are some who have trained themselves and only know small spells. Those are simply called magic users."

Andron's eyebrows rose as he sat down on a stone by the fire across from Sh'on. His concentration was fierce, and he intended to find out as much as he could.

"What is the difference between a mage and a wizard?"

"A wizard has more power because they are born with it. Often, they are not aware of it until they reach the age of maturity, but then they find they can conjure spells and feel a remarkable power within them. The power is so strong that if they do not harness it and learn to control it, it can destroy them…and everyone surrounding them. This is why they carry something to control their power, a way to channel it in a controlled manner."

"A zylek," Andron whispered.

"Yes…many use a zylek, or a scepter of some sort. Each one is created to the type of magic that they hold so it is best used for them."

"And a mage?"

"Mages are not born with magic; it is something that needs to be unlocked within them, or through other means. Some study for years in an attempt to gain control of the power. For some, there is a flicker inside of them that if they find they can harness and control. Mages are not as powerful because a hidden force of magic within us doesn't tear through our defenses when we reach maturity. Instead, we have to seek for it and grasp it with all of our might. Therefore, once we claw at it and grasp it, we are already in control. Think of it like this: Wizards struggle to keep their power inside of themselves. That's why they have zyleks, to release the magic that desperately wishes to escape when they are in need. With mages, we have to search for it and grab it before we can release it. This makes what we do not nearly as powerful as a wizard, but sometimes it does make it more controlled."

"I see," Andron muttered, glancing away from the mage.

"Met a wizard, have you? Would it by chance be Karceoles?"

Andron quickly turned back to face the mage with flickering eyes. "Yes…you know him?"

Sh'on's face lit in a sly grin. "A distant cousin. I would very much enjoy seeing him again. It's been many an age since I've seen that sarcastic fool."

"Ah, I see you have met him."

"What about the others?"

"Warlocks are either wizards or mages who have turned to the dark magic. They are really powerful whether they were a wizard or merely a mage. The dark magic is powerful, but it comes at a price. There have not been mentions of a warlock for a very long time, yet these times are starting to darken. I very much hope it stays that way."

"Sorceresses and witches?"

"Both are women that can wield magic. Sorceresses are powerful and often use a scepter whether they are born with magic or must learn it. Women are complicated creatures." He looked over at Starlyn with a grin. "They always feel like they must be in control, which is why they use a scepter. Witches study the dark magic as well, yet in this way they are different than warlocks. Not all witches are dark themselves, like warlocks. Women can control their minds better, and some witches only study the dark magic without letting it control them. Still, they are dangerous because many choose not to use a scepter for control."

Andron studied the mage for a long moment. His green eyes were the most unsettling about the mage. Blond, almost yellow, hair hung straight down past his shoulders onto a green robe, the same hue of his eyes. His eyes seemed to glow with a fiery light to match that of the green smokeless fire on the ground in front of him. He seemed direct unlike the wizard who only divulged what seemed like riddles. Sh'on seemed more in control of his emotions and had patience. Karceoles seemed to be an old impatient man who always fought for irrational decisions and swift strikes. It was hard to believe that Karceoles was the more powerful one with how serene Sh'on appeared to be.

"So tell me," Sh'on said, breaking Andron from his thoughts, "what has my fool cousin been up to?"

"Karceoles is with a captain named Searon. He is helping us gather warriors for a march against the draeyks."

"Ah, so he is hoping to start a war, is he?" he asked, shifting his glance toward Starlyn.

Her head shook in annoyance, "The old fool is trying to."

"Have his manners got to you, Starlyn? Do not pay him any attention. He has always been crude toward women. I do believe one of his parents dropped him on his head decades ago," Sh'on chuckled, his yellow hair bouncing on his shoulders as he laughed.

Andron chuckled as he thought back to his memories of the wizard. He did seem like he was the most hardheaded person in the entire land. His warm humor dissolved as he stared back around at the village. The destruction was overwhelming, and he was done with foolish questions. He looked back up to the mage with a grim expression on his face.

"What happened here?"

Rubble scattered the roads, making it nearly impossible to walk a straight path. Wagons were burned and charred. Skeletons scattered the ruins without a single one being spared. Andron's teeth clenched along with his fists as he surveyed the carnage along with Sh'on.

"I came because of a vision I saw of this place…I was too late. The draeyks have destroyed it. I have found a few of these creatures hiding inside this village. I could smell them, but rest assured, I have sought them out and destroyed them. That's when I stumbled upon you two…or you two stumbled upon me."

"You were too late? So everybody is dead." Andron's shoulders sank as he turned away from the mage.

Reality began to sink into his mind. His wife and children…had they perished in the attack like everyone else? A single tear swelled in each eye and slowly trickled down his face. He glanced at the dirt below his feet, and with anger built up inside of him he kicked it with enough strength to cause a large dust cloud to float around him. Hiding his anger and weakness, he quickly swelled his chest with pride. He was a warrior; he could not show weakness. Weakness on a battlefield was certain death. If that was what the creator wanted for his life, then so be it. He would become like Searon, hard and strong, seeking only one thing: revenge. Sh'on met his eyes, swirling pools of emerald blazing like fire, they made Andron's hard focused eyes loosen slightly.

"Not so fast on judgment, Andron. With my magic, I sent a message to this village to another magic user. I sent warning of this attack.

By the looks of this village and the three south, it seems warning had reached in time. A stand was made here instead of each village that was destroyed. There was resistance, but from the looks of it, it was only a distraction. It seems this village was set in defense to allow more time for the people to escape. A city lies to the north, I believe, and I believe that we will find survivors there."

"There is still hope," Andron whispered, looking toward the ground. He lifted his face up and looked directly into Sh'on's fierce burning eyes. "Let's be off then and make for Wesiet."

He tried to hide his fear of losing his family deep inside of himself. It was hard because it made his heart throb with each beat. He also tried to hide his hope of them still being alive. Instead, he tried to numb his feelings. No matter what the outcome, he would be prepared, but was that going to be enough? He felt at the painting hidden securely beneath his armor. It brought warmth to his soul as he felt it and re-membered the picture of his family.

Sh'on put his hand on his shoulder as he studied him. "I under-stand you are eager, friend. Yet it is late, and I know you have traveled all day to reach here. I am weary as well and could use some rest. Let us sleep this night, and when dawn arrives we shall leave for the city. It will not be long."

"Of course...you are right. We are in need of rest. I am ahead of myself. In the morning then."

Sh'on nodded and leaned back into the stump behind him. Within minutes, he seemed to snore, but his eyes were still open. The haunting fiery-green glow was lessened, making his eyes almost a normal green. Starlyn shivered as she shifted over to Andron by the stone.

"Do not fret, Andron, this man can be trusted."

"Then why are you afraid of him?"

Starlyn turned to look at him, surprise in her eyes. "The things I have seen him do. He is powerful. Whether he be an ally or not, I fear anybody with more power than I understand."

"I do as well. Get some rest, Starlyn. I will take first watch. There are too many thoughts in my head for sleep right now anyway. I will wake you halfway through the night."

She nodded but scooted closer to him and rested her head upon his shoulder. He put his arm around her for comfort. She shivered every few seconds, and he removed his cloak to cover her. A smile touched her lips before she slipped into a dreamy state.

He looked up at the stars, glittering in patterns and shapes far above him, and pondered. It would not be long now until he found out if his family was still alive. What would he do, what would he say when he found out? He sat there for most of the night pondering his reaction and thinking of what to expect.

Chapter Twenty-five

After three more days of traveling, they passed by two more villages before coming to a towering city. As they approached, they slowed down to gaze upon its beauty. It was the evening of the third day as they approached, and Searon's eyes were wide with the view of the city. Nearly fourteen years had gone by since he had seen the place, and the changes were astounding.

Before, there had been many large stone, brick, and wooden buildings, all finely made. Now there were towering buildings hundreds of paces into the sky, and they were all made of brick and stone. One of the towers was taller than them all and seemed to be hexagonal in shape and gray in color. The entire city was circled in a stone wall that was thirty paces tall. Searon only remembered it being twenty paces in height when he lived there.

They approached the gate and noticed four guards stationed there clad in ring mail armor. Each of them wore a steel helm where their faces weren't visible. Long swords in scabbards were attached at their waists. Two stepped forward holding their hands out clad in metal gauntlets. The other two stayed back with hands on hilts of their swords watching the company.

"What is your business in Legain?" a husky voice demanded.

"We have come to speak with Noraes," Karceoles said up, as Searon was at a loss for words.

"What are your names?"

The sun shone from his metal to blind the eyes of the four of them as they tried to look at him. Xython dismounted and walked over in a few hearty steps. A wide grin was planted on his face.

"Brexhar, is that you?" Xython asked.

The guard shifted his eye to see better. "Xython, what brings you here? And who are your friends?"

"This is Searon, and his friend Karceoles. I have come here with them, with my sister."

"Why are they here to see Noraes?"

"Searon is Noraes's brother."

Brexhar's eyes went wide, and he looked toward Searon and nodded. He turned to another guard, "Go inform Noraes that his brother has come to speak with him."

"Yes, sir." The guard saluted and headed through the small door next to the gate.

Xython and Brexhar shared a conversation for a few minutes before the guard came back. He approached Brexhar and whispered in his ear.

Brexhar nodded and looked to Searon. "You may enter. He is in the barracks on the eastern side of the city. Do you know where that is?"

"If it is the same place it was fourteen years ago."

Brexhar's head tilted. "Yes…but if it's been fourteen years, then a few changes have been made."

"I can already see that."

"Open the gate!" Brexhar called behind him.

The metal drop gate began to rise, and Searon rode in followed by his three companions. People scurried through the streets on their busy tasks without paying notice to Searon and his company as they rode in. A few did stop to stare for a moment at his horse, but other than that everybody's business seemed to be more important. There were hundreds of homes and businesses scattered throughout, if not thousands. It was a gigantic city with a handful of towers and a large castle on the southern side. Most of the houses were brick or stone, as protection against sieges, but there were a few wooden homes and businesses. Yet they were thick and strong with stain to match the rest of the city's rustic appearance.

171

The Crimson Claymore

Warriors patrolled the ground between all the civilians that were traveling from one place to another, either trying to buy food from merchants or visit their friends. Food stands were set up everywhere, and many attempted to get Searon's attention with porridge or fresh fruits, but he didn't stop. The people were beginning to dwindle as the sun set in the west, and they cleared as they passed through the stands and markets.

They passed blacksmiths, bell makers, shoe makers, lumber mills, and several other businesses. The barracks was an octagonal shape and close to the castle next to a large blacksmith and stable. Searon rode to the stable and handed the stable boy two gold coins to take care of the four horses.

"You three should find an inn. I wish to see my brother alone." He handed a few gold coins to the wizard.

He didn't give them a chance to respond and began walking toward the barracks. A dozen warriors stood outside to guard it when he walked up. They looked at him for a moment, studying him, before one of the men's eyes grew large.

"Searon? Is that really you?"

Searon smiled. "Is my brother inside?"

"Yes, I have heard you came back, but I didn't believe it."

"May I enter?"

"Yes, oh, sorry."

He moved away from the entrance along with the other few guards. Searon nodded and smiled to him before stepping inside. The interior was full of wandering warriors either studying books on tactics, or weapons that hung on the walls. Various types of armor hung on the walls, too, from leather, plate mail, chain mail, scale mail, and ring mail. Each seemed expertly crafted and held slightly different designs than their counterparts.

Nobody seemed to notice him except for a woman who smiled and walked over. She was clad in brown leather armor with a bow over her shoulder and dagger at her sash. Her smile was intoxicating, with a perfect balance of teeth showing through her soft thick lips. Long auburn hair fell down her face in braids of black and red. Her nose was thin and crooked with small freckles on it. Cold gunmetal eyes stared deep into his without a blink.

"What are you searching for, stranger?"

"I am looking for Noraes."

"He awaits you in the practicing arena." She pointed to a thin stone door without a window.

"Thank you." Searon bowed his head slightly.

Inside the door was a vast area that looked like wilderness. Stones, trees, streams, and grass flourished through the area. For a moment, he thought he was back outside in some hidden place within the city. A warrior rushed by him, ducking from stone to stone with a keen eye out into the wilderness. When he thought he was clear, he leaped out, and three arrows struck him hard, and he fell. Searon rushed forward to grab him when three more warriors leaped from seemingly nowhere and went to his aid. Two went forward to pull him to safety while another guarded them in front with a large wooden shield to protect from three more arrows that bounced off.

Searon noticed that the arrows on the ground weren't fixed with sharp tips but smooth stones. He walked up to the squad of warriors, shaking his head.

"What is this?" he asked.

"The training ground, sir," a man in thick leather armor and short black hair said.

"What is your objective?"

"To reach the captain on the other side."

Searon scanned the area, noticing the large field had little cover. A few stones were scattered throughout that provided little protection against arrows. The archers were in three separate points in the farthest reach of the arena. He could see their eyes over stone and knew they were being watched.

"Is he done?" Searon asked, looking at the man who got hit by stone arrows. He was rubbing his chest where he was hit. Welts probably covered the areas.

"Yes, more than two arrows hit him."

"Crossguards," Searon smiled.

"Yes...the same rules apply."

"Sometimes in Crossguards, a sacrifice must be made."

"Can you beat this?"

"Yes...I know these rules. I also know the style of play being used. Do you see those two close stones on the far side? Three archers hide behind those. Do you see the two stones on the sides? The swordsmen wait behind those to ambush."

"How do we get past that?"

"Simple, you fight. Grab another shield, and have two of you carry shields to guard the other two as you make for those two rocks. Expect the ambush, and one of you drop a shield to defend." He studied their hardened wood swords and shook his head. "Meanwhile, those archers will meet their ends, and I'll meet back with you."

Each looked at his claymore in turn with wide eyes. He only smiled. "Do not worry, I will not kill them."

He waited until the four of them dashed into the opening. Arrows began soaring but were easily blocked by the two shields. They ran straight toward the two large stones, and when they were twenty paces away, Searon dashed from his coverage. He went a different path along the side of the clearing. His feet carried him quickly, and by the time the battle was in full force he was there behind the archers. He drew his claymore as he looked at the three. None of them saw him and he gently tapped the blade against each in turn.

"Dead," he said.

The three looked at him with wide eyes but set their bows down and bowed to him. He nodded and came from the clearing to where the three were still fighting. The one with the shield had been struck down. There were four opponents, but none of them noticed as Searon came from behind. He still held the claymore in his hand, and he tapped each of them in the back with his weapon. The four turned to stare at him and dropped their swords in turn.

"Dead," he grinned.

A horn erupted through the quiet air, and over a dozen men entered the field. Each stared wildly at Searon. Some whispered to each other and pointed. Searon stood motionless but stared at each one of them. He gently placed his claymore back in it scabbard and crossed his arms.

A man stepped through the crowd of men in full scale mail that glittered blue in color. It didn't appear to be battle worn in the slightest, as if it was new armor or newly refurbished. His blue-and-silver helm was secured on his head. Searon could only see his deep hazel eyes, thick bronze eyebrows, long eyelashes, sharp nose, and pursed lips. Suddenly, the captain smiled and took off his helm. His dirty-blond hair was just past his ears, and his face was clean, except the scruff of a beard that desperately wanted to show but was still near invisible. A large brown mole rested on his face above his left eyebrow, a birth-mark.

He walked up to Searon and lay a hand on his shoulder. "Brother, it's been a long time."

Chapter Twenty-six

Andron made sure the three of them were packed as soon as the sunlight touched the sky in the morning. The dirt roads were clear and open through flat terrain with only a few slopes of elevation. No animals or people crowded the abandoned roads, and that thought brought chills to Andron's spine. The sea beyond was always visible as they traveled, and a constant reminder of more pleasant thoughts. Starlyn's eyes didn't seem to waver from the sea on the west of the road. It seemed that her eyes were glued, and several times she bumped into Andron with an apology, but soon after her eyes glanced back to the sea.

"Is this your first time seeing the sea?" Andron asked.

Her head seemed to shake from her thoughts as she glanced back toward Andron. "I have never been this far from my land. This much water…it's incredible."

"Yes it is…truly a sight to behold," Andron whispered.

She blushed and turned her face back toward the sea, leaning in close. The sparkling from the water seemed to shimmer on her face, escalating her astonishing beauty. He only looked at her for a moment before continuing through the land. Wheat and grain grew on the land for leagues along each side of the road with large wooden farm houses and barns. Everything seemed well overgrown without maintenance, and the houses were abandoned. The only sound was that of crows and ravens that flew through the skies to land on the farms and feast on the vegetables that were left unguarded. Some birds were kept at bay by large menacing scarecrows, but a few scarecrows were destroyed and tossed into the overgrowing gardens.

The roads stretched for leagues until they reached the city of Wesiet by twilight. There was little else to the journey but farms with fruits, vegetables, wheat, and grain. Everything was abandoned, even those the closest to the city walls of heavy slate. The gate by the city was guarded by a force of thirty men heavy in armor and weapons.

Andron frowned as the neared the city gate. Normally, the city was only covered with two men on the outside and a small force within. It was not a city that was full of people to defend. Wesiet was only a transport village of supplies and held as little as the last village. Most of the things made and grown were transported to other cities and villages in trade for other supplies or coin. The army that Wesiet had was little more than militia.

He noticed the guards at the gate were of varying appearance. There were many different crests on their breastplates from the various villages to the south as well as that of Wesiet itself. The four different crests consisted of a crow, an eagle, a vulture, and a wagon. Hope restored in Andron's mind as he saw the four crests of the various villages before the city. He hoped everybody had made it inside of the large city. Yet he wondered if there was room for all there.

"Halt, who comes to Wesiet, and what business do you hold here?" A guard stepped forward with a large crest of a wagon of Wesiet in gold on his chest.

"I am Andron, my family is from Guerettos. I have come here to see if they have made it safely."

"And these with you?"

"This is Starlyn, a kheshlar from the kheshlarn city in the woods. And this is Sh'on, a mage from across Calthoria."

The captain's eyes grew wide, and he unsheathed his sword, pointing it inches away from Sh'on's face, whose green eyes glowed with shimmering fire as his hand began to glow with a color to match. The rest of the guards unsheathed their weapons as well and took a step forward.

"Magic is not welcome in our lands; leave this place."

"I have not come here to harm but to help."

"There is little trust in those who can use magic."

"Please, stop. Violence is not necessary," Starlyn said, stepping forward.

Each guard in turn stared at her openly from her dazzling blonde hair and pale serene face, and lingered as they took in the rest of her shape. The captain stepped forward and opened his mouth, but no words came out.

"Captain?" Starlyn asked.

The captain cleared his throat with a few coughs before removing the sword from next to Sh'on's neck. "I am sorry, m'lady. I have never seen a kheshlar before."

"And what do you know of kheshlars? Are kheshlars liars?"

"No, m'lady. Everything I hear is that kheshlars do not speak a lie."

"Then I will tell you to stand down. This mage does not threaten you or your kin. He has fought the draeyks before with me, and he has come here with me to do the same. Do you doubt my words?"

"No, m'lady."

"Then let us pass."

He reluctantly turned to his comrades as if looking for approval. None of them looked at him but instead stared toward the kheshlar in awe. Shaking his head, he sheathed his sword and took a step back.

"You may pass."

Each of the other guards sheathed their swords in turn. The tall metal gate rose through the stone with the guards in towers on the inside turning the wheels. Starlyn took the first step with Sh'on and Andron following her as they walked inside of the large city.

Inside the gate, the city looked like no other. Nothing appeared to match as many buildings were of gray or brown stone while others were made of wood of various stains. There were also plenty of brick buildings of every color. Most were businesses of various sorts from herbal shops, leather shops, and any other material that might prove useful. Homes were scarce throughout the large city, and it was empty of most travelers. There were no merchant stands of any sort. Streets were bare instead of like normal cities or villages that would be covered with people. There seemed to be only one pub on the main street, and it seemed crowded beyond anything Andron had ever seen.

A soldier patrolled the streets and nearly walked past them before Andron caught his arm. The man didn't look pleased and brushed Andron's touch from his bicep. His face wore a grim expression with a thick red goatee and square jaw.

"Excuse me, sir, do you know where the survivors from Guerettos are?"

The warrior's expression changed from anger to sorrow as he inspected Andron and the two others. "Most are in the third bunker from the west, near the sea. They wished to stay as far from the gate as possible and the closest to the sea."

Andron nodded. "Thank you."

He continued on with his mind set on his goal. Everything around him seemed to be a blur. Even the whispers of both Sh'on and Starlyn were but hazy murmurs in his mind. His one focus and thought was of seeing his beautiful wife and children again. Everything else around him was clouded in darkness without a thought. He traveled from alley to alley until finally the buildings grew scarce with open terrain. The sea was plain in sight, and he had to clench the excitement within him so he wouldn't run toward the bunkers. There were dozens of them; each was created to store wheat and grain until ships were arrived. Another reason they were built so securely was in case of an attack, but never in their wildest dreams did they think they would actually be used for such a feat.

He walked slower once he reached the entrance. Seagulls scattered the sky above him toward the sea. The sunset was to the west across the glistening water. A blanket of steaming mist covered the water for a league before the sun's blinding reflection. Above the sun were streaks of clouds that glinted yellow and orange with gray and black clouds in the shadows on the north and south side. The sea created a peaceful scene, with perfectly still waters catching the reflection both sun and clouds.

Andron watched the sunset for a moment before walking down the steps of the third bunker from the west. Each bunker only showed a few paces from the ground. The majority of the stone buildings were built underground so the cool dirt of the land would keep everything cold. In rumors, there were also hidden levels that went beneath the main level to hide goods or people in case of dire need.

With heavy breaths, he stopped at the tall white stone door. For a long moment, he stood there looking at the door before him. His breath slowed as he stared for what felt like hours. He held his hand in the air in front of the door, and it twitched as he kept it raised.

"Andron?" Starlyn whispered.

His mind cycled through every possible outcome that could occur if he opened that door. He wasn't sure if he was ready for any of them. Turning around, he looked at Starlyn's beautiful eyes. She stared back at him with wonder and quickly stepped up to him to embrace him in a hug. At first, he was taken aback, but soon his arm was around her in an embrace.

"It will be okay, Andron. Whatever happens, both Sh'on and I will be here for you."

"Thank you."

With another large breath, he turned back around to face the door before knocking against it loudly. After a few minutes, a rectangle of stone at eye level was removed from the door to be replaced with two eyes. The eyes were brown in color and surrounded by a wrinkly face full of wisdom.

"Who wishes to enter?"

"It is Andron. I am looking for my wife and kids. Ketharine is her name. Is she in here?"

"Yes, child, your family is inside."

The empty rectangle was replaced with the stone, and the door opened. Standing before them was an elderly woman in gray robes. She had short white curly hair and a smile of treasured gold. Motioning for them to follow, she led them down a hall where stone doors appeared every fifteen paces on each side. Finally after what seemed to be half-way down the immense hallway, she came to a stop and motioned to an unmarked doorway.

He nodded his thanks and took a deep breath as he pushed open the door. Inside were a large rocking chair and two smaller chairs of well-crafted wood. A woman with long curly red hair sat in the rocking chair with a young baby in her arms as she sang him to sleep. The two other chairs were occupied with two young girls that watched their mother. One had a head full of red hair and wore a white dress while the other had black hair and a light-blue dress.

When the three of them saw Andron, they gasped, and the two young girls leaped from their chairs to run at him. Both giggled as they hugged at his legs. He knelt to the ground and grabbed the both of them in his arms.

"Daddy!" they cried.

"My dear Kierra and Adreamera, I have missed you so," he said as tears came to his eyes.

The woman in the chair stood up and laid the sleeping baby on a mattress on the ground. She walked a few steps and looked at Andron with fierce eyes. The two girls looked back at their mother and cringed as they saw her.

"Daughters, go to your room."

"I love you, Daddy," both of them whispered into his ears before disappearing into another room.

He smiled as he watched them go with their dresses twirling, and they dashed out of sight. When he turned back to the woman, he flinched slightly. She walked up to him without a hint of joy or concern painted on her face. He stood expectant of her reaction as a hand smacked his face hard. Wincing in pain, he knew better than to rub his sore cheek. Another slap came on the same cheek that caused him to cringe.

"How dare you!" Her voice was shaky.

"I'm sorry."

Another slap crashed against his left cheek that caused him to rub it in pain. She went for another slap, but he caught her arm and stared into her eyes. Tears swelled up in her deep hazel eyes.

"How dare you leave us to worry about you? Do you know what it was like to wonder each and every day if you were alive or dead? Do you have any idea what you have done to this family?"

She shook with tears as she stared at him. He clasped his arms around her and brought her in for a hug. She fought against him at first but finally caved into his arms sobbing uncontrollably.

"It's okay, my love. I am here. I am back."

She pushed him away and took a step back, "Okay? How dare you say that! It is not okay. I can already see it in your eyes. I know you, Andron, and I know that you are not coming home. You are not coming back to us. I can see it in your eyes; you will leave us again. Do not say it will be okay."

"I love you all very much, but now that I know you are safe, I need to go."

"Please, Andron…Please don't leave us again."

"I know it has been a while, but we no longer have a home. It will not be safe for us to go back until this threat is gone. I am with people now that seek for an alliance to defeat these creatures. I must leave and help them."

"Surely, you don't have to leave right away."

He turned to look at both Starlyn and Sh'on. Both stared back at him with warmth in their expression.

"I am sure Searon wishes to visit with his brother a few days as well. Stay here with your family; Sh'on and I will find this barracks and whatever warriors are here in an attempt to ask for their support."

Andron turned back around and saw a smile on Ketharine's lips. She leaped into his arms and kissed him passionately. He was taken aback by her abruptness and the fresh sting that swelled on his cheek. Bringing his hand to her face, he tangled it in her hair and kissed her back just as eagerly.

"Good, it has been far too long that I've slept in a cold bed," she whispered with a smile.

Starlyn and Sh'on both bowed before leaving the room for Andron and Ketharine to be left alone. He smiled back at her with a twinkle in his eye.

"It has been far too long."

Chapter Twenty-seven

Searon watched his brother with keen interest. It had been many years since he saw him last, and so many things had changed. Yet at the same time, there were so many things that were the same. His hair was short and dirty blond with stubble on his face. Years back, when he was young, it seemed no matter what he tried no facial hair would grow. Searon smiled at the fond memories.

"How have you been, Noraes?"

He stared around the lively pub that his brother had taken him to. Serving maids patrolled the dirty green wooden floors, dodging spilled mugs of ale to bring fresh ones to customers. Several of them flinched as their bottoms were pinched, but none shrieked out. It appeared to be a too common thing for them that they were used to sore bottoms. The crowd cheered at the juggler as he tossed seven small silver balls up on the stage. Next to the juggler, a woman in a long green cotton dress played a fiddle.

"I can't complain, I've brought myself a long way since the last you've seen me. Perhaps I've matured a little."

Searon barked a laugh as he studied his brother. He changed out of his armor into a short sleeve blue cotton shirt that shone his tight fit muscles at his arms down to his hands. The muscles were as large as Searon's, yet for his thin frame they were impressive. Noraes rubbed at his chin, feeling at his whiskers.

"Since when have you been able to grow a beard?"

Noraes laughed. "I still cannot, but this keeps my face a little warm in the winter."

"So have you found yourself a wife yet?"

No matter how much his brother had claimed to change and mature, he still couldn't see him settling down. He knew his brother to have the same compassion and loving nature as himself, but he was still a wild spirit. Searon had almost forgotten his compassion that he once had for his family and friends over the last few years of being alone. Now that he was seeing his brother once again, those feelings began to swirl back.

Noraes sighed, and his face grew grim. "No, I just haven't found the right one," he chuckled and leaned back in his wobbly chair. "How is Victoria?"

Those were the words that Searon was dreading to hear. They tore through him like a sharp knife through fresh bread. He closed his eyes and rubbed his index finger and thumb against his forehead. After taking a deep breath, he opened his eyes to his brother's worried expression. His brother had known how much he had cared for Victoria and wouldn't go anywhere without her. Noraes began to look around as if expecting to see her come from a corner of darkness. He knew his brother cared for him deeply and would ache when he told him. Searon shook his head and sighed. Noraes studied him for a long moment with concern flashing in his green eyes flecked with hazel.

"She is dead."

Noraes's eyes flared as he stared at his brother. Searon's heart pounded with fury as flashbacks entered his mind. He clenched his fist and put it to his forehead as a splitting migraine overcame him. Shivering, he opened his eyes and brought his shaky fist onto the table. He clenched the pint of ale in his hand and began to chug it. Normally, he wouldn't drink ale because he wasn't as fond of the taste as he was of harder alcohol. However, it was his brother that had ordered the drinks, and it was one of those rare occasions where he preferred the bitterness.

"Creatures called draeyks killed her…and my son. Scaly reptile beasts they are, with long snouts like a lizard and tails behind them. They are black in color, though some have speckled variations under their jaw and on their chest and abdomen. Noraes," Searon paused, "they look like dragons in the storybooks we read as children, except they are our size and without wings."

"I am sorry, Brother. I do not recognize these creatures. We have a threat of our own down here. From the look in your eyes, I can see that you have already come across a few daerions."

"Yes, I have. They are vicious beasts, much stronger than draeyks."

"Then you already know of my dilemma."

"I do. Yet you do not know of mine. I have been lost, my Brother. For the last forty-one months and eighteen days I have been wandering without knowing what to do. Every fiber in my body has been seeking revenge upon these creatures. A little over two months ago, a wizard approached me and scolded me for being so selfish. I welcomed death and embraced it as I struck down creature after creature seeking revenge for the past three years. He has offered me something different, a path to these creatures—destruction instead of tearing them apart one by one. Together, we have begun an alliance to strike the heart of these creatures."

"How many do you have in this alliance?"

Searon sighed. "There is only the old wizard, I, Xython, a kheshlar named Starlyn, and a cunning human warrior named Andron."

"A kheshlar?"

"Yes, Brother, they really do exist."

"I know all too well that they exist."

Searon's eyebrows rose, but he didn't voice his question over the subject. "The wizard and I split with the kheshlar and human to travel in two different paths to begin forming an army for an alliance. They went to the northern cities where Andron's kin lies to find an army. The wizard, Karceoles, and I…have come down to these southern cities."

"Ah…you have come to find me."

"I hate to put you in this situation, Brother, but I do need you. I am rejoiced in seeing you alive and was surprised the wizard knew more of your whereabouts than I. I know you are commander of an army down here, and I was hoping you would join me and fight alongside me once again."

"It is not that simple, Searon. I am not only the general over the Legain army. My title is grander than that. I am in command over all the armies in this province of Lorgaeth. There are seven cities and nineteen villages here under my command. It is not official yet, but there are votes going on to make me grand duke of the land. The king is sick and is without an heir since his only son fell from horse and carriage two years ago. There are many who think without a king of the land that I would be sufficient in his stead."

"You...king?" Searon asked before bursting out into laughter.

"As I said, my Brother, nothing is official. Yet you can see why I cannot leave. For me to leave, even in absence of war during these times, would show that I abandon my people. I feel that if I remain here I may be able to do some good. Even if it is only as grand duke."

Searon downed another pint of ale that the serving maid had just left as he listened to a bard on stage. He was singing of a young boy who killed his three brothers to become king but grew old as a king without an heir. Searon wondered if it was about the current king or a fictional story. Gently setting the empty mug on the table, he studied the pub with interest.

Most of the men at the other tables were too drunk to talk in normal speech anymore. Many slurred their words and were too drunk to pinch the serving maids' bottoms anymore. A few had fallen asleep at the tables, snoring loudly. The juggler dressed in white-and-black striped silk sat at a table in the corner, talking to two serving maids. Both seemed interested in his talents.

As he looked to other men, warriors, they seemed to peer at Noraes from time with time with signs of great respect. Their serving maid came back to the table, and Searon watched with interest as she bowed courteously toward Noraes and flashed her best smile. He indeed was a popular man in the city.

Searon noticed the double wooden doors pushed in at the entrance of the pub. An elderly man stepped through with a staff in his hand, followed by a broad ebony man wearing leather armor. He smiled as he saw his two friends notice him and began walking over. Karceoles stopped to whistle at a serving maid that passed by.

Noraes tilted his head toward the entrance, "Don't tell me...that's the wizard."

Searon grinned. "Sadly, it is. I understand that you are busy, Noraes, you have your work cut out for you. Perhaps you cannot join in this fight, or perhaps you weren't meant to. However, if there is any help you could offer..."

"I must stay in charge of the city's defense, as well as the province. However, the council of elders has spoken of forming an army for an offensive strike against the daerion threat. Perhaps I can speak with them, but you have to promise the army would not be for your personal gain to destroy the draeyks. They are to be a force to not only battle the draeyks but the daerions that threaten us as well."

Searon stared at his brother for a long moment as Xython sat down in the chair next to him. He sighed and reluctantly nodded. "Yes, I agree, of course. At first, I admit I was selfish in coming here. Xython here knocked some sense into me when I ran into him in Erdunadir."

Xython smiled as he nudged Searon's shoulder with his elbow. "That I did. Searon will always be the headstrong captain ready to jump to conclusions before using his brain." He looked around, finally finding a serving maid and yelling into the wind. "Ale! My good lady, I need ale, three pints for me, and two more for my friends here."

Noraes returned his smile. "It is nice to see you again, old friend."

"As always," Xython replied.

Searon looked around in an attempt to find Karceoles and shook his head as he saw the old man leaning against a pole, speaking with two serving maids. When he turned back around, he saw Noraes raise an eyebrow and Xython chuckling loudly with a cheery laugh. The serving maid returned with five pints of ale that she gently set on the table before she took the empty glasses.

"Searon, there is one condition you must complete before I will go to the council and bid to them that I have a good general for the task."

"Anything, Brother, of course."

Noraes smiled. "I must see you can still play the game. If you are to lead my men, I would like to know it would be victory and not death."

"The game?"

"I believe when you left the last time, I was the one victorious."

"Crossguards," Searon whispered with a chill running down his spine.

"Yes."

"Brother, I have not played since that day."

"For my support and my men…you will have to beat me. Otherwise, you will have to find your help somewhere else."

Searon nodded. "Let the games begin."

Karceoles stumbled into the chair next to Noraes and sat down with a grin. "What game are we playing?"

Noraes turned to the old man. "My brother tells me you are a wizard."

"He is correct. Has he also told you about my ravishing good looks and brilliant mind as well? For those were the three things I told him when we first met."

Noraes grinned. "Prove it."

"Prove what? My charm? Did you not just see me with those two serving maids?"

"Not that, prove that you're a wizard."

The old man looked to Searon with a questioning eyebrow raised. "Just do it," muttered Searon.

Karceoles looked around a few times to make sure nobody was watching as he held his zylek with his right hand and pointed it to his left as it made a cup. His eyes turned to orange fire as the surrounding air heated around him. A small fiery ball a centimeter in diameter rotated in his palm. With a sheepish grin, he looked at Noraes as he raised an eyebrow.

Noraes raised his left hand and glided it over the wizard's palm. An eerie chill filled the air to diminish the heat that surrounded them. The wizard's eyes flashed in surprise when his hand was covered, and he jerked it away. He clenched it and rubbed it with his other hand as a small clinking noise echoed on the table. A small round ball of blue ice spun on the table where the wizard's hand was. Noraes reached out and grabbed the small globe and dropped it in his ale.

"Unbelievable," Karceoles whispered. "You can wield magic."

Searon grinned now. He was aware of his brother's ability but was surprised the all-knowing wizard was shocked. "I thought wizards knew everything."

Karceoles shot him a look that only caused Searon to laugh.

"Noraes, your skill has improved," Searon said.

"I have been studying and training for many long years since you've been away."

Noraes snapped his fingers above his head. Within minutes, a serving maid appeared with a wink and a smile directed at Noraes. "What do you desire, m'lord?"

Searon studied her and noticed her dress was different from the other serving maids. Each serving maid had a dress half white and half black separated down the middle with large white cotton balls as buttons at the bosom. The maid in front of them was wearing a black-and-white silk dress cut past the knees with cotton fringes and balls rather than all cotton like the rest. She appeared to serve only the most important men in the pub, and besides one other table it was only Noraes to whom she directed her attention.

"Another round of ale for my friends and me, and please, bring us a Crossguard board."

She bowed. "At once, m'lord." She turned around and quickly walked away.

"Excuse me, miss," Karceoles beckoned.

She turned to look at him from the corner of her eye even though she faced Noraes.

"May I bother you to grab me a bag of dry roasted peanuts, as I traveled through this city I could not help but hear everyone boast about the quality of the peanuts here?"

"Of course, I will be back soon with your ale, game…and peanuts." She turned around and strode through the crowd.

Noraes gave the wizard a blank stare with an eyebrow raised.

Chapter Twenty-eight

The stars were out, glistening above the dark city as they reached the outside of the bunker. Starlyn smiled as she looked at the glowing specks in the sky. Her thoughts were warm after seeing Andron reunited with his family. The look on his face was priceless when he glanced upon his children again. She was taken aback when his wife came up to him to slap him. It was strange to her, but Andron had warned her of his wife's temper. Anger seemed to replace the love and loss of her husband instead of dread and sorrow.

Starlyn found the behavior of humans strange. Many of the kheshlars would be rejoiced in celebration when their family returned. Instead, it seemed Andron was punished. She only hoped they would be able to make up before he had to leave again.

It was strange seeing Sh'on again after so many years. The last time she had seen him was at the end of the draeyk wars. He had been there to help her capture Arria. Without him, she might not have ever caught her sister. But Arria could not be held for long, and she had escaped after killing two male guards. Starlyn shook her head in disgust with what she had done to them.

When they neared the barracks, Sh'on grabbed her arm. She turned around to look at him. His eyes seemed to blaze, and a smile set on his lips.

"Take your leather armor off, and put your battle armor on."

"Why?"

"Because your bosom looks better in chain mail."

"Excuse me?"

"Starlyn, please keep in mind I have already seen every inch of your flawless body before today. There is no need for embarrassment. That washed away the moment I saved you from those cells long ago."

"What are you getting at?"

"These are humans, not mere kheshlars we seek help from. Enough kheshlars drool when they stare at your body. Think of how these human warriors will react. If we are in need of allies, the best course of action would be to tempt them to follow. The way you look in chain mail and armor is nearly the most tempting thing these men could ever see. Besides, I believe a display of your fighting skills will get these men to crawl over themselves to help you."

"What you suggest is wrong, for me to use my body to inspire these men to fight; it is not something a kheshlar should do."

"Ask yourself this: To fight these creatures, to find your sister, how far are you willing to go? Without the help of these men, if they deny you, how long do you think you will survive against the overwhelming number of foes we shall ultimately face?"

Starlyn gritted her teeth. She knew the mage had a point, and a strong one at that. Even Andron's eyes could barely contain themselves from her body, and he was faithful to his love. She looked around, but nobody was in the small alley they both stood in.

"Could you shield from wandering eyes?"

"Yes, of course."

A shimmering green glow encircled them in a globe. She could see outside of it in a hazy green mist, but she knew that nobody could see within. Sh'on watched her as she unpacked her armor from her travel bag. She nearly removed her light leather armor before staring deep into his eyes.

"Do you mind?"

"Sorry, I suppose the memory has my mind craving for another glance. I will give you privacy."

He turned around with a smirk on his face and closed his eyes. Starlyn rolled her eyes as she dropped her leather armor to the ground and began securing the chain mail and plate armor. She secured her hammer on her belt and felt at her pouch with shurikens. When she was satisfied, she nodded.

"All right, Sh'on, let's go meet this army."

His green shield faded, and the two of them stepped from the alley to greet the two warriors guarding the black stone barracks. Both looked from Sh'on to Starlyn where their eyes set. She felt exposed as their eyes traveled across her entire body. A flush of red came across her cheeks as she stepped forward.

"Halt, what is your business here?"

Starlyn bit her bottom lip as she stroked the breastplate of one of the guards. "I am here to see the captain. He would not wish it if I were denied. Would you take me to him?"

The guard looked to the other before quickly nodding. "Yes, m'lady. I would be honored."

As she entered, she heard the guard behind her halt Sh'on. She turned around to raise an eyebrow at the other guard.

"Who is this?"

"That is my bodyguard; surely you wouldn't want me walking into a barracks of men without protection."

"Of course not, m'lady." He withdrew his arm and let Sh'on pass.

Once inside, they went through darkened corridors that seemed to stretch endlessly. They made many turns through the maze until finally reaching a door of finely carved stone and design unlike any other. For a city without much people or an army, they had one of the largest barracks she had seen. Of course she had not seen any other human cities, only villages.

The man pounded hard on the door with his steel gauntlets. Silence followed, making an eerie silence before the sound of shuffling papers could be heard from within. Loud clinking of boots could be heard nearing the door.

"Who disturbs me?"

The guard looked frightened and stared back at Starlyn. He seemed to snap out of his daze of lust into realization that he didn't know.

"Starlyn," she whispered.

"My Lord Etherond, Lady Starlyn wishes to see you."

The door creaked open, and a head popped out. "And who exactly is Lady—"

His breath caught as his eyes fixed on Starlyn. They seemed to travel from her boots all the way up to her face slowly, as if studying every detail. When his eyes finally reached hers, he smiled.

"Please forgive me, m'lady; do come in."

The door opened farther, and he backed off inside. Starlyn stepped in first, followed by Sh'on and quickly shut the door. She saw the puzzled look on the captain at the man in green robes behind her, but his attention quickly turned back to her.

"Starlyn, is it? I am Etherond and the captain of the army here in Wesiet. How may I serve you?"

She studied him for a long moment. He had gray plate armor over chain mail with green lining. A broadsword hung at his hip in a scabbard next to a collection of throwing knives. He had medium bronze hair that fell into his gray eyes in curls. His jaw and nose were pointed only slightly, and his face was absent of facial hair. He didn't look young but seemed wise and clean shaven. His appearance would have probably made many human women weak in the knees. A small crescent scar marked his face to the side of his right eye. His shoulders were broad and his arms muscled, but his stature was that of a leader, proud and defined.

"I am here in hope of creating an alliance between the cities to destroy the threat of draeyks from this land."

He rubbed his chin as he thought and took a seat behind his large oak desk. "Please, sit."

She sat in the only chair that was in front of his desk and glanced at the stacks of papers and maps. Several fragrant candles littered his desktop, and they spun a wide aroma of cinnamon and spice. He shuffled another handful of papers and pushed them to the side of the table along with his ink and pen.

"A kheshlar. I have not seen one of you in these parts before."

"This is the farthest I've been from my homelands."

"Tell me then, kheshlar, this alliance you seek, does it have the full support of the kheshlars?"

She shifted her gaze but didn't speak.

"Ah, so not all the kheshlars have the same hate for these creatures as you do. Why is that?"

"I hold a personal grudge for what they did to my sister."

"Ah, it is a matter that holds close to the heart. It gives you more strength than the rest. I have lost my brother to these creatures, so do not think you are the only one."

"Please help us. Join with us and strike into their lands to destroy them once and for all."

"You come to me as two and expect me to drop everything and follow you? What for, when you can't even offer the support of the kheshlars?"

Starlyn gulped. "I believe that the kheshlars will join once they see an army united…and there are three of us."

"Who is the third?"

"A warrior named Andron who left from the village of Guerettos to fight the creatures."

"So only one of that party has returned. His fighting must be impressive."

"It is."

"Still, what have you got that we do not? If I charged my own men out of here to strike without you, how would we be any less successful?" he asked.

"We have a wizard, a mage, a captain, and me. Match me against your best warrior if you wish, but I will be victorious."

His eyebrow rose as he studied her. "Is this your wizard?"

Starlyn smiled and turned back to look at a surprised Sh'on. "No, this is our mage. He is both wise and powerful."

"And your wizard?"

"He is foolish and powerful. He rides to the southern cities with our captain to strike an alliance with them."

"I see." He paused for a moment to glance at her bosom. "Still, our defenses are needed here; we cannot simply abandon our duty."

"I am not asking you to. I am asking for an army that you can spare, from this city as well as the few to the north. With enough men to march against this threat, we may be able to extinguish it."

"You do not seem as if you are much of a threat," Etherond remarked with a smile.

"Try me."

"I would enjoy nothing more." His grin broadened before he cleared his throat. "I have a proposition for you."

"Speak it."

"I will battle you, and if I win, you will join my forces to fight the draeyks."

"And if I win?"

"If you win, I will appoint a new captain in my place and gather a strong force of warriors to follow your lead."

"I accept."

He nodded and rose to his feet to the corner of the room. That side of the room was empty except for a wooden door on brass hinges that he opened. Starlyn followed him with Sh'on closely behind.

The room was ten times as large as the small office he kept his desk. It seemed to be a battle arena with weapons and pads for practice. All of the pads were worn from constant training.

"I practice my sword four hours a day; you will not find defeating me to be easy."

"I like a challenge." She smiled.

He unsheathed his broadsword as Starlyn removed her hammer. His eyebrows rose as he saw her choice of weapon. Sh'on kept back by the door as he watched with interest.

Etherond leaped forward with two overhead strikes, one on each side. Starlyn easily brought forth her hammer to block both strikes. Raising his eyebrows again, he sidestepped her and slashed at her side with a quick strike. Starlyn shifted her weight to her right and slammed her hammer on the incoming blade on her left. The broadsword pierced the matt at the ground, and she leaped toward him to strike. As he saw her, he let go and rolled backward across the mats. She leaped for him with a strike, but he ducked and tripped her. While she fell, he locked both his arms around her elbow, causing her to drop her hammer.

He stood with her hammer in his hand and a smirk on his face. She leaped away as he slammed the hammer where she just was. Her speed outmatched his, and he had to chase after her. She dived to the ground and grabbed his broadsword in her hands. He bashed the hammer at her in an array of flows from the battle-scarf form. His attacks were barely deflected and dodged by her. She was impressed with his skill with both the sword and hammer.

His anger showed, and his attacks became fiercer. The hammer seemed to shimmer with each strike, but each one was deflected with an even faster defensive blade. Starlyn held the hilt tight and slammed the sword down hard on top of her, hammer causing his entire body to shake from the force. She leaped into the air and climbed up her hammer and his arm until she sat on his shoulder with his broadsword's blade pressed against his neck. He dropped her hammer, and the ring-ing of metal echoed through the room.

"I win," Starlyn whispered.

Chapter Twenty-nine

Searon sat at a fine dark-stained oak table in front of a board game. The sound of a rocking chair squeaking in the background echoed in his ears. Karceoles sat in the rocking chair, puffing on his pipe as he watched the two of them play Crossguards. Noraes lived in a stronghold just outside of the main city so that he wasn't bombarded by traffic. It was well protected, as he was the duke of the city, but his residence wasn't overwhelmingly large. After all, he was just a duke, not a prince or a king.

Searon observed the large castle behind brother's stronghold. The duke was to protect the king of the land, and so the stronghold was placed in front of the castle in order to protect it. There were a handful of other strongholds that defended against invasion as well as the overwhelming moat that surrounded the entire gray stone castle. Most of the strongholds were made of sturdy wood that made it hard to siege. Only the castle was made of thick stone with a drawbridge and moat surrounding it. It was the size of at least three of the strongholds that surrounded it.

Noraes's stronghold appeared to be the strongest and sturdiest compared to the other four, but it was still dull in comparison to the castle. A large wall was built around the perimeter of the stronghold, and it consisted of trees standing vertical, tied together with strong twine. Peasants and serfs maintained the grounds as well as a few servants of the king while Noraes kept to his duties from within. There were only a few bedrooms inside the structure that were designed primarily for guests of the house rather than serfs or servants. Searon stayed in one while Karceoles stayed in the other. Xython didn't wish to stay in a room under Noraes and instead chose to stay in the city at an inn.

Cinnamon and clove mixed together in an exotic aroma inside the small study as Searon moved an archer into position on the board. He gently puffed on his cedar pipe with the borrowed tobacco from Karceoles. Noraes didn't care for clove spice inside his own tobacco and rather preferred a strong unflavored blend to go with his coffee drink that brewed hot in a ceramic mug. Noraes claimed to have found the beans on his travels and took to grinding them down and brewing them with hot water, much like he'd do with tea. Searon noticed the flavor was much different than tea and a lot stronger. It seemed to bring awareness to him with each sip. The effect was reversed with Noraes, where it relaxed his normally hyper personality.

Searon didn't much care for the flavor of the black strong coffee and chose to add a small amount of milk and honey to it. It sweetened it slightly to make the taste not as strong, though the strong effect didn't seem to affect Noraes or Karceoles, who had also taken a liking to the brew. He lazily rolled the dice two times, winning each turn and in place defeating one of Noraes's pikesmen. His brother scowled as he removed the piece from the board before moving his last crossbowman in position against Searon's only swordsman. His roll failed against Searon's, and the swordsman lived.

"You two have been playing for neigh a week," Karceoles bickered.

"Do you wish to have my support or not, old man?" Noraes asked.

Karceoles shifted in the rocking chair and began puffing on his pipe once more.

Searon finished his second cup of coffee and pushed it away. Within minutes, a woman appeared to clear the mug. She wore a simple slate tunic with a purse at her belt. She had deep-black hair, coppery skin, and bright brown eyes. After curtseying to both Noraes and Searon, she made her way back to the hot coffee for a refill.

"No thank you," Searon said.

She turned back to look questionably at both Searon and her master as she froze in place.

"Tea, please, if you don't mind."

She nodded and began to set a kettle of water over the fire in the wood stove. Searon watched her carefully, admiring her hard work in cooking, cleaning, and other household chores she provided for his brother. She was the only one who had her own room in the stronghold, and for a long while Searon suspected both her and Noraes to be involved.

When the kettle began to whistle, she removed it carefully and poured a mug full with a bag of black tea. She returned to Searon and handed him the mug before disappearing to do more tasks around the home. He spooned a bit of honey to stir into his drink before returning his gaze to his brother.

"What is her name?"

"Sophie. She is the housemaid."

Searon could smell the aroma of chicken and vegetables boiling in a large pot above a fire that Sophie was beginning to cook for their supper. He wondered if his brother appreciated her as he should. It had been many years since Searon had anybody tend to him, and he missed it dearly.

"When I first came in here, I was wondering how you kept this place so organized," Searon smiled.

"Come now, Brother, we both know I'm more organized than you."

"Organized in chaos. Admit it: without Sophie, this place would be a mess between pipe tobacco and coffee."

Noraes only smiled before returning his gaze to the board game. He wore blue slacks without shoes and a long-sleeve silk shirt with pearl buttons. Searon wore less noble attire with a long sleeve crimson cotton shirt with silver buttons and black breeches. Both were only slightly similar in appearance but it was their nature that they were defined as brothers rather than appearance.

"It may or may not be true. Since she *is* here, we will not have a chance to know the outcome of my existence without her."

Noraes rustled his hands through his medium-dark-blond hair, and he pondered a move on the board. After what seemed like a struggle of internal debate, he finally moved his general across the board. Searon noticed the move to conquer his archer and quickly shifted them away. With a few more moves between the two of them, Searon was able to position a cavalry piece to protect his archers.

The Crimson Claymore

Noraes scratched his brow just below his rounded brown birthmark. He had no choice but to fight Searon's cavalry even though he had no desire to. After a series of seven rolls, Searon inflicted three damage points to his brother's general. Three hits killed his cavalry, and the leftover roll was won by Noraes's chance turn with his general. It left the general with only one life, making Noraes quickly back it away from battle. However, what he didn't see was that Searon had lined up, expecting the retreat, and he moved his general piece forward to meet his brother's. After only two rolls, Searon's general defeated his brother's and created a remarkable lead for Searon.

The game still wasn't over, as the only way to truly win is to defeat all your opponent's pieces while keeping your general alive. However, for Noraes, there was no chance to win. Instead, he would have to keep the chaos of his leaderless men in check to create a stalemate like a game of tic-tac-toe without a straight line. In order for him to accomplish it, he needed to focus all of his attacks on Searon's general. Searon knew this and was swift to remove his general from the chaos of battle on the board. In many ways it was like a real battle, if your leader is down, the only way to not surrender is to take the opposing general.

"It seems you do still know how to command a force."

"Just like throwing a spear at a boar; no matter how long it has been, the talent will never diminish."

"Is your childish game over at last?" Karceoles asked, rising to his feet.

"It is still far from over. Searon still has a lot of my pieces to kill."

"Can we put these childish matters aside for now and discuss plans?"

"I still haven't decided whether to help you yet, old man. Searon has not won the game yet."

"Biscuits, you two. Well, do you at least have a map of Calthoria I may look at so I may ponder what I am to do?"

"It took you long enough to ask," Noraes said.

Noraes smiled and pointed to a rustic bookshelf stained dark mahogany and filled with books. Many of the books had leather or cloth covers and were arranged by color rather than what was inside. The shelf second to the top held books with blue binders, and the colors descended to red, green, black, and gold. At the top on the highest shelf were scrolls arranged by color of ribbons in the same manor except from left to right.

"It is but one of my many bookshelves, however, the largest scroll with a black ribbon is a well-crafted map of all of Calthoria."

Karceoles nodded and slowly walked to the beautiful bookshelf, admiring many of the books as his fingers grazed them gently. He puffed on his pipe as he inspected several of the titles before snatching the scroll from the top shelf. After opening it carefully, he wandered over to a medium rounded table and sat down, spreading the map out.

He gasped as he studied it. "Where did you get this?"

Noraes raised an eyebrow as he studied the old man. "During my travels, I came across an odd man with long blond hair, intriguing me with it. He claimed it was the most accurate map and wanted a hefty amount of gold for it. As I am a lover of literature and scrolls, I was more than content to haggle over the price only slightly before purchasing it." He ran a hand across his chin, stroking it gently. "Why do you ask?"

"This is more than a simple map of Calthoria. It is a magical map of the land that changes as things happen. I thought he destroyed the last one of these to prevent it from falling into unwanted hands...it seems he is more intelligent than I give him credit for. Instead of destroying it, he gives it to the one unlikely person that would so happen to help us on our quest where we're in need of such a map."

"Who is this person you speak of?"

"A mage. Both he and I created this map decades ago. It was actually he who came to me to request my knowledge to create such a map. He wanted to help the kheshlars in some war, and I was reluctant to oblige, but I trust him."

"I met a mage? That is interesting. I knew I could sense something odd about him."

"With practice and study, you could learn how to harness your energy where you'll be able to sense who has magic and how much they possess."

Noraes smiled. "I do not have the time for all of that, old man, I am the duke here, remember? A duke that some people wish to make king. I'm afraid any free time I have is spent relaxing."

"Or playing childish games."

"As I said...relaxing."

The Crimson Claymore

The sound of soft droplets of water began to clatter against the thin tin roof on Noraes's sturdy wooden stronghold. Before long, the rain grew louder and seemed to pound against the roof as thick crackles of thunder echoed throughout the room. Searon looked up from the game and frowned before moving a crossbowman.

"Supper is ready," Sophie called out from the dinner table across the room.

Karceoles rushed to be the first one seated despite having been farther away than both Searon and Noraes. He rubbed his hands together in anticipation. The table was set with fresh loaves of bread, chicken vegetable stew, butter, honey, milk, and a strange tan cream. They seemed to eat like kings for the week that they stayed with Noraes. He was the duke after all, but even he didn't eat so luxurious except on occasion. Having Searon back home was such an occasion, as he proclaimed.

"What is this?" Karceoles asked, pointing his dull silver butter knife toward the tan-colored cream.

Noraes smiled as he sat down. "I do recall your fascination for peanuts, and so I took the liberty of having my chefs create a peanut cream for your bread. They have only recently come up with the idea by mixing it with vegetable oils. Try it with a little bit of the apricot jam."

"There's apricot jam?"

Noraes laughed as he slid a bowl with a small spoon from behind the butter. Karceoles swiftly snatched it and sliced a piece of bread. Most of the meal was eaten in silence except for the wizard's loud chewing. Searon was only able to try a small portion of the peanut cream before Karceoles finished it. The food was excellent, with a fair amount of leftovers that Noraes had Sophie deliver to the serfs and peasants after dishing herself a plateful.

A sudden knock at the door shifted Noraes's attention for a moment. He got to his feet and wiped his mouth with a thin white cloth before setting it back on the counter. Sophie opened the door and bowed to a young man wearing bronze chain mail with a long scabbard at his hip. Rain frantically bounced from the chains on his armor, and his short red hair was soaked to the top of his head. He smiled and curtsied low to Sophie before standing up straight and winking at her. She giggled and moved aside for him to enter.

"Lord Noraes, I have come upon request," he said, holding out a parchment.

"Very good, Phoenix. I would like you to meet my brother."

Searon stepped forward and extended his hand, which Phoenix took immediately. A smile came across the man's broad lips as he scratched at his red goatee.

"A pleasure to be sure, my lord; your brother has spoken high of you over the years since his return."

"His return? Where has he been?"

"I'm afraid that is something he will not say." Phoenix grinned as he watched Noraes from the corner of his eye.

"It is not of importance where I went off to. What is important is that I'm here now, and I am your commander."

"Yes, my lord," Phoenix bowed.

"I want you to be a captain under my brother's army. He is in need of help, and who would we be not to assist him?"

"We would be ill-suited hosts indeed, my lord; what is the mission?"

"His intention is to remove the threat of the daerions…and another creature called the draeyks from this land. To cleanse them from being a threat."

"Excellent, my lord, I have much desired to be a part of such a party."

"It will not be easy, and your responsibly will at least double from the small command you have under me. Do you think you are capable?"

"Yes, my lord. I am more than capable, my lord. I will not fail you."

"Good, see that you don't. Not only will you be in charge of ten thousand of our men, but you will be advising the spies and scouts as well as communications so that if you are needed elsewhere you will be well informed."

"Ten thousand?" Phoenix whispered along with Searon and Karceoles.

"Will it be enough?" Noraes asked.

Searon stood straight, making sure his back didn't slouch in the slightest. "It will be plenty, my Brother, and I thank you for such a generous offer."

"Brother, I know these draeyks are top in your mind because of what they did to your family, but I only give you this many because I trust that you will return if we send word. If we are attacked, we will need assistance. I have left enough for us to defend, but if too strong of a force appears, I will need you."

"I understand."

"I have spoken with the king, his advisors, and the council. They all agree that this threat of the daerions is strong enough to rally an alliance to oppose them. They were also intrigued that you have a wizard with you and kheshlarn support."

"Only one kheshlar is in support of our cause."

"Shh, they don't know that. Besides, I know you'll find a way to turn that around."

Searon smiled.

Phoenix stepped forward. "A wizard?"

Karceoles smiled and stuck out his hand, "I am Karceoles the Wise. I am a wizard graced with the task of keeping young Searon here alive."

Phoenix shakily put his hand in the wizard's. "You're not going to turn me into a toad, are you?"

"A toad? Butter and salt, my boy; if you upset me that much, I will turn you into a slug and sprinkle salt on you."

Phoenix gulped, but Karceoles only laughed. "Come, young Phoenix, let me show you our plans on this map."

"So you have decided to help?" Searon asked in a whisper.

"Don't think you've got off so easy my brother. You still have to finish beating me. Besides, it will be near another week before all the forces will be ready to march. They are coming all from all over the province. Would you like to hear your numbers?"

"Surely, I would, so the battle tactics in my head can begin."

Noraes smiled. "Two thousand pikes, two thousand long spears, two thousand swords, one thousand maces, one thousand crossbows, one thousand cavalry, five hundred archers, and five hundred javelins."

"That is quite the force to match. I've never seen such high numbers with these creatures. Let us hope that with one swift strike we can all safely return home."

"That is the idea, my Brother, but I fear that there is much more going on than we can see. My heart tells me that such a force isn't enough. Let us only hope that it is."

"Dare we send for Xython?" Searon asked.

"He will learn of it soon enough. Besides, let him visit with his family for a bit longer before the lust of war clouds his judgment." Noraes brushed his hair back before grinning. "Besides, we still have a game to finish. Are you ready?"

Searon smirked. "Aye, you will not survive long without your captain."

Chapter Thirty

Starlyn stood on a grassy hilltop that looked over most of the land. Only she, Andron, Sh'on, and the human captain, Etherond, stood on the hill. Behind them, a force of nearly eight thousand men camped. She was surprised that young Etherond was able to mass such a large force in only a few weeks, yet at the same time she could sense the aura of leadership about him. Most of the men were barely warriors, as nearly half were holding pitchforks, but there still were a large amount of pikesmen and maces. The cities to the north weren't wealthy in any way, and so there were few swordsmen, less than a thousand in the army. She only hoped their determination and heart could replace what they lacked in skill. While their task had been successful in bringing numbers and heart to their cause, Starlyn still didn't feel it would be enough. She hoped that Searon had been more successful when he met his brother in the south.

There was an elderly gentleman with a sword that invented a concept weapon called a protosword. It was a wooden club shaped like a sword with sharp edges fastened with chunks of glass and obsidian. They were easy enough to make and were given to the new recruits or those without weapons. Every day there were people outside practicing with wooden swords, preparing for war.

She stared at the lavender-and-scarlet sunset of the third day they waited for Searon's return. It was true that they had expected him days ago, but she didn't fret the delay. After all, it had been years since he had seen his brother, and she was sure Karceoles was doing all he could to hasten things up. She smiled at the memory of the bitter old man and his sarcastic remarks. Being so long without seeing the two of them, she actually missed some of his bitter remarks.

As the last light dipped below the horizon, leaving the sky in twilight, Starlyn sighed. Another day had come and passed without sight of Searon. She hoped that he was all right and nothing had gone amiss. The men were growing impatient for battle despite their readiness. Etherond being the worst as his blade almost seemed to twitch for battle. Out of all the men, he was the most capable, as she noticed his skill not only from battling him once firsthand, but also from the many spars that both he and Andron engaged in each day. Both seemed matched in skill, although Etherond came out ahead more often than not.

She walked down the hill unsteadily to the company of men. Etherond and Andron had already gone back to the games and activities while Sh'on accompanied her back to camp. He seemed as anxious as her to get things moving, but she was unsure if it was to be in battle or to see his old cousin the wizard. The mage had always been much of a mystery to her, and even after the years of knowing him, she still didn't fully understand him. It had been decades since she'd even seen him, but from what she could tell he hadn't changed in the slightest.

"If he doesn't appear tomorrow, we'll have to send scouts," she whispered.

"Yes, I believe we should have sent a few today."

"Sorry, I have been going by his word when he should return…I should have realized that things could have come up. I will send scouts in the morning."

"Do not fault yourself, Starlyn, you have trust in this young man…a human. How are you fairing with the likes of them?"

"At first, I wasn't sure what to think with the rumors through Sudegam about the hastiness, hatefulness, and stupidity of them. However, after meeting both Searon and Andron, I have also found compassion, love, and wit. They are more intelligent than kheshlars give them credit for, and their compassion and love is something that the kheshlars could do with."

Sh'on flashed a smile. "I am glad you have chosen not to discriminate against them as so many of your kin have done."

"Discrimination is only for those who choose not to take the time to get to know someone. I have a friend who is discriminated against only because of what she is, when she has no choice in the matter. I protect her, and if need be, I will protect Searon and the others from the discrimination of the rest of the kheshlars."

"Kind words. I hope this Searon treasures your friendship."

She smiled. "He does."

Etherond walked up with an impatient look upon his sturdy face. "Still no sign of this army?"

Starlyn felt his deep-gray eyes stare deep into hers. "Not yet...they will be here."

"I say we strike. There is plenty of damage our force can do to the draeyks, instead of all this endless waiting!"

"Relax your bloodthirst; you will have it soon enough," Sh'on remarked as he stepped forward next to Etherond and collapsed his hand on the man's shoulder.

Etherond flinched at first, but his scowl quickly turned into a wide grin. His hand released where it clutched at his sword hilt, and he clasped Sh'on's shoulder in turn. He shifted his bronze curls from his eyes. "I'm famished."

"Let's eat," Andron suggested as he walked up next to Etherond from behind.

The two humans had seemed to form a bond in the past few weeks. Starlyn noticed that Etherond was still reticent to approach her on most matters, but she was happy that Andron was at least able to form a friendship with him. The two seemed to have a lot in common—from their love of families to morals to their respect for the creator. Etherond was constantly preaching about following the creator in his wishes and willing to speak to anybody willing to listen. Andron was most interested, as he shared the same beliefs in everlasting life in another world. Starlyn wasn't quite sure what to make of it, as kheshlars hadn't created sin as the humans proclaimed to have happened to them. Perhaps that was why the kheshlars were still gifted with eternal life, but she wasn't sure and didn't feel like getting involved. The only thing the kheshlars worshipped was nature, and respected all those whom lived among it.

"Do so away from me," Starlyn grumbled as she looked away from the men.

Without saying another word, she disappeared from sight and walked back up to the top of the hill where she sat with her legs crossed. Her mind became filled with her thoughts, and her breathing slowed so that it was too low to be heard by anything other than kheshlarn ears. A soft breeze tickled her long ears and brought a chill to her face. The last bit of light disappeared from the sky and was replaced with darkness.

Starlyn loved the night more than the day, as nothing could compare to the beauty of the stars. Her blonde hair always seemed to brighten in the starlight. It was a calm night with only a few clouds in the sky in the distance. Lightning zipped from the clouds off in the distance with a few crackles sounding nearly thirty seconds later. She was glad that the storm was far off as it would have covered the beauty of the stars. The small crackles and pops of lightning almost sounded like music in her ears. Sighing heavily, she lay down on the hill and ate a small piece of bread to settle her stomach.

She wondered where Searon was and if he was safe, yet beyond that she wondered where her sister was. It had been a long time since she had seen her sister. She was surprised when she had appeared to taunt both her and Searon. Before that encounter, it had been a few decades since she'd seen her last. She wondered if there was anything she could to do to bring her sister back to the light. Surely, there had to be some way, a hidden piece of a puzzle, that once shifted into the right place would complete it once more. She closed her eyes as she remembered the times she spent with her sister as a child. Back when the two of them were innocent, playing in fields and catching dragonflies and butterflies. Often, she wished she could return back to that time, but instead her mind faded to a dream where she felt like she was reliving it.

* * *

Starlyn awoke to a hazy pink sunrise through thick fluffy clouds. Birds glided through the sky, allowing the brisk wind to carry them on their journey to new lands. She still lay upon the top of the hill where she strayed during the night. All was silent around her except for a few murmurs between the men at the bottom of the hill in camp. A warm smile came upon her face as she whistled into the wind at the birds. There were four in the distance, but one was apart from the others, and when it heard her call, it immediately soared toward her. Its beauty was unmatched by any other bird in the sky with its head as white as the clouds and its body as brown as the bark on evergreen trees. It was a bald eagle and the proudest of the sky.

The large bird landed on her outstretched hand and blinked its eyes at her. It cocked its head as it watched her, making its beautiful bright-yellow beak glitter in the sunlight. She stroked it a few times gently on the back of its neck as it watched her. Footsteps echoed behind her, and the eagle tensed up but soon relaxed. Starlyn turned around to notice it was only Sh'on, and he smiled back at her but kept his distance.

"Can you do me a favor, oh proud one?" she whispered.

The eagle considered her for a moment before nodding its head. She smiled back at the bird and stroked its neck some more.

"Fly south, and find an army, a large army. It will have a general in red plate mail with a giant claymore sword. With him will be a foolish wizard wielding a zylek. You should notice the horse with the black-and-white stripes. Can you find them and come back to me and tell me how far away they are?"

The eagle's beak seemed to form into a smile as it nodded and leaped from her fingers and into the air. It flapped its wings and flew up high until it found a wind path in the sky, heading south. Sh'on quietly walked up and gently rested his hand on her shoulder. She didn't turn around to observe him but kept her eyes attached to the direction the bird flew.

"I was going to suggest sending a few scouts, but it seems your idea will be swifter," Sh'on laughed.

"I would go myself, but I'm afraid to leave."

"And you should be. You are needed here. Etherond is a great captain, but if anything happens and it falls to him to command everyone, I feel chaos will be his fighting style. Andron has yet to grasp any leadership himself, even though I believe he would make a great captain."

"He is young, but yes, I am in agreement."

Starlyn took one last glance south before heading down into the camp. She explained to Etherond that she sent a scout to search for them, but she withheld that it was an eagle she sent. Andron would understand because he had seen her with birds before, but Etherond would most likely question her abilities. He seemed to accept her response and didn't seem as on edge for battle as he was the day before.

Throughout the morning, he and Andron sparred each other, coming out with an equal number of winnings. Starlyn observed a few battles, but she had quite a few offers of engagement herself. It seemed many of the top swordsmen wanted to test their skill against a kheshlar. They figured they were at higher odds since she used a hammer rather than sword, but as they found out they were sadly mistaken. She even took the opportunity to really show off and battle a few of them at the same time. There were stunned expressions everywhere as they saw her defeat two or even three opponents.

Chanting began for Andron and Etherond to pair up and face her. Both the blade masters smiled at the thought but disregarded it, as if they would be too much of a challenge for her. It was that motion that sparked Starlyn's interest. She was never one to back down from a challenge, and even she admitted that facing the two would be one of her most difficult tasks. The two were masters of the blade compared to the rest and had different fighting styles that would complement each other as allies.

Starlyn faced the two of them and bowed with her hammer clenched in her hand. Andron frowned, but Etherond smirked at the chance to have a rematch with her. He stroked his bronze-hilted broadsword before flashing a few fancy maneuvers through the air. Cheers erupted throughout the crowd louder than before as everybody circled around the three of them.

Etherond leaped forward with a quick, high thrust followed by a lower one. Starlyn avoided the first by sidestepping. She slammed her hammer onto the top of the blade on its low strike, causing the weapon to embed into the ground. Andron circled onto her other side with a few rapid strikes of shimmering metal. She avoided strike after strike with a few defensive maneuvers with her hammer. When Etherond reached her other side, she grasped the shield that she seldom used that hung on her back and brought it forth to block a strong impact from Etherond's broadsword.

She didn't use her shield often except in dire need, as it slowed different attacks she could accomplish by using two hands. The shield formed into a large star with two leather straps in the back where she slid her arm through and held the top tight in her palm. It appeared silver but instead was crafted of titanium, which was one of the hardest metals the kheshlars had found. A golden trim surrounded it to match the rest of her armor with a golden *S* in the center of the outside.

Both Etherond and Andron appeared surprised when they saw her shield and frantically searched for an opening through her tightened defenses. She didn't let even an inch of play through her hammer or shield. Sparks surrounded her as they fell from her shield and hammer. Dead grass at her feet ignited in flames from sparks from the clashing weapons.

The crowd was no longer cheering or rowdy but instead was stunned into silence as they watched with disconcerted eyes. They opened the circle even farther to give them more room to fight. Most wore their jaws wide, as well as their eyes, as they studied the different moves. She only hoped that they learned a few tricks as they watched, to better prepare them for the battle ahead.

Etherond's blade broke her defenses once to strike her shoulder, and as she dashed to the side Andron's sword tripped her. As she stumbled, she threw her shield toward them, where it hit Etherond in the gut. She tossed it so the points wouldn't pierce his flesh. When she rose back to her feet, she parried with Andron for a few moments until knocking his sword down with her hammer on her left side and leaping into the air to kick him in the jaw, causing him to release his sword and tumble back. She reached down and grabbed his sword and leaped into the air into a dropkick against Etherond's chest. He tried to recover from the wind that had been knocked out of him as her foot stomped on his shoulder. She looked down at him and smiled. He sighed and let his head collapse onto the ground.

Nobody cheered, but everybody watched her intently. Andron walked over to her and bowed. She held her hand out for Etherond, who grabbed it and stumbled to his feet. Smiling at the two of them, she handed Andron his sword back and picked up her shield. As they stood there in silence, she could hear something distant in the air. She looked up and saw the eagle appear from high and glide down toward her.

Starlyn smiled and held her arm out. Everybody watched in amazement as the eagle landed on her outstretched fingers and began to chirp lightly. She nodded with acknowledgment, and the bird flew off into the air.

"What is it?" Andron asked.

"Searon is a day's march south…with an army of at least ten thousand."

"Dare we wait?" Andron asked.

Etherond smiled. "I say we rush to meet thy army; thy men are restless, and thou be ecstatic with this task."

She turned to Sh'on, who appeared through the crowd. He smiled at her and nodded. Everybody around her was still as they awaited her command. She had never commanded so many—or any humans before, and now they all looked to her. Her mind traveled as she thought; she was excited to see Searon as well and finally get everything started.

She grinned. "We march south."

Chapter Thirty-one

After a while, Searon, Karceoles, and another young man came up the hill and met with them. The army stayed down the hill and waited.

"Is this your brother?" Andron asked, trying to find the resemblance between the two men but somehow missing it.

"No, my brother wasn't able to make it; he's managing the defenses of his city. This is his captain, Phoenix."

Phoenix held his hand out and shook it with everybody there.

"This is Sh'on, a mage, who once helped us kheshlars against the draeyk," Starlyn said.

Sh'on bowed and shook Searon's and Phoenix's hands. Then he stood in front of Karceoles. "Hello, Cousin."

"How have you been, Shronan? I haven't seen you in a very long time."

"I've been traveling the universe; I always have to be where something is happening. So when this world doesn't need me, I travel to another."

"How exactly?" Karceoles raised an eyebrow.

"Ah…now that is my little secret."

"It's nice seeing you again; are you ready to get this started?"

Sh'on nodded.

"Are we going to head out in the morning?" Etherond asked.

"Who's this?" Karceoles asked, bewildered.

"My name is Etherond; I'm leader of these 'ere men," Etherond said, pointing over the hill.

"Let's give our army a day's rest; so we'll leave day after tomorrow's morning," Karceoles announced.

"The men are well rested and ready for battle."

"Ours are not; one more day isn't going to strain you, Captain Etherond."

"Let us not be bitter but instead rejoice in the presence of each other. Tonight, let there be a feast—and ale!" Xython stepped up and clasped his hand upon Etherond's shoulder.

During the night, there was a celebration of the armies. There were some who drank too much, but most only drank enough to feel a slight relaxation. Most knew that at any given moment they could be attacked or be called for an attack. Andron and those from his town pulled out the pipe weed and shared with anybody willing to try it.

In a large crimson tent around a table sat all of the captains of the armies. Searon sat at the head with Starlyn and Karceoles on his sides. The wizard was smoking his pipe with the newfound pipe weed that Andron had introduced to him. Sh'on sat next to Karceoles, watching the wizard as if he were watching a child. Beyond that, it was Andron who sat next to Starlyn with Phoenix by his side, followed by Xython, Dennark, Mattenyi, and Extodus. On the other side next to Sh'on were Etherond, Leinard, Drahcirch, and Nhorjah.

The fourteen of them sat around the table as they ate quite the feast. Many discussions were going on about battle tactics as well as the course of attack that would make the most sense. The table and tent that they sat in were removed from one of the large wagons so they could make a command center. In the morning, it would be taken down after they decided their course of action. The decisions were to be made during the course of the meal.

"I don't understand why we can't strike the heart of the filthy creatures," Etherond said with gravy dripping from his mouth and fist pounding on the table.

"Only fools rush in…you fool. What you desire will kill many more men than is necessary. There are other ways to approach this," Sh'on said.

"The element of surprise would be effective; we should bash their heads in!" Drahcirch said as he brushed his medium chestnut hair from his eyes.

"The effect could be catastrophic. What if these creatures are expecting us, or notice our large army approaching?" Mattenyi asked, scratching at his thick orange-and-white beard.

"Shall we concentrate on one focal point, or would it be best to strike in sections?" Leinard asked.

Leinard and Drahcirch were the only two who weren't wearing breeches. Instead, each wore a wool kilt, Leinard's being red, black, and white, appearing in a plaid pattern. Drahcirch's was green, black, and white with the same pattern. Both of them were from separate armies of men that joined them from far-out lands away from the city. They weren't as civilized as many of the other folk, but their fighting tactics were extraordinary. Most wielded axes or blunt weapons, but the few who held swords were powerful fighters and held large broadswords.

"If we focus too much on one location, what stops them from attacking our homes?" Nhorjah asked.

Searon sat silent, twisting his left arm back and forth while fiddling with his two pearl buttons on his crimson silk shirt. He wasn't used to wearing silk, and the texture felt odd to him. Karceoles insisted that he dress as a general when he'd be more comfortable in either his armor or a plain button-up cotton shirt. Out of all the men sitting at the table, only Searon was dressed in silk. It gave him the presence of leadership compared to the rest. Both Sh'on and Karceoles were the only ones in robes while most of the rest wore leather armor or plate mail. Searon felt lost without his crimson-crested claymore secured tightly in its scabbard. His eyes drifted to the corner where it rested on his dresser.

He was eager for the meeting to be over so he could attempt sleep once more. It didn't come often for him because of the nightmares that broke his silent dreams every night. Sometimes, it felt like he could sleep for weeks, especially with the newfound stress of leading an attack, but once he lay down, his conscious wouldn't allow him.

He found the conversational arguing between the men of different lands humorous. Most of them didn't look his way as if they were afraid to see what his opinion would be. Instead, they constantly bickered between each other in an attempt to persuade Searon one way or the other. Instead of focusing on words or ideas of what they had to say, he focused on their actions and tone. It was the best way to tell the leaders from the followers, as well as those who would be too hardheaded to control.

"There are two outcomes that could come forth from either plan. If we choose to attack as one large force, we will be able to dominate settlement after settlement of both of these creatures. However, there is the likelihood that while our backs are turned there will be losses of our own. This is the swiftest route to destroy all the creatures that spawn in this land. However, a more effective, and safer, route would be to strike in small groups, scattered, in order to keep them on edge and too afraid to separate their armies to attack our cities. It would be a constant battle of trying to feed them to our larger force. The time it would take and the strategy would be overwhelming." Karceoles paused to study Searon for a moment as he puffed his long-stem pipe. "However, it is possible, and would be more effective, as it would prevent as many losses from both our armies as well as the citizens in villages and cities."

"A valid point and wise words. I am quite impressed with you, wizard," Starlyn said softly into the silence.

Sh'on chuckled. "There are oftentimes even my cousin surprises me. Usually, his thick head and dry wit are his undoing. However, there are times I think he only uses his personality as a front to his actual knowledge."

"Can ye handle such a task, Master Searon?" Leinard asked.

"If it pleases this council, strategy has always been in my favor in Crossguards," Searon grinned.

The comment received chuckles from half of the group while the others sat in silence and seemed to stare at him in disbelief. Searon didn't understand the seriousness of some people; without a bit of fun or jokes in life, it all seemed too bland to want to continue on. Karceoles sure kept things entertaining, but he seemed borderline insane sometimes.

"If you expect us to put all our trust into one who is skilled at a child's game, then we are surely doomed," Drahcirch said.

"Have you such little faith in one who not only a wizard supports, but a mage...and a kheshlar?" Karceoles challenged.

"I have faith in you, wizard. I'll put my trust where you see fit, but don't expect me to trust foolishness."

"And what would you have us do, if this were your war to lead?"

"For one, I would not treat as a mere game. This is a war, not a mere scrimmage. This a full-scale war. There be casualties, extreme ones, and it is expected many of us will die. Let us not walk into battle blindly; let us go steady with solid aim."

"Well spoken, Drahcirch." Searon said. "I am not as playful as you would assume. I was merely trying to lighten the mood. I do have experience in leadership and tactics. Never before have I led such a force, but I am fully confident in my capabilities, as are those who sit around me."

"I accept your leadership."

"This is agreeable. If there is anywhere you think I lack, I would be more than happy to accept advice," Searon said.

"My first advice? Do not trust wizards," Drahcirch said.

Searon smiled. "That, my friend, is excellent advice."

"What is your course of action, Sir Searon?" Andron asked.

"We will scout to find the largest settlement, and when it is found we will strike it with our full force. After they are destroyed, we will separate into smaller forces where we will weaken the smaller settlements to prevent them from breaking away to savage our villages and cities."

"A fine course of action, my lord," Etherond said, shattering the silence.

Everyone seemed to agree in either nods or low murmurs. Whispers began to erupt through the tent with captains talking among themselves. Searon sat back and closed his eyes, letting the darkness consume him. A swirling image broke the darkness—of Victoria's face. At first it, was sweet and innocent, with a smile. Soon, however, it transformed into some sort of demon dripping blood, and Searon tore his eyes open, flinching.

"Are ye all right, my laird?" Leinard asked.

"Yes, yes I'm quite all right. It's only a memory of the past. Leinard, you and Drahcirch pick some men to scout south. Andron, the same north, and Etherond, you pick some of your trusted men and search east."

"What about the west?" Nhorjah asked.

"Starlyn and Sh'on will search west and meet the kheshlars. While there, make sure they are safe, and if there are any kheshlarn allies you think may help, at least pass on the knowledge of a brewing war to help protect their land."

"It will be done." Starlyn nodded her head with a toothless smile.

"This meeting is adjourned, please report back to me first thing in the morning with some news."

Everyone bid Searon farewell and exited the tent one by one. He took off his silk shirt and tossed it onto the floor, exposing his muscular chest and abdomen. His chest was covered in thick hair as well as some of his stomach. Instead of putting something else on, he walked around to his desk to begin writing battle schematics. Karceoles was the only left in the tent, and instead of leaving, he walked up to Searon and put a hand on his shoulder.

"That was well done, boy."

"If it was so well done, then perhaps you should not call me a boy."

Karceoles grinned. "Do you expect problems from Drahcirch?"

"Of course."

"Are you worried?"

"No."

"Why is that?"

"Because, despite his lack of respect for the leadership, this party has chosen, and I do not blame him in the slightest. I still don't understand why I'm to lead this expedition. His opinions of what our ultimate goal is in compliance to mine. No matter if he kills me in my sleep to usurp me as a commander, his goal is still the same. The extermination of the draeyks. That is all that matters. So long as it is finally done, it should not matter who is the one to lead these men to victory."

"Wise words from a leader."

"Wise? No, not wise, foolish. Foolish words from one who holds nothing precious in life. There is one thing left for me in this land, Karceoles, and it is not friends or family. Those are gone. I am here for revenge. If I die in the process of a good cause to avenge my family, then so be it. All it will mean is I will go with the creator sooner, and back to my family that already awaits me in the paradise land."

"Even after what happened to your family, you still believe?"

"Should I not? It is the last ounce of hope I still possess, that when this life is over, I may have the opportunity to be with them again. Do you doubt, wizard?"

"I have no doubts."

"Let me rest now, Karceoles, I have much work to do."

"As you wish…my lord."

Searon smirked as he watched the old man leave the tent. His head began to hurt with the haunting memories. They seemed to be coming out of his dreams to torment him during the day. He didn't have to last forever, just long enough to start the war. After that, it wouldn't matter who was leading them. He massaged his temples and closed his eyes to enjoy the silence. Yet inside his head, there was no silence; it was broken by the constant screams of Victoria.

* * *

At midafternoon the next day, Searon stood on the tallest hilltop, looking south. The scouts from the north and east had already returned. There was still no news from anyone from the south or west. Searon expected Starlyn and Sh'on to remain in Sudegam for a bit to visit with other kheshlars, yet the scouts from the south should have returned soon after dawn. He ordered more scouts be sent, one from each captain's party, to find those that traveled south. There was still no word from those scouts either.

"What do you think is postponing them?" Searon asked.

"I do not know, my lord; those are my best men. I am afraid there is a reason they haven't returned," Leinard said.

"I should ride south to find them," Searon said before whistling to his horse.

"No, my lord, let me send someone." Leinard grabbed his arm.

"These are my men out there, if they are in danger, then I need to be there for them."

Stripes trotted up the hill until coming to a stop at its peak. In the distance, a lone man on a horse trotted forward with three arrows wedged between his armor in his chest, stomach, and shoulder. He was still a league off and seemed as if he was being chased. Searon didn't waste any time; it did not matter to him how many were following him. The information the wounded warrior had would be useless if he fell to his foes. He didn't wait to speak to the members of his council, although he did hear their objections from behind as he galloped forward.

Searon knew those behind him couldn't see as well as he; his vision was beyond that of any human and even exceeded some of the kheshlars. He saw at least three daerions chasing the poor warrior and wasn't sure how many more were trailing behind. They almost seemed faster than the man's injured horse. If Searon didn't arrive soon, he would be lost with whatever had happened to him and the rest of the scouts.

As he galloped, he noticed something pass him from behind, or someone, rather. When he focused his eyes, he noticed that it was Starlyn with her hammer already out. Her speed excelled that of his horse, and it was a good thing she arrived just then as she blocked an incoming strike that nearly took the scout's head off. He tumbled to the ground instead as Starlyn stood over him, blocking the strikes of the three savage creatures.

Searon arrived and promptly hopped from his horse to better wield his glowing crimson claymore. Both he and Starlyn fought in unison with each other without a word from either. She seemed focused, and he imagined the news from her wasn't going to be well received. After only a few minutes the rest of his guards and council members arrived and made short work of the three creatures.

Breathless, Searon sat on the ground with the tip of his claymore embedded in the dirt. Starlyn looked down at him with a grim look upon her face, but he dare not ask her anything. Instead, he turned to the dying scout.

"What news do you bring from the south?"

"Invasion…Legain," he said with less breath than Searon.

"How many?"

"Thousands," The man said in a whisper.

Searon cursed under his breath before turning to his men. "Take this man away; get him medical attention."

Wiping the sweat that was covering his brow, he turned to Starlyn. "Are there any better tidings from you?"

"I'm afraid not. The kheshlars may not be part of this war, but they keep a close eye on the happenings of the draeyks. All their camps have been abandoned."

Searon cursed again. "Everybody pack; we're headed for Legain."

"My lord, if they've already attacked, we may not be able to make it on time."

It hit him to the heart that in his absence to seek revenge that he may have condemned his brother to death. There was no water on the planet thicker than blood, and he was not about to abandon his brother.

The Crimson Claymore

"Watch us," he whispered before pulling Stripes's reins hard.

Chapter Thirty-two

Searon pushed everybody to their limits, even himself. Everyone followed him without question, even those that were in doubts only days before. There wasn't anyone who wasn't growing weary, but they all kept their mouths shut. They knew that it was more important to reach the city in time. Many of those men were kin to those in the cities and villages of the south. The rest had already developed friendships with those of the south and were welcoming them to their homes and pubs for feasts in the north after destroying draeyks.

Most of their journey was silent because using breath would be using too much energy that could better be conserved for travel. Searon had a hard time staying behind with his men when he had Stripes that could gallop faster than any of the men could run. He knew it would be a foolish act because he wouldn't be able to fight an entire army by himself, no matter how much he wanted to. Even with Starlyn keeping his pace – the two of them were still no match. Searon did ride ahead with Karceoles and Starlyn by his side. Many of the human captains weren't far behind on their own horses as well as a few thousand cavalry.

It was impressive to say the least at the progress of the men on foot. None of them seemed to take breaks but continued walking throughout. Many had canteens and dried meat in their packs that they used while they marched. They knew it was their duty to protect the people of Calthoria and wouldn't give up hope due to tiredness. Searon was quite proud of the effort and continued to push them.

What should have taken the army two weeks by foot ended up only taking just over a week. Searon and Karceoles had made it to Legain in little over a week by horse, and yet they took several breaks between. There was no time for such luxuries on the second journey. He wasn't sure if his homeland was already being attacked or if the raids had just begun. Nothing was clear in the scouts' words other than before he could reach the cities he would be intercepted by the creatures. Either way, Searon knew that he was going to be late to come to his brother's aid. During the travel, the ravens had come with letter after letter of assistance needed near Legain. Searon cursed his luck as he read each one.

The weather became hotter the farther south they traveled. It didn't seem as hot the last time Searon passed through, but water scattered the ground in a fresh rain that seemed to bake in the sunlight. The humidity was nearly unbearable as it caked his skin in pounds of water that soaked into his cloth riding gear. He felt suffocated in a mask of a blanket that wrapped around, him yet no matter what he would do, it would never tear off.

He had taken his armor off the instant the heat rose from the morning and attached it to his saddlebags. There was little doubt in his mind that with his armor still on he would have been baked to the back of his horse like a fried egg. The heat didn't slow him or his men, though, as they trudged through the unbearable heat and rough terrain.

Birds seemed to keep a constant chirp around him that was very different from the birds around the kheshlarn capital of Sudegam. Instead of being in chorus with each other with soothing melodies, they seemed to be in competition to see who the best singer was. It was still soothing to Searon's ears as he'd rather hear that than silence. The sound of birdsongs gave him enough inspiration to continue on without giving up. Even some crickets began chirping, which added a more soothing effect.

Only when Searon danced his head around to the beats of the animals did he realize the effect was making him tired. Without but a few minutes of sleep here and there while being on top of his horse, he was growing weary. He turned to his side and noticed the wizard puffing on his long-stem pipe. Searon cursed as he forgot where he had hid his own pipe and nudged his stallion toward the wizard's horse. Without speaking to Karceoles, he snatched the pipe out of his hand and began puffing.

"Excuse me, human, what is it that you think you are doing?"

"Smoking, what are you doing...wizard?"

"I was smoking until some human brat stole my pipe!"

"Perhaps you should have held onto it better; besides, you don't need the tobacco nearly as much as I. How much longer until we arrive?"

Karceoles huffed and pulled some more tobacco out of his pouch and held it in a ring between his index finger and thumb. "Two days at this pace."

"What are you doing?" Searon asked.

"Being ingenious."

The brown tobacco burned orange, and the wizard sucked in his breath, taking the smoke into his mouth. He inhaled deeply before puffing it out into large rings. Searon only shook his head in amazement.

"Two days," he whispered.

He looked over to his side and noticed Starlyn with a lone bead of sweat trickling down her brow. Searon cursed, wishing he could be so lucky. His entire face was soaked, and his hands pruned as if he had spent hours swimming in a pond. Still, Searon knew kheshlars weren't even supposed to sweat, and so he knew that Starlyn was tired. She didn't show it, but he could tell after having known her for a short while already. It was obvious to him while other humans would be oblivious to it. Sweat was a sign of tiredness for a kheshlar, same with the expression of dread. Her lips were closed tight together, and her eyes stared straight ahead. She didn't seem to glance about to inspect her surroundings as she normally would.

He studied her as a few more beads of sweat came across her face, almost making a light coating. It was still nothing compared to that of the humans surrounding them. Even Karceoles was drenched in sweat with his salt-and-pepper hair slick against his neck. Starlyn shivered and quickly turned her head east. She shook her head and turned her face forward once more. Her head jerked to the east once more, and she looked up to Searon. She stopped in her tracks and looked to the east indefinitely.

"There is no wind…" she whispered.

Searon had to bring his horse to a stop and trot back toward her. When he reached her, she still didn't look at him, but her hand was on the hilt of her hammer.

"What?" he asked.

He tried to follow her gaze and comprehend her words. His mouth moved to form what she said. *There is no wind.* He knew there was no wind; wind would have made the heat bearable for him. Without the wind, he and all of his men were drenched in layers of sweat. He noticed more sweat caked against Starlyn's nearly flawless face and studied her.

"I can hear the leaves," Starlyn said quietly. She dared not turn to look at Searon but continued to stare at the bushes at the edge of the forest.

He turned to the bushes where she stared with caution. There was a pair of sapphire eyes glaring through the trees. They were staring at Starlyn with such ferocity that it rendered her speechless. It was shocking that such a beautiful blue could be considered so deadly.

"Daerions!" Starlyn yelled.

Realization dawned on Searon. They were at the edge of the forest, almost out of it. Had they continued on and left the forest to the downward slope toward the first city by the river, they would have been exposed to an attack from behind. The attack would have been devastating because they would have had to fight uphill and would have been caught by surprise from behind.

He could still only see the sapphire eyes, but he trusted Starlyn's judgment. She already had her hammer drawn and clenched tight in her hands. Searon withdrew his claymore from its scabbard and stared into the trees. The crimson glow sparkled through the shady trees, and everyone looked up at him.

"Weapons!" Searon yelled.

All of the cavalry and captains on horses pulled their weapons and formed into battle ranks. Many of the warriors on foot were still a league behind, with a few scattered between to keep rank. Still, Searon knew he couldn't count on them for this battle and hoped the cavalry troops were worth their salt as warriors. Karceoles had his zylek already out glowing orange in anticipation. Andron and Etherond were a league behind with the rest of the men to help lead them, and he wished they were up front. Searon knew of Andron's skill already, but he had heard from several men that Etherond had bested Andron on numerous occasions.

He watched as a few hundred sapphire eyes appeared and rough-skinned blue bodies appeared from the bushes. It was a strange sight to see blue creatures able to disappear through the shadows of green bushes. If he hadn't seen it in that moment, he would have never believed it. He rushed forward to meet the creatures in battle and crossed his blade against a spiked mace. The two of them danced in a flurry of attacks both high and low. Each strike was expertly defended by the other. Searon wished the blue-skinned creatures were as pathetic as the draeyks in fighting, but these put up a hard fight. It almost seemed as if a master at arms was the one who had trained them. Finally, he was able to slide his metal between the creature's defense to slice off one of its horns, followed by its head.

When he turned to his left to block an incoming creature, he failed to notice another come from his right. A blunt mace caught him at the ribs at half force that knocked him from his saddle. He was glad for his horse's movements to try and avoid the attack, or it could have been much worse. When he rose to his feet, he spit dirt out of his mouth and tried to get the dry taste from his mouth. His claymore was still clenched in his hands as he stepped forward. Stripes trotted away from the battle, though he still remained useful. When a daerion would stray, Stripes would kick it hard with his hind legs before dashing away in another direction.

Searon stepped forward, welcoming a daerion to come toward him, but instead of only one, three stepped forward. He clenched his teeth. *So be it.* He fought gallantly against the creatures but was barely able to hold his own. A few times, he was able to inflict a few slashes against the faces of the creatures, but there was little more than that he could do.

At his side, a strange flashing green light flickered where nothing stood. He watched it from the corner of his eye for treachery and nearly froze in shock with what appeared. A man with thick eyebrows and yellow hair as bright as the sun appeared in green robes. He was weaponless, but his hands flared an emerald green to match his cold eyes. The same glow encircled the three daerions in front of Searon before what seemed like a strong wind tossed them backward.

"Could you use some help, Master Searon?" the man asked.

"Sh'on? I thought you were at the back for defense."

"I was...though it seems I am much more needed up here. I could not entrust your life with the likes of that wizard. He won't even notice you in the heat of battle. Besides, it does not take too much energy to teleport up here."

"Nothing better happen to our back lines on your watch," Searon muttered.

"Spoken like a true general, I commend you on your effort. I know we have not been properly introduced. I am Shronan Onderon, mage of Calthoria, and old ally of Starlyn during the draeyk war."

"Not that I mind introductions, but I hardly feel this is the time."

"Yes, I understand; what is our plan to defeat these creatures?"

Searon looked at him and then back to where the majority of the battle was being fought. Karceoles shot flame after flame at creatures, burning them to a crisp and turning their blue-skinned bodies black. Between uses of magic, he used his zylek as a staff and fought against the blunt weapons of the creatures.

"Are you as powerful as Karceoles with magic?" Searon asked.

"No, but I am wiser in how I use my power. Fire takes up a lot of energy; I would never be able to do such a feat as he. Instead, I use simpler spells. Air takes up less energy, and the highest I'll go with elements is ice because it's more effective in smaller doses than fire."

"Follow me, and use your knowledge to slow the creatures that I fight and anyone around me fights."

"As you command," Sh'on said.

Searon dashed forward and fought against the three daerions that the mage had pushed back. It was so much more effective with Sh'on behind him as his magic froze a few attacks and tossed other ones backward. A battle that should have taken nearly half an hour only took a few minutes before all three creatures lay dead at his feet. The mage was right that his power was used wiser than the wizard's. It had a larger area of effect while Karceoles only shot down one creature at a time. Karceoles couldn't even create an area of effect with his fire otherwise to cause damage to their own men.

"Reckless fool of a wizard," Sh'on said under his breath as he looked to Karceoles.

The wizard was shooting fireballs that appeared to be getting out of control and harming the humans surrounding the creatures. Many had to flee back to roll on the ground and put themselves out. Searon stepped up to Starlyn's side, and both fought next to each other in almost a rhythmic dance to defeat creature after creature. There were only a few hundred, and the more Searon thought about it the more he came to the conclusion that the force was only meant to slow them down and cause them casualties rather than destroying them.

The battle was going in their favor, but there were still many casualties that Searon wished hadn't occurred. There was limited archer support with many of their archers farther back. Some had caught up and began supporting them since they were able to travel faster with their limited armor. Starlyn seemed preoccupied as she battled looking away from the foe in front of her to another in the ranks. Searon glanced to where she was looking and noticed a larger more muscular creature seeming to bark unintelligible orders to the others. He had no idea such creature would have a commander, although it would make sense. His assumption had been their commander would have been a human or kheshlar or something with higher knowledge. He wondered how intelligent the creatures were.

"They have a commander," he whispered to the mage.

"I assume so, as their attack is coordinated," Sh'on whispered.

"Southeast thirty paces, the larger one with a scimitar, do you see him?"

"Yes."

"A leaderless army is chaos, can you create a path to him?"

"I can," whispered Sh'on.

"Do it."

He turned and looked at Starlyn, who only nodded. She stepped back and let him lead the attack with the length of his glowing claymore. From her sash, she removed a handful of shurikens. She glanced around and studied her opponents hard before releasing them. Searon smiled as he noticed the daerions surrounding the commander began falling. Many were only injured rather than killed by the shurikens, but with them weak they would be easier quarry. Air surrounding a dozen of the creatures became thicker and turned green before they were raised off their feet and tossed across the ground.

Searon turned and noticed on the other side Karceoles led men to keep them away from him as a distraction. He doubted the wizard knew what he was doing, but he dared not convince him of battle tactics. Searon sliced down daerion after daerion as he made his way toward the captain. Men rushed in behind him to finish off the injured creatures that both he and Starlyn had weakened.

Starlyn stood next to Searon as they faced the daerion captain. Its eyes seemed to sparkle before a twisted smile came across its face. The scimitar rang as it pounded it against its chest before diving toward both Searon and Starlyn. Starlyn tried to throw shurikens at the creature, but each one was either deflected or dodged. The daerion captain put up quite the fight with Searon and Starlyn, showing its superior fighting skills.

The creature's scimitar grazed Searon's elbow, and he cursed, wishing he had his plate mail on. He knew that in the heat it would be of little use and would only succeed in tiring him. Starlyn crushed the creature's left hand in a swipe with her hammer, but the act only enraged the monster, causing it to push both Searon and Starlyn back.

"Sh'on!" Searon screamed.

He turned to see the mage up against his own band of foes. At least three daerions surrounded him, and he continued to use magic to knock them away, but only more sprang at him. Still, he turned and saw Searon in peril and held out a glowing left hand that shot energy at the captain daerion. The creature only faltered a step back rather than being knocked airborne, but it was enough for Searon to dash forward and sliced its left hand off. The advantage only lasted for a moment as the creature dashed toward them and moved its blade so swift that it was barely noticeable.

As soon as a break came, Searon stepped back and looked for a weakness in the creature's attack. It was unlike the rest of its comrades in that its attacks seemed almost flawless. He couldn't quite place it, but he knew there was a weakness in there. Starlyn dived and rolled around several attacks before rushing to his side.

"His confidence," she whispered.

"Excuse me?"

"You're looking for the creature's weakness. Confidence; it has too much confidence in its ability."

"Do you want the kill?" Searon asked.

"You have a plan?"

"Yes, don't fret on my fall; use it to your advantage, but do not think you do me any favor by acting foolish over it."

She smiled, already knowing his plan.

He dashed forward with a slash that was easily deflected, before stepping back. The creature snarled at his taunt and sprang toward him. Starlyn stood on the side, offering a few blows. Its focus was on Searon, and while it contained Starlyn it stepped toward him. He kept his attacks steady and stepped forward with a clumsy foot that twisted in the dirt, causing him to stumble. Without missing a beat, the creature took advantage and knocked the claymore from Searon's hands. He stepped back with a gulp before tripping over his own feet. The creature drove Starlyn back before turning to Searon that lay on the ground. Two slashes were dodged by Searon before jumping to his feet and pulling a dagger from under his leather that he stabbed through the sword hand of the creature. It shrieked loudly before turning around and into the square of Starlyn's hammer that crushed its skull in.

Echoing shrieks came from the surrounding creatures as they saw their leader fall to the ground. Daerions everywhere stopped fighting and dashed through the forest north. When the attack first began, there were nearly three hundred creatures, and yet it was less than a hundred that retreated.

Sh'on stepped forward and clasped his hand on Searon. "Well done."

"Tend wounds where you can, and continue forward. There is little time to waste," Searon said.

He turned, and his horse came trotting up to him. With a sigh of relief, he hopped up on the animal and continued the rest of the way out of the forest. When he broke through the clearing, what he saw brought chills to his bones. Black smoke rose in the sky from Erdunadir by the river. The village appeared in ruins, although its damage couldn't be determined from such a far distance.

"No time to waste," Searon whispered as he urged his horse forward to a gallop.

Chapter Thirty-three

The city of Erdunadir lay in ruins. Stables were burned, and homes were thrashed. Bodies littered both the streets and homes where they fell. The smell of vinegar lingered fresh in the air from the blood that scattered the ground. Corpses were horror-struck, and the dried blood was only a day old.

Everybody was silent as they marched behind Searon. He was too late to arrive at Erdunadir, and despite their defenses they had been no match for whatever force desecrated them. He felt sick from the carnage. It took a long time until anything could be seen besides mangled human bodies torn limb from limb. Searon noticed first and rode toward it. A daerion lay on its stomach where it had been bested by two warriors. Both of those warriors lay dead just beyond the creature.

"I should have never left," came a raspy voice from behind him.

Searon turned around to see Xython grabbing at his short, curly black hair. His bright teeth were gritted behind his ebony lips. He looked around at the carnage in disgust as he clenched the hilt of his mace.

"You would have been dead as well," Searon whispered.

"An honorable death, with more than just one creature dead around me."

"At least ten would have been dead by your spiked mace, old friend, but it would have done everyone little good. You are much more valuable alive. Now you will be able to kill much more than ten, and with enough deaths you can avenge all those whom we lost today."

Xython cursed under his breath, "Yeah, you are right. I still don't like it."

"Neither do I."

Karceoles urged his horse forward, where he stopped by the sign of the Dancing Donkey. It had fallen off the brass chain that kept it above the door and lay crooked on the ground at the step. Most of the walls had been burned down, and dozens lay dead near half-charred tables. The wizard didn't get off of his horse but led the animal into the ruins of the bar, where he poured himself a tall mug of ale from the only untouched barrel. When he finished, he slammed the mug on the bar, where it crumbled underneath his touch and collapsed to the ground.

He turned to the stage where a lone body was burned and bloody under a tangle of black hair. Karceoles got off of his horse and walked slowly forward with his zylek shaking in his hand. He rolled over the body, and recognized the face as Annettera's, one of the dancers. She must have been entertaining during the attack.

Searon walked up next to him and clasped his shoulder in comfort. He offered the pipe he had stolen from the wizard, which Karceoles took violently. After a few puffs, the wizard drew in his breath and sighed.

"Are you all right?" Searon asked.

"Where is Berethana?"

"Who?"

"Her sister, the other dancer. She should be here with her sister if they were on stage together."

Searon looked around but saw nothing. "I do not know, my friend."

Karceoles began frantically looking around, moving around rubble as he searched. There was a determination about him that Searon knew he wouldn't be able to mellow. Instead of fighting it, he began to look around as well, joining the search with the wizard; the other warriors began searching as well. A small group of men went up the creaky steps to search the rooms of the inn.

Within a few minutes, a man hollered from upstairs, and the team of them came down holding a naked woman with blonde hair who shivered in their arms. Tears fell from her eyes, and blood streaked her face. A few scrapes and tears fell across her naked body but nothing severe. It seemed she had survived the attack almost unscathed.

"Please…" she whispered. "Please, don't rape me, please, please…don't."

Karceoles walked up and took her out of the warriors' arms. "Quiet, girl, nobody here will harm you. I promise you."

She looked up into his eyes and brought her shaky hand to his face. "Wizard? Is that you?"

"Yes, Berethana…it is I. Everything will be okay."

"It was horrid, fire was everywhere, people burned—my sister…she screamed from the fire that consumed her before those creatures came in and…and—"

"The fire came first? Why are you not burned?" he asked.

"I-I don't know. It was all around me. My clothing was caught on fire, but I didn't feel the heat. When the creatures came, I hid, but the only place I could hide so they couldn't see me was in the fire."

Karceoles's eyes flickered, and he looked around until settling his eyes on Searon's. "Shh, it's okay now. Everything will be okay."

He brought her over to his horse and tucked her in blankets before turning around to look at Searon. After a long breath, he walked forward with his eyes glancing around at the others surrounding the warrior.

"Survivors…search the village for survivors," Searon said. "Go, now!"

Everybody scattered out of the pub and into the streets. Searon took a step toward the wizard while glancing at the young dancer bundled up in blankets. He looked around at the carnage and the smoldering wood.

"What's wrong?" Searon asked.

"She's not burned. She hid in the fire…and she's not burned."

"What does it mean?"

"It means that my seed is inside of her. The seed of fire."

Searon nodded. "So what does this mean?"

"She must be protected. Fire cannot harm her, but our enemies can. She is the first to hold the seed of a child in near a century."

"What happened to the rest? I know for certain that she has not been your only conquest."

Karceoles's face turned grim as he looked toward Searon. "They have disappeared, or the seed hasn't taken. It is already very rare that a seed will hold; not all wombs are suitable for wizards."

"Disappeared?" Searon asked.

"Killed sometimes, or vanished. Wizards are a near-extinct race. Besides a few novices or those who keep themselves hidden, I am the last remaining wizard."

"Will you protect her?"

"Yes, she will be safe with me."

Searon nodded and walked out of the pub. He nearly walked into the mage in the chaos of the village. Everybody scurried from one place to another, and to Searon's surprise survivors were being found everywhere. He watched as they were being pulled from crumbled buildings and rubble.

"How many survivors have been found?" Searon asked.

"Thirty one, five of whom won't survive the night," Sh'on said.

Searon nodded. "Give those five a tall mug of ale and some food, and make them as comfortable as you can with bales of hay. Then we march; there is no time to waste."

"One is a small child, a girl, no older than the age of twelve."

"A child...Charlotte..." Searon whispered.

"Charlotte?" Sh'on asked.

"Nobody, do not worry about it, she is not from this village. Is there nothing you can do? All this magic that both you and Karceoles have, and you can't even save a small girl?"

"I am limited with healing, Lord Searon; what I can do I must save for those who can survive. Besides, I can only heal what is there...and some of her insides are...missing."

Searon's stomach twisted in disgust, and he spat on the ground. He sighed heavily until shaking his head and turning to the mage. "I will see to her, but you must take care of these other four. If there is to be any chance of Legain surviving, we must make haste."

"As you wish." Sh'on bowed and pulled his cloak to his side as he turned and strode off.

Chapter Thirty-four

Searon stared into the distance toward the gates of Legain. An army of daerions crowded its front gates, laying siege to the walls, and yet relief spread across the captain's face. They hadn't broken through the gate yet, and Legain's defenses were strong. His brother had made sure of that. He watched in pride at the crossbow men along the wall's crenellation as they fired down upon the creatures. He knew they wouldn't be able to hold long as fires had begun on the stone. In the midst of all the blue creatures, he noticed something amiss. There was a lone person on a black stallion with a long staff who appeared to command them.

The number of daerions was more than Searon could have imagined. At least three thousand fought at the gate of Legain, and many of them tried climbing the thick walls. Whoever sat on the horse appeared to be a magician and used his power to create black fires on the walls of the great city. The gate seemed to be weakened, and a few hundred of the creatures carried crossbows that killed several of the humans atop the walls and towers. He watched as the hundreds of creatures trying to break down the gate suddenly moved away. The magician stood alone against the gate and shot magic from his staff that shattered the gate into a thousand pieces of metal and stone.

"A dark wizard?" Searon whispered.

"A warlock," Karceoles said at his side.

The thousands of creatures began flooding into the gates of his home city. Rage pulsed through Searon's veins. He was already uneasy as he watched the young girl die just the other day in the small destroyed village. There was little he could offer her except comfort and a small taste of the wizard's last jar of peanut paste.

He turned around and raised his claymore to cavalry and infantry alike. "Men, these creatures are slaughtering your families. Show them no fear, show them no mercy! Destroy them all! Charge!"

Searon quickly sheathed his weapon and kicked the side of his striped stallion. He was hoping to delay for a time while the rest of the men on foot could catch up, but there was no longer time. The gates of his former city had been demolished, and to make matters worse, some sort of warlock appeared to be leading them.

Starlyn ran at his side and thrust her golden hammer into one foe after another. She pulled her shield up high to deflect scimitars as the strikes came at her. Rain began to fall from the cloudy sky and covered her in large droplets of water. Searon wondered why she cared so much. He knew that she was desperate to find her sister, but she had bonded with him and the rest of the humans. She would protect them with her life and he wasn't quite sure why. Lightning illuminated her golden shield with scattered designs of blue leaves across the front. Searon fought by her side, making sure that she was well defended.

Searon slid on his crimson-and-gold helm before making his first slash with his glowing claymore. In the heat of battle, he looked like every other warrior, with no significance toward his leadership. He was careful not to be on the front lines to bring attention to himself, although his cunning swordplay as well as the striped stallion he rode gained him enough unwanted attention. Starlyn stayed by his side on the ground and kept him well defended as well as a few of his guard. Karceoles the wizard wasn't too far away, either fighting alongside the mage Sh'on with complimentary magic spells, though each focused on different directions.

The daerions were strong creatures in spite of how short they were. Most carried short swords, yet their brute strength was all they needed. Searon watched as one of the daerions reached and grabbed one warrior off of his horse by the neck and crushed the man with bare hands. Arrows soon took the creature, but it took nearly a dozen before it dropped to the ground with dark-sapphire blood pouring from its twisted mouth.

Etherond and Andron fought east of Searon and brought a lot of attention to themselves as Etherond blew through a ram's horn. The sound rallied his men to him to fight in an oval, and yet at the same time it caused the creatures to suspect him as a leader. Searon wasn't as worried about delivering deathblows as he would have been in the past. He knew there were warriors behind his ranks that had the sole task of making sure fallen foes caught their last breath. His mission was to injure them and knock them onto their feet.

No matter how hard they fought the creatures from behind, it did little to stop them from flooding into the gates of Legain. The warlock was in their center, but he stayed by the gate to usher the creatures in. He shot magic out of what Searon could only assume was his zylek toward any human that seemed to be a threat. Searon wasn't so sure he could stop the magic, and was wary about approaching the dark magic user. He knew that some form of defense was needed to prevent as many of the creatures as they could from entering the gates. Noraes would have his defense ready for sure, but against the savage beasts the casualties would be hefty. There were a few thousand of them, and while Searon had at least four times the number, his men were still forming rank toward the city with many still a league away. He looked around until he spotted both the wizard and the mage.

Searon rode his stallion up to the mage. "Can you reinforce the entrance to Legain?" He half screamed to be heard.

Sh'on turned to look at Karceoles, who only nodded in response. The wizard clutched his zylek tight and shot a flame of orange energy into the daerions that caused them to separate long enough for both Karceoles and Sh'on to ride through the middle of their ranks toward the gate.

When he turned back around, he noticed Starlyn was fenced in by five daerions and having a tough time defending herself with only a hammer and a few humans around her that seemed to drop like flies to a frog. Searon jerked his stallion's reins, causing his companion to gallop back toward the kheshlar.

He reached the kheshlar in what seemed like the nick of time as he decapitated a creature that she hadn't noticed behind her. Her eyes bulged as she stepped over the severed head to dodge another strike.

Six humans lay dead around her; that had died protecting her. Searon pushed a few of the creatures back, but it wasn't until Leinard appeared by their side in his green-and-black kilt that the tide seemed to change to their favor. Leinard had a claymore similar to Searon's except its hilt was silver and green in color and its blade didn't glow crimson as Searon's did in battle.

Half of the daerions seemed to be through the broken entrance before the wizard and mage reached it. A small flash of greens, oranges, and blacks appeared as they fought the warlock before the man garbed in black cloaks backed off with his black stallion. He didn't appear to want to fight against two with magical powers.

Karceoles began weaving his zylek into complex patterns, creating an orange horizontal barrier in front of him in place of the shattered gate. Sh'on spent his time sending green flurries of power out in front of them to push oncoming daerions away. He didn't bother using large amounts of energy when it appeared he would need to save his strength for whatever the wizard had planned. Searon knew that they would need help and Sh'on would eventually have to combine his powers with the wizard for a secure defense.

He galloped his striped stallion forward and grabbed Starlyn by the elbow as he did, lifting her onto the back of his steed. At first, she protested, but he didn't allow her an opportunity to object further. Searon rode back north and away from the force of confused daerions.

"To me, to me!" he cried. "Create a path to the gate; we must defend it!"

With that order, Leinard broke off with his men, and a few hundred men in kilts charged through the center ranks, carving a path toward the mage and wizard. They didn't bother killing anything in their path but focused on injuring to increase their speed. Daerions were driven back on each side while others stepped in to battle against them. Searon strode his horse right behind Leinard until he stopped in front of Sh'on and Karceoles. They were on the other side of the magical barrier, but no longer did Sh'on have to distract himself with the creatures.

Searon saw through the gate and saw his brother surrounded by a dozen men fighting inside of the city. A rapier was in his right hand while his left glowed a deep blue with magical energy. He seemed to toss daerions across the yard with his magical fist as he sliced others down with his rapier. His speed with the thin blade made all the difference against the heavier weapons and slower creatures.

A shriek and snarl shattered the battle cries, and the man on the rider with the black cloak reared back on his horse. His horse stood on two legs and kicked the air in rage as he shouted. "Kill them! To the gate, kill them, and destroy the city!"

"Now!" Karceoles yelled.

Searon turned back around and began holding the defenses of the gate with Starlyn by his side. Behind him, a flicker of green formed that seemed to intertwine with the horizontal magic in a vertical pattern that created a series of off-color magic boxes. Everything vertical was green while all the horizontal magic was orange. Where the two magic forces met, it was a mixture of the two colors – making it a black with green tint.

The daerions didn't seem to consider the magic as they charged. There was little regard for the defenders and their weapons as the creatures seemed to charge right over them and into the magical gate. When they came into contact with the magic, they seemed to catch fire and freeze at the same time. They became a fire that shattered into a thousand pieces of broken ice. Searon thrust his claymore into any that came close to him, and soon the creatures turned away in fear.

A loud crackling of black lightning thickened the air and shot out in every direction. Searon watched as many of his men fell victim to the charged energy and fell to the ground, lifeless. Enough of the magic came toward him to cause him to stumble as well as those around him. Even Karceoles and Sh'on were affected and lost control of their spell. However, a cloud of black smoke appeared until it became a great fog, and when it disappeared – so did the warlock.

"Torches," Karceoles muttered.

Most of the daerions outside of the gate were missing as well, and after their army slaughtered what was left, they entered the city. Searon stepped up alongside his brother, Noraes, as they finished off the creatures inside of the city.

Soon swords were raised, and men began chanting, "Victory!"

Searon took off his helm and attached it on his armor and clasped his brother in a hug. Noraes's armor wasn't so far different from his brother's. Rather than crimson and gold it was silver and blue, but much of it was the same style. His rapier didn't glow blue as Searon's claymore glowed red, but his hand took care of the complimentary colors when it filled with magic.

Karceoles's brow was full of sweat as he stepped up and shook Noraes's hand.

"Well fought," Noraes said.

"I'm sorry, Brother, I should have kept better scouts," Searon said.

"Nonsense. You could not have foreseen this. They had a wizard with them."

"Warlock," Karceoles corrected. "Wizards are better looking."

Noraes smiled. "Warlock. He probably saw you and waited until you were too far away before he began his attack. This is no folly of yours. However, Brother, I will need men back now. I can't fall victim to this again and must reform my defenses."

"Of course. As many as you need, both north and south men alike."

Noraes looked at the army before him and seemed in awe. There were near twenty thousand men and the largest force to be under one banner that the land had seen in centuries. Small house flags were held by banner men, and yet most were the red flag and gold claymore. Searon Claymore they called him, and hung his banner high and proud.

Starlyn walked up next to Searon before removing her golden helm. Her lovely golden hair fluttered behind her head and sparkled in the twilight. Noraes seemed taken aback and turned to gape at her. Only when she finished untangling her hair with her hand did she notice him, and he lowered his gaze and coughed. Her cheeks seemed to turn a slight shade of red, if only for a second.

"My lady," he shifted, "I am Noraes, captain of Legain."

She smiled. "I'm Starlyn of Sudegam."

He extended his hand to her, and when she took it he brought it to his lips and kissed the ring mail gloves upon her hands. She blushed as he nodded to her and smiled.

"It is a great pleasure to meet you, Lady Starlyn, to be sure," Noraes continued, still not letting go of her hand.

Searon smirked. "I hate to shatter your thoughts, dear Brother, but our men are tired and hungry."

"Of course, of course. There will be a huge feast to celebrate our victory," Noraes announced, turning to his brother and finally releasing Starlyn's hand.

Chapter Thirty-five

Searon sat at the crowded oval table, staring across to look at Noraes and Starlyn as they conversed with each other. He found it odd how quickly the two seemed to form a bond. His brother had always been quick to sway a woman in his direction that he had interest for, and yet it still surprised Searon that a kheshlar could be affected so. It was the kheshlars that were supposed to be the fair folk that all others toppled over themselves to please. Instead, it was Starlyn that seemed to blush with embarrassing smiles at his brother's remarks.

Surrounding them were the primary captains of the battle scattered about feeding themselves thick slices of ham and mashed potatoes. Andron sat next to Etherond and talked about the creator while Sh'on and Karceoles spoke about magic on the other end. Karceoles only had a plateful of bacon and a jar full of peanut spread with a wooden spoon.

Starlyn seemed uneasy to be so close to the thick smell of meat, and yet it didn't seem to bother her as much as she sat in Noraes's company. Noraes didn't have any meat on his plate in respect and only ate the bread, corn, and potatoes as she did. Searon hadn't told him that kheshlars didn't eat meat, although the folklore about the species stated it bluntly enough.

Most of the rest of the army was out in the streets in Legain, opening barrels of whiskey and ale to celebrate. Searon only hoped that their celebration wouldn't be too hard in case there was trouble throughout the night. They had won the battle, but the war was far from being over. All of the human captains seemed content with talking about the war and different battle tactics they could use to destroy the savage beasts of the land. Searon lost focus and began eating. Nobody seemed to talk to him, and he didn't much care for trying to talk to anybody. The only thing on his mind was food. He did begin tuning into his brother and Starlyn.

"Are all the kheshlars as beautiful as you?" Noraes asked.

"All kheshlars are a distinguished race of beauty," Starlyn respond-ed, yet she couldn't help but to smile as she did.

"Still, I doubt any compare to you," he smiled with his eyes fixated on hers.

"How would you know, have you ever met a kheshlar?" Starlyn asked. "You'll just have to find out for yourself."

"In fact, I have met a kheshlar, several of them, truth be told. Yet that is another story from a faraway land. I have not met any of your kin, and perhaps one day I will. For now though, my responsibilities of this city keep me here."

Searon scowled at that as he lifted his glass of red wine and drank a mouthful. His brother never told him that he'd seen kheshlars before. He began to wonder what all his brother had been up to in the past few years.

"Can all kheshlars fight as well as you can?" Noraes asked.

"Most," Starlyn confessed as she nibbled on a piece of bread.

Everything became a blur to Searon as he unfocused his attention from reality and let his mind consume him. Memories of his son and wife flooded into his mind like a downpour. Nothing around him seemed to matter at he focused on her face. He missed her so much, and some days were harder than others. When he fought, he was able to release his emotions once more as his blade slashed into the air and through bodies. It was his release of anger and frustration of his loss that kept him close to sane.

Forty-two months and eight days had passed since the slaughter at his home. He still didn't know how the number stayed in his head. Somehow, he just knew, and that was the fact that scared him. No mat-ter how much he could accomplish during the day and no matter how many of the creatures he slaughtered, he still could not forget exactly how long ago it was that he lost his family. That at its core was what tore him up inside. He thought if he could at least forget the number, the internal clock that continued to tick with each passing second, that he might be able to cope and move on. However, something in his mind wouldn't allow him to do so.

He got to his feet, stumbling as if he was drunk, and yet it was only a bottle of wine that he drank. Everything swirled in colors around him as he wearily walked from his brother's keep. People stared at him uneasily, and yet he did not seem to notice. Nothing mattered in his mind, nothing except for fresh air. He couldn't breathe as the memories haunted him. His face turned red with the shortage of breath, and he stumbled from the room and into the brisk cool night air.

The stars were especially bright that night. They always seemed so every time Starlyn was in a bright mood. He wondered if there was any significance to that aspect and her namesake. Nobody seemed to be outside in the streets, and he wandered aimlessly until tripping over something and crashing to the ground. His stomach twisted as he released its contents. Everything he had eaten was now before him in a steamy pile that gave off an ill scent. He heaved two more times before crawling forward and resting his back against a short wall of stone brick.

Noraes walked up and stopped a span from Searon to stare in disgust. He walked around the bloody vomit until he sat down next to his brother. His hand clasped Searon's back before he sighed.

"Is everything all right, Brother?" Noraes asked.

Searon coughed, "The memories…the nightmares came back. As they often do."

"It is a terrible thing that you have gone through. I wish there were words I could use to ease your mind. All I can say is give it time. How much, I do not know. Yet I think this war will help you find the peace that you so desperately seek."

"All I want is this war to be over; it grows tiring," Searon confided, clasping his face in his hands and running them through his thick hair.

"I thought there was to be no rest for you until every last draeyk had been stricken down."

"I still plan on it, yet I haven't rested in so very long. I miss my peace, my family, but I will never have that again. What happens when this war is over? If I'm still alive after we've hunted down every last creature to see their dying breath? What am I to do then? Right now, this rage inside of me is the only thing that keeps me going. Without it,

I would be consumed by the nightmares, curled up into a little ball, clutching at myself and never wanting to move. Will that be what I turn into once I'm done with this? Will all my energy be vanquished when I'm through? What could I possibly turn to in order to be all right?"

"I will always be here for you, Brother. When you're done…come home. There will always be a place for you here. You have taken care of me for so long, don't you think for a minute that I'm not here to help take care of you when you're going through rough times," Noraes said, squeezing his brother's shoulder. "You know," Noraes sighed, "when you left, I envied you for the longest time."

"You envied me?" Searon asked.

"I saw how happy you were with Victoria, the joy that she brought into your stone heart. I envied the love that you two shared together. I've never thought I would be able to find such a thing, such passion."

"There is someone out there for you, and one day, you will meet her."

"I hope so, Brother," Noraes said, "I grow tired of being alone. I think I'm about ready to find myself a wife and start a family."

"That is something I never thought I'd hear you say," Searon laughed.

"I never thought I'd say it either."

Searon got to his feet and stretched out his arms. Noraes followed his example, and they both stood there for a moment in silence. Finally, Searon stepped forward and grabbed his brother in his right arm and brought him in for a hug.

"Thank you for being here for me," Searon said.

"Come, Brother, it's time for us to get some rest." Noraes smiled.

Chapter Thirty-six

Searon woke up early as he always did without much sleep between the nightmares he had throughout the night. He yawned, wishing he could get a full night's sleep at least in the comfort of his brother's home. Yet he didn't know if he'd consider lounging on some fancy furniture in the main room comfort. Still, it beat sleeping on the hard ground, which he'd grown accustomed to during his travels. Nobody seemed awake, and he wasn't too sure where Starlyn had run off to, and so he decided to step outside and enjoy some fresh air.

The air was crisp and almost bit through his white button-up cotton shirt and brown breeches. He almost considered turning around and seeing if his brother had anything warmer to wear. Imagining himself in blue silk made him quickly dismiss the idea. Most of his brother's things were more elegant than he liked due to Noraes's position as duke. Outside was peaceful as he wandered from the stronghold toward the city. He found his stallion in the stables and rode into the city he once called home.

Nobody roamed the streets except a few peasants. A near-total silence pervaded the air, and he enjoyed nothing more. Searon liked the peace and quiet; it gave him more room to think. He wasn't sure what he liked thinking more about, his past or his future and heading into the war. Neither appealed him much more than grief.

As he walked, he notice a few of the stores were open, and he came to a stop in front of one that intrigued him. Vines cascaded from the top of the building only a few spans tall and veered into every crack of the brown stone. Hanging from the door was a large red sign with carved letters that read, *Magical Enchantments*. He slid from his horse and tied the reins to a post outside before pushing through the swinging stone doors.

Inside, the shop seemed plain enough with a bunch of mechanical gadgets hanging on hooks up the walls and a few thin metal shelves with knickknacks. The floor seemed worn from generations of travel, almost as if the shop had been there longer than the city itself. Behind a marble countertop he saw an elderly man fiddling with some sort of mechanical device with a screwdriver. His head was bald except for the sides where long strands of white hair tangled down to his shoulders. Suddenly, a spring from the device slipped from his control and shot out and hit Searon in the center of the forehead.

Searon nearly lost his balance from the impact when it hit him. He stumbled and grabbed onto a shelf in the story to keep himself balanced. A large welt formed on his forehead where he had been hit. It pulsed rapidly until he rubbed it.

"Oh, I'm sorry, sir," the old man said with a deep voice through his large spectacles.

"Just don't do that again," Searon said as he rubbed his forehead.

"I won't, at least not to you. Is there something I can help with you today?" the old man asked as he pushed his spectacles up his large nose.

"I'm just looking around. I have never seen a shop such as this before." Searon glanced toward the gadget still in the old man's hands.

"Ah, a newcomer, and by the looks of you I'd say you are a warrior, cunning and proud."

"I am leading a force to strike against the draeyks."

"Ah, a leader," the man said as he rubbed at the white stubble at his chin. "There are plenty of things we have in here that you may find useful. Tell me, do you have a ranged weapon, or only that gangly claymore."

"My claymore is the only weapon I need," Searon said with aggravation.

"Yes, yes, of course it is. However, there may come a circumstance where you might be in a bind and in need of something with more…range. Here, let me show you something," the old man pleaded.

He walked out from behind the counter until he reached a shelf on the wall. On the shelf were various shortbows, crossbows, throwing axes, and daggers. He searched through all of them carefully until picking up a medium-length dagger in a thin leather scabbard and handed it to Searon.

Searon studied it carefully, feeling the tip of the titanium blade that was a span long. There was no handle to it, and the curves fit perfectly into his hand. Its balance was near flawless, and the rubies sparkled almost as bright as Searon's own.

"That is a nice throwing dagger, but I'm afraid it only has a one-time use. I am not going to be able to retrieve it after a throw," Searon commented and attempted to hand it back.

"Ah, but that is the beauty of it. The blade and scabbard are enchanted; you will not lose it so long as the scabbard is secured to your sash."

"How much?"

"Seven gold coins."

"Seven? You are trying to rob me. I can sleep in a good inn for half of that."

"Yes, you can. But can you sleep in an inn every night that comes back to you with an enchantment?"

Searon sighed, knowing the price was bloody high, and yet if the old man's story were true, the dagger could prove useful. Normally, an entire throwing dagger set cost only a quarter of the price. He grabbed his pouch full of gold coins and set seven on the counter. It had been so long since he'd spent any of his money that losing a few gold coins didn't matter.

He fastened the dagger to his sash and headed out of the door. Outside was no longer so quiet, and people walked about from every direction. It seemed a busy day for the shops. Strangely, he didn't notice any of the commotion while he was inside of the shop. He turned around only to find out that the building he had just been in was no longer there. Somehow, the shop had vanished from sight, and he didn't know if he would be able to ever find it again. Only an empty space stared back at him, and when he felt the space where the building should be, his hands only passed through air.

Searon shook his head and found his horse wandering toward him. The post that he tied Stripes to had vanished along with the shop, but at least his horse had somehow found him. He sighed and mounted his stallion before trotting back out of the main city toward the country and his brother.

Chapter Thirty-seven

"**W**here did you go?" Noraes asked.

Searon already brought his horse to the stable and was walking up the steps to his brother's home. Noraes didn't seem worried, but only mildly curious. He had been out and about for half the day, and it already approached late afternoon as he sat next to Noraes.

"I went for a walk this morning. The air was refreshing."

His brother looked at him with genuine concern, and Searon began to wonder what was so strange about his whereabouts. He started for the door but was blocked by Noraes. The look on his brother's face was stern and stubborn.

"You have been gone for half of the day...are you all right?"

"Have I?" Searon responded, still distracted from the events of the day.

"Yes, you have."

"I found a shop called Magical Enchantments," Searon claimed.

"Magical Enchantments? There is no such shop in the city. In fact, I have never heard of such a shop."

"I think what I need is a drink," Searon murmured.

"I concur, come inside."

Searon nodded and walked inside the house. He took off his scabbard and placed his helmet on an end table before he noticed Starlyn sitting at the dining table. She wasn't wearing her typical steel armor or even her leather armor, but instead wore a dress of light blue that fell just above her ankles. Her feet were bare, and it was the first time Searon had seen her perfectly shaped toenails. He wished his were as clean and trim as hers as he stared in bewilderment. The dress was most likely of human make because Searon couldn't imagine where she would stash such a thing. It was made out of the finest silk he'd ever seen and he could only assume that Noraes was the one who found it. Her hair was tucked behind her ears and for the first time Searon was able to study them carefully. They were similar to human ears but the very tip had a slight point, and unlike the rest of her pale complexion, her ears were slightly pink.

"Searon, we have been worried about you," Starlyn announced and got to her feet.

"I am fine; I was only wandering the city for some fresh air."

"Would you like to join us for some tea?" Starlyn asked.

She stepped from her chair and opened the cabinet to grab some fine china that Searon hadn't even realized his brother had owned. Her mood seemed abnormally happy compared to how he'd normally seen her, and he took notice right away. He watched as she fiddled with the china with a grin upon her soft face.

"What is going on?" Searon asked. "You're not normally this chipper, Starlyn."

"Is it noticeable?" she asked with concern spread across her eyebrows.

"By the brightness of your face and the gracefulness in your movements, it is quite noticeable."

She blushed and whispered. "Don't tell anyone. I have lost control of my emotions as of late."

He smirked. "I am glad to see you happy, Starlyn."

"It is wrong for a kheshlar to lose control like this," Starlyn confessed.

"It is all right, Starlyn. I understand that it is hard to suppress your emotions."

"It isn't only that…kheshlars are forbidden from being with humans," she cautioned.

"Ah, I see. Do no fret, Starlyn; nobody will know," Searon said, taking his tea and blowing on it lightly.

Starlyn gently sat back down in her chair, but her hands shook lightly as she held her cup of tea. Noraes walked over to her and rested his hands on her shoulders for a moment. He bent down to kiss the top of her head before walking away to his bedroom. Starlyn's face noticeably lit up with a small toothless smile as he did, and she blushed. Searon scooted his chair closer to Starlyn and whispered in her ear.

"I know this is more than only losing control of your emotions."

She turned to him with eyes wide in horror. "Excuse me?"

"The way you look at him – the way your face lights up when he is around."

"It is not allowed," Starlyn argued with panic reaching her voice.

"Rules cannot prevent what the heart wants, Starlyn. Every rule I knew told me I should have left Victoria in that village…yet I could not."

Noraes walked back out from the bedroom in a change of clothes. He no longer wore his casual home clothes but had a formal blue silk shirt and black slacks. Starlyn stood up as he walked over to her, but when he tried to put his arms around her waist and kiss her, she pushed him away. She quickly dashed out of the way and turned to face him.

"I must go," she squeaked as she looked deep into his eyes.

She walked over to grab her armor while trying her best to avoid Noraes's gaze. Her wide eyes met Searon's for a moment as she gathered her things. Noraes walked up closer to her and grabbed her arm.

"Not so fast," he said.

Noraes ran his hand through her hair as he kissed her lips. She tried to pull away at first, but he wouldn't have it. Soon, she sank into the kiss, and the two were caught up in passion. She cut it short and stepped back in a flush.

"I really must go," she said before taking one last look at the two of them and rushing out the door.

Noraes turned to look at Searon. "What was that all about?"

Searon smirked as he took a sip of his tea.

Chapter Thirty-eight

Searon stood against the breeze at the gate facing the wilderness beyond Legain. He gave half of his army back to his brother as well as a quarter of the north men to help defend. His own force would be a lot smaller than before and would be forced to make swifter strikes. It wasn't what Searon wanted, but he also didn't wish to leave his brother as defenseless as before.

He embraced Noraes in a half hug with a partial smile. As Noraes hugged him back, he slipped something into Searon's sash. Noraes did it in such a way that nobody surrounding them noticed the motion except for Searon. He shook his brother's hand before peering into his sash to find a single white rose.

"Give that to her for me," Noraes whispered.

"I will," Searon smiled.

"I will miss you, Brother. It has been too long, and yet our ways must part. We both live such different lives, and must go down such different paths."

"Take care."

Searon turned and mounted his stallion before galloping to the head of the army. Starlyn and Karceoles awaited him there along with a protection of guards. He edged close to the kheshlar and kept his hands from view by his guards or the wizard. After one hard look toward the wizard, Karceoles swiftly avoided his eyes and turned his horse away. Searon pulled out the single white rose and handed it to Starlyn. She looked around quickly to make sure nobody was watching as she snatched the beautiful flower from his hand and smelled it before tucking it into her breastplate. Her gaze strayed away from Searon to look back toward the city where she most likely searched for one last glance of Noraes.

"Thank you," she murmured.

Searon nodded and led his stallion forward, motioning his army to follow. The journey ahead of them was to be long, and he scarcely planned to stop any place for too long. All the men were ready for another long journey with thick blood pumping for another taste of battle. They did not complain, as they traveled with scarce breaks, but continued on for duty.

After a fortnight, they left the southern cities for the wilderness to the north. Searon varied from his original course to the west where he knew of a small village he had visited in the past. It seemed like such a long time ago that he traveled to the village of Augealia, and yet the memory was a fond one. He had been there long before he had followers, back when it was only him searching for stray draeyks to slaughter. After Augealia was when he had met the wandering wizard.

He hoped by coming to the old village he could discover if there were any draeyks nearby. After all, he had done them a favor the last time by destroying the savage beasts that attacked the village. Searon didn't wish to bring the entire army into the small town. He knew there wouldn't be enough provisions, and it might frighten the townsfolk. Instead, he pulled aside Starlyn and Sh'on.

As they walked from the camp and onto the worn road surrounded by farms, Searon noticed that not as many farmers were out and about. The farms on the sides were bare, and he only noticed two farmers that were in the gardens. Both of them looked drained of life and barely moved their shovels.

When Searon reached the gates, he noticed that there were no guards outside and the doors were shut tight. He tried to pry them open, but they were shut solid and nothing he could do would make the gate budge.

"A little help, mage?" Searon asked.

Sh'on smiled and raised a hand that glowed green, and soft sparkling left his palm that blanketed the gate. In one fluid motion, the large doors snapped open a crack. The three of them had to use their strength to pull one door far enough to slip in.

As they walked through the village, it almost looked abandoned except for a few of the guards patrolling the streets. The village was small with only a handful of shops that all appeared closed. Searon didn't notice the shops he had seen in the village so long ago. It had been such a lively place the last time he had been there, but now it seemed so lifeless.

One of the guards Searon had recognized from the gate so long ago approached them. His sharp chin and pointed nose were unmistakable as well as his attitude. Richard was his name, and Searon remembered him all too well.

"Still killing draeyks for coin, Sir Mercenary?" the guard asked sarcastically.

"No coin needed. I have decided to raise an army to strike the draeyks in their own camps."

"You seem to have come a long way from a mercenary."

"Only as far as is necessary to defeat these creatures once and for all," Searon said as he looked down the streets again to see only emptiness. He noticed that many of the merchandise at the markets was still out, and yet nobody was at the businesses. "Where is everybody?"

"We are in lockdown. There are draeyks outside of the village that we cannot defend against."

"How many?" Starlyn asked.

Richard paused as he looked at Starlyn. "A real kheshlar. I always thought they were only from stories. I didn't know you ever left your forest. Tell me, kheshlar, why have you left your home?"

"How many?" she repeated.

"I would say over two hundred, yet less than three."

"We'll take care of them for you," Searon said.

"With only three?"

"As I've said, I have an army under my command now. A mere three hundred is nothing to us after how many we've already slaughtered."

The guard raised his eyebrow and studied the three of them. "If that is the case, by all means."

Searon nodded and turned around to walk out of the village. They closed the gate as they left, and Sh'on locked it. When they were far away from the village and the farms surrounding it, Searon placed his hand on Starlyn's shoulder. She turned back to look at him and seemed to understand what he wanted right away.

"Find where they are, and come back to camp."

Starlyn nodded and silently took off in another direction. Searon and Sh'on continued back to camp where they explained to Karceoles what was going on. They began preparing the army for battle. Searon sat down on a stump as a large force of men prepared for battle and took his knife from its scabbard to feel the blade. The titanium was smooth and crafted with such perfection that it didn't seem like a mere human could have made it. The sharpened blade was exceedingly fine, and he knew if he were to graze his bare skin with it that the blade would turn red.

After only half an hour, Starlyn came back to the camp where she walked through a crowd of men to reach Searon. He watched as all of the men that parted for her continue to stare as she passed. She knew as well as he that with her being the only female in the army that all sorts of advances were to be made. Searon knew that she was more than capable to take care of herself, but he also put word out that if she were to be touched that a noose could be easily found.

"Did you find them?" Searon asked.

"Yes, they are northwest of the village. We can travel through the forest to find them so we don't draw attention to ourselves."

"Perfect, how many?"

"Three hundred and forty-seven."

"How many men would suffice without large causalities?"

"Five hundred, at least a hundred of them archers, and we should be able to make short work of them."

"Etherond, Xython, and Sh'on, with me. Find your best men to complete this task. Andron and Karceoles, stay here with the rest of the army as we dispose of this small force of creatures."

"As you command," Etherond smirked and turned around to speak with his men. His bronze cloak glittered in the sunlight as he walked away barking commands.

Searon gathered himself together and got on his stallion with Starlyn at his side and led them toward where she saw the creatures. In a matter of half an hour, they had arrived at the camp that was filled with slaughtered animals and cook fires. The clearing was small and yet crammed with all the creatures as they fought with each other for scraps of food.

Etherond gathered his men behind the second row of trees and told them to hold fast and prepare. Searon and Sh'on organized the archers behind the first rank of trees until they were scattered enough so every archer was open for a clear shot. Sh'on looked at Searon, who nodded back at him.

"Loose!" Sh'on whispered.

Arrows shot out of the trees in a flurry along with wisps of green magic. Many draeyks fell, but a lot of the arrows bounced off the scales of the creatures and tumbled to the ground. Searon held onto his claymore tightly, awaiting the attack that would head his way. As he suspected, the creatures became outraged and began charging into the forest where Searon already had his defenses set.

Archers continued to fire until the reptilian creatures neared the forest, at which point they ran back to the third line of trees and behind the swordsmen. Some of the men were knights, cavalry, and others were swordsmen or men with axes and maces. The trap ensnared the draeyks perfectly as the creatures ran past the first wall of trees to the second. Searon stayed behind a thick tree on the first rank and watched as the creatures ran past him. Starlyn stood at the tree nearest him, and both prepared to attack from behind once the last of the creatures broke through the forest.

The draeyks fought gallantly but ultimately met their demise. Many were hard to kill because of their thickened scales that were as hard as some of the men's armor, but between the mass of arrows and warriors they began to fall one by one. Searon jumped out and fought hard against their back ranks with Starlyn by his side. Her thick hammer crushed snouts and heads one by one as she swung it about. Some draeyks were skilled enough to block her first few strikes with axes before being crushed under her blows, but none compared to her caliber of skill.

Etherond fought like a madman with loud echoing laugher as he went from one foe to another. His skill was impressive to say the least, even at moments taking on three of the creatures at once. He fought a line from the front ranks all the way to Searon where he formed in a triangle with both him and Starlyn. The three struck down anyone that came at them. Since the draeyks had been on the offensive, none had rushed into the forest with crossbows ready, and so the three hundred creatures with axes fell in a span of a quarter of an hour.

Searon inspected the injured and dead and was quite happy to have only three deaths. There were over thirty injuries, some severe, but most were light. Everyone would be able to make it, and Sh'on and Starlyn quickly attended to the injuries.

All of them traveled back to the camp, where Searon decided to give his men a rest. He asked Starlyn to accompany him back into the village in the morning to tell the guard of their progress. With the news, hopefully they would be able to settle the minds of the villagers so they could come out of hiding once more.

Searon yawned and decided to get some rest before heading out in the morning. He lay down next to his horse where he kept warm under some wool blankets under the stars. Before he closed his eyes, his memory flashed back to Victoria, and he knew he wouldn't get much sleep.

Chapter Thirty-nine

When dawn arrived, Searon left silently with Starlyn. He rode his stallion with Starlyn at a trot, enjoying the brisk sunshine that warmed his face. His heavy armor stayed back at camp along with his helm, and he wore only his red-brown leather armor. Starlyn only wore her dark-brown armor rather than gold metal so she would be lighter.

The village gate was open, and so Stripes walked through. It seemed even emptier than it was before without even guards patrolling the streets. They continued on until they reached the village's barracks where he saw the same guard that had sent him out. He was surrounded by at least twenty more guards, and the one closest to him was a captain. Searon recognized the captain as the one who gave him a sack of coin to fight the threat of draeyks the last time. His hair was short and spiked of a dirty-blond hue and he had two large gold hoops in each ear at the cartilage. He raised an eyebrow as he stared at both Searon and Starlyn.

"The draeyk threat is gone now. You can tell everyone it is now safe to come out," Searon said.

The captain only shook his head and smiled as he looked behind Searon. Searon abruptly turned around to see a man with a long black beard with white flecks that hung past his waist. He wore a black cloak with purple robes exposed in the front and gold jewels that pinched his long beard together in three spots from top to bottom. His hair hung down his back near to his rear where it was a curled mess. There was no hood to the cloak, and his red eyes were haunting to stare at.

"It is never safe," the guard whispered from behind Searon.

Searon didn't turn around but continued to stare at the strange man in front of him. He held what appeared to be some form of zylek, but unlike Karceoles's it was metal instead of wood with four spikes that looked like a hand holding a small skull at the tip. The skull's eyes seemed to glow red while the rest of it appeared to glow white. At first, Searon assumed it to be some form of wizard or warlock until he saw the skeleton that stood by its side. The skeleton was a full body of bones completely attached and a head shorter than the man beside it. It held a cleaver in its left hand and a bone shield in its right.

Searon knew what it was as soon as he saw the skeleton. He whispered, "Warlock."

The warlock held a dead scorpion in his pale-white left hand. His eyes seemed to flash and shine brighter as he looked at the scorpion. More than the man's retina appeared red, but it was his entire eye that seemed to take flame. They almost appeared like small balls of fire that seemed separate from his face. He blew a green mist that surrounded the scorpion before waving his zylek about the creature in three turns. The scorpion levitated in front of his eyes and began to glow a dull yellow.

Suddenly, the ground shook all around them, which caused Starlyn to stumble and fall. She reached to Searon and grabbed his shoulder to keep from falling. He was barely able to keep his own balance and held onto her tightly as they both watched in horror as the scorpion grew in size. It continued to grow larger until it reached three heads taller than a human. Six red eyes glared toward Searon and Starlyn before blinking a few times. The creature stood on two thick hind legs with four arms at its front and two pincers. A stinger came from its rear and curled up so it floated near its mid-back.

"Kill them," the warlock whispered.

Searon pulled out his claymore in a stride ready to face the creature. At that moment, his stallion reared and knocked both Starlyn and him from saddle. The horse galloped away from both Searon and Starlyn toward the gate of the village. He stood up next to Starlyn, who already had her hammer held tightly in her grip. Searon rushed toward the creature first, and after two slashes was blocked by pincers. The creature's tail slammed against Searon's chest, causing him to fly backward into a stone building.

Starlyn stepped up next, but instead of attacking she seemed to wait for an attack with a defensive stance. She stood so that her side was facing the creature rather than her entire front. It took a moment before the scorpion decided to lunge forward with both pincers snapping where Starlyn's head was only a moment before. She ducked and rolled toward the creature, bringing up her hammer to crush against a pincer. The other claw came at her and slammed against her hammer. Her weapon flew from her hands, and she watched as it skidded across the dirt. The scorpion brought its tail toward her, and she dove into the air to avoid it. She landed on the middle of the tail and ran all the way up it before jumping off. As she fell toward the ground at its back, she took three shurikens from her pouch. The first bounced of the hardened shell of the creature and sprang back toward her face. She only had enough time to tilt her head to the left, causing the star to slice of a long strand of her bright-blonde hair. The creature turned to her when she landed, and she threw another, but the creature easily deflected it with a claw. Her third shuriken soared past the creature's defenses until it penetrated into one of the scorpion's six eyes.

Starlyn didn't waste a second of time as she dashed away from the creature and toward Searon. He was back on his feet, and when he noticed her coming toward him, he put his claymore back in its scabbard. His arm secured around her, and they turned around to see the scorpion walking slowly toward them.

Searon led Starlyn between the shops and into the alleyways that he remembered in detail. When they thought they lost the creature, they noticed the guards appear in front of them with swords out. There were five, and each one had glowing red eyes. Searon let go of Starlyn and stood in front of her as he unsheathed his claymore. He felt her shiver behind him, and her eyes were wide with terror. She seemed clueless at what she could do, and the sight of her frightened Searon. He never imagined that Starlyn could be afraid of anything, but for once she seemed as human as he.

He clashed blades with the first two men and ducked as a third slashed a high sword at him. His left hand dropped from his handle and grabbed the dagger at his sash. He threw it forward, and it struck one of the humans in the neck. The man's eyes turned from red back to brown as he fell to the ground. Searon only glanced at him for an instant before going back into defensive posture against the other four men. He was able to catch one of them off guard and struck him through the chest between plates. It dropped another, and yet it was a mistake as a sword slammed onto his right hand, cutting deep through his leather gloves. He dropped his claymore and fell to his knees. Swords came at him from all directions, but he rolled on the ground, covering his bleeding hand as he dodged one slash at a time.

Starlyn remained still as he ran up to her and stood by her side once more. The remaining three rushed at him, and both he and Starlyn dodged several attacks. A sword hilt hit the top of his head as he dodged the blade, and he crashed to the ground with his face in the dirt. Starlyn dove and rolled to Searon's claymore.

She reached Searon as they did and was able to deflect their blows. Even though her primary weapon was her hammer, she was still able to quickly slice one down with Searon's large sword. The remaining two were excellent swordsmen and rushed at her from both sides. She defended against them easily enough, but she wasn't used to the length of Searon's claymore and so wasn't able to mount an effective attack. His weapon was better suited for power rather than speed, and that was something she wasn't accustomed to.

Searon shook off his dizziness and began crawling toward them as Starlyn battled. He was able to grab one of the human's feet and was surprised to find that it felt limp in his hands. The man stumbled enough for Starlyn to rush forward and strike him down. Her attack was swift, and yet it let her guard down enough for the other to knock her down. She dropped the claymore as she fell upon Searon, who was still too weak to support her.

The captain was the remaining swordsman standing, and he smiled at the two of them. His golden loops sparkled in the early daylight as he walked closer, dragging one leg. He smiled as his eyes grew redder and brighter to match the color of flames. Searon and Starlyn didn't have enough time to react, and he stood atop them, ready to strike the deathblow. Before he could bring his sword all the way down, a sword pierced through his heart from behind, and he crumbled to the ground.

Behind him stood Andron with his sword covered in a hazel blood with Phoenix by his side. Searon barely recognized his brother's captain, but was thankful to see the young man. Andron gave a partial smile as he held his hand out for Searon to take. Phoenix helped Starlyn up, and the four of them looked around. Searon nodded his appreciation as he grabbed his claymore to sheath the weapon.

"Let's get out of here," Searon said.

As they turned to leave and run through the alleys, the large scorpion blocked their escape. The creature stood at the exit of the alley, and its pincers clamped furiously. Its ebony shell shone the reflection of the sun into their eyes.

"Go, we will slow it down," Andron declared.

He gulped as a bead of sweat cascaded down his scalp. His hand shook on his sword, and Phoenix looked as nervous as he. Searon clutched at his claymore, ready to draw it.

"Go!" Andron shouted.

"You can't hope to destroy that thing," Searon objected.

"Just go, get the others. You cannot die; without you our cause is lost. Either we all die, or Phoenix and I will make a sacrifice. Starlyn and you are too important. Perhaps we can delay the creature long enough for your return, but you must hurry!" Andron spat and took a step forward.

Searon grabbed Starlyn's hand and jerked her through another alley as Andron and Phoenix twirled their swords in unison to face the creature. He knew that it was against all hope for them to defeat the creature, but he knew that Andron was right. The new threat was a surprise, and the others needed to be warned of it. Perhaps the mage or wizard could come up with an idea on how to destroy the creature. There was no time to waste.

Chapter Forty

S earon and Starlyn were out of breath by the time they made it back to the camp. Both dripped in sweat and tears as they reached the wizard, nearly collapsing at his feet. They panted as they tried to catch their breath but were unable to overcome their exhaustion.

"Where are Andron and Phoenix?" Karceoles asked.

"Back…in…the village," Searon gasped. "They probably didn't survive."

"Draeyks?" Sh'on asked.

"Worse," Searon quivered, "The dead rise and attack."

"The dea—" Karceoles said.

"No time, hurry, everybody with us!" Searon barked.

He was near out of breath, but he knew that he dared not rest. If there were any chance to save Andron, he knew he had to act swiftly. Luckily, he found Stripes, who had galloped back on his own. He bounded onto his steed, with Starlyn at his back. She held on tight as he led the way back toward the village with the army at their heels.

When they arrived, the village seemed abandoned and appeared as if no battle had taken place. Searon slowly got off his stallion, with Starlyn behind, and they walked into the town with footsteps that echoed against the silent terrain. Karceoles walked up to them from behind with zylek in hand and looked from one to the other with squinted eyes.

"What exactly happened?" he asked.

"We ran into the captain, however, he seemed different. It appeared as if he was possessed, and he rushed to attack us. Dead bodies and skeletons began to rise and strike. We were already overwhelmed when the warlock used magic on a dead scorpion, bringing it to life to tower twelve spans over us."

"A warlock?" Karceoles asked.

"Yes, he held a metal zylek in his hand," Starlyn admitted.

"That was no warlock; a necromancer is the type of sorcerer that can command the living and the dead."

The warriors searched the village, but all the houses were empty. Phoenix's body was found lifeless, decapitated with his head not too far away, but Andron wasn't anywhere to be found. Starlyn's prized war hammer vanished, and none of the people, skeletons, or necromancer were to be found either.

"Andron was worried about you," Karceoles admitted, sitting down next to Searon and bringing out his pipe that he stuffed with an exotic weed. "He said he had a bad feeling about you two heading off alone, and he wanted to go into town to check it out." The wizard sighed. "I paid it no attention and told him he was welcome to go. Phoenix tagged along with him."

"It is not your fault; you couldn't have known. What he did saved our lives, and we are grateful. All there is to do now is honor his memory, both of their memories."

"A life-sized scorpion raised from the dead, you said?"

"Yes," Searon admitted. "One of the most terrifying things I've witnessed."

"That is new. I've never heard of a necromancer bringing forth a nacropis."

"Nacropis?" Searon shivered.

"Yes, at least that would be what I would call such a creature. This must be a powerful necromancer to conjure such a creature. I can only hope they don't decide to bring forth spiders next."

"Why is that?" Searon asked.

"I hate spiders, frightening creatures."

"A wizard, scared of a little spider?"

"How would you like to be wrapped up in a giant spider's web?" Karceoles asked.

"A valid point," Searon admitted.

"The nacropis is extremely powerful. Neither Starlyn nor I could defeat it."

"A new foe is always a difficult task to overcome. Think back to how difficult draeyks were when you first encountered them. I can only imagine the challenge of this foe. Starlyn still looks pretty shaken up over the experience, and that's saying something for the foes that she has faced in her time as a kheshlar."

Searon snatched the pipe weed from the wizard's hand and took a few puffs of the exceedingly long-stem pipe before passing it back. He forced his scattered thoughts into a tight ball in his head and slowly relaxed with help from the slow inhales until he could think clearly. Starlyn had been equally afraid, of that he could clearly see now, but for some reason he'd imagined her stronger than he, without the need for comfort.

Away from the crowd, sitting alone with back turned to everybody and helmet off to her side, was Starlyn. After a deep breath, Searon got to his feet and strode over to Starlyn, where he sat by her side. For a long moment, he didn't dare speak but sat next to her in silence, watching her as she stared blankly at her trembling hands before her. When she couldn't stand to look at them anymore, she slumped over and rested her head on Searon's shoulder.

"Are you all right?" he asked.

"I only miss Sudegam. Things were simpler there. I didn't expect all of this. Even when I marched out the first time, I was overwhelmed, but it was nothing like this."

"When we reach the kheshlarn capital you can go back. I am not going to force you to be here. Your presence is heartwarming for many humans, but without full kheshlarn support it is little comfort to them."

He continuously did his best to comfort her during the travels, but in his heart he knew that she was not meant to be in the wild. Her place wasn't mixed in the middle of humans, and sometimes she seemed out of place; she wandered away from them often to be by herself to meditate, or enjoy the nature surrounding her. There was a warm, welcoming place for her back in Sudegam, and she should be with her people.

"I know that," she said. "I want to stay with you. My place is with all of you in this battle against these foul creatures. Somewhere, sometime, we will run into my sister again. I feel she is involved in this somehow, and when we do—I want to be there."

"Are you sure?"

"Yes, do not worry, my friend. I will be fine. I've fought in a war before, but the last time I never followed it through to the end. It was a false end last time, and this time I want to make sure the war is truly over."

"I will make sure of it. I despise these creatures as much as you do, and I will not give up until every last one of them in buried into the ground."

"What are you to do when it is all over?" Starlyn asked.

"That I do not know. My life has been full of revenge, and I'm afraid there will be little left of me besides an empty shell when this is complete. I do know that I've made some great friends along the way." He smiled.

"It is a shame what happened to this village. I only wish we could have saved them from this chaos. I can't help but think of all the help-less women and children at the mercy of the necromancer." Starlyn shook her head with eyes downcast.

"Children…" Searon whispered.

"What is it?" Concern streaked Starlyn's face.

"Children!" Searon shouted, nearly leaping to his feet.

Before Starlyn could stand up, Searon was gone, shouting through the alleyways. She didn't know what was going on in his mind and could only imagine it had something to do with his past. It had never been her purpose to bring up such a heart-wrenching subject. Starlyn trailed after him.

"Charlotte…" Searon whispered, collapsing to his knees and drop-ping his head in his hands.

"Charlotte?" Starlyn asked.

"Yes…Charlotte. She was this poor little girl I met here long ago. She had to steal for food, and I gave her coin for her to find the captain for me. She was so young…so very young," Searon whispered, tracks of tears melting onto his face.

Starlyn seemed to approach him to offer comfort but held back as she pondered how to do so. Children weren't something she was famil-iar with, and she knew that it tied closely to the warrior's heart. His heart had already been devastated with the death of his own children, and so the feeling of possibly losing another child that he'd aided along his journey seemed a heart-breaking thought. Without a better thought coming to mind, she tumbled forward, clasped her arms around him, and embraced him in a comforting hug. It seemed to work at first when he gripped her tight, but the moment was lost when he suddenly backed away.

"I have to find her…I have to know." Searon turned away with a look of eagerness about him. It seemed he was lost in thought as he wandered through the alleyways, leaving Starlyn behind.

She stood there for a moment, watching him search desperately all through the alleys. He rummaged through body after body, searching for a girl that resembled the precious Charlotte, sickened at the sight of the bloody and battered corpses. Most were grown men or women, but there were many children, and that aspect alone sickened Searon beyond anything he could ever imagine. None of them looked familiar to him, except when he saw a poor boy and girl that he remembered helping out their mother. That sank his heart, but the body of Charlotte still was nowhere to be found. Disgust crusted his face as he tore through the bodies, one by one, through every alley, home, and clearing, and yet not once was he slowed by the carnage.

"They deserve a memorial," Searon said at last.

"There are too many bodies to bury them all, Searon," Starlyn replied.

"We can at least burn them and celebrate in their memory."

Starlyn appeared to object at first but quickly closed her mouth and nodded. "As you wish."

Searon seemed to barely notice her as he disappeared into a home and dragged bodies out. When he returned outside, he noticed that she was gone, but it was only moments later that Starlyn reappeared with a team of warriors to help bring the bodies to the center of the village. After several hours, all the bodies were piled in the center of the town. Andron's body was still missing, and Searon's precious Charlotte seemed nowhere to be found. Both Karceoles and Starlyn walked up next to him, the wizard with his zylek at the ready and his face full of contempt—while Starlyn's face seemed pleading.

"Did you find her?" the kheshlar asked.

"Her body is not among the dead," Searon whispered.

"If that is so, why is there so much disappointment on your face?"

"I would like to know where she is…if she made it."

"It is possible she escaped."

He looked from her to the destroyed homes and pile of bodies that nearly stacked seventy spans high and shook his head, disappointment masking his face with tears swelled at the corners of his eyes. "It is unlikely, but you're right. I should still have hope."

The three sat together for a long while until twilight arrived before Searon solemnly nodded to the wizard. Karceoles rose to his feet, used his zylek to create a blazing fire over the bodies, and withdrew his pipe to take a few puffs. All of the warriors found places to stay for the night, many outside, but still more found empty homes or shops to stay in. Some even found barrels of ale from the pub and inns of the small village and began to drink in memory of the citizens.

Searon seemed the only one who didn't move from his spot as he sat on a barrel of grain directly in front of the large fire, staring into the flames. Memories haunted him of that fateful night with his family and the carnage of his home village afterwards as he explored it. He shivered as those thoughts came into his head, yet they wouldn't leave his haunted mind—until finally when Starlyn sat down next to him and put her head atop his shoulder. Only then did the haunting daydreams seem to disappear, replaced with feelings of comfort and friendship. How long it had been since he could consider somebody as a true friend, and yet here was Starlyn, asking for nothing in return, but comforting him nonetheless. His heart warmed at the thought, and only then did his eyes close for the night, and the peacefulness of rest finally consumed him.

Chapter Forty-one

The company traveled through the vast wetlands before them: full of shallow ponds, winding murky rivers, short red and yellow grass, and the smell of thick dirt all about them. Off in the distance in the north were the Shayli Mountains, masked in a coat of snow at their tips. There were only three peaks, but they were so massive that everybody dreaded the moment when they'd have to cross them. The way was faster than any other as Karceoles pointed out with his maps, and yet the trek it would take to get there would be grim.

They lingered in the village for a day in hopes of finding any draeyks or the necromancer that disappeared, but there was no such luck. Searon, more than anything, wanted to come across the little girl that haunted many of his thoughts. Yet he knew that he dared not remain in the village too long. In order to be effective against the draeyks, they needed to strike soon.

Searon looked up to the sky where a rainbow still spanned the horizon, and he watched as an eagle gracefully glided across the clouds. He smiled at the wonderful bird, admiring its beauty and wondering how peaceful it would be to be an eagle. It was the king of the sky, without worry or fret, no wars to mask its center of peace, and could travel wherever it chose.

The way was rough and hot with gnats and mosquitoes along the way. Everybody became irritable, but most were ready to be across— and prepared to end the war as soon as possible.

Soon, the marshes became dry, and they wandered into the midst of the Teyyuar desert, where water was scarce. This was the way that the wizard had suggested, although he knew it would be hard on the men, many of whom never wandered into the dry heat. It wasn't as vast as the Aedth Eastern Desert on the other side of the Benora Mountains. Nobody was sure how large that desert was because the mountains went from the northernmost border of Calthoria all the way down to the south, and nobody had ever claimed to cross it. Nobody seemed foolish enough to try. The desert they walked into was only twenty leagues by measure.

Karceoles made sure that they stopped at the last pond of the marshes before they continued on to the desert. The water was murky and questionable, but wet nonetheless, and each man filled his water skins to the rim before continuing on.

By the time they reached the desert, it was morning of the next day. Even Searon had a rough time crossing the terrain, and his poor horse couldn't carry him for long. Horses were meant for the long meadows and forests but were useless for much more than a place to keep saddlebags throughout the desert. Even as resilient as Stripes was, he, too, was discarded in the midst of the desert for rest. Searon knew that he could probably keep on the horse, but he didn't want to bring his old friend to exhaustion, and so he willingly began walking the rough path.

At first, there were shrubs and bushes throughout the outskirts of the desert, many of them herbs like sage and thyme, but as soon as they crossed out of the cloud coverage and far enough away from any ponds or rivers there were only cacti as far as the eye could see. Many were spread so far apart that they only appeared close together from afar. The ground was flat with gravely rocks scattered across its surface, making everybody's feet sore through leather and steel boots. Animals weren't to be seen in any direction except for the few lizards and snakes that crossed their field of vision before quickly disappearing into nothingness.

The terrain was flat; there was nothing to be seen to the northwest toward which they traveled except for the three Shayli peaks at the end of their perilous journey. Some of the cacti that they passed held beautiful flowers of orange, pink, and blue, but the wizard warned of their poisonous nature, and so many stayed away. Starlyn appeared mesmerized by the beauty of them, and stood for long moments admiring several of the cacti with flowers. Many more had barbs and needles that many of the men found quickly to be more than an inconvenience when tripping on them.

In the distance, a mirage could be seen, black in color, almost appearing like smoke because as they got closer it seemed to disappear. Karceoles called them water mirages, claiming that the mind in such dry air without moisture craves water and creates an image in your mind to remind you of your dire need for the substance. Even as it would disappear as they neared it, the image continued to move farther out, creating a never-ending cycle.

A large number of the men came close to exhaustion and nearly passed out as they traveled. Men surrounding them helped them out by giving them physical support, water from their skins, and attempts to cool them off by fanning them. Starlyn seemed the only one who handled the heat well. She'd only taken one sip of her water skin throughout the journey; being a kheshlar she was better built for weather conditions than humans. Exhaustion didn't take her as it did the men, but from her appearance it could be deciphered that she was wearing out. The heat even tore at Karceoles and Sh'on, not as quickly as the humans, but not nearly as slowly as it tormented Starlyn.

Once they passed the center point of the desert, most of the men had emptied their water skins. Karceoles bid them to stop as he and Sh'on walked ahead alone. The wizard swirled his zylek at the ground, and after a few minutes water appeared to come to the surface. Sh'on channeled his own green magic to steady the floating water and duplicate it. Men came rushing forward, overjoyed, as they filled their water skins. Both the mage and the wizard appeared drained, and so Searon bid Etherond take charge and lead the men as he stayed back with Karceoles and Sh'on.

"Thank you," Searon said.

They only nodded back to him, most of their energy seemingly drained from them. Searon withdrew his water skin and gave them each a sip before getting between them and helping them forward and back into the ranks of men.

Many grew anxious as they saw dozens of wandering scorpions crawling around and hiding behind rocks as they passed. Starlyn seemed the most uneasy at their appearance, still with the nacropis fresh on her mind. For many, it wasn't the scorpions that made them uneasy, but the constant circle of vultures that soared in the sky above them. It seemed they were expecting a meal, a meal that they most likely were always sure to have.

Without Searon's confidence and leadership, they wouldn't have continued through the desert at such a consistent speed. Breaks were seldom as they traveled through the desert, as he knew that if they stopped for too long, nobody would be able to get back up to their feet. They weren't fast as they traveled, but they were consistent in pacing themselves. So long as they moved they created a false breeze across their face that would not be there had they remained motionless. Nothing helped their dehydration much, but so long as they rationed their water properly, and took small sips only every once in a while, they could survive.

They took a break as the sun began to set. Searon kept everybody moving during the day because the heat was too much if they stayed still, and without shade they were better off moving than staying still. They couldn't move fast, but neither could they stay and bake in the sun. The half moon was by far more welcoming to the men than the scorching rays of the sun. However, the atmosphere didn't cool down as much as they desired, and while the night air felt crisp compared to the daylight, it was still dry and hot. The heat seemed to continue to rise from the ground where the sun had baked it into the dirt. They no longer felt the heat from above, and for that they were grateful. However, they weren't grateful for long because soon all the heat left the rocks and the desert became bone-numbingly cold.

Searon only let the men rest for less than half of the night with most of them taking turns on watch. Many were upset with him because they needed rest but quickly stifled themselves when Searon showed his authority and asked them if they'd rather travel longer in the sun or get closer by continuing through some of the night.

As dawn approached, they were nearing the edge of the desert, and cacti became less prevalent and were replaced with sagebrush and palm trees. The weather was still dry and hot, but it wasn't nearly as terrible as the center of the desert. Clouds scattered the sky instead of the brilliant blue brightness that the desert held. Still, most were bright white and fluffy without much precipitation. Most of the men were out of water and barely dragged on, but the sight was more welcoming than where they had just been, and so they pressed on with new motivation.

As they continued on, the sun rose higher in the sky and hid behind clouds of gray rather than white. The sight was welcoming, and many prayed to the creator for rain. No longer was the desert flat terrain, but it now held a vast variety of rock formations. Some simple scattered rocks from large to small, but others appeared as arches and small mountains. Everybody's feet began to ache from the rough ground, but it didn't slow them much, as determination was their focus. On their right they noticed a small canyon that fell leagues into the ground. It was by far the most beautiful sight in the desert, but they dared not approach it, despite knowing that a river created it, because it was too far a climb for such a little pleasure.

Nobody thought about the water that could be at the bottom of the canyon for long because soon it began to sprinkle, and everyone was overjoyed with mouths open and tongues sticking out. Cheers erupted through them, and they stopped in their tracks to try and catch some in their water skins. The sprinkle didn't last long, as it turned into a downpour so ferocious that it pelted blisters underneath many of the men's armor. Everyone held their water skins tight trying to get as much water as possible inside of them. Searon struggled, pushing them forward to keep pace through the rain when so many were overjoyed with its presence. He claimed that the rain would stretch on for a long while and that it would be better for them to be farther along before the heat came back.

When the rain finally stopped, they were thankful for Searon's rashness at pushing them forward. The heat amplified through the water when the clouds disappeared and felt even hotter than the central desert.

It wasn't until dusk of that night that they reached the end of the desert near the peak of the mountains. They rested for the night before beginning the long trek across the Shaylis in the morning. The pass didn't look as bad as it had from a distance, and although the mountains were large, there seemed to be a pass between them that Karceoles directed them to. There was still a climb, but not as daunting as it was first made out to be. After nearly another half day, they climbed through the mountains and reached the other side that opened up to a valley.

Small hills and mountains surrounded them in the valley on each side, but none as large or daunting as the ones they just crossed. The trip down was fast as gravity hit them with each step, and they welcomed the grass on the other side and the breeze from the rivers and lakes that could be felt with the new humidity. They smelled the scent of fish and wildlife. When the mountains were far behind and the grass had become thicker, they welcomed it under their feet for much-needed padding. A gentle valley breeze swept across them that brought tears of joy to the warriors' eyes.

They came to rest at the edge of the valley next to a small lake before it ended with a large mountain that they had to climb to be within draeyk territory. Wildlife roamed the valley, and many of the men, deprived and hungry began hunting them, and so Searon took Starlyn out of the camp to the edge of the western hills to find fruit. A tree seemed to call to them, holding golden-yellow apples with such a sweetness to them that they nearly melted in their mouths. Starlyn found a few various vegetables growing through the valley, which they shared as they talked.

"Will you be ready to face the draeyks tomorrow?" Searon asked.

"Yes, though I do not feel right with this sword."

Searon looked at the new scabbard at her hip and bronze-hilted broadsword. The blade itself was of a fine human make and one of the better swords in his ranks of men, and yet it did look odd on her. He was most accustomed to seeing her with her hammer that had disappeared in the town with the necromancer. Instead, she carried the sword of the fallen Phoenix, whom they had found when they came back to the village with an army.

"I'm sure Phoenix would have wanted you to have it." He tried to reassure her with a comforting hand.

"I know that...but it's just wrong."

"Yes, I know, being with the sword brings back the memories of what happened that day."

"Yes," Starlyn admitted, looking down to the half-eaten apple in her hand.

"When you return to Sudegam, have another weapon made for yourself, and bury that one in Phoenix's memory."

Starlyn smiled and brushed the hair from her eyes. "Perhaps I will."

They stayed a while longer, enjoying their meal and pleasant conversation about life, before heading back into the midst of camp. Searon had already bid the wizard to dispose of any bones before they arrived, and while the smell of cooked meat remained, nothing was to be seen. All the men respected Starlyn too much to flaunt about the meat they had enjoyed. Most of it had been packed up in animal hide and cloth in order to take with them, some packed in saddlebags and whatever else they could find. Searon gave Starlyn a hug goodnight, and she kissed him on the cheek before leaving off by herself to sleep away from the men.

He continued to a small orange campfire and sat on a rock next to the wizard who pulled out two large steaks for him. Both were still warm and nearly melted in his mouth as he tore at them with bare hands and teeth. The vegetables and fruit filled him more than he expected, but he still devoured the desired meat.

"Thanks," Searon said.

"Get some rest; I will take first watch," Karceoles said.

* * *

When Searon awoke the next morning, everybody was packed and ready to go. His exhaustion was understandable, and everybody decided to let him sleep. Most knew that he continuously woke up through the night because of his nightmares and any sudden movement that he decided to check on, which was one of the disadvantages of being a leader.

By midafternoon, they had reached the top and began the journey back down the small mountain. When they looked north toward the draeyk settlements, they found a strange sight. All seemed deserted. Searon looked questioning at the wizard, who shrugged nonchalantly. An eagle flew by, which Starlyn called to with a great whistle, and after it circled around them once, it came to her and landed on her outstretched hand.

"Tell me, king of the sky, why are these settlements deserted; where are the creatures who inhabited them?" she whispered.

The eagle nodded to the south before it leaped from her hand and took off again. Her eyes widened in dismay as she turned to listen to the bird whistle in the air. She shifted south and stared disbelievingly before turning to Searon with her mouth agape.

"What is it?" he asked.

"They are heading south," she said.

"How many?"

"Thousands, all of them from this region."

"Where are they heading?"

Karceoles stepped up and stared into the south with repulsion. "Where else…Sudegam."

"That is not all," Starlyn whispered.

"What is it?" Searon asked.

"When the eagle left, he told me that not only do these northern creatures head south, but the southern beasts do as well, and a new creature, a desert creature, marches with them as well."

"The daerions…and the nacropis? How many total?" Searon had the chills.

"An eagle does not count the same as you and I, but if I were to guess I would say thirty thousand."

"So it is as I feared; the races have united," Karceoles whispered.

Etherond stepped up to Searon, hand gripped tightly on the hilt of his sword. "We are many, but even I don't know if we are a match."

"We will stalk them to kheshlarn territory and attack from behind when they least expect it. Once they enter the land of kheshlars, they will have no choice but to fight them," Karceoles said.

"We won't survive," Etherond gasped.

Karceoles turned to Starlyn. "Go, and warn the kheshlars about this."

Starlyn looked to Searon, who nodded, and she began running south at a speed none of the men knew she had. She took a path to avoid running into the army but she still seemed cautious about her every step. Tears masked her face of fear as she ran with all speed toward her homeland.

"What if the kheshlars come too late when we attack them…or what if they don't come at all?" Etherond asked.

"That is a chance we are going to have to take. We can no longer win this war without the kheshlarn support. We can either defeat this common enemy with their aid, or die slowing them down and causing enough damage to make it easier for the kheshlars to be victorious. I suggest that you begin praying to your creator," Karceoles said.

Etherond gulped as he took one last look toward the south. Searon stepped beside him and placed his hand on his shoulder.

"Will you join me in prayer?" Searon asked.

Chapter Forty-two

Rest felt like something of the past as Searon pressed forward with his stallion between the vast hills heading south. He had to make sure his army stayed far behind him and kept quiet, a task that he presented to Etherond in hopes that his loud mouth could stay silent if for only a time. Only Karceoles kept pace with him on his own horse, and the two of them kept an eye on the steady army of draeyks and daerions that headed south. They would arrive at the forest soon, and it would prove even harder to keep an eye on them without being seen or losing them. Searon knew that he would have to place scouts through the forest, but he hoped that they would not be discovered, otherwise their surprise attack would be in vain.

Through the midst of the army, there appeared to be a man in black robes mounted on a tall ebony stallion, zylek in hand, and barking orders to all the creatures surrounding him. There was a familiarity about him, and after a moment Searon recognized him as the same man from Legain. Before, he hadn't noticed that he was a wizard because he was hiding in his hood without a zylek to be seen, but now his hood was down and dark-gray hair tangled down past his chest. In his hands he held a twisted wooden zylek warped in shadows to match his dark attire.

Soon, the thin pine trees and autumn maples and oaks became thicker pine, and they knew they were drawing closer to the kheshlarn territory. With the abundant amount of large pine, it made it easier for

278

them to hide in the shadows behind the army. It was not difficult to track them with how primitive they were. They were also able to resume conversations at a quiet whisper without fear of being overheard.

"They have a wizard," Searon said.

"No follower of the dark is considered a wizard," Karceoles said trotting next to him.

"Dark wizard?" Searon asked.

"Dare I call a kheshlar one of your kind, a dark human?"

"I suppose you could, that is, if you really wanted to. I, however, find that fallen or wicked would fit nicer."

"Wicked?"

Searon smirked, "Yeah, wicked wizard."

"If you want to act a fool, then yes you may call him that. However, a warlock would be what he truly is. A corrupted wizard that has fallen to the darker powers of magic where power means more to him than preservation of life."

"Warlock, got it."

"His name is Zergiel, once he was a guardian of peace – a part of the magic council that protected these lands," Karceoles said.

"There is a council that protects Calthoria?"

"Not anymore, it has long since disbanded. Long ago there were dark times where there were far more evil than mere draeyks and daerions tormenting the land. The last effective use of the council would have been the battle against the dragons. There are few of us left, Shronan and I are all that is left I'm afraid except for Zergiel. Most of the mages and wizards have since been lost or destroyed, and if there are any druids left they have not let themselves be known."

"Druids?"

"They are more a legend now than a reality; once they roamed the land through the forests, protecting the wildlife with magic and being one with nature. This was back when kheshlars did not fear magic, but practiced it with druid help. Nature was more alive when they were about than ever."

"So what happened to Zergiel?" Searon asked.

"He betrayed the guardians, killing many of them, craving power in the end before he disappeared."

Searon left the matter there as he saw that the topic didn't seem to be one of the wizard's favorites. The forest continued to get thicker around them as they entered in kheshlarn territory with trees so tall that they made all the men appear insignificant in comparison. He decided to wait for attack until they were far enough in the kheshlarn territory that would leave no choice but for the kheshlars to defend their land, but not too far in that harm would come to them. There was a long stretch of kheshlarn territory that many roamed before entering the capital of Sudegam.

Nobody else knew when the ideal moment would be because even Searon hadn't decided yet. Everyone followed his judgment and actions without question except for Leinard, who traveled close behind with a few mutters under his breath about what actions he would take that would be more productive. An opening presented itself a mile north of Sudegam when the army stopped to plot their attack rallying around the warlock. At that moment, Searon knew that it would have to be then or never to begin his attack, and it would be best to catch the dark force unaware.

Reaching down to his sash, he felt at the wrong side absently for his weapon and found a scabbard of his large throwing knife. Surprise filled him as he felt that the weapon was back in place. The last he remembered, it was still embedded in a human in the haunted village. He had never gone to pull it out, and yet there it was back in place, and it wasn't until then that he began to believe its enchantment. Withdrawing it from his sash, he galloped forward.

"Charge!" he yelled into the twilight air.

Hair fluttered about his neck where it draped through his crimson-and-gold helm that he secured atop his head. Blood boiled through his veins with the electric feeling of heading into battle. His stallion was in the front for only a short time as the rest of the cavalry caught up and rushed ahead of him for protection. As he neared the force, he heaved the long throwing knife at a daerion where it penetrated through the veins in its neck and collapsed to the ground.

The dark army was caught completely unaware as the cavalry blasted through them, knocking down ranks of creatures to never return to their feet. Searon only kept a few ranks back as he sliced at the creatures as well as he could with the long claymore in his hands. Most humans would not be able to wield such a large weapon while mounted, but his strength and agility was exceptional for a man. Many of the others held lances and pikes as they charged the ranks, with short swords attached to scabbards at their hips for extra protection when they need-ed it.

All around him, creatures fell as they tried to form rank to the sur-prising attack, but many of their defensive warriors were on the far side and closest to Sudegam as they were supposed to be the first ranks to strike the city. Instead, most of their crossbow soldiers were in the back and crumbled under ranks of cavalry and men as they rushed in. The advantage seemed theirs as they pressed in, losing few men and striking down the creatures three to one.

Searon paid little consideration to the battle tactics, as he knew that his captains would be working things out with everyone. He wished that Andron were with him now, and the thought of his old friend brought a wrath to Searon that he hadn't known since the slaughter of his family. One after another, the creatures fell before him, pounded into the ground; any that attempted to get up were smashed by the men with maces and hammers behind him.

Etherond trotted up next to him with his brown stallion and fought alongside the cunning general, fueling off Searon's intense drive, and the two of them formed an impenetrable V that zigzagged as they rushed forward. The broadsword nearly mirrored Searon's own attacks, and besides, the sword itself looked very similar in design with a crim-son-and-gold hilt slightly smaller and a blade as thick except for its length being considerably easier to handle from horseback. Not every-one could use a broadsword with such skill and maneuverability to strike in such a way to make each curve of the blade effective, but Etherond had years of practice. His ability to catch attacks by twisting his weapon so either an axe or machete would snag between the curves, more than making up for his lesser swordsmanship skill than Searon.

Together, they galloped forward, breaching a path toward both the wizard and the mage on the east to place a defense in front of them. Orange energy spiraled out of the wizard's zylek into flame that encir-cled all the surrounding creatures. Another blast left his zylek in a zig-zag pattern that forked from the main stream to slam like lightning into the bodies of a dozen more creatures. Thunder blasted with an echo as the orange electricity pulsed through the draeyks and daerions alike. Each new creature that stepped too close to the others became en-twined in the magic as well and fell to the ground by their comrades, convulsing.

The Crimson Claymore

"You look a little fried!" Karceoles shouted. "There isn't quite anything like fried lizard," he chuckled as he used his zylek as a staff to smack creatures as he sped past atop his horse.

"Reckless fool," Sh'on muttered with rolled eyes atop his own mare.

The wizard didn't seem to care what his cousin, the mage, thought as he continued to blast forth flames, lightning, and spheres of orange light to any creature around him. There seemed to be excitement in his eyes as they glowed brighter than a child on their birthday. A sinister grin formed upon his face as he released energy that he spent so much time trying to contain. The only time he truly looked happy was when he was in the midst of battle.

Searon and Etherond positioned themselves to contain the flow of enemies on the front side, which caused the wizard to change his direction of spells to his right. Now that he was no longer alone with Searon's charge close at hand, he reined in his spells, and they became less chaotic and more focused. He seemed to focus on a greater area of the enemy with his new attacks, calling forth magical rainfalls of fire that fell amid the ranks of draeyks and daerions. Many of his newer attacks were as simple as knocking opponents down to let the surrounding warriors finish them off. It seemed he did know how to play it smart and use little energy when the task called for it, yet it seemed that whenever the battle started, he contained the need to impress.

Sh'on fought on Searon's left side, casting a dazzling series of simple flows of green magic. He maneuvered his hands in patterns, causing them to glow with a green hue as he directed his spells toward the draeyks and daerions. Most of his magic was used to knock creatures forward or back in order for the surrounding human warriors to strike their foes down with ease. His enemies would highlight in emerald as his magic touched them before they were cast aside to fall upon a piercing or blunt weapon.

In the midst of the opposing army, he created a crater in the center, causing them to concave into a V, making a gap that became easily accessible for the charging cavalry. There seemed to be no need in using powerful magic for the mage, as the wizard seemed so fond of using, when there were hundreds of warriors galloping forward to strike down the foes that he tossed to the ground with magic. It was a strategy that he already discussed with them in detail before the attack, one that Karceoles fought hard against but ultimately accepted.

Sh'on seemed to notice the fire rain that the wizard created and appeared to get an idea of his own. He strained as he focused his energy into a sphere that glowed with more passion than anything previously seen, and after a few enchanted words he shot the globe of magic into the clouds. At first, nobody could tell what he did, but when a brilliant white cloud turned green and fell over the middle ranks of the creatures they could see the thick ice rain that stormed down. Everything that descended appeared as green snow, but when it fell upon the rough skin of the daerions, or the scales of the draeyks, it seemed to freeze them ever so slightly so that their movements grew sluggish.

The mage's productive spell was short lived, however, when a laughing Karceoles blazed an orange flame from the tip of his zylek that spiraled forth, catching hundreds of the creatures and setting them afire, but at the same time many humans were affected that screamed into the wind as they burned from head to toe. The spell proved as effective is it was foolish.

Searon observed as Sh'on watched the wizard and nearly let a lone daerion rush toward his blind side. "Shronan!" he screamed, hoping the mage would notice.

The mage raised his hand in the nick of time for his magic to surround and freeze the blue-skinned creature in place, its scimitar only inches from his face and its horns twitching ever so slightly as it huffed through its mangled snout. A green glow surrounded the daerion as Sh'on lifted his arms out and continued sprinting forward. The creature rose above his head, and he dashed under it. His hands regained their proper hue, and the beast plummeted to the ground behind him in a thud.

Searon fell well back, behind both the wizard and mage that cleared the ranks ahead on both sides. He was amazed by their power and didn't want to get too close to their spells, and so both he and Etherond fought alongside each other in the center ranks behind a force of their own men. Their tactics and element of surprise had them at an advantage, but he knew it would not last for long against the vast numbers of draeyks and daerions.

The warlock was stuck behind the vast amount of creatures in what appeared the back of the battlefield. He pressed forward, trying his best to maneuver through the ranks of his army in order to better attack the force that caught him by surprise. Some of his allies did not move quickly enough for his liking, and he knocked them aside, sometimes using his magic to kill a few until they parted for him. Too many were clustered together, which put him at a disadvantage.

Searon continued to fight well, attacking two or three draeyks at a time with a daerion between. The reptiles seemed to outnumber the blue creatures three to one but were an easier foe to overcome. Welts began to form all about his body where attacks struck him, and although his heavy armor protected him from anything fatal, and Sh'on's protective magic stopped a few when his plate mail sparkled green, many blows still got through. There were too many creatures to defend against, and Searon couldn't stop them all.

After striking down at least a dozen draeyks, a daerion leaped out at him and caught him unaware. Without having the time to think, he pulled out his throwing knife and hurled it at the creature's soft spot between its jaw and curved horn on its neck. After a fierce roar, it came crashing down, colliding with Stripes and causing Searon to tumble onto the ground. Once he rolled and came back up to his feet, he noticed he was surrounded by draeyks with a handful of injured humans on the ground around him from the collision. He held his claymore high and awaited an attack, the ferocity of his blade glowing a brighter crimson than ever seen before, a feat that gave him confidence in his abilities. Two dashed at him that he quickly outmaneuvered and struck down only for the gap to be replaced by three. He took a step back and looked around for an exit.

When Searon looked about, he noticed Etherond charging toward him with a battle cry and a force of five cavalry. They reached him in the nick of time as he defended himself against the growing number of creatures. Etherond led the charge, holding his flamberge tight as he struck down the surrounding creatures with such precision that they had little chance of defending themselves.

Once Etherond was by Searon's side, the two of them fought off a new charge of daerions that rushed at them, creating a blur of deep blue to match the ocean. The captain's skills against such a foe was impressive, as the two of them fought the creatures one by one and after only a little resilience they overcame the force. For most men, it would have taken several to strike down only one of the blue-skinned creatures.

A force of humans charged past them to fight the oncoming ranks, leaving only Searon and Etherond alone in a field of dead reptiles, blue-skinned creatures, and more humans than they wanted to count. Etherond took off his golden helm and smiled as he held out his hand, which Searon gratefully accepted and mounted the horse behind the captain.

"How do we fare this battle?" Searon asked.

"We lose many; at first it looked as if we could win, but now that their ranks are set in place I doubt we will survive the hour. Where are those bloody kheshlars?"

"Do not fear; they will come. Starlyn would not fail us."

"I know you trust her, but if she doesn't return soon with a force, we will be obliterated," Etherond said.

"I know."

"Your stallion is injured. I sent him back to be cared for. Do you wish another horse?"

"No, I will continue from the ground. Take me to the wizard and mage."

"As you wish, my lord." Etherond galloped off through the ranks of dead men toward the battle.

Searon could see the progress as they neared the battle, and he watched carefully at how their number dwindled. Everybody fought well, but there were just too many of the creatures to be successful. Their archers were doing an excellent job plummeting arrows into the ranks of daerions and draeyks, but so were the draeyk crossbowmen who felled enough humans to rival. Even with the archers standing on a slope, firing down into the ranks with a few bushes and trunks to cam-ouflage them, they were soon outflanked. Swordsmen stood at the bot-tom of the slope to protect them, and they returned the favor by help-ing shoot down their enemies, yet still the draeyks broke through their defenses to the archers, causing them to face close opponents.

On the other side, the warlock, Zergiel, finally broke through to the front lines and got off his black horse, raising his zylek high into the air and slamming it to the ground, causing black swirling magic to shatter from the soil and toss humans like toys throughout the crowd of battle. He began to target humans with magical abilities that Noraes had sent with them, and one by one he showed them that the power of their magic was insignificant compared to his own. Many magical barriers that were on a few of the more cunning warriors collapsed when the men died who created the protection spells. Without the protection of the spells, they began to fall, creating even more openings for the savage creatures to break through. Nobody seemed able to cause a scratch to the warlock, and many of the warriors didn't dare try; those that did became mutilated with dark magic.

Both Sh'on and Karceoles were on the opposite side of the battlefield and more than doubled their efforts by working together as they headed toward Zergiel. Despite their skill, both got cut up as there were simply too many draeyks and daerions for them to fight. Searon noticed what the two were trying to do and urged Etherond forward to reach the mage and wizard, rallying humans as they passed to join them.

With a force of at least fifty cunning warriors behind Searon and Etherond, they were able to carve a path through the thick pool of creatures. When Searon finally reached the mage and wizard, his companions separated out into a triangle of protection around them. Their position wouldn't hold long, but it would be long enough for what Searon wished to accomplish.

"Follow us," Searon told them and rushed out with his claymore without further explanation.

Neither of them doubted him and kept up on his heels, Sh'on withdrawing a short sword from a scabbard at his side, highlighted in green and hidden between his robes without anybody knowing he had it. Karceoles continued to limp with use of his zylek for a cane against the forest slopes.

As Searon tore a path in the front, he didn't bother making any killing strikes, instead focusing his attention on swinging his claymore with such a fury that he blasted through their defenses, clashing into armor or legs tripping up his foes, making it easier on the warriors behind to finish them. Together, they tore a path without Karceoles or Sh'on having to use much magic except for a few blasts of air to help clear the way. Their progress inspired all of the surrounding humans to fight even harder, creating a push on the dark army to match the start of the battle.

Within minutes, Searon neared Zergiel, headstrong and brave, in all readiness to conquer the battlefield, and he pushed on in hopes to take on the dark wizard himself. Before he could reach the warlock, the warrior noticed the alteration of his zylek that now pointed to him and switched his claymore to his left hand as he felt for the throwing knife at his sash. As Zergiel called magic, Searon launched the small weapon through the air, creating a high-pitched whistle that throbbed his ears. When knife and black lightning bolt collided, time seemed to freeze, and seconds felt like hours until finally an explosion shattered in a white light that knocked everybody in the surrounding area off of their feet.

Dust fluttered about everywhere, falling from the heavens and covering all the warriors, creatures and humans alike, in such a thick soot that everybody appeared to be of the same gray color, with only protruding snouts of lizards or horns of rams defining the races. Violet sparkles drifted to the ground in a powder that made many sneeze as they inhaled it. Even the warlock was knocked from his feet, and Searon seized the opportunity to approach the weakened man.

His claymore sprang forth, glowing crimson with shaking intensity as he reached Zergiel, who still lay across the ground, yet it wasn't fast enough as the warlock rolled out of the way of the strike. As Searon struck a second time, Zergiel was able to pull out his long sword for a block that created echoing sparks, which dazzled to the ground about them. The warrior kept his attack too heavy for the warlock to get to his feet and caused him to drop his zylek in order to defend himself against Searon's raging attacks.

Etherond and the rest of the accompanying warriors kept their distance from the mage but formed a circle of defense around them as they sparred, with Karceoles's and Sh'on's help. Most were out of reach of Searon's vision as he fought, but he felt safe with the protection surrounding him.

After a long few minutes of keeping the offensive against the warlock, he inflicted a few scrapes to draw blood. Many of the strikes were deflected whether they were overhead or slashed from the side, but Searon was able to slice both forearms. Zergiel, desperate, dashed and crawled out of the way, grabbing a fighting draeyk and tossing it toward him. His claymore sank right through the creature's stomach, soaking the crimson glow in black ooze. Zergiel rushed over to his zylek, and shot a quick blast of black flare toward Searon that struck him in the shoulder and tossed him back into a draeyk.

Karceoles and Sh'on quickly stepped forward as Etherond helped Searon to his feet. Colors of green, orange, and black magic flashed everywhere from ice, fire, and lightning. There seemed to always be a point where one of them was blasted off their feet from magic. Zergiel appeared to be losing the battle even though he appeared more powerful. Both the wizard and mage were faster to strike, and with two of them they overwhelmed him. They closed in on Zergiel and didn't allow an exit.

The warlock kept his spells ready as he stumbled forward, drenched in blood, and beaded in sweat that dripped down his pale face. He was wearing down, and it was showing, but he did his best to show an exterior of strength. Even though he appeared to be losing his battle, the draeyks and daerions all around him were tossing humans like a pack of wolves closing around a farm of sheep.

With great concentration, he seemed to catch a blast of green ice from the mage that he directed back toward him, followed by a fireball of black from his own zylek. The deadly duo of magic tossed Sh'on hundreds of feet back into the crowd of humans soaked in water. Karceoles stepped forward with a sigh to duel the warlock. They knew they could not defeat the dark army, yet their goal wasn't to win but to postpone the inevitable until the kheshlarn army could arrive. *If* they would arrive in time.

Both Zergiel and Karceoles seemed to have a constant battle of canceling magic that faded each time it collided. Magic was really all about predicting elements, and as a fire spell hit a water spell it would simply evaporate. However, sometimes a bit of the water from the magic would continue on to strike its foe, depending on how powerful the spell was. It continued on like this for a long while with small residue of spells striking each other with light drizzles of water, insufficient spurts of lightning no more powerful than a positive striking a negative charge when two people touch, or even a small puff of flame that held no more burn than moving a hand too close to an ignited pipe. This kept on until Karceoles shot an ice spell as Zergiel released one of water that blanketed around the ice but froze as it continued on toward the wizard. Zergiel leaped the out of the way, dodging the ice, but Karceoles was not as lucky as the blanket of water became a storm of raging ice that froze him and a dozen draeyks and humans around him into solid ice.

Zergiel grinned as he walked toward the frozen form of Karceoles. He attached his zylek to his robes and withdrew his sword from the ground where it had fallen. With slow approaching steps, he made his way toward the wizard. He raised the sword up high and slashed it down hard in hopes to shatter him; everybody seemed to stop throughout the battlefield to watch. As the blade came crashing down, Searon, who was still injured and watching the battle from the pile of bodies nearby, leaped forth with his claymore out. The warlock's blade clashed with Searon's claymore hard, sliding down the length of the blade and colliding with the side of the warrior's helm, tossing him back into a tree where he hit the back of his head. His body remained motionless as his limp body slid down the tree onto the ground seeing nothing but darkness.

Chapter Forty-three

Starlyn strode up to the king's chambers only to be blocked by the guard withdrawing two scimitars. The king's guard, Vil'ek, stepped forward, eyebrows raised, as menacing as a jaguar prepared to protect its kin. No thoughts protruded into Starlyn's mind other than the fact she had to plead with the king to listen to her demands to help Searon, her friend. Everybody was in danger, even the kheshlars, but she knew that it would be nigh impossible to convince the stubborn king. There was little hope that the kheshlars would rally behind her again after the last time she drove them into battle, yet that wasn't what she wanted. Even though she hated to admit it, she felt that even losing the wizard would be a blow to her heart. She knew Searon well enough by now to know that no matter if the kheshlars came to help or not, he would lead his men into battle in an attempt to at least preserve the kheshlars as long as he could.

"Let me pass," she demanded.

"What is your business with the king?" Vil'ek asked.

"A threat approaches the capital. I must speak with him."

Her breath came in gasps since she'd reached Sudegam in a matter of only a few hours. Nothing dared get in her way or slow her down, not even the hand of the kheshlarn king. She stepped forward toward the golden doors of the throne room

He stared at her for only a moment, searching her eyes before sheathing his weapons and stepping aside. The doors clambered open, and the scraping metal echoed throughout the chambers. Vil'ek kept at her heel, trying to cease her speed but failed as she ran up the steps to the king.

Elsargast pondered scrolls as he sat upon his golden throne, without a look of fret upon his ageless, wrinkleless face. Annoyance stained his expression as he glanced up from his studies toward Starlyn, who swiftly bowed before him.

"What is it, my child?" Elsargast asked with distaste in his mouth.

"An army approaches our land, my king. Thousands strong, both draeyks and daerions amid the ranks."

"How have you come across this information?"

"I traveled north with Searon and the wizard to the draeyk settlements. Abandoned...all of them. He keeps pace with the rear of their army, but they press on directly toward us. Searon plans to strike them from behind, my king, as soon as they enter our territory, but he won't be able to stop them. There are too many."

"Are you sure of what you've seen?"

"Do you not trust one of your own, my king?"

"Not one that holds the company of a human. Especially when traveling with a wizard who desperately wants me to join this silly war of his."

"Karceoles might be outspoken and rash, my king, but foolish he is not. He saw this war coming and did all in his power to stop it. Nobody took him seriously, and now an army approaches our land."

"Will this human army weaken them so, that when they strike we can easily finish them off?"

"I beg of you, my lord, there is little time. If we don't help them out, they will be no more. Is that what they deserve for trying to protect our race? They will be slowed and weakened attacking us, but it will still happen. If this is a full-scale war, any allies we can get will be useful."

Elsargast calmly rolled up his scroll and neatly tied the purple ribbon onto it before placing it on the ground with the rest. Footsteps rang through the hall, and three kheshlars entered the throne room, each bowing in turn to their king. Vil'ek stepped between them and the king with hands on scabbards.

"My lord," one of them said, "a threat approaches our northern borders. Draeyks and some blue beast. They appear to be marching toward us."

"Very well," the king sighed. "Vil'ek, head into the city, and seek anybody willing to fight on such short notice. Have them join together north of Sudegam. Lead a force against this army, and protect our lands. Wedge them between you and this human army at their head, and destroy all between."

"Yes, my lord." Vil'ek bowed.

"Starlyn?"

"Yes, my king?"

"I am sorry to have doubted you. Join Vil'ek under his command, and show him to this force. Plan with him the best way to strike this upcoming foe. And when this threat is no more, I want you and any living human leaders to report directly back to me."

"Yes, my king."

Starlyn followed Vil'ek out the palace, but instead of keeping with him as he rallied the kheshlars, she parted and traveled by herself outside of Sudegam toward a small lake. She hadn't realized how much she'd missed her home until she returned. The kheshlarn territory was peaceful, animals scurrying about, birds chirping in peaceful melodies.

She stopped at the foot of a small cottage surrounded by blue jays and chipmunks, and she smiled at their welcoming sight. The cottage seemed separated from everything else around the kheshlarn capital—this was solitude, and it had been a while since she had visited this place. After a deep breath, she knocked on the door, breath caught as she wondered how long it had been since she'd seen her friend.

The door opened slightly where a pair of silvery-emerald eyes appeared with a smile before it opened fully. A kheshlarn woman emerged with long brunette hair that she pushed from her face with a blush. Her skin was a pale green rather than the pale blue of most kheshlars. Tall rounded ears with only a slight point at their tips broke through her straight hair on each side.

"Starlyn, it's nice to see you," she smiled.

"Anaela…there's no time; I need your help," Starlyn pleaded.

A mask of concern replaced the kheshlar's smile. Starlyn hated to ask aid from her friend, but knew that she needed to. Time was desperate, and there was nobody more skilled. More importantly, there was nobody she could trust more than her dear friend.

"What is it?"

"I need you to come fight with me. I know you were hoping to stay out of battle, but a threat exists in the kheshlarn forest. You are the best archer there is."

"Let me get my armor," the woman said as she closed the door.

Within minutes, the woman opened the door back up, dressed for battle with chain mail covered with green plate mail lined in silver that nearly resembled leaves. The two rushed back into the city where they found Vil'ek awaiting them with a force of over six thousand kheshlars armored and ready for battle. There hadn't been such a sight in decades, not since the last time Starlyn had led her brethren into battle.

"Lead the way to your…friends." Vil'ek nearly spat the last word out.

Starlyn did not care for his judgment and only concerned herself with the fact that he was going to help her save her friends. Nothing else mattered. Hope remained. They left Sudegam and Starlyn led the way to the north where they traveled less than a league to hear the clatter of battle. As soon as the creatures were spotted, kheshlars rushed forward, raising weapons high and screaming a battle cry to the mother to aid them in their fight.

Starlyn raised her own sword and noticed Phoenix's blade in her grasp. Tears formed around her eyes for the fallen hero that had saved her life. "For the mother!" she cried and ran forward.

Although a sword wasn't her preferred weapon, her skill with it was near flawless. She parried foes with such precision that many fell before her. Draeyks and daerions fought hard against her, and many were hard to oppose with their hardened scales, but Starlyn knew of their weak spot just below the jaw and targeted it. As she pressed on, she saw the impressive magic that had frozen Karceoles in a statue of black ice. A wizard in black robes rushed at the frozen form with a sword held high, and Starlyn cried out. Before the ice could be shattered, Searon leaped forward and blocked the blow, only to be thanked by being knocked away as easily as a moth.

The dark wizard turned back around with a sickening grin appearing on his face when he looked at the frozen statue of Karceoles. He raised his sword high and slashed it down, but before the blade could make contact, a blast of green energy zipped through the air and struck his palm, knocking his weapon from his grasp and into the sky where it disappeared with a twinkle. More magic pressed onward toward the dark wizard in lightning bolts and water blasts, but many were cast aside as he raised his zylek to deflect them.

Kheshlars pressed forward through the ranks, many unheard because of their soft steps. Vil'ek fought gallantly next to Starlyn with his two scimitars, and the two of them sliced through many ranks of creatures. The draeyks and daerions outranked the humans three to one, but now that the kheshlars arrived, the numbers were well balanced. It took little effort for the kheshlars to break through the dark army's defense, but after a while they reformed and created a wall that made things more challenging.

Starlyn felt uneasy with the sword in her grip and dearly missed her hammer. She fought well with the imbalanced weapon, but knew that she would be more successful with her own steel. Kheshlarn weapons were better balanced, and there was always something about a hammer that she craved. Swords were meant for elegance and precision, when all she wanted to do was slam through defenses. She pushed through the ranks with the kheshlars surrounding her. Kheshlars weren't that much better warriors than the draeyks and daerions, only swifter with better balanced weapons. The creatures had been trained well, and many kheshlars underestimated their foe, paying with their lives.

A harsh battle transpired between Sh'on and Zergiel. It took them far from most of the action. Zergiel shot a black spell at Sh'on that formed like a skull coming toward him. Sh'on shot two small green fireballs from his palms that blasted into the skull, and both magic disappeared into a swirl of smoke. Both of Sh'on's hands glowed green, and within moments so did Zergiel. With a smile, Sh'on raised his hands into the air and slammed them down, causing the warlock to float up into the sky and crash into the ground in a thud.

Zergiel got back to his feet, grasping his shoulder with clenched teeth, and shot a bolt of black lightning toward the mage. Sh'on's body lit up ebony, and his white bones could be seen through the shock as his body convulsed. While being electrocuted, Zergiel shot another blast of magic—a black fireball—that caught Sh'on's green robes aflame. He spun around, shaking his body and trying to put out the fire as an arrow killed a daerion beside him. The beast collapsed on top of Sh'on, putting out the fire but trapping him under it.

Zergiel laughed and rushed forward toward the kheshlarn army. Determination plastered his face that showed he wasn't about to lose the battle because of the arrival of the kheshlars. Dozens of black skulls burst forth from his zylek that claimed the lives of many kheshlars as he charged them with his black horse. The kheshlars scattered out of the warlock's way, including Starlyn, but when she looked over her shoulder she noticed Vil'ek hadn't budged. He stood alone as Zergiel charged for him, zylek raised and a surge of three black skulls that shot toward Vil'ek. Starlyn shrieked out in alarm, but Vil'ek didn't turn. He braced his two scimitars in a cross as the magic neared him, and to everyone's surprise, the black skulls vanished as they encountered the blades. Vil'ek smirked and rushed toward the warlock, dove and slashed his weapons onto the legs of the horse, causing the animal to trip and fall to the ground with Zergiel sliding into the dirt.

Vil'ek rushed toward the fallen form of the warlock. Zergiel didn't have time for another spell and pulled out a sword that hid within his robes and deflected the kheshlar's weapons. The two battled each other with such skill that it amazed all the kheshlars and humans surrounding them. Their weapons hit so hard against each other that sparks silhouetted the air everywhere. They seemed equally matched opponents, and neither could break through the other's defenses.

Starlyn reached the frozen Karceoles and stared at him in disbelief. She felt the cold chill of the ice and looked at the blank expression on his face. His jaw was agape and eyes large as if he expected the worst to happen to him. Starlyn circled him, battling anything that came near. She tried looking around for Searon, but she couldn't find him and hoped he was all right. As she battled furiously at the daerions to her front, she didn't notice one that came at her from behind. She gasped, realizing she didn't have the time to stop it. Suddenly, an arrow with a black tip flew past her face and into the daerion's skull. It dropped to the ground without a sound. She smiled as she searched for her friend, seeing her a hundred paces away with bow in hand. Starlyn's mind eased as she noticed more and more arrows killing draeyks and daerions around her, making her only have to attack one at a time.

The draeyks and daerions were dropping hard with all the kheshlarn support in battle. The once-massive army was getting smaller and smaller, until it held a lot less fighters than the kheshlars and humans. Zergiel appeared to notice and knew he wasn't going to win the battle. He ducked from a blow from Vil'ek and then rolled forward, knocking the kheshlar down. He set his sword back in its scabbard and got his zylek out. A large black skull shot into the air that exploded and created black fog that surrounded the entire battlefield.

When the fog cleared, Zergiel and all of the creatures were gone. Starlyn looked through the wilderness and saw them all running back up north, already a league away. Sh'on came up to her, being freed of the daerion now. He stood by Karceoles and his put hands on the cold ice. His hands glowed green, and steam rose from them. Slowly, the ice around Karceoles melted away. He didn't melt it too fast because the sudden change of temperature might be harmful to even a wizard. When he collapsed free of the ice, Starlyn caught him and held him in her arms in an effort to warm him. Sh'on held onto his robes, heating them up and drying them. As soon as he was done with that, he also helped warm him up slowly with magic. Karceoles was unconscious but alive, and they set him on the ground while they searched for other survivors.

"Where is Searon?" Starlyn asked, concerned.

Her heart caved in a little as she realized she couldn't find him. She remembered him saving the wizard's life and being tossed back. Shivers spread through her body as she searched for him, unable to imagine him being gone.

"I do not know; last I saw he tumbled into a tree after being hit by Zergiel," Etherond responded, walking up to her.

Everybody began searching around for him, but he was nowhere to be found. Etherond dug through piles of draeyks and daerions on the ground. Starlyn searched for him through the whole area hurriedly, trying to find any glimpse of him.

The sweat and worry of all the warriors was astonishing. Without Searon, they had no idea what to do or where to turn next. They all seemed to look to Starlyn for orders but realized she was just trying to find Searon. Now everybody joined in. The kheshlars had left the battlefield, already heading back to the capital.

Drahcirch seemed unconcerned about Searon's well-being and gathered a handful of followers that he began to order about. During the battle, he led a sizable force to victory against overwhelming odds and brought even more to his favor.

Bodies were overturned and set into piles by race. Some daerions still drew breath but were swiftly silenced by the men.

"Here he is!" Etherond shouted.

Starlyn turned around and rushed to where Etherond moved around carcasses. She helped him pull Searon out from under a large daerion that was atop him. They carried him to a clearing and set him down. She pulled off his crimson-and-gold helm. Dried blood streaked down both sides of his face. His dark-brown hair was died red, and Etherond lifted him to a sitting position. Starlyn looked at the back of his head where there was a large gash. He wasn't bleeding anymore, but a lot of blood had been lost. She took off his gauntlets and felt his wrist with her fingers.

"Is he alive?" Etherond asked.

"His pulse is very slow, but yes, he is still alive," Starlyn said.

"That's good." Etherond was relieved.

"Help me, we must get him to Sudegam, fast," Starlyn said.

Chapter Forty-four

Searon awoke with his chest bare and a searing pain that traveled up his spine. His eyes opened and were nearly blinded at the brightness of the white room. He lay upon a bed with his head propped atop soft pillows and red-stained white sheets that he knew came from his wound. Dizziness overtook him when he tried to sit up, and that caused him to fall back to his pillow and made him want to curl up in a ball from pain if he only could. A glass of cold water seemed to shine in his peripheral vision that had him grasping for it in a heartbeat. Thankfully, his arms worked well enough for him to grab the water and take a few sips before the rest spilled all over him. His dizziness began to fade as he set the glass back on the white table next to him upside-down.

The door cracked opened, and a beautiful brunette kheshlar wearing white robes entered the room. She stalked up to Searon and gazed at him with sparkling silver-emerald eyes. Concern masked her face as she sat at a stool next to him and felt his forehead with her palm. Her skin was different than the other kheshlars; it was a pale green instead of blue.

"How are you feeling?" she asked.

Entranced. Mesmerized. He began to wonder for a moment if he was dead, and this was the paradise realm of the creator.

"A bit…dizzy," he confessed.

"That is to be expected." She came up to the bed and sat next to him as she checked his bandages.

He watched her carefully as she inspected his wounds. Most were minor, but dried blood scarred most of his arms and face with a few on his chest. Her eyes wandered across his half-naked body for any other wounds she might have missed.

"What is your name?" Searon asked.

"Anaela," she shared, slightly smiling.

She unraveled the bandage from his head and cringed as the cloth fell. Her fingers moved to his chest where she pulled the cloth off next to expose black-and-purple bruises. He looked down and shook his head as he saw what shape he was in. Anaela ran her fingers over his chest, and he sucked in his breath to mask the pain. She pushed with her fingers at certain spots on his flesh that nearly had him wailing in pain. Her hands abruptly shot back, and she bit her lip as she looked down at him with concern.

"Don't stop," Searon whispered.

Her touch had felt divine against his bare skin, and he craved it despite the intense pain that it caused; it was worth having her soft skin upon him. He began to wonder what it would be like to have her hands travel the distance of his body, but he quickly shook his head to dismiss the notion.

She grinned as she secured his wounds back in bandages, careful not to hurt him. His eyes held hers in a long moment that seemed frozen by time. Her grin turned to a halfhearted smile as she studied him. It no longer appeared as if she were studying his wounds, but his appearance overall. He remembered doing the same the first he saw the kheshlars and wondered if this woman had ever seen a human. Her eyes lingered on his muscles, and her cheeks reddened before she turned away.

"You need to keep these bandages on for another week," Anaela blurted toward the empty glass of water.

"How long have I been out?" Searon rubbed his eyes with a yawn.

"Five days."

Five days of no memories. He shivered as he thought about it. He wondered if she had been there taking care of him for the past several days. Soon, his mind wandered to his companions, and he wondered if everybody was all right. Shivers drenched his body with chill bumps to match.

"Wow," he whispered.

He gazed around and noticed crushed herbs and vials of colorful liquids on a desk at the far side of the room and gaped. There were so many potions and herbal remedies, some of which he recognized from when Starlyn had him picking plants and flowers with her for healing Andron. His attention shifted back to the kheshlar, who studied him carefully. Her ears were rounder than the other kheshlars but still had a sharp tip, and her eyebrows weren't as silver as other kheshlars.

"Are you a healer?"

"More so than other kheshlars. I cannot explain it, but I somehow know more about the plants. They call to me and tell me how to use them. Your injuries...I did not think they could be healed, but Starlyn was insistent that I cure you."

"Starlyn, she is well?"

"Yes. It was she who brought you aid. She asked me to help, and I am here. But now I must leave."

She stalked to the door with a hand on its handle before turning back to Searon with a long face and pursed lips. Her breathing slowed but deepened, and she bit her lip. Searon shifted to sit up as he admired her beauty.

"Don't go," he pleaded.

His mind clouded in a mist of pain, confusion, and happiness. He didn't understand the emotions, but for the first time his internal time clock no longer ticked. No longer did he remember how many days and hours it had been since his wife and child had been slaughtered. He mourned for them terribly, but they did not dominate his thoughts anymore. A great pressure that always kept his mind compressed felt lifted from him, like a burden that he could barely handle had been given to another. The memory of his wife and son would be treasured forever, but the sorrow and constant grief seemed to flow out of him, and made him a free man. He didn't understand it but felt without a doubt that they were connected with this woman before him. Whether it was her healing remedies or something deeper, he was unsure.

She blushed. "You have a visitor who wishes to see you."

Her heart pounded through her chest, and she clenched her fists as she touched the door handle. She dared not turn around to face Searon, but he needed no confirmation from her with his excellent hearing and close attention to detail. He smiled as she left.

The door opened almost instantly after she disappeared, with Karceoles striding in. He paused, turning back as if studying something peculiar before entering the room. His zylek held stiff in his hand as he steadied his walking with it until he could sit at the stool next to Searon's bed.

Karceoles frowned as he looked at Searon from head to toe. "You look like two draeyks were playing lizard in the loop with you."

"Lizard in the loop?" Searon asked.

"Like monkey in the middle, except if the middle lizard catches you, you get eaten."

Searon grinned despite himself. "I'm a bit dizzy, but it's getting better."

"That's good," Karceoles said.

"How about you?"

He studied the wizard, who seemed to be in a lot better shape than Searon. No external damage appeared on his skin from bruises or frostbite. A lot better than it could have been had he been chopped into a thousand chunks of ice over the battlefield. The thought of losing the wizard surprisingly terrified Searon. He knew it would be peaceful at first without the massive amount of sarcasm and recklessness, but overall the wizard had been helpful. Even if some of his ideas were stupid, they did always work.

"I am doing well, now that the frostbite went away," Karceoles admitted.

"Ah...frostbite...good times. So tell me, how do you like your payback?" Searon smirked.

"Ha, ha. I left you relatively healthy when I froze you. It is not quite the same."

"And yet I feel so much better knowing that you have gone through the preservation process."

Searon attempted to rise, but his strength failed him, and he caved back into the pillow behind his head. Karceoles rose and attempted to aid him, but after a moment's consideration Searon shook his head.

"No, I need to build my own strength."

"There is a celebration tonight, if you feel like attending," Karceoles encouraged.

"That sounds better than being trapped in this bloody room all day," Searon chuckled.

Karceoles strolled to the armoire and opened the doors carefully to display clothes ranging from robes to cotton shirts to brown breeches to and light leather armor.

"That kheshlar that was in here, Anaela, she is very beautiful," Searon admitted.

"Do not get any ideas, Searon; you do realize that she is way out of your league. Now I may have a chance, but you aren't even in the same realm of my awesomeness," Karceoles grinned.

"Now, we'll just have to see about that, won't we?" Searon smirked, finally getting to his feet and limping over to the wardrobe to peruse.

* * *

Later that night, Searon strode into the commotion in a long-sleeve shirt and dark-red vest. Everywhere around him were kheshlars drinking wine and men drinking ale. A collection of kheshlars played lovely music with a quartet of string instruments, some of which Searon recognized. He made small talk with a few of the kheshlars and humans as he walked around and let everybody know that he was feeling better. His leg was still bothering him from the fall, but it hardly showed with a slight limp as he enjoyed the celebration.

Anaela stood alone near the orchestra, swaying back and forth to the beat of the instruments. She wore a dark-green dress cut low on her lower back just above her hips where her soft skin was exposed before it traveled all the way down to her sandals. Her straight hair hung just below her shoulders, tied at the top with a green ribbon. Most kheshlars kept their hair longer, but Searon liked hers, as it was not too long or too short.

He walked up to her as she turned to face him and blushed. Her features seemed to light up, highlighting her freckles that were adorable upon her innocent face. The same feeling overcame him as the last he'd been in her presence, and he didn't understand it. He'd never felt nervous around someone, and now it seemed his heart raced at a pace to match a sprinting horse. It seemed he was finally able to accept that Victoria was gone, and he could never be with her again until after death, if the creator chose to be nice to him. He'd never considered looking for another, but now that Anaela stood in front of him, he became entranced by her beauty and character.

He barely knew the kheshlar and didn't know why his feelings about her were so strong. All that he knew was that he hoped to get to know her better. She seemed innocent, sincere, polite, friendly, and intelligent. The most intoxicating part about her, though, was her smile. That was odd for Searon, as he usually noticed lips or hair first, and although he did notice her soft glittery lips and perfectly straight hair, her smile was what entranced him. He shook his head in an attempt to dismiss such thoughts.

"Hello, guest of honor," she smiled.

"May I have this dance?" Searon held his hand out.

Her face reddened, and she stepped back. She seemed to ponder the thought of dancing with him and blushed even deeper before a shiver traveled up her. Her gaze left his, and she looked at the ground, biting her lip.

"I shouldn't," she paused. "Nobody else is dancing."

"Let us be the first," Searon smirked.

He knew that she was interested, but scared, and he wasn't sure if it was because she was embarrassed or worried about what the other kheshlars would think. She was still mysterious to him and differed from all the other kheshlars with darker hue and shorter ears. He hoped he could bring her out of her shell and learn more about her.

"I do not know," she protested.

"I'm the guest of honor, correct?"

"Correct."

"If that is so…then I should be granted a request."

"True."

"I request that I have this dance, with you," he smirked.

"All right, but only one," she said, defeated.

He reached for her right hand and placed his other on the small of her back. Her body shivered with chill bumps as he brought her close enough to smell the melon scent of her hair. At first, he began slow, leading her through the rhythm of notes with grace, but he picked up the pace by spinning her and twirling her around him. The kheshlars with instruments seemed so thrilled by the display of dancing to their music that they began to step up the pace. Soon, more and more people, both men and kheshlars alike, came over toward the orchestra to dance. Many smiled and cheered for Searon and Anaela, disbelief in their eyes at his skill.

A magical feeling came across Searon as he danced with her. Together, they held such perfect form, and felt like they'd been dancing partners for centuries. Both seemed to know what the other would do next. He studied her face as they danced and was pleased to see her relaxed and loose. Her face lit up in red heat, and she giggled as they moved from left to right, front to back. No longer was her face serious as if afraid to get involved with a troublemaker named fun. Searon smiled as he realized that it was the most pleasure he'd had in a very long time. The war wasn't on his mind; he did not contemplate what to do next, but ceased in the moment. Passion overwhelmed him. How long had it been since he gave into passion? For once, he lived in the moment, and he loved it.

Anaela's eyes closed as the song neared its end. Searon brought her in close until her head rested upon his shoulder, where they held each other until the melody faded. She continued to hum the tune under her breath, and he continued to sway her with the beat she chose for several long moments before leading her away from the crowd, still holding her hand.

Another song began as they left, and nobody bothered to pay them any heed as they walked through some bushes to stand before a lone fountain. He led her a bit farther into the clearing, where the moon shone brightly in the sky, before helping her down on the ground. Together, they lay on their backs and stared up at the stars.

They talked for what seemed like hours about nothing. Small things they learned about each other, and yet neither of them dug too personally into the other's life. He noticed her beauty intensify with the light cast from the stars and moon. A yearning to kiss her filled his heart that he dared not act on.

He wondered if she struggled with the same thoughts. Both of them had gone silent, and their faces were only inches apart. Her eyes appeared downcast, as if staring at his lips. He couldn't help but stare at hers that only seemed to sparkle more under the stars. She shifted closer, and he responded, making their lips only slivers apart.

Her body tensed, and she flushed a deeper scarlet than she had before. She pulled away and swiftly got to her feet to take a few steps back. Searon stood up with her too quickly for her to escape. He gently stroked the hair from her face and tucked it behind her ear. His touch made her suck in a deep breath and freeze. Her heart raced, he could hear it, and he could feel it. He stepped closer, lips only breaths away from her. She abruptly fell back, dodging the gentle touch of his lips as they leaned for her.

"I should go." Anaela bit her bottom lip with an intake of breath.

"Do you want to?" Searon asked.

"It doesn't matter; I need to," Anaela whispered.

"Please don't," Searon begged.

"I'm sorry." Anaela stalked off into the night.

Chapter Forty-five

Starlyn sat on the front porch of her cabin and watched the sunrise. Hummingbirds flew all around her, sucking nectar from flowers; she smiled and held out a finger. One bird looked at her sideways, only inches from her face, before it settled down on her outstretched hand. Not many people could calm animals like her. Even many kheshlars couldn't keep a busy hummingbird still for long, but Starlyn had learned from her friend Anaela. Wood kheshlars seemed much more a part of nature than high kheshlars. She wished she knew more, but as far as anybody knew, Anaela was the only one.

The air was calm and her surroundings clear. Peace. If anything, Sudegam represented peace. Although she was just outside the gates of the city at her cabin, she was still close enough to enjoy the serenity that surrounded the city. She realized how guarded the kheshlars were from the outside world. The king didn't let them stray to the human territories or to any common foes. He seemed to keep his people contained and oblivious to anything outside their own realm. Starlyn wished everything were simple again, without threat, and only stillness. Yet she wondered how boring such a life would seem now.

She looked up as the scarlet humming bird leaped from her finger and fluttered into the air while her dearest friend approached wearing a white dress. A pearl necklace hung around Anaela's neck, and a single azalea was tangled in her hair. Starlyn still remembered the day she found Anaela: alone, bloody, and scared surrounded by the mangled corpses of her brethren. She had been the only survivor of her race. At least, that was what everybody believed. Her memories were lost prior to waking up and seeing Starlyn, and her company that stalked the draeyks searching for her sister. That had been a long time ago, and ever since the two had remained close.

"Anaela, what brings you here?"

"Does one need a reason to visit an old friend?"

"Yes, one does."

"Very well…it's about your charming friend Searon," Anaela admitted.

Starlyn could hear the way she rolled his name off her tongue. A clear compassion, yet fear shook the wood kheshlar's speech. She coughed before looking away and turning scarlet.

"Do you like him?" Starlyn raised an eyebrow.

She knew her friend well and could see the interest in the woman, but Anaela remained so caught up in the rules of the high kheshlars. Starlyn didn't blame the woman since she remained under study after arriving as the only wood kheshlar seen in hundreds of years; the last one seen since their falling out with the high kheshlars. She looked into Anaela's eyes and saw that they didn't look at her, but through her, swirling in galaxies of memories and passion.

"It does not matter whether I do or not. We are kheshlars. It cannot be. In time, he will pass from this world to his creator as the mother continues to give me life until time itself stops."

"What if things were different? If we could choose…haven't you ever wondered?" Starlyn asked. Memories of her own swirled through her mind, of times spent with Noraes.

"Every day…what is your fascination with the human?" Anaela asked.

For a long time, Starlyn had wondered what it would be like to be with a human. She pursued Searon for a short time, intrigued by him since he was the first she had ever seen. Yet she soon realized he was too damaged for her, and his interest wasn't there. Elsargast had forbidden any such activity, and yet there had been no logical reason for it. It seemed only foolish because humans had such short lives. Still, it should be a choice.

"It's not him, it's...nothing," Starlyn paused. "Searon is a good friend to me; he's saved me, and I care about what happens to him as much as I care about what happens to you."

"He is a good man," Anaela smiled. "Handsome and charming too, but things cannot change. I need him to stay away from me."

"Is that for his benefit, so he won't get hurt? Or is it that you're afraid of yourself?"

"Starlyn...please," Anaela pleaded.

"Very well," Starlyn sighed. "And I suppose you want me to tell him."

"Just kind of push him in the other direction for me," Anaela sneered.

"If his mind is made up, there is no way I can change it. He can be...hardheaded," Starlyn half smiled.

"He was there at the lake during the night...and I think he's still there," Anaela mentioned.

"I'm sorry, Anaela, but men will be men," Starlyn said. "I do wonder why he went there."

Anaela nodded and stalked off. Starlyn stared after her, knowing the real reason why her friend was there. If she wasn't interested in Searon, she would have been straightforward about it. Instead, she came to Starlyn to keep him away because she knew she wasn't strong enough to. She liked him and was afraid she couldn't resist temptation. Starlyn had already fallen to temptation, and she wasn't planning on preventing her friend from it. She smiled. *Fate is unexplained and sets its own course. It happens if it's meant to be.*

* * *

Searon awoke under a purple-and-crimson sky with a stick lodged in his side. He rolled over to see Karceoles above him shaking his head as the sun rose. The sight spooked him, and he flinched backward.

"Get up, you useless scarecrow," Karceoles said.

Searon sighed as he got to his feet with a yawn. He looked around and realized he wasn't in the hospital bed he had fallen asleep in. Instead, he stood beside a lake and remembered wandering to it late in the night.

"Why were you sleeping next to a pile of deer waste?" Karceoles asked.

Searon leaped up from the ground, searching the area but seeing nothing. He continued searching the ground, even glancing at his armor but neither saw nor smelled anything.

"Made you look," Karceoles chuckled.

"What are you doing here...besides annoying me?"

"Do I need another reason?"

"Fine." Searon brushed off his shoulders and began to walk away.

"Searon," Karceoles called.

"Yes?" Searon turned around.

"Starlyn wishes to talk to you; find her at her cabin."

"Okay."

Searon hadn't ever been to Starlyn's cabin before, but he knew where it was, near a lake enclosed with trees. However, it happened to be on the other side of the lake and quite a walk. He admired the simplicity of her home as he neared it. It was all but secluded without anybody neighboring her, and a thin stream curved in front of it. Searon had to cross a wooden bridge to her porch where a lone rocking chair sat swaying in the wind. He cautiously walked up to the door carved in patterns of stars with holly hung above it. He knocked gently.

Starlyn answered the door with a smile and gestured for Searon to step inside. He complied. All around, the walls were a display of maps, scrolls, and paintings. One fresh painting caught his eye on a canvas by her desk. A hungry crow floated over a battlefield, where a warrior held a kheshlar in his arms as he tried to escape his foes. Starlyn swiftly covered it in cloth when she noticed him staring at it. He only grinned in return.

"I heard you were at the lake," Starlyn said.

"Something woke me up last night, and I went for a walk."

"So you could find Anaela?"

"Not partially. I only meant to get some air. So she saw me?"

"Yes, and she wants you to stay away."

"I didn't know she was there. I walked to the lake to enjoy the view. However, I did not know which view I would come by."

Starlyn smiled, and she walked to her kitchen and grabbed two wooden goblets. One she handed to Searon while she took a drink from her own. He stared at his for a moment, admiring the craftsmanship of the wood; up past the stem were carvings of a moon and stars.

Searon brought the goblet to his mouth for a slow sip and was surprised at the taste.

"Wine?"

Starlyn only smirked as she finished her goblet. "I'm not asking you to stay away from her. Only tone it down a little. She'll come around."

Searon grinned and nodded. He finished what was the strongest red wine he had ever had, making his body feel numb, and most of his pain sped away.

"Is there anything else?"

"Yes, where are you staying? They told me you grabbed your belongings from the infirmary."

"I don't know, but I don't want to be there any longer. Everything is too white. Where is the rest of the army?"

"They are just outside of town on the east. Sh'on is staying with them, as the rest of the captains are in guesthouses. They are growing tired of eating vegetables and fruit, but that is all we will allow them to eat around Sudegam's borders," she said.

"I reckon I will go stay with them."

"No, you can stay here. There is plenty of room out here while I sleep in the back," Starlyn insisted.

"I don't want to impose."

"Do not be silly, Searon. Besides, you need time to heal, and wouldn't you rather be closer to Anaela?"

"If you insist," Searon responded, half grinning.

"I do." Starlyn tossed him a wool blanket and left toward her room.

Chapter Forty-six

Birds chirped in a chorus with each other, awaking Searon in the morning. He lay on a couch with his eyes opened as he took in the melody of the various birds outside. They were soothing to him as he struggled to his feet. He could not remember a more peaceful night of rest. The wine had really relaxed him, and he was thankful. The sun shone brightly through the cabin, and he wondered what time it was. It appeared nearly midday, and he couldn't remember the last time he slept so late.

He walked around wondering where Starlyn got off to. She was nowhere in the main room of the cabin or outside. Cupboards were partly open throughout as if she left in a hurry. He went to the back room and knocked gently, feeling the hardened wood under his knuckles. Everything was quiet, and after a moment he tried knocking again before giving up and stalking back to the front room. He took a deep breath, inhaling pine that soothed his nose and throat. The cabin smelled like it was still fresh, and even although pine always held a fresh smell compared to other woods, he wondered if her cabin was alive and still growing. He shook the thought from his head and grabbed his claymore as he paced out the cabin.

Something unsettling rolled inside of his belly as he left. He couldn't think of any reason for her departure without telling him, and he began to worry about her whereabouts. She drank as well, so her tolerance of the dream wine must have been much higher than his own because it put him right to sleep. He stopped in his tracks as he realized he hadn't had any dreams of Victoria or his son. It was one of the few times he hadn't had nightmares of the draeyks' attack. Shivers traveled down him as he looked around.

He stood inside Sudegam on a gloomy day; the sun hid behind luscious white clouds in an overcast sky. Wind gusted across his face, giving him chills, and he continued walking into the city.

Searon stopped when he found a shop called Herbal Enchantments and decided to go inside for a look. Outside, a pile of gray stones stacked tightly together to make an oval building. At the door, a rectangle of real grass grew while all around it was dirt. Searon wiped his feet on it and opened the door.

Inside, shelves were everywhere with herbs and flowers of every color. They ranged from green to red to blue to white to yellow. Each had labels and was categorized as either seasonings, medicinal, conditioning, or essence.

"May I help you?" a tender voice asked.

Searon turned to stare at the counter where he saw the strangest kheshlar he'd ever laid eyes on. Her appearance differed completely from any other kheshlar. Her skin didn't match the pale blue of the kheshlars, or even pale green of Anaela, but instead was dark milk chocolate. At first, he wasn't sure if she even was a kheshlar until he noticed her silver eyebrows that didn't seem to match her shoulder-length ebony hair. She smiled, showing her beautiful white teeth that nearly blinded him.

He walked over to the counter and put his hand out. "My name is Searon."

"I know, you are well known, even for us kheshlars. My name is Aliuqa. Is there anything you are looking for?"

"I am just looking. I have never been in a shop like this before," Searon admitted.

"Ah, well, there are some herbs that may be useful to you on your journey; follow me."

She walked into a back room through a maroon sheet that hung on the wall. Searon followed, and she pulled the sheet out of the way for him to step inside. The silk brushed across his arm and gave him shivers as he entered.

Inside were no windows, but the entire room was lit by candlelight. Lavender candles filled the shelves at every corner and let out a flowery scent. The aromas of the candles and all the herbs were causing Searon lightheadedness. Most of the smells were lovely separately, but as they blended together it caused him dizziness.

Aliuqa stopped at the last shelf where four small containers sat with different herbs. Each was in a glass container, making them clearly defined. She handed them to Searon, where he inspected each one in turn.

"What are these used for?" he asked.

"The green leaf is called ammoresh. Mix it with water and crush to lightly slather over external wounds. The red is snaothoeth. Mix it with wine and feed to somebody for healing internal wounds. The blue is enneth. Mix with pipe tobacco to prevent fatigue before a battle. Last, the purple is called camorea. Mix a small amount with pipe tobacco to relax you after a battle and numb you from injuries. The kheshlars often use this for celebrations."

"I believe my friend Andron had some of that, although it wasn't as deep purple as yours."

"It isn't as strong either. His he could smoke by itself. However, this I suggest a small amount with your regular tobacco. These are all helpful; however, don't abuse them."

"Thank you, but how much will this cost?"

"Do not worry about payment, I owe Starlyn, and she wouldn't want you to pay."

"Well, thank you again." He looked one last time into her beautiful silver-hazel eyes beneath long black lashes before leaving the store.

Searon continued walking through the city until he came across a sparring field. He was entranced by the beauty and grace that the kheshlars fought with. Each strike resembled art rather than a calculated attack. Beyond those sparring were a few kheshlars that practiced archery from a small hill. He walked through the trails that zigzagged through the field so he could observe the kheshlars as they practiced.

When he came to the archery field, he noticed a kheshlar farther away from the others, bow held high as the wind rustled through her brunette hair. It appeared as if she wanted to be alone and away from the rest while shooting her arrows at a lone target. The kheshlar appeared as if she and the bow were one as she withdrew an arrow with more speed than the others. She held it and sucked in a breath as she grazed her thumb against the white owl feather. Her bow was crafted from cherry wood with designs that were so different than the other kheshlars. The arrow's shaft appeared to be made of hickory, and the tip sparkled in the sun, making Searon think it wasn't stone or steel.

She paused and took the arrow from her bow. Instead, she switched it with another that had a steel tip. At incredible speed, she drew her bow and released. Searon watched as it flew through the air at unbelievable speed. Her accuracy surpassed the other kheshlars; at even a hundred paces her arrow struck in the dead center of her target.

Searon smiled as he walked toward her. He studied her armor and admired its uniqueness and pattern. Chain mail covered her from shoulders to toes skintight; two-piece forest-green plate mail covered her chest and waist in a undergarment fashion. The edges of the armor were silver along with a few matching swirls upon the center of each breastplate. She released a few more arrows, and each hit the center perfectly.

"Nice shot," Searon complimented with a smile.

Anaela tensed as she turned around, eyes widening as she stared at Searon. She backed up a pace and raised her eyebrow.

"You know, you are quiet for a human," she admitted.

"Only when I want to be."

She smirked with heated cheeks.

"May I?" Searon asked, holding his hand out.

"You might want to move closer," she taunted.

He tilted his head and pursed his lips together, silently waiting until she handed him the bow. She sighed and handed him her bow before taking a step back. He held the shaft in his hands, impressed with its lightness. He looked at his target, still a hundred paces away. Anaela withdrew an arrow with steel tip and handed it to him, eyebrow still raised as if she waited for him to make a fool of himself.

He held the arrow in his hand and inspected it. The craftsmanship was beyond anything a human could make, and he nodded approvingly. Her bow was handcrafted, and only then did he notice the green metal leaves around its top and bottom. He positioned himself and pulled back its string with more ease than any human bow would allow.

"It's been a while since I've used a bow," Searon warned.

Anaela rolled her eyes.

Searon grinned as he turned away from her and stared at the target. He held the string steady and fit the arrow. Memories traveled through his mind from his marriage to Victoria all the way through the recent battle against draeyks. Thoughts scattered his mind next about how his feelings for Anaela made his memories of Victoria good ones instead of nightmares. He pushed all his thoughts and memories away and concentrated on the target. His eyes focused, and he watched as the target seemed to leap toward him and appear only a dozen paces away. He sucked in a breath and released the arrow as he exhaled. The arrow leaped through the air and struck the center just outside of all of Anaela's. He nodded and handed the bow back to her.

"I'm impressed." She shot him an uneven glance.

"Bows are not for me. I will spar you though." Searon smiled.

"I am an archer. I do not practice swordplay."

"What is that sword there for?" Searon pointed to her scabbard. "Is that just for looks like that pretty face of yours?"

Her cheeks burned red as she pulled her emerald-and-silver hilted sword and twirled it in her grasp. The sword was short, only a little longer than a short sword, obviously a backup weapon.

Searon drew his claymore and pointed it toward her with a nod. He pulled his crimson-and-gold helm from his back and secured it over his head before walking toward her.

"We are not supposed to spar on the archery field," Anaela cautioned.

"Then you'd better push me back to the sparring area." Searon came toward her.

His steel blade clashed against hers, causing crimson and emerald sparks. He tried two overhead strikes, one on each side, but she easily blocked both of them with perfection. When that didn't work, he changed his form to the snapping snake, issuing a swift combo of uppercuts and side swings that were just as easily deflected and evaded by her. An opening formed in her defenses that made him stab directly at her, but instead of flying through her defenses she leaped into the air over him.

He turned around to find her running away, with sword hung low, its tip inches from the ground as she went. She grabbed her green-and-silver helm where she did her archery and placed it on her head. As he caught up with her, she turned around and blocked his incoming strike.

His attacks stayed on the offensive, with each strike calculated with precision. He fought differently against a skilled opponent than he would on the battlefield. Dueling was an art when compared with his chaotic strikes on the field against several foes. Being reckless on the battlefield worked for him because it enabled him to slice through a handful of opponents at the same time.

He did well against Anaela and was able to push her farther into the archery field. Arrows flew to targets all around them, some even flying only inches from their faces that they had to dodge.

Anaela finally got an edge against him, and when she did she withdrew a long curved dagger that was attached to her leg and fought with both weapons. Her attacks were swift and cunning, but even with her kheshlarn speed, Searon was able to block every incoming strike. However, she was effective in pushing Searon back and taking control of the duel. He was pushed back all the way to the dueling field, where the battle broke even once again.

Searon delivered some offensive attacks that made Anaela have to dodge and cartwheel away from. She came back at him with sword and dagger, making complex spins and twirls that should have overcome any human. He not only deflected them with ease but came back with his own offensive strikes that nearly broke her defenses.

Every kheshlar on the field ceased their own attacks to watch the two of them battling. Many seemed impressed with his skill and studied him carefully. Each movement they made seemed to match each other without flaw. Anaela looked stunned that he was able to match her speed, especially because of his much larger two-handed weapon.

Searon knew that he had to prove himself now with all of the kheshlars paying attention to him. Many did not believe that a human could match them with sparring, and he was ready to prove them wrong. All of them doubted him as a leader and disapproved of what he stood for. The war was no longer about revenge, at least not anymore. He stood for peace and justice. The time had come for humans and kheshlars to take back control of Calthoria.

He lunged forward with an attack toward Anaela's face. She blocked with ease, and he followed with a high strike that was deflected just as easily. Searon ducked as she slashed high and rolled forward with a leg swipe. She fell forward onto the ground, her face colliding with the dirt. Searon stepped atop her, sending swift strikes in an attempt to finish the battle. She rolled, defending against his blows with difficulty.

He kept his attacks steady and fast, not allowing Anaela a chance to get up. His strikes kept speed when he added a couple of spins that knocked the dagger from her hand. He didn't slow as she was reduced to one weapon, making her have to steady her sword with both hands. A lone raindrop fell through the front of his helm onto his nose, and he looked up as more began to fall. At first, only a light sprinkle fell, but soon it became a flood of rain.

Anaela used the distraction to wrap her legs around Searon's ankle and twist her body, causing him to tumble onto the ground. She unraveled herself and gained the advantage on top of him, producing strikes. It became harder for Searon to defend himself because of the length of his weapon, and lack of elbow room for proper blocking. Anaela found her opening and shot three swift strikes, two high and one low. The last blow struck the hilt of his weapon, his grip loosened, and his claymore flew fifteen feet. Lightning flashed in the sky, and thunder came soon after, pounding so fierce that it could be felt through his chest.

She smiled through her helm, hair stuck to her face, in apparent victory. Searon refused to give up and already had his dagger where he struck her hand hard with its hilt. She dropped her weapon, and he hit it again, knocking it to the side. He grinned, tossed his dagger aside, and wrestled Anaela to the ground, until she lay on her back and he on top. She struggled, but he held her arms down.

Searon looked around and noticed that they were alone. The storm had grown, and it seemed the rest of the kheshlars went home. Only he and Anaela remained. His mind wandered, and while it did, Anaela kicked him and sprang an arm free. They rolled on the ground until both helmets fell off and Anaela pushed him down to be on top. Her soaked hair fell in front of her just above her breastplate. She looked down at him and grinned in victory. Searon struggled for a while until he gave up and let his body go limp.

She looked around and also noticed how uncomfortably alone they were. Searon smiled as she looked back down at him. Her soft lips perked in a silent feminine snarl. He put his hands behind his back and pushed himself up and stared into her beautiful eyes. She froze as she looked deeply into his.

Suddenly, she jumped onto him, lips compressing onto his own, light at first but quickly sinking into it. The kiss became passionate with both of their hands finding each other's hair. The rain refused to slow, and both were drenched as they tore into the kiss like animals.

As he kissed her, something inside of him awoke, and he'd never felt so alive. At first, the rain made him cold, but after her lips met his, burning warmth spread throughout his body. His heart felt as if it was barely contained inside his chest, pounding so hard that his armor seemed to vibrate to its beat. Her lips were softer than he ever imagined, and he found it impossible to tear himself away.

He gave into his desires and kissed her even more passionately, and she didn't dare stop him. She moaned when he pressed harder onto her lips. Searon felt like he glowed as he kissed her, and strangely it seemed as if she did as well. The moment did not last, though, and soon she pushed him away from her. She stared at him for a long moment before getting to her feet and running off. He sat there for a moment more before closing his eyes and sinking to the ground. In his mind, the moment came back, and he cherished reliving every second on it.

Chapter Forty-seven

Starlyn saw everything, from the two of them dueling to kissing at the end. Most wouldn't expect such an event from a human and a kheshlar, but Starlyn knew it was inevitable. She knew Anaela wasn't strong enough to resist Searon, and only a matter of time would have her losing control. However, it did happen sooner than Starlyn thought. Kheshlars were weak when humans were involved. There were no rules with humans, and they were full of temptation. Freedom wasn't evident until humans came in the picture. Without rules, there would be chaos, and that's exactly what humans were: chaos.

She needed to be break free of the bonds that held her. In Sudegam, she was a pawn to the larger picture of the kheshlars. How would they look at her if she left? Fear clouded her mind, and yet she could feel the pull that drove her away. She knew if she stayed there would be nothing for her but death. Flashbacks of her mother growing ill and dying illuminated her mind. Tears painted her face as they fell in streams. She had to be strong; it was something she had to do. There was no other way.

"Starlyn," a raspy voice whispered.

She spun and stared at her friend. He was the only one she knew she could trust. For years, he had been there for her when she needed him the most. He came only in times of need, but so many years ago he had saved her life. She owed him. The forest around her cabin looked lonely with only the two of them standing there. He had found her…somehow he knew.

"Starlyn, you need to at the least say goodbye to him. He cares for you, as a friend, like a sister. If anything, tell him you will see him again," he said.

"Shronan…" Starlyn whispered.

"He deserves that much, Starlyn," he insisted.

She knew the mage was right; he did deserve to know that she was leaving, even if she could not tell him why. That was the reason she dreaded it so—because she didn't know how to tell him. How could she put into words the gratitude that she felt for him, for all the things he showed her, for uncontested friendship? She knew that she could trust him to not ask questions or tell anybody if she asked. Saying goodbye to him would be the hardest thing she'd ever done, and she dreaded it.

"I know…and I will," she sighed, wiping tears from her face.

* * *

Searon sat alone on Starlyn's porch as he smoked from his cedar pipe. The smoke kept him warm on the cool morning while he pondered his thoughts. He continued to think about the previous night that he spent with Anaela. She kept him infatuated but seemed to stay distant. At least, she'd tried to until she leaped at him with a kiss. Searon hadn't thought she was interested in him, or at least not enough without pursuit. He smiled when he remembered the night. Warmth spread through him at the thought of her; there was something about her that kept his heart and mind racing.

The peace and quiet appeared short lived when the wizard walked up to the porch. Karceoles sat down at Searon's side and lit his own long-stem pipe. Smoke encircled his face with a long puff before his exhale turned into a bow and arrow. Searon smiled at the smoke representation and rather enjoyed the extra company, especially since the wizard hadn't opened his mouth yet.

"So…how does she taste?" Karceoles asked.

"Excuse me?" Searon shot a glance at the wizard.

"Anaela, how does she taste?"

"You saw us?"

"No, but you've been grinning like an idiot. By the serene look on your face, which is a first time I've seen you happy since your wife.

Adding to that the way you can't take your eyes off of her shows me that she would make you happiest. Then of course the fact you are sitting on a porch alone, and she isn't here, and the fact that you're smoking a pipe. This leads me to believe she didn't spend the night, but something else happened with you two last night, the final conclusion being a kiss. So I ask again...how did she taste?"

Searon's eyebrows rose, impressed to be read like a book. Generally, he kept his feelings hidden. Anaela seemed to bring the personality out of him. He liked the wizard better when he kept his mouth shut, but since he knew it was unlikely, he sighed. Karceoles would continue to press on him until satisfied with an answer.

"She tasted like cool watermelon and sugar; it was the most intoxicating thing I've ever experienced." Searon smiled.

"What did Starlyn taste like then?" Karceoles asked.

"That was different." Searon frowned.

"I know, but the taste...I am curious," Karceoles admitted.

"She tasted like a hot glass of apple cider."

"Interesting, isn't it?"

"What?"

"How each kheshlar has a unique taste."

He had never thought about it before, but it did seem odd to him that Starlyn had the taste of spiced apples, but he never paid it much attention. Now that the wizard pointed it out, he did notice that both had distinct tastes and smells. When he was with Anaela, he hardly paid attention because he was so ecstatic that they kissed. He never considered adding the fact that she tasted sweet as well, and that both tasted of exotic foods that weren't similar to each other.

"Is that true?" Searon asked.

"For the females, yes, it is. It is part of their mating. The male often finds a soul mate with one who has a taste he can't resist. They get a slight hint of it when they kiss their hands in introduction."

"There is so much to know about kheshlars."

"And nobody will ever learn it all. They are mythical creatures."

* * *

Searon wandered the city all day; he watched the kheshlars spar in the field and read from the vast collection of books at the library. They were a fascinating species, elegant in their own way and completely different than humans. Despite all of his wandering, he never found the person he truly wanted to see, Anaela. After their kiss from the previous night, when she ran off, she hadn't strayed too far from his mind, and despite his best efforts she could not be found. Although all evidence pointed against it, he truly hoped he hadn't upset her.

He returned to Starlyn's cabin at twilight and saw her sitting on the porch, serene in posture, alone with hands in her tangled hair, and tracks of her tears dried upon her pale face. Carefully, he strode up the steps and sat next to her. At first, he sat there silently, but when she didn't speak, he decided to put his arm around her and embrace her in a comforting hug that she accepted gratefully. He wasn't sure what bothered her but knew that it would be best to let her unload when ready. She felt cold against him and so he held her tighter in an attempt for his warmth to spread through her.

Starlyn remained still, quiet, accepting his comfort, but not yet wanting to open up to him. He didn't bombard her with the questions spinning through his mind but remained silent as he held her. She moved closer and put her arms around him; tears steadily flowed down her face, and he embraced her even tighter. Searon had never heard of kheshlars crying, and to his knowledge such things were rare, but Starlyn differed from others. She remained more open with her feelings than any other kheshlar Searon had knowledge of.

"I have to leave, Searon. I have to travel far away from here."

"Why?"

"You are a friend, a real good friend of mine, but you must understand I cannot tell you. I cannot tell anyone." Starlyn sniffed.

"Is the fault mine?"

"The only fault this is…is my own."

"Is there anything I can do to help? Perhaps I can have someone accompany you on your journey."

"This is something I must do alone, but I will have company though," she revealed.

"How far do you have to go?"

"A long journey. I will be gone for a long time, but when the time is right, I will see you again." Starlyn smiled.

"Promise?"

A single tear washed down her face, and she smirked. Even so sad, her smile warmed Searon's heart. He couldn't imagine never seeing her again and only hoped to see her return soon. Her journey was a long one, but he hoped one day to see her face again, and to see her happy. The tears that stained her face were upsetting to him.

"I promise," she said.

Searon stood up and took three steps back from her and got on one knee. He released something from his sash and held it in both hands as he bowed his head and handed it to her. She looked bewildered as she removed it from his grip. In her hand she held a throwing knife and pouch.

"Searon...I do not need this. I have shurikens."

"Ah, but shurikens do not find their way back to you. Your journey is farther than mine, and I wish for you to have it. May it remind you that no matter where you go, my spirit will be with you."

"Thank you."

"I notice you've acquired a new hammer."

"Yes, it is the metal of Andron's. I melted it down so it would better serve me. It is not quite as large as my old one, but it will do."

Searon leaned in and gave Starlyn a tight hug before grasping her hand and gently kissing it. He smiled, took a few steps back, and released her hand.

"May the stars shine upon you, Starlyn, and let my creator and your mother watch over you on your long journey."

Starlyn smiled. "And may your blade never dull, your creator never stray, and my mother keep an eye on you, always."

She turned toward the incoming wind and whistled. Footsteps echoed through the forest that grew louder with each passing second. A white Bengal tiger appeared from the trees and sprinted toward them. The tiger knelt before Starlyn, and she stroked the beast just behind the ears before climbing on and looking back to Searon.

"Goodbye, my friend."

A single tear surprised Searon's face that he promptly wiped away. "Goodbye," he whispered.

He stared in disbelief as Starlyn and her tiger fled into the night. An eerie cold overtook his naturally warm body as he stared up at the sky to find a shooting star. He closed his eyes and said a wish to his creator, asking for a safe journey for both Starlyn and himself. When he opened his eyes, he looked toward the ground where he spotted a single white rose. One eyebrow rose as he bent to the ground and picked it up, twirling it in his fingers as he stepped inside Starlyn's cabin.

Epilogue

Searon sat alone on the porch of the abandoned cabin with pipe in hand. He smoked his tobacco as he wondered where Starlyn could have gone. A week had passed, and he hadn't dared speak of her departure with anybody. Everybody wondered where she disappeared to and why. Searon kept busy making preparations for his army so they could head back into the wilderness. After the last harsh battle, he wondered if he would be able to defeat the draeyks and daerions, especially without the kheshlarn support he hoped to bring with Starlyn.

There appeared to be powerful leaders against him, Zergiel the dark wizard being one, but also rumors flooded of Starlyn's sister, the undead kheshlar, being behind some of the training. He shivered as he thought back to when he met her face to face.

He hadn't seen Anaela since the night they kissed, a truth that haunted him dearly; she made it blatantly obvious that she wanted to avoid him—and her feelings. At least that was what he kept telling himself; he couldn't bear the thought of her not wanting to be with him. The kiss they shared showed him otherwise, or at least it felt so. Every now and then, he would catch glimpses of her, but she would disappear as soon as he spotted her.

Searon knew the kheshlars' hospitality would only go so far, and so when he received a polite message from the king to leave his land, he began packing his things. Starlyn remained the main reason they had been tolerated for so long, and now she was gone. An alliance shattered with the disappearance of one kheshlar.

He sighed as he fingered his weapon, circling around the crested rubies before getting to his feet. Everything was already prepared with the messages he sent to Sh'on and Etherond. He prepared himself to meet with Elsargast and thank the king for the little hospitality shown, and say goodbye. Wind crept over the cabin, and he took one last look. It reminded him of his own home so many years ago, a place that he wanted to live when the war was over, if he survived.

Searon shook his head and stalked off into the city where Elsargast awaited him. Vil'ek stood by the king's side, serene in appearance and hands far from the hilts of his scimitars—a small measure of trust about him. They waited for him by their keep, gold circlet and armor secured upon the king.

Anaela stood near them, confident expression on her face, yet she dared not make eye contact with Searon. She appeared more beautiful than ever with hair hung straight past her shoulders, except for a small piece near her face braded in green beads. A forest-green dress without straps fell only a few inches below her hips. Searon stared in awe for a moment before he shook himself out of it to nod to the king.

"Searon, I am sorry to see you leave, and yet I am content with your departure," Elsargast admitted.

"I appreciate you letting us stay so long."

"Starlyn wouldn't have wanted us to cast you out until you were healed and organized," Elsargast admitted.

"Yes, she is an amazing person."

"I wish she were here; her whereabouts are still unknown. Have you heard from her?"

"No...no, I have not." Searon sighed.

"Where is Karceoles? I thought he was supposed to be here to say goodbye as well."

"He is supposed to be here, but I do not know where the old wizard is."

Searon shrugged and held his hand out, and Elsargast took it and held firm, his hand so much softer than Searon's own, which was full of calluses. He looked around for a moment, but when nobody showed he nodded to the king and turned to leave. Before he could get a few steps, he heard quickened footsteps in the distance. A mix of iron and copper lingered in the air that Searon knew too well as fresh blood. Karceoles appeared from the southern gate, running toward them with a limp, using the zylek to help him along. Strapped over his shoulder was a flaccid warrior with long ebony hair.

At first, Searon figured it to be a swordsman in his ranks, or perhaps even a scout that caught wind of something. He hoped it wasn't a scout because it would mean something bad approached. Searon shook his thoughts as the wizard advanced, out of breath. He stopped and looked at the man; something familiar about his appearance fell just outside of his grasp. Searon moved the long hair from his face and noticed a large jaw with clef chin and scruff where a beard usually didn't grow covering his face.

It dawned on Searon and he gasped. "Is that—"

Karceoles pushed Searon aside and crept toward the king, where he stopped and bowed his head only slightly. Anaela rushed forward, face covered in a mask of horror as she scanned over the man's wounds all across his shattered plate armor.

Searon pushed everyone aside and studied the man once more. He knew it was him, although he had no idea how or why his life had been spared. His hand shifted to the man's neck, where he felt a slow but steady pulse. Relief drenched Searon's face as he noticed the young man continued breathing.

"Andron," he choked.

Andron's black-and-blue eyes opened slowly to glance at Searon. He attempted to smile but tensed as he realized how much it hurt. Instead, he coughed a few times and looked back up to Searon.

"I'm glad you made it out of there," Andron coughed. "General."

"You saved my life," Searon said.

Andron only nodded and closed his eyes, his head falling down limply. Karceoles turned to Elsargast, staring deep into his silver eyes, causing a look so intimidating that even the king seemed to shrink at the glare.

"This man needs medical help, now!" the wizard shouted.

Elsargast turned to Anaela, who had remained still with eyes wide. Her eyes bulged, and she looked around to each person surrounding her, and each in turned looked to her. She flinched and burned red but looked around, unsure what to do.

"I will need help for this," she informed the group.

Without another word, she sprinted off into the city. Everyone remained still as they watched her leave. Once she disappeared from view, they all turned to Elsargast.

The king sighed. "Bring him into medical."

Karceoles nodded his thanks and turned to run toward the kheshlarn infirmary, with Searon chasing close beside him. Elsargast followed with Vil'ek at his side, and both held hands gently on their hilts.

Once they were inside the white room, Karceoles gently laid Andron on the bed. The former white sheet stained scarlet in mere minutes as they removed his armor. Everyone tried their best to contain his wounds, but it seemed ineffective. Searon held onto Andron's hand tightly in comfort and to feel his pulse.

"What happened here?" Elsargast asked.

"I found him in the forest, struggling to get here to us," Karceoles said.

"And you know him?" Vil'ek asked.

"He was our captain; he sacrificed himself to save me," Searon confessed.

"I see. Well, we will do our best with him," Elsargast said.

The door sprang open, Anaela and Aliuqa rushed in, holding bottles of elixirs and herbs. Aliuqa wore a dark-purple dress down to her toes crested in blue sapphires, and her hair fell down in waves and shone darker than ever before. They arranged a table and gently set everything down on it before inspecting the injured warrior.

Weapon marks from axes and machetes were the least of Andron's worries; bite marks and claw marks also covered the human's body. Anaela and Aliuqa began mixing colorful liquids with herbs to spread across the wounds. Andron cringed with pain, clenching his fists as he grunted, but he dared not move as they cared for him. Sh'on and Karceoles lent what little healing aid they knew through magic, but the rest was left for Anaela.

"We need to have a council meeting, Elsargast," Karceoles said.

"No, we don't; nothing has changed," Elsargast said.

Andron stirred in the bed, mouth opening as if ready to speak, but gave up and rolled his head to the side. Anaela rushed to him and gently put a pillow under his head so he could see everybody.

"It's going to take him a while to recover; he is in bad shape," Aliuqa announced.

"Not...soon enough," Andron choked.

"What is it, my friend?" Searon asked.

"They are coming," he said.

Karceoles took a step back and stared at Elsargast. There was no objection the king could make now. He clutched his green cape as he stormed out the room with Vil'ek at his side. Everybody watched him leave until the door closed shut, and an eerie silence lingered in the thick air.

"They are coming..." Andron whispered one last time as his eyes closed and he fell into a deep sleep.

Author's Note:

Join my mailing list for an exclusive short story, "Victoria's Grave," and I will also keep you informed of new releases as they come out!
http://www.craigaprice.com/email-list.html
As an indie author, reviews are really important to me. If you enjoyed this story, please leave a Review. I would really appreciate it.
http://www.craigaprice.com/review-me.html

Why are reviews important?

When a potential buyer goes to an author's book's Amazon page, one of the first things he or she does is look at the star rating and the number next to it (number of reviews). The higher the number, the more likely the trust in taking a chance on a new book he/she hasn't heard much about. *Social proof.*

What can you say about the book if you liked it?

You can say what your favorite part is. Did you like the plot? A particular character? The themes of the book? Did you think it was well written? If you feel like you read it too long ago, just think back, and if you remember you liked it, try to remember the general feeling. Did you read it all at once? Did it make you cry or laugh? When you were finished, did you want to read more? Who else might enjoy the book? Give a recommendation (e.g., If you like____, you will love this book, **or** I recommend this book to anyone who likes____)

What if the book isn't quite for you?

Can you at least give the book three stars? You may certainly leave bad reviews, but remember to leave *fair and constructive reviews* if you go this route. If you dislike a book because that's not the kind of book you enjoy, but it was well written and you think a different audience might enjoy it, say that. "This book wasn't that appealing to me, but it was well written and____ would probably enjoy it." If the book is full of spelling errors, but the story is good, say both.

The Crimson Claymore

If you like this story, please check out my others:
"The Mage and the Freckled Frog" and
"Diamonds Under a Hickory Tree"
or
For a complete list of my published and unpublished novels and information about my works in progress go to this link:
http://www.craigaprice.com/novels.html

Craig A. Price Jr.
Acknowledgments

There are a lot of people I am thankful for as I begin my journey as a writer. The first person I want to thank is my Aunt Ann Kriss. Without her constant belief that I can make it as a writer, her kindness, and her donation, I would have never been able to get all of this done. I am very grateful and thankful to have her support. My wife, Amanda, for being so supportive of me and being with me every step of the way. My mom, for always believing in me and for showing me what it means to love and never give up on my dreams. My son, for being my inspiration. All of my followers on Wattpad, for all the wonderful comments and critiques that have made me a better writer.

A special thank you to Kyle Bradford for letting me use his character name "Ehterond." Phil, for the use of his character name Zergiel. Shawn Williams, for being an inspiration for the sarcastic humor, and for coming up with the full name for the character based on your name, Sh'on, or Shronan Onderon. Thanks to Ben Worcester for helping coming up with the name keshlar/kheshlar, and thanks to my fans on wattpad for deciding they liked kheshlar best.

My son insists that our cat, Tiger, is a large inspiration as well. I would like to thank Jason Whited whose wonderful edits made this novel come together. I would also like to thank Treasure Scarbrough for creating this wonderful cover for me. I want to thank Joyce Scarbrough for all of her help with my print edition.

I would also like to thank my followers on Wattpad; a few in particular have been very supportive: Emily Klimczynski, Carl Alvey, and Lilia Loewenberg. And to the following Wattpad users who left wonderful comments on my novel: @roostergirl56 @AaronMeadows4 @redbirds96 @JanetBates @kirley3656 @sueqqqq @FranklinCherry @JedMolyneux3 @UwannaVaughn63 @TerryKenny @mankloy @borjieporgy @Sean68 @SandraEjeh-Eze @graverage1973 @JeffreyThomas0 @RaymondCarles @bildek @rougue434 @RichardIJenkinsSr @kanha001 @KenRider @AzieSyafiqDayyana @Dulceblue @KyleMichaelBradberry @ShaneHussey @mousa2828 @GrEysQueling @Giddeon510 @omniaetnihil @Nachosoflife @JohnMcBride4 @MebiusBrave @MebiusBrave @AmyPoppe @NicholasJones932 @LawrenceDavids @Hierophant18 @FatherofFour @stochx @Starlynpearl @spider881424 @alisa3232

The Crimson Claymore

@racjuly @MartyOneill @JoshuaMichaelMiller @AweleUtomi @Alantson @PietPompies @amswarriors88 @reddragon16091972 @MatthewHaslund @Bullwhip4 @ray321 @ChrisDavis6 @djhan1992 @manocha @JackanorySMurphyy @arunmechie @richjoycelyn @Otterblue @Evalau @leavesrloony @MemantotAlcazar @EmilyAlyssa17 @Archangel_Azriel @josephmpaterson @mla031 @guambum @cjo1964 @JardeRiccardoRiekert @lucario912742 @kesstra @glittleman @raymack70 @spider881424 @Coastal @mathif @AmpieRomero @JoseAlfredoArteagaSo @LoraGomez @darksythe @redbirds96 @baker75 @iloveoreos101 @JosephLeblanc @AndrewWhite065 @Frankylopez @alancnelson @pitboss1600 @Rich1986 @Captshan @JosephFloydCarrier @JasmyneSpearson @PatrickSaril @ovelikon @Nomad_03 @Alzo77 @Floyd_Chaffee @NormanMcNeese @BobNovak @Gangerdr @HansFransen1 @WinkerRrague @Nick2803 @ferdy0 @BornToRoam @bosvold @5ParkerY5 @BinaryWarden @BethLowe @ShannonMarino @viba2311 @Hayesbo @RobertPatrickTacker @ShannonBergamin @Zipper_Head @TimMcFarlane @LawrenceDavids @DilanRees @janetgarza86 @SissaRomanova @BlakePatnoe @VictoriaRBock @bibliophile3 @FranklinCherry @E0347050 @renethuh @penric55 @bosvold @NancyParsons2 @Valkrye @AwesomeSophie @JoelKJannenga @kanha001 @tripitaka33 @SusanTester @Dulceblue @carolyndymit @LJACOB2 @mrsward1983 @MattKemper5 @KealebogaBogopane @ClaudiaInTheClouds @deanmceachern984 @AgnesdeOcampo @fernandojadormeo @doumams67 @bookaholic71 @shad0021 @eddie21 @gravestone12 @beastman6 @Sulay12 @AubreyMarie @clevelandclunie3 @MihirGonsai @Scottry49 @tracyscole @Ezio21

Without all of them, this story would not have been possible. Lastly, I would like to thank all of you that have read this book. I hope you will continue to follow my work in the future.

Please visit my website:
http://www.CraigAPrice.com
Free Stories by Craig A. Price Jr. (Wattpad is also an app!)
http://www.wattpad.com/user/CraigAPrice
Need an editor? Check out mine:
http://www.jason-whited.com/editing/

Characters

(In Order of Appearance)

Searon: (Sear-on)

Human - 37 years of Age
Birthplace: Legain
Appearance: Shoulder length wavy dark brown hair, thin side-burn going to beard and mustache, green eyes, and clef chin. Wears red stained metal with gold lining.
Weapon: A large Claymore sword that glows slightly crimson as he wields it.

Charlotte: (Char-lott)

Human - 13 years of age
Appearance: Medium blond hair and blue eyes.

Karceoles: (Car-see-ohh-lee-s)

Wizard – 937 years of age
Birthplace: Unknown
Appearance: Salt and pepper hair down past his shoulders in a tangled mess. Clean shaved. Wears orange robes that are so dirty and faded that they appear brown. Carries around a zylek for a weapon to help aid in channeling magic.

Starlyn: (Star-lynn)
Kheshlar - 320 years of age
Birthplace: Sudegam
Appearance: Bright Blond hair, electric gray-blue eyes, thin eyebrows, cunning smile especially when the stars are about. Pointed chin and high cheek bones with the fullest bosom of all the kheshlars. She wears midnight blue chainmail under golden bronze and blue hued plate mail.
Weapon: Large steel hammer with spike on backside.

Victoria: (Vick-tor-e-uh)
Human - 28 years at death
Birthplace: Tiermera
Appearance: Straight glossy brunette hair just below her shoulders.
Firm lips with bottom lip twice the size as her top and swirling
chocolate eyes.

Kellen: (Kel-n)
Human – 10 at death
Appearance: Shaggy brown hair, son of Searon.

Arria: (Arr-ee-uh)
Undead kheshlar - 420 years of age
Birthplace: Sudegam
Appearance: Long pearl white hair in waves that flows past her but-
tocks, dark black eyes, medium white eyebrows. A sinister smile
when she is amused. Her bosom is also fuller than most of the
kheshlars, yet not as full as Starlyn's. Tight black plate mail on top
with silver and black leggings on her thighs. Her boots are tall past
her knees with three spikes like daggers extruding from both boots.
Weapon: A long Flamberge with black hilt and gems.

Andron: (An-draw-n)
Human - 26 years of age
Birthplace: Guerettos
Appearance: Long straight black hair, pointed jaw, clean cut face,
slanted nose. Leather armor.
Weapon: sword with diamonds encrusted.

Vaelmirr: (Vael-murr)
Kheshlar – 420 years old
Birthplace: Sudegam
Appearance: Shining silver hair, gray eyes,
Info: Leader of the high kheshlars in the hidden cities outside of
Sudegam.

Erenuyh: (E-ren-yah)
Kheshlar - 220 years of age
Birthplace: Sudegam
Appearance: Redheaded with high cheek bones and few freckles.
Weapon: Kheshlarn Bow

Ketharine: (Keth-ar-ine)
Human - 26
Appearance: Fiery hair and freckles, kind and gentle, yet fiery temper.
Andron's wife.
Weapon: Temper.

Kierra: (K-eye-error-uh)
Human – 9
Appearance: Fiery red hair and freckles. Andron's daughter.

Adreamera: (Ad-re-mer-uh)
Human – 5
Appearance: Long black hair, freckles. Andron's daughter.

Aneldon: (An-L-don)
Human – 1
Appearance: baby with few red hairs.

Berethana: (Ber-eth-anna)
Human - 23
Appearance: A blond dancer from the dancing donkey. Holds the seed of fire.

Annettera: (Ann-et-erra)
Human - 22
Appearance: A brunette dancer from the dancing donkey.

Xython: (Zy-th-on)
Human - 35 years of age
Birthplace - Legain
Appearance: Ebony Skinned, Thick black beard, double wide appearance with broad shoulders and large belly. Thick and big boned, full of

hearty muscle. Bushy Eyebrows, and a faint scar from his left eye to his jaw. Purple glinted Scale mail.

Weapon: Ball spiked Mace.

Taasheka: (T-a-a-sh-e-ka)

Human - 22

Appearance: Ebony skinned, long black hair. Xython's sister. Small rounded nose, large lips, piercing brown eyes.

Shronan Onderon (Sh'on): (Sh-ro-naun On-der-on / Sh--on)

Mage - age unknown

Appearance: Long straight blond hair, green eyes, green robes, dark green magic.

Weapon: Molecule based magic

Brexhar: (Br-x-har)

Human – 22

Appearance: White hair, silver eyes. Guard at Legain.

Noraes: (N-or-ace)

Human - 30 years of age

Appearance: Dirty blond hair, bushy eyebrows, extremely long eyelashes, large mole on his forehead above his left eye as a birthmark. Has blue and silver plate mail.

Weapon: Silver hilted Rapier. As well as learned magic he can cast from his left hand.

Etherond: (Eth-er-on-d)

Human - 38 years of age

Appearance: Bronze hair and gray eyes. His jaw long and pointed as well as his nose, and a half moon scar above his right eye. His eyes are slanted with long eyelashes.

Weapon: Broadsword

Sophie: (So-f-ie)

Human – 19

Appearance: black hair, coppery skin, and bright brown eyes. Maid to Noraes.

Phoenix: (Fe-nix)
Human – 26
Appearance: Bronze chainmail, short red hair.
Weapon: Long Sword

Dennark: (Den-nark)
Human – 41
Appearance: Gold Hair, beady eyes.
Weapon: Staff with small spiked flail balls on each side.

Mattenyi: (Mat-en-yai)
Human – 50
Appearance: Thick orange and white beard.
Weapon: Axe

Extodus: (X-toe-dus)
Human – 57
Appearance: Gray hair and beard.
Weapon: Flail.

Leinard: (Line-ard)
Human – 46
Appearance: Green, black, and white kilt.
Weapon: Broadsword.

Drahcirch: (Dra-cir-ch)
Human – 39
Apearance: Medium chestnut hair. Red, black, and white plaid kilt.
Weapon: Axe

Nhorjah: (Na-h-or-ja)
Human – 37
Appearance: Black hair & beard.
Weapon: Pike.

Richard: (Rich-ard)
Human – 28
Appearance: Spiked blond hair with a large gold hoop earring. Captain of Augealia.
Weapon: Sword

Vil'ek: (Vil-ekk)
Kheshlar - 420 years of age
Appearance: Long black hair, muscular shoulders. Was once the lover of Arria before she became an undead kheshlar. He is the right hand of the kheshlarn king.
Weapon: Two long curved daggers.

Elsargast: (L-sar-gast)
Kheshlar – age unknown
Birthplace: Unknown
Appearance: Straight blond hair to shoulders with silver locks blending in. He is the king of Sudegam.

Anaela: (An-uh-L-uh)
Wood Kheshlar - 320 years of age
Appearance: Long straight dark brunette hair, deep green eyes, dark green and silver armor over chainmail.
Weapon: Kheshlarn longbow sung from the trees.

Aliuqa: (A-lick-uh)
High Kheshlar - 520 years of age
Appearance: Chocolate skinned, brown eyes, and straight black hair to her shoulders with long eyelashes.
Weapon: Two long double bladed daggers, and brown magic.

Races:

Wizards:

Wizards appear like men but as they have been around for so long, most wear robes instead of armor and have long black to gray hair if not white. They must channel their power through a device such as a staff or zylek in order to control it. The magical ability they are born with, yet with so much power inside of them they are dangerous if they cannot tame it.

Mages:

Unlike wizards, spellcasting to become a Mage can be learned. Most are born with a small spark and can learn to define and tune it. Yet their power is so far less than the wizards that they need no device to channel the energy, and can instead shoot straight from their hands.

Warlocks:

Warlocks are wizards or mages that turn to dark magic with a selfish desire of power. Even without the strength of a wizard before turning, they can become powerful warlocks because dark magic is stronger, but it comes with a price.

Necromancer:

Necromancers are magic users that study specifically in raising the dead. Most of them tend to lean toward dark magic, but there have been cases of "good" necromancers.

High Kheshlars: (K-hesh-lars)

High Kheshlars live in the cities within the forest on the eastern side of Calthoria, most dwell in its capital of Sudegam where the kheshlarn King sits. They are oldest and wisest of the species, and have tall diamond shaped ears that match the leaves of some bushes. Their life is everlasting so long as poison or blade doesn't claim them.

Wood Kheshlars: (K-hesh-lars)

Wood kheshlars make homes within the forests, although much of their nature was lost in the last few hundred years, as nobody has seen any come from their dwellings except Anaela, and her memory fails her after being ambushed by a squad of draeyks and found by Starlyn. She has never been able to find her way back home. Deemed the best archers in existence.

Draeyks: (Dray-ecks)

Reptilian creatures with long snouts, sharp teeth, and tails. Black and scaly in appearance, some with spots of color on their underside. Stand tall on two legs like men, wielding mostly axes as they fight. A few can hold crossbows. Some believe them to be a long descendant of the long extinct Dragons.

Daerions: (Da-air-e-ons)

Ram like creatures with horns spiraling from their large forehead towards their jaw black in color. They stand short on two legs at only five feet with leathery blue skin and splendorous muscles. Some have learned the art of magic and all have mastered the short sword, some carry maces and others bows.

Caestlycs: (C-uh-a-s-t-a-licks)

Crystal appearing beings. Cannot be seen well as they are transparent like crystal.

Nacropi: (Na-c-row-pie / Na-c-row-piss)

A Nacropis is a larger than human-sized scorpion, brought back from a dead scorpion by a necromancer. Not much is left except for their bloodlust; they come in all shades and sizes, depending on the original scorpion.

Land & Cities

(In order of appearance)

Calthoria: (Cal-thor-i-uh)
The large landmass that is surrounded by ocean and everything takes place.

Sudegam: (Sude-gam)
The capital of the kheshlars deep in the western forest. Their king lives there and most of the population of high kheshlars.

Kazna'renth: (Kaz-n-uh--ren-th)
Capital city of the draeyks. Northwest corner of Calthoria.

Lenor Lake: (Len-or)
A large lake in the southeast that a large battle between humans and daerions took place hundreds of years in the past.

Guerettos: (Gwer-tous)
A medium village in the north just below the sea at a bay. Famous for their growing of Klitheaur leaf, a weed that has many qualities of healing and soothing of pains, as well as the soothing of stress. When smoked in a pipe it relieves stress, pains, and gives a sense of bliss.

Teyyuar Desert: (Tey-yar)
A small desert south of the Shayli Mountains. It is often crossed when going from southern to northern villages.

Brekaes Noielyna: (Breck-ace Noy-lena)
A lost kheshlarn city. Palaces and buildings of stone everywhere, many that appeared like rocks themselves rather than stone. A different type of kheshlars lived there rather than wood or high, although the idea of them have been lost.

Tiermerra: (Tier-merr-uh)
Once only a large village, now a strong neighboring city of Legain and ally. Located in the south of Calthoria.

Legain: (Lee-gain)
Large human city on the South Eastern side of Calthoria. It is governed strong and was the home city of both Searon and Noraes.

Erdunadir: (Er-dune-uh-dir)
A small village on the southern side of Calthoria below the great kheshlarn forest. Buildings of mostly rustic stone of gray and tan. Since it is the border village it gets raided from time to time by daerions. It has a pub called, *The Dancing Donkey* that is full of upbeat music and dancers.

Gythero: (Guy-th-ere-oh)
A small village in the north of Calthoria below Nygenquy before the bay. Made of wood with a gate of tree trunks.

Nygenquy: (Ny-gen-qu-i)
A small village above Gythero, but below Igurilena in northern Calthoria before the bay.

Wesiet: (Wess-i-et)
City in north Calthoria just above the village of Guerettos on the bay.

Igurilena: (I-gurr-i-lena)
A small village above Nygenquy, but below Guerettos in northern Calthoria before the bay.

Meshsylic: (Mesh-si-lick)
A large city on the southern side of Calthoria down the southern path from Erdunadir. It rests on the ocean and is largely a tourist spot for those wishing to see the vast ocean.

Lorgaeth: (Lor-gay-th)
Province of land in the south of Calthoria, containing both Legain and Tiermerra.

Augealia: (Aug-eal-i-uh)
Village of the Robin, where Searon met Charlotte, located near the

mountains on the east above Legain.

Shayli Mountains: (Shay-l-i)
A mountain range on the eastern side consisting of three peaks from west to east, sometimes used as an easier path to travel between the southern and northern territories.

Aedth Desert: (A-deth)
East of the Benora mountains, the largest desert in Calthoria. It is vastly unexplored. Nicknamed *a death* desert.

Benora Mountains: (Bee-nora)
Exceedingly large mountain range on the furthest east explored in Calthoria that ranges near the top of the land all the way south.

Glossary

(In order of appearance)

Zylek: (Zi-leck)
channel of energy - A wooden or metal staff, crafted to control magic that wants to release from the body of a wizard or warlock.

Adueur: (A-due-r)
Purple flowers, helpful with healing, rare ones are deep blue with green lining near the stem and are more potent for healing.

Klitheaur: (K-lith-aur)
A weed that grows generously in the northern cities, used for healing and relaxation when smoked with tobacco in a pipe.

Crossguards:
A board game much like chess, but more detailed with different types of warriors to take the field.

Ammoresh: (A-more-shh)
Green leaf, Mix it with water and crush to lightly slather over external wounds.

Snaothoeth: (Sn-a-o-th-oath)
Red leaf. Mix it with wine and feed to somebody for healing internal wounds.

Enneth: (N-Eth)
Blue leaf. Mix with pipe tobacco to prevent fatigue before a battle.

Camorea: (Ca-more-uh)
Purple leaf. Mix a small amount with pipe tobacco to relax you after a battle and numb injuries.

About the Author

Craig A. Price Jr. lives on the Alabama Gulf Coast with his son and wife. He spent most of his life in the Pacific Northwest before moving to work as a pipefitter. He has finished 4 novels and has seen a lot of success on Wattpad, where his book The Crimson Claymore has seen over 2.5 million reads and was a featured read for over two years. On his free time he enjoys to write and read novels, especially of the fantasy genre.

He is your typical fantasy author: He has a beard, a typewriter, he enjoys the occasional tobacco from his long stem pipe, and he loves listening to classical music on his record player.